A
Song
of
Sixpence

Judith Arnopp

A CIP catalogue record for this title is available from the British
Library.
Cover photo: DianaHirsch@istockphoto.com
Edited by Cas Peace

Dedication

I wish to dedicate A Song of Sixpence to the memory of the late M.M. Bennetts, an author whose support and encouragement has made me the writer I am today. She is very much missed.

Chapter One
Boy

London — Autumn 1483

Ink black water slaps against the Tower wharf where deep, impenetrable darkness stinks of bleak, dank death. Strong arms constrict him and the rough blanket covering his head clings to his nose and mouth. The boy struggles, kicks, and wrenches his face free to suck in a lungful of life-saving breath. The blanket smothers him again. He fights against it, twisting his head, jerking his arms, trying to kick; but the hands that hold him tighten. His head is clamped hard against his attacker's body. He frees one hand, gropes with his fingers until he discovers chain mail, and an unshaven chin. Clenching his fingers into a fist, he lunges out with a wild, inaccurate punch.

With a muffled curse, the man throws back his head but, keeping hold of his prisoner, he hurries onward down narrow, dark steps, turning one corner then another before halting abruptly. The boy hears his assailant's breath coming short and sharp and knows he too is afraid.

The aroma of brackish water is stronger now. The boy strains to hear mumbled voices, low and rough over scuffling footsteps. The ground seems to dip and his stomach lurches as suddenly they are weightless, floating, and he senses they have boarded a river craft. The invisible world dips and sways sickeningly as they push out from the stability of the wharf for the dangers of the river.

The only sound is the gentle splash of oars as they glide across the water, then far off the clang of a bell and the cry of a boatman. The boy squirms, opens his mouth to scream but the hand clamps down hard again. The men draw in their breath and freeze, waiting anxiously. There's a long moment, a motionless pause before the oars are taken up again and the small craft begins to move silently across the surface.

River mist billows around them; he can smell it, feels it seeping through his clothes. He shivers, but more from fear than cold.

He knows when they draw close to the bridge. He can feel the tug of the river; hear the increasing rush of the current, the dangerous turbulence beneath. *Surely they will not shoot the bridge, especially after dark?* Only a fool would risk it.

The boy wriggles, shakes his head, and tries to work his mouth free of the smothering hand. He strains to see through the blinding darkness but all is inky black. The boat gathers pace and, as the noise of the surging river becomes deafening, the man increases his hold, a hurried prayer rumbling in his chest.

The whole world is consumed in chaos, rushing water, clamouring thunder, biting cold. In the fight for survival, the boy continues to battle fruitlessly for breath, struggle for his freedom. The body that holds him hostage tenses like a board and beneath the boy's ear beats the dull thud of his assailant's heart. The blanket is suffocatingly hot, his stomach turning as the boat is taken, surging forward, spinning upward before it is hurled down again between the starlings, shooting uncontrollably beneath the bridge.

Then suddenly, the world is calmer. Somehow the boat remains upright on the water. It spins. He hears the men scrabble for the oars, regain control, and his captor relaxes, breathes normally again. Exhausted and helpless, the boy slumps, his fight defeated.

All is still now; all is quiet. The oars splash, the boat glides down river, and soon the aroma of the countryside replaces the stench of the city.

His clothes are soaked with river water; his stomach is empty, his body bruised and aching. As the man releases his hold, the boy slumps to the bottom of the boat. He lies unmoving, defeated and afraid.

He sleeps.

The world moves on.

Much later, waking with a start, the boy hears low, dark whisperings; a thick Portuguese accent is answered by another, lighter and less certain. This time when he blinks into the darkness, he notices a faint glimmer of light through the coarse weave of the blanket. He forces himself to lie still, knowing his life could depend upon not moving, but his limbs are so cramped he can resist no longer. He shifts, just a little, but it is too much. His kidnapper hauls him unceremoniously from the wet wooden planks.

The boy's legs are like string. He stumbles as they snatch off his hood and daylight rushes in, blinding bright. He blinks, screwing up his face, squinting at the swimming features before him, fighting for focus. He sees dark hair; a heavy beard; the glint of a golden earring— and recognition and relief flood through him.

"Brampton!" he exclaims, his voice squeaking, his throat parched. "What the devil are you doing? Take me back at once."

Brampton tugs at the boy's tethered arms, drawing him more gently now to the bench beside him.

"I cannot. It is unsafe."

"Why?" As his hands are untied the boy rubs at each wrist in turn, frowning at the red weals his bonds have left behind. He pushes Plantagenet-bright hair from his eyes, his chin juts forward in outrage. "If my father were here ..."

"Well, he is not."

Brampton's tone lacks respect, but the boy knows him for a brusque, uncourtly man.

"But where are you taking me? What is happening?"

"To safety. England is no longer the place for you."

The boy swallows, his shadowed eyes threatening tears. Switching his gaze from one man to the other, he moistens his lips, bites his tongue before trusting his breaking voice. "Where is my brother? Where is Edward?"

Brampton narrows his eyes and looks across the misty river. He runs a huge, rough hand across his beard, grimaces before he replies. His words, when they come, spell out the lost cause of York.

"Dead. As would you be had I left you there."

Chapter Two
Elizabeth

"Sing for us, Bess, and I'll give you a fat sixpence."

The court falls silent at the king's voice and all eyes turn expectantly toward me. My father, King Edward IV, slouches in his chair, his fingers slick with grease as he shreds flesh from the fowl before him. I do not see the pouches on his cheek that others see, nor the shadow of death beneath his eyes. He is my hero, my king, and to me the epitome of manhood.

With a smile, I rinse my fingers daintily and wipe them on the cloth before sliding from my seat and taking my place before the assembled court. I do not ask what song I should sing. I know the king's favourites and the players do, too. With a nod to the minstrel the music begins, and I break into a merry tune about a cuckoo and the onset of summer. The company, replete with meat and wine, sway in their seats as I sing for them. The royal fools begin to dance with hands on hips and pointed toes in a parody of their betters.

Sumer is Icumen in,
Loudly sing, cuckoo!
Grows the seed and blows the mead,
And springs the wood anew;
Sing, cuckoo!

When I reach the part about the cows, the fools moo and snort loudly, turning my performance into a farce. Father is rolling in his seat now, mopping his face with a big kerchief, and my own voice trembles with suppressed laughter. At last, when my song is done and the applause has died down, the king asks for another.

Hidden in my chamber, I have a vessel of coin earned by these means. My sister Cecily says if it were hers she would buy a new hood or a pair of hunting gauntlets. She thinks I am soft to give my earnings to the poor, but I have a deep concern for the ordinary people.

Sometimes, when I am safe and tight in my bed, I think of them shivering beneath inadequate covers, the roofs of their houses leaking, the rain and wind gusting in beneath the doors. I am always aware that but for the whims of fate, I too could have been born a pauper instead of a royal princess of York. I've learned that a princess's first duty is to charity, but sometimes I fear it is a lesson that has passed my sister by. We have never known want, our bellies have always been full, but that doesn't mean I cannot imagine the misery of poverty. If England is to remain a merry place, those in our position should do all they can to ease the hardships of the poor.

My father and his supporters fought and won wars for the privilege of ruling over England. For years men died and women wept but now all that is over, and under York's rule the country is at peace and likely to remain so. The people love my father and cry out in cheer when we ride through the streets, although it is not so for my mother.

Father was criticised when he married her secretly, undermining the control of his guide and mentor, the Earl of Warwick. Mother is not only a non-royal but the widow of a man who fought and died for the cause of Lancaster and, to add insult to injury, she was already mother to two small boys.

Warwick had set his sights on a foreign princess for my father; a union to secure our position on the throne of

England. But my mother, with her silver-blonde hair and merry laughter made a fool of the great Earl and snared herself a king. She has proven more fruitful than even Warwick could have dreamed.

Now Warwick lies unmourned in his grave, killed in anarchy against his king, and the royal York nursery is teeming with children. With two strong sons and a bevy of princesses, my father's hold on the crown is unshakeable.

York is here to stay. Our claim is strong, our line legitimate, and the days of Lancaster are over.

My song comes to an end and as the music tails into silence, the minstrel bows and I curtsey low to the king amid wild applause. My father beckons me to his side for a kiss and I skip toward the dais to give him my salute. When I press my lips against his cheek, his hands slide about my waist and he pulls me onto his knee. "Ah, Bess," he whispers. "You are just like your mother."

Father signals for a stool to be brought and I squeeze between my parents and look across the hall, my heart light, my cheeks pink with embarrassed pleasure. A trio of fools flip upside down across the hall, leaping and bounding like deer from the hounds. Father leans forward and presses a coin into my hand and I turn to thank him.

But as I go to speak, something changes. His cheeks begin to blur and the whole scene begins to dissolve before my eyes. The people in the hall are silent now. Darkness rushes in from the periphery of the room. I call out his name, spin around to find they are no longer there. I am alone.

They are gone. Father is gone, the royal court has disappeared, and only Cecily is weeping in the darkness of our chamber. I sit up in my bed and look around at the humped shadows, the dying embers of the fire. It was all just a dream. My happiness seeps away as reality washes over me. The first streaks of morning are showing in the east and with the dawning of the day, the living nightmare that my life has become begins again.

As my mind re-engages with the present, I remember with sickening clarity that Father is dead and my royal brother has been deposed. My father's children are all bastards now and Uncle Richard, who stole their crown three years since, has marched away to defend it against the spawn of Lancaster; Tudor. Henry Tudor.

Tudor has sworn that, once he has gained his rightful throne, he will marry me and merge his house with mine, finally putting an end to the wars of York and Lancaster. But I loathe Henry Tudor; his very name turns my stomach and makes me want to spit.

I am Elizabeth of York and it should be me weeping in the dark not Cecily, for should Lancaster prove victorious, it is I, the eldest of my father's daughters, who will be served like a pig on a platter to the triumphant king.

*

"Stop crying, Cecily. It won't change anything."

At my cruel words her tousled head emerges from beneath the covers and she sits up, wipes her nose on the back of her hand.

"How can you be so calm? Things had just begun to go right for us. At least King Richard was treating us with some respect. If he loses the fight and Tudor is victorious, do you think a Lancastrian will do the same? He might well throw us all in the Tower."

She is red-eyed and snotty, and Mother would be horrified at such loss of dignity. I pass her a kerchief.

8

"What would Mother say, Cecily? For goodness sake blow your nose, wash your face and behave like the York princess you are. We are not defeated yet."

She scowls at me and snatches the kerchief, blowing her nose loudly as her shoulders continue to shudder. There is no use in tears. I wept too many when my father died and my siblings and I were made bastards. Our Uncle Richard took the throne for himself and kept my brothers close in the Tower. I could not comfort them. I could not distract my brothers with tales of King Arthur or try to explain to Edward that Uncle Richard thought he was acting for the best.

I railed against Richard at first, spoke scathingly and unwisely of his actions, and when Mother plotted against him, I did nothing to prevent it. Most kings would have had us taken up for treason, but Richard is quite unlike other kings.

It was a dark day when he came to us in Westminster sanctuary. My mother and sisters were still deep in mourning for the sudden loss of our father and were not expecting a visit from the *'vile usurper'* as Mother labelled him.

We were gathered in a gloomy chamber about a lazy fire when some small sound made me look up from my needlework. Richard hesitated at the door, absorbing our hatred, understanding our sense of betrayal. He moved through our bitterness to sit among us and try to make us understand why a child could never hold England's crown.

His features swam beneath my tears as he spoke quietly and rationally in a voice so soft I was forced to lean forward to hear him. Cecily was weeping noisily and the children were restive.

"An infant prince has never thrived in England..."

9

Mother leapt to her feet.

"Edward is no infant. God curse you, Richard!" she cried, as if she were still queen. "God damn you and all your heirs."

With a look that would wither nettles, she whirled on her heel and marched imperiously from his presence. Richard remained seated, regarding me as if he expected me to follow her, but I tarried and listened to his words.

The firelight fell upon his sleek dark head, shadowing his face, his occasional glint of tears testament to his regret. And as we sat together, I began to see a glimmer of reasoning behind his ruthlessness. But I hated him still.

"If I could have the time again," he said, "I'd do all I could to prevent your father's death and keep England merry, as it used to be."

Cecily left us, mumbling words like *hypocrite* and *usurper* but I was not so quick to judge. I knew more than Cecily. I was aware, as she was not, that our father made some harsh decisions too... for the sake of the realm.

Of course, Richard's apologies didn't make me resent his actions less. The throne belonged to my brother by right of birth. He was raised to be Edward V and had my father lived just a little less extravagantly, perhaps his son would have held on to his crown.

"You have named us all bastards. How are we to trust you?"

He sighed and looked away, shamed and sorry, but made no answer.

"Can I see my brothers?" I asked with great daring. Richard raised his sad eyes to me and slowly shook his head.

"Not yet, Elizabeth. Not until everything is settled. You can see them then."

"They will be frightened ... grieving!" I stood up, my book falling to the floor, and Richard stood with me. He reached out and clasped my wrist gently.

"They are safe in my care, Elizabeth. I would never hurt my brother's sons but I cannot allow them to be a target for my foe. I must keep them close."

I trusted him. He was their uncle, as he was mine, and the Plantagenet bond was unbreakable. I gave the ghost of a smile and did not fight for my brothers.

I told myself there'd be time for that later.

When the boys disappeared from the Tower our hearts broke afresh, for the king would not tell us their whereabouts or even confirm they were still living. It was hard to bear so soon after losing father, for even if they lived, estranged from us, they were as good as dead.

Mother swathed herself in mourning and lost no opportunity to smirch the reputation of the new king. She took some sort of theatrical joy from refusing to leave sanctuary and return to court. She cursed Richard as a usurper, the abductor of her sons, and the destroyer of her reputation. Her hatred for him was ungovernable, verging on madness. Her mood swung from violent rage to cold, calculating scheming. One moment she wept, the next she called for parchment and pen and began a desperate correspondence with our erstwhile enemy.

So, when she agreed to release us from sanctuary and into the care of our uncle, the king she professed to hate, Cecily and I were astounded.

*

My sisters and I poured from the grim sanctuary walls like birds from a cage. After so many months of austerity and boredom we embraced life at court with alacrity. It did not matter that we were no longer called 'princess' but simply 'lady'. It did not matter that our aunt Anne now sat as queen in our mother's place. The younger children were absorbed into the royal nursery while, with the selfish, thoughtless enthusiasm of youth, Cecily and I burst onto the royal court with a zest for life and fine clothing and romance inherited from our dazzling parents.

Within weeks, Cecily had embarked on a round of flirtation that raised the eyebrows of the gossips. I let her go her own wild way and took little notice, for my own romantic interest was sparked by someone far more unsuitable and closer to home.

When I was small and my uncle Richard came to my father's court, I would sit on his knee and shriek with laughter when he discovered coins behind my ears or pulled acorns from my nose. He was the first man, apart from Father, to guide me gently around the dance floor. He had the goodness not to remark upon my faltering steps or less than serene grace. He was like an elder brother, another father, someone I could rely upon to keep my childish indiscretions secret. My father had trusted him, too. Of all the men in the kingdom his brother Richard was the one he depended upon ... above all others.

That is why, when my childhood hero transformed into Herod and stole my brother's throne and saddled me with the stain of bastardy, my heart was broken.

I thought our relationship was over.

But on our arrival at court, Richard sought me out. I looked askance at my father's crown glittering on his dark hair, but I curtseyed low before him.

He gave me presents and both he and Aunt Anne made it very clear that they regarded all my father's children as their family. Despite my sorrows it was good to be back at court, hailed among the highest in the land again, albeit of bastard stock.

With a belly full of fine food, a soft bed to sleep in and a closet of new clothes at my disposal, I began to overlook his sins. Gradually the old avuncular relationship between the king and I began to recover.

And then, one night, I had a dream. A disgraceful, passionate, impossible dream that meant I would never be able to look upon Richard in the same light again.

There was no indication that he felt the same, but I could not stop thinking of him. My eyes followed him about the hall. I absorbed his every word, reading meaning where there was none. And each time I lay down to sleep, his image would rise before me.

This man in my dreams was most unlike my Uncle Richard. The man, the king of my imaginings, was wild and ruthless with desire for me. His mouth pressed close to my ear whispered of forbidden things, my skin burned beneath his imagined touch.

It was an ungoverned passion, a longing that was impossible to conceal, and soon people began to notice. I gave myself away in a million different ways. Soon, the gossips began to whisper in the shadows and, like a dirty stain, the tale spread across the country.

They spoke of a lecherous king giving court to his niece under the nose of his ailing wife. Had Richard truly planned to wed me I'd have fallen at his feet, but none of it was true. He never once indicated that he felt anything for me but the love of an uncle for a niece. He loved Anne deeply and treated me as he always had, with gentle deference and amusement. It was only my treacherous heart that betrayed him and provided the court gossips with fuel for their filthy fires.

Poor Aunt Anne, she didn't know what to believe and she died miserably, eaten up with disease and jealousy for an incestuous act that had never taken place outside my own imaginings. But, once ignited, gossip becomes rampant and people went as far as to accuse the king of poisoning her for want of marrying me.

Richard, who at first shrugged the rumour off, grew angry. He brooded at table, his conversation became clipped as if he was afraid that any word he spoke would be taken and twisted out of truth. And to make things worse, he barely looked at me.

I almost died of shame when Richard was forced to speak out and deny me before the world. He could have demanded that I refute it too, but he spared me that dishonour. I know now that I should have confirmed I'd never known the touch of his hand or had the honour of his kiss. I should never have pretended I had. I can only blame the folly of youth, the unfulfilled desires of a lovelorn maid.

In those days I was full of love for him, but now that love has turned to terror, terror that he will die on the battlefield today and I will have no choice but to wed the man who rides against him.

*

"Where do you think our brothers are?" Cecily asks for the hundredth time. "Are they still living? Do they know about the battle? Who will they root for; Uncle Richard or Henry?"

"How do I know? Either way it will mean little difference to them, if they still survive."

She shrinks away from my sudden anger, and impatiently I turn from her and stand on tiptoe to see from the tower window across the vastness of the

Yorkshire countryside. There is a sick feeling in my stomach to know that miles away men are pitting their strength against each other, wounding and slaying their own countrymen for the sake of power. England is the prize and I will become the property of the victor. For years there has been war; war and bloodshed. For longer than I can recall the men of my family have ridden out to kill and maim their neighbours. There was a time when I thought it was over.

Cecily is slumped on the edge of her bed. I hold out my hand and pull her to her feet. "Come," I say. "I will comb your hair. Once we are up and about we will feel better. There is no point wallowing in grief. When life sends you conflict it is better to face it in full armour than to hide like a toad beneath a rock."

Despondently, she sits before the looking glass while I tease the tangles from her hair. The household is stirring. A hearth girl comes in to stoke the fires and footsteps are scurrying up and down the winding stair. Cockerels wake and begin to call in the morning, dogs are barking in the bailey, and soon the matins bell will ring calling us all to prayer.

*

I am following the train of Cecily's gown up the twisting stair. Her step is heavy; she is wishing we were back at court not packed away to the country for safety.

Sheriff Hutton castle holds the royal nursery where the King has the children under his care held in safety. Cecily and I, seeing ourselves as women grown, are insulted to be treated as infants. As well as my sisters and I, our cousins Margaret and Edward of Warwick are also 'kept safe.' Their father, George of Clarence, was murdered when we were children, some say on my father's order.

When we first came I feared she would resent us, but when we met Margaret's smile was warm and I realised that she too has grown up to understand the ruthlessness of kings.

We gather in the solar where her brother Warwick shows me his kittens, piling them in my lap and pointing to his favourite and telling me all their names. While they clamber with stiff tails and mewing mouths about my skirts, Margaret looks on with a slightly anxious frown. He grins up at me, his face alight with innocent pleasure. He has no concept of our position, no idea of the raging battle that will determine all our futures.

Margaret and I exchange glances and I see her eyes are full of tears. She fears for him as I fear for my own brothers.

"We've not lost yet, Margaret," I murmur and our eyes meet over Warwick's head. "Even if Tudor wins the battle, he may not win the war. York can fight another day."

It has always been so. A great see-saw of power with the crown as the fulcrum. Sometimes it seems there will never be peace in England. As for us, the children of York, every one of us is vulnerable and easy prey for power hungry kings.

Chapter Three
Boy

The boy looks up at the vast sky, the wheeling gulls, and the angry, scudding clouds. His soul is filled with the sounds of the sea; the strain of the rigging, the slapping of the sail, the crashing of the great waves against the hull.

I should have been born a sailor, he thinks as he clings to the ship's rail, his legs splayed to effortlessly ride the surging deck. The wind is laced with tiny shards of glass that sting his face, turning his cheeks scarlet, but he doesn't mind the cold.

A few feet away a lad not much older than himself is scrubbing the deck, the soles of his feet are black, his clothes tattered and bleached by salt and sun. The boy moves forward, pushes back his cap and tucks his thumbs into his waistband.

"Is that hard work?" the boy asks. "Can I try?"

The cabin boy looks up warily, shakes his head but makes no reply. He keeps his eyes cast down and quickly returns to his task.

"What is your name?" the boy asks but before the cabin boy can answer, a hand falls hard upon his shoulder. Brampton turns the boy to face him, stooping so as to hiss into his ear.

"Didn't I tell you not to talk to anyone? Keep your mouth closed, your accent marks you out. You are supposed to be my servant yet here you are strutting about like a lord. Get below and do as you are told."

The boy jerks his arm free.

"He is only a lad. I am bored with being below deck. There is no air, nothing to do. I want to stay here and feel the air on my face. No one on board cares who I am."

Brampton screws up his face.

"Any man on earth will carry tales for the right price. We don't want the crew spinning yarns about a bright-haired lad taking ship from Bristol port; a lad with a lordly accent and hands like an untried girl."

Grabbing the boy's collar, Brampton bears him off. Once in the cabin he throws off his hat and collapses onto the bed. "You are my servant now, you'd best get used to it."

The boy, narrowing his eyes, slides down the wall and brings his knees to his chin. He flexes his fingers and examines his palm.

"I don't have hands like a girl."

Brampton emits a bellow of laughter and thumps his straw-filled pillow into some semblance of comfort.

"You certainly don't look like any sailor's lad I ever met. Keep away from them. You stick out like a pearl in a bowl of pig swill. Land can't be far away. If you don't do as I say I'll make you walk every step of the way to your aunt's court; maybe that will humble you."

"My aunt?" The boy is alert now, his mind quickly assessing. "In Burgundy? Is that where we are going?"

"Sshh." Brampton springs from the bed and clamps his hand over the boy's mouth. His face is so close that when he speaks the boy flinches from the fumes of his garlic-laced supper. "I have said too much. Forget I spoke."

He releases the boy, who turns away, folding his arms and heaving a sigh. He feels they've been travelling for months, yet it is only a matter of weeks. A few days at a country manor where he befriended a servant girl with pretty red hair; a week on the road, darting from one sorry tavern to the next. He is tired of it, tired of Brampton, tired of travel. He wants his sister; he misses her songs and stories of knights and chivalry.

"I hate being your servant," he spits but he keeps his voice lowered, knowing Brampton is his only friend. He owes his life to the man.

Brampton from his bunk glares back at the boy. "Maybe I should have let Buckingham have you then. Maybe I'd be living the high life, dallying with loose ladies at court instead of here in this shit pit with an ungrateful cur."

"You can't speak to me like that." The boy's face is scarlet, his eyes ablaze with resentment. Brampton laughs and turns his back on the boy.

"Sure I can. You are no one, nothing … until I say you are."

Chapter Four
Elizabeth

<u>Sheriff Hutton Castle —August 1485</u>

I am bored, we all are. The babies are fractious, the infants beginning to quarrel; even Cecily and Margaret had a falling out earlier over a game of knucklebones. Only Warwick seems content, tormenting his kittens with too much love.

Allowing my sewing to fall to my lap, I stretch my arms and heave a hefty sigh. "This day is endless."

Margaret looks up from her book. "Word will come soon enough."

"Let us hope it is good news when it arrives." The tone of Cecily's reply leaves us in no doubt that she fears it won't be. We subside into silence again and brood until a sudden scream from my little sister makes us leap from our seats.

"Bridget, let go!" She is clasping a handful of Catherine's hair and has forced her sister to her knees, her mouth wide and her screams piercing. The nursemaid rushes forward.

"Oh, I am sorry, Madam. They are so naughty today."

I wince as she spanks Bridget's hand and Bridget immediately opens her mouth to add her cries to Catherine's.

It is as if the children sense our tension. In other circumstances such domesticities would be a welcome interlude, something to laugh about later, something to add to a letter to make Mother smile. But today I am so

21

distracted I offer them comfort with more impatience than empathy. I just want them to be quiet, to sit and be silent so that I can fret in peace.

When the children are calm, I summon the nursemaid from her corner. "I think they need to rest; they are fractious because they are tired."

Amid wet kisses and sticky waves goodbye the children are ushered out, leaving Margaret, Cecily and I alone. I move to the window and look out across the battlement to the road beyond, where a puff of dust on the horizon betrays the approach of a small band of horsemen.

"Someone is coming."

The girls hurry to the window, jostling for a view.

"Who is it? Can you see? What badge do they wear?"

As yet, they are too far off to determine. We watch as the horses grow larger and the shapes of the men slowly detach from the dun coats of their mounts. With a sick thumping heart I screw up my eyes to identify them, but their badges are obscured and they carry no flag. Cecily's shoulder is pressed against mine as she strains to see.

"Tudor would come with an army. He'd not come with a small retinue like that."

I turn away, smooth my skirts and try to arrange my thoughts.

"Tudor would not come at all. He would send a messenger, as would my uncle."

I clench my fists, pray silently and rapidly that Richard is safe. If York should fail, my life, all our lives, will change beyond recognition. Soon, although it seems like hours, there are sounds of arrival in the bailey. A trumpet sounds and a door slams far below and someone shouts for a groom. A dog runs out barking frantically, setting off the others. I watch and wait, my heart a sickening throb in my throat. Blood pulses in my ears, and I know Cecily and Margaret are just as afraid as I. I can hear their high rapid breathing as we stand in the centre of the room, side by side, with our clasped hands hidden in our skirts.

Footsteps on the stair outside are followed by a curt command, and the door is thrown wide. "Sir John Willoughby," my page announces. "And Sir John Halewell."

Two men enter, draw off their helms and make a hasty bow.

Lancastrians.

York has lost.

My heart turns sickeningly.

I loosen the girls' hands and move forward to stand behind my chair. I lift my chin, bite my lip and remind myself who I am, the house I represent.

It isn't the end, I tell myself. *It isn't the end. Richard will rally and fight again. It isn't the end.*

Unsmilingly, I hold out my hand while they bow their perspiring heads. They are ripe with the stench of horse and sweat, the megrims of the ride.

"Well, my lords?" I say at last. "What is the outcome?"

Willoughby throws his gauntlets onto the table with a satisfied flourish. "Richard of Gloucester is dead and Tudor is victorious."

The world swims but I clutch the back of my chair tighter, my nails digging into the carved wood.

"Dead?" I hear myself say. "York is vanquished?"

"Most certainly. Like a fool, Gloucester took one last insane risk and tried to fight his way through to the king. Luckily for us, Stanley, changing his allegiance at the last, moved in and his army beat the usurper down. I watched myself as Lord Stanley plucked up the fallen crown and placed it on the rightful king's head."

As he delivers this good news he beams around the room, nods familiarly at my sister and cousin as if they are tavern wenches and not of royal blood.

I am confused. His rightful king and mine are two different men. The news that Richard has fallen refuses to take root in my mind. I had thought that even if the battle was lost, we would fight another day. The see-saw of York and Lancaster has ever swung up and down, and up again, but now, now … who is left to fight on?

With my brothers in hiding or dead, who does that leave? My cousin, John Lincoln? My little cousin, Edward of Warwick? Neither are strong enough and neither have experience at rallying men. Richard *cannot* be dead.

While my mind pushes away the fact of Richard's defeat and whirls with possibilities for York to regain power, Willoughby's voice continues. I drag myself back to the dreadful present.

"We are sent to bring you and your sister"—he nods in a perfunctory manner in Cecily's direction—"to London, and the boy, Warwick, too."

A sudden movement, a boyish yelp of protest, and Warwick emerges from beneath the table. He has been there unnoticed all along and heard every word. For once I am glad he lacks the wit to fully understand. He struggles to his feet, still clutching his favourite kitten.

"I don't want to go to London; I like it here."

With a cry, Margaret swoops toward him, guides him as far as she can from the men who have come to detain us.

"We must do as the king says," she says gently, for the benefit of Willoughby. "The king in his wisdom knows what is right and best for us."

I realise then that she is trying to guide me, subtly beseeching me not to argue with them. *We must not grieve for Richard, we must do all we can to pacify this new king. ALL we can.*

I know she is right. There is little point in protesting. We must ride to London on the orders of this Tudor king and face whatever fate awaits us. Whether I find myself a prisoner in his Tower, or bedded as his wife, I have no choice.

*

In August the roads are dusty, the plants in the hedgerow are setting seed, and the farmers getting ready to slaughter their stock. The winter will be hard, the wind will howl and the snow will fall. Many will suffer, many will perish, but as we are hurried past their humble, ill-thatched dwellings I find myself longing to be ordinary. Better to be an out at knee rustic at the mercy of nature than a richly clad princess at the mercy of her enemy.

I pin my hopes on Mother, who will be waiting to greet me. She and Henry Tudor's mother, Margaret Beaufort, have known each other for years, sometimes friends, sometimes foes, but Mother is Queen Dowager. She will speak for me and see I am treated fair.

Although it is many hours until dusk, I call to Sir Willoughby and beg that we may stop awhile. "We are tired," I tell him. "We are unused to travelling so fast. You must think of the boy ..."

"The king bid us make haste. There is much unrest in the land and he wants to get you to safety as fast as he can."

I pull my mount to a complete stop and look down my nose at him. "We were safe at Sheriff Hutton, the people of the north would never harm *us*; perhaps you should have left us there."

He reaches out and takes hold of the reins. "I do as my king instructs. You must save your remonstrations for him."

And so we ride on through the heat of the afternoon, my fingers on the reins are slick with sweat, my thighs aching, and my skin thick with the dust of the road. When we stop for the night at a priory I fall into bed, and for the first time since we heard of Henry Tudor's landing in Wales, I sink into a deep, undisturbed sleep.

The next morning, after Mass and a swift breakfast, I climb groaning back into the saddle. Warwick is whimpering. His kitten has fallen sick after being taken from its mother too soon, and it hangs over his arm like a ginger fur cuff. Margaret clucks at him in sympathy and he wipes away a tear.

"Cheer up, Edward," I say, trying to boost him. "We can get you another kitten."

As I kick my horse into position in the column, his tears start up again. "I don't want another kitten, I want this one."

And I can sympathise. I don't want this life. I want my old one.

As we draw closer to London, we are joined by a great cavalcade of ladies and gentlemen who treat me with great deference. We become a procession, a royal entourage to demonstrate how well the Tudor king treats the women of his vanquished foe.

Warwick is held behind and we are told there will be no triumphant entry into the city for him. He will be borne separately to the Tower; although he is a boy, and a backward one at that, he is too great a rival for Tudor's peace of mind. When they are separated Margaret cries out in protest, but she is taken firmly in hand.

"Be quiet, my lady," Willoughby hisses. "You will see your brother later; he will come to no harm."

I reach out, take hold of her bridle.

"Hush, Margaret, do as they say or it may be worse for Edward. I am sure Tudor will not harm a boy. If I am able I will do all I can to protect him."

And with all my heart I hope that is true.

*

We are reunited with my mother, lodged at the home of Henry Tudor's mother in Coldharbour to await the pleasure of the king. For days, I dress in my best and wait for him to come. In the end I grow tired of waiting, tired of being cooped up indoors. Outside the summer is slipping into autumn and I crave fresh air, to stretch my legs in the garden and say farewell to the swiftly ebbing sun.

Mother is resolute. "It is all going to plan," she says. "I have always thought Henry would make a good match for you."

"He has not come near me; how can you think it is going to plan? And since when did a Tudor become a fitting match for a daughter of York?"

"Hush, hush, my dear. You know your father suggested it once, to bind the houses of York and Lancaster and put a stop to the endless war."

She pushes me into a chair and begins to play with my hair, pulling it away from my face and tying it into a thick braid. She leans forward and speaks rapidly and quietly into my ear. "He will come. He needs you. He cannot hope to hold England without you. Many Yorkists who fought for him at Bosworth did so only because of his promise to join with you."

"Then why hasn't he come?"

She curls the end of the braid around her finger and smiles, maddeningly calm.

"He is punishing you for being who you are. You are his superior in all things; that is something he hates and so he is flexing his muscles, trying to make you suffer. When he comes, you must be indifferent. Not cold, not overjoyed, just cool and perhaps a little reluctant. That way he will want you more. He will want to master you and he cannot do that until he has made you his wife."

Her words, or perhaps it is her hands that continue to move in my hair, make me shudder. "Now, now," she whispers, "it won't be that bad. He is just a man with a shiny crown. If you want to have any influence over him you must make him worship you."

"How? How can I do that?" I turn to her and she grips my wrists.

"Be humble and reverent. He has been raised in obscurity and will be a stranger to adulation which all men thrive upon. Give him a taste of it and in turn, he will worship you. That is always the best way to control a man, be he king or commoner."

I have a sudden memory of her looking at my father with all the love in the world in her eyes. For the first time I question it.

"But … you didn't do that with Father, did you? That wasn't a feigned affection?"

"Oh no." Her eyes mist over, and a dreamy look spreads across her face. She is still beautiful, despite the suffering. "That wasn't feigned," she says, as her fingers absentmindedly resume their work. "I would have loved your father were he king or swineherd."

*

28

It is late and I am about to call my women to help me to bed. The fire has slumped in the grate and an autumn chill is creeping into the chamber. I put down my book and draw my shawl about my shoulders. Just as I am about to rise there is a sound at the door and a terrified maid stumbles over the threshold, almost falls as she bobs a hasty curtsey. "Sorry to disturb you, my lady but … the king is here."

I am on my feet, fumbling for my shawl which has fallen to the floor, snatching up my cap and pulling it on to cover my hair. Realising I am wearing only one slipper, I kick off the other and hope he will not notice I am barefoot.

Before I can delay him, the maid is grovelling on the floor and a man is coming quietly toward me. His face is in shadow, I can only see his outline. He is smaller than I'd imagined, not kingly at all and half a yard shorter than my father. Forgetting all my formal training I stare at him open-mouthed before remembering to curtsey. I crouch on the floor, short of breath, my heart hammering. His feet appear before me; black, square-toed shoes, his hose slightly wrinkled at the ankle.

I feel his hand on my shoulder and he bids me rise. I obey slowly and moisten my lips, fumbling for something to say. "Your Grace …" I croak at last.

He laughs at my confusion but not unkindly. "You were not expecting me?"

"No, Your Grace, or I should have gone to more trouble."

"No need, no need. I would see you as you really are."

We shouldn't be alone, not before we are wed. I make a sudden movement. "I should summon my mother …"

He puts up a finger to stop me and his eyes close slowly; every movement he makes is slow and considered, like a snake before it lunges.

"I sent her to her bed. I wanted to meet you alone, away from the eyes of the world."

"I see."

He is standing close. I can hear his breath whistling through his nose, and when I raise my eyes I see his skin is glistening, the pores open, as if he is overwarm, although it is chilly in the chamber. He is afraid and as wary of me as I am of him. My confidence rises a little and I lift my chin while he makes his inspection.

"They said you were beautiful."

"I am sorry to disappoint."

He laughs again, recognising the irony in my tone.

"Oh no, not disappointed." He lifts a strand of my hair that has slipped from the confines of my cap, and rubs it between finger and thumb as if he is a draper testing the nap of a velvet gown. I feel like an ox on market day. "You are very fair."

"Thank you."

He turns to the table and fills two cups with wine, offers me one which I accept, although I do not drink from it.

"Do you welcome our marriage, Elizabeth?"

Richard's face flickers in my mind and for a long moment I look down at the red, glutinous liquid in my cup. There is only one answer I can make. The only way to keep my family safe, my mother, my sisters, my uncles, my cousins, my brothers ... is to agree.

"Oh yes," I hear myself reply. "I have longed for our union for years ... ever since Richard of Gloucester stole my brother's throne."

Detesting myself for a base liar I gulp from the cup, suppressing a cough, tears springing to my eyes.

"Ah yes; your brothers," he is saying. "Where are they, do you know?"

I shake my head and look into the dying embers of the fire. He comes to stand behind me. I can feel his breath on my neck.

"If we are to marry, I must revoke the act that made you illegitimate. I cannot wed you while you are labelled bastard. If I revoke the act that made you so then I legitimise your brothers too and in turn, make them my rivals ... and dangerous. You must see that cannot happen."

My throat is blocked with grief. I nod my head. "I understand," I croak.

"Are they still living? You must tell me if they are. And if you know their whereabouts you must tell me that, too. It is your duty ... as my wife and subject."

Our eyes are level; his are grey, like steel, and mine are awash with tears. I let my chin tremble as I lie to him and betray Richard one last time.

"I fear they are dead," I sob. "My poor, poor brothers, they were defenceless in the face of Gloucester's greed. They never stood a chance."

I drag a kerchief from my sleeve and sob into it, feeling him take a step closer.

"There, there," he says, reaching out to pat my shoulder. "You must not weep; we have had our vengeance on him already."

He draws me closer and I go stiffly into his arms. His chest offers little comfort. It is not vast and soft like my father's, nor hard and muscled like Richard's. It is narrow and bony and beneath it I can feel the pattering of his heart. He is as afraid as I am.

31

Chapter Five
Boy

<u>Brussels – December 1483</u>

It feels strange to be on firm ground after the swelling and rolling of the ship's deck. The boy stumbles and almost falls into a stack of barrels. Brampton laughs, tosses a pack onto his shoulder and moves into the crush of people. "Bring the luggage, boy," he says.

The boy watches him disappear into the crowd. He is tempted to ignore the order and hesitates. Men pass to and fro, coming between him and his guide until all he can see of Brampton is the top of his cap.

Brampton is a rogue and a fool but he is all the boy knows. He snatches up the bags and staggers after him, the hard edges of the pack digging into his thighs. He calls out to him, people turn and look, and Brampton, who is deep in conversation with a shabby-looking fellow, scowls and growls at him to be silent.

It takes a while to barter for two down at heel nags. The horses stand heads down in the shade of a spindly tree, their ribs like hoops, their hooves split, and the droppings behind them too wet to be healthy. The boy waits, tired and thirsty, overwhelmed by the voyage and the strange clamouring harbour town. It is very different to travel as the servant of an adventurer than as a royal prince. There are no comforts, no easement. At first he was full of questions but now exhaustion is making him accept whatever comes – he snatches at memories of his mother, his sisters and the love they once offered, but their faces slide away before he can grasp them.

When Brampton tosses the saddlebags over the neck of the largest horse the boy is surprised the beast doesn't stumble. As he waits to be helped to mount he wonders if the poor creatures will last till sunset. Brampton doesn't even look his way; he swings himself easily into the saddle.

"Aren't you going to help me up?" the boy demands. Brampton turns and looks at him, one eyebrow disappearing beneath his curly hair.

"Nope," he replies and kicks his horse into a shambling trot.

The boy drags his reluctant mount to a tumbledown wall and heaves himself aboard, his legs flailing. Before he is properly settled the horse begins to move off, forcing the boy to scramble to keep his seat. "Hey wait," he calls. "Wait, I say." But Brampton's back is disappearing into the trees.

The boy has ridden since he could walk; fine blooded specimens with coats brushed to a sheen; their hooves oiled, their manes and tails pulled and laundered. He has never known the trials of an ill-fitting saddle, an ill-mannered, over-bred, broken-down, grass-bellied mare. By the time they've travelled five miles he is exhausted, his fingers are blistered from hauling at the reins, and his buttocks are sore from a tear on the saddle.

Brampton seems unconcerned although he too is used to finer steeds. He sits loose in the saddle, his cap pushed back and his legs jutting forward as if taking his ease in a brothel.

"How far is it?" The boy flaps his legs, urging his horse to Brampton's side, and the man turns.

"I don't know. Far enough. Now, get behind, remember who you are supposed to be. I am tired of reminding you."

34

The boy falls back but every so often Brampton glances over his shoulder and smiles at the lad's discomfort. The next few years will be hard. Brampton has told him he is a good boy, better than his brother and should make a better man than his father, but he has been spoiled. His softness needs sharpening. Brampton is determined to rough him up a bit and turn him into a soldier – more like the Plantagenet prince he was born to be. The boy shies inwardly from the prospect.

At night they lodge in shambling inns, eat rough bread and sup rustic soup, and Brampton insists they rise early before the other travellers are on the road. As they leave the town behind Brampton trades in their broken mounts for horses of better blood. The journey becomes more comfortable, and once they reach less travelled roads, Brampton relaxes.

Now there are fewer folk to see, the boy can ride beside him. He has learned not to speak too much but he listens, unwittingly absorbing lessons from Brampton's tales of war and leadership. The man has lived a colourful life, travelling the world, seeking his fortune. And he has left it all behind to give his service to a dispossessed boy.

The boy has discovered it is fruitless to quiz the man about what has happened to his brother, yet he is desperate to know the plan. He doesn't know where they are going or what is going to happen. "When are we going to go back to England?" he asks one day, but his companion makes no answer. He squints into the horizon, along the endlessly winding road.

"Wait and see," he grumbles.

'Wait and see' is the only reply the boy ever hears.

*

Evening is almost upon them, the shadows are long, the birds quietening, the bats beginning to flit in the darkening sky. Without warning, Brampton turns his horse from the road and leads the boy down a long grass track.

"Where are we going?" the boy whispers. He keeps his voice low, sensing the need for stealth, although he knows not why.

"Wait and see," Brampton growls.

The track is overgrown and seldom travelled. They follow its dwindling path until they reach a dwelling; a house and a cluster of farm buildings. There is no one about. Weeds grow in clumps around the water trough where they let the horses take refreshment. Brampton slides from the saddle and, with his hand on the hilt of his sword, looks around.

Silence. Even the owls are quiet. Brampton jerks his head at the boy who dismounts and obediently leads the horses into the barn, out of sight. There is hay in the manger. He removes the saddles, rubs a fist over the sweaty patch beneath, and then creeps from the barn to find Brampton.

The door to the house is ajar. Warily, the boy steps over the threshold and looks around the dim, empty room. Brampton has thrown open the shutter and is reading a note by the fading light of the back window.

The few sticks of furniture are swathed in sheets, and when Brampton pulls them aside the boy is surprised to see good quality stuff. There is a strong oak table with good serviceable stools and, before the vast fireplace, a settle with cushions. This is no poor man's home.

"What is this place?" the boy asks. "Who lives here?"

"Wait and see."

Brampton opens the pantry door and emerges with a fresh loaf, a roasted fowl, a flagon of wine and some apples. It is the best they've eaten for weeks and the boy falls upon the food as if he has never known better.

"Is it your mother's house?"

"My mother's house? Why would you think that? Do I sound Burgundian bred?" Brampton chews, wipes a trickle of grease from his stubbled chin. The boy shrugs and pokes another chunk of bread into his mouth.

Brampton is Portuguese. He still bears the accent of his homeland and his looks are dark and swarthy, and he wears an earring like a pirate. The boy remembers him from court, laughing with his uncle, drinking with his father and earning the approving royal tag as the king's 'loyal friend.'

Deep down the boy knows Brampton is a good man, his devotion to his father continuing long after his death. That is why he is here with him now; Brampton must have promised either his father or Uncle Richard to protect him, no matter what. But, in the past, he has heard other whispers about Brampton.

His brother Edward, God rest him, liked to frighten the boy with dark tales of murder and intrigue. "Brampton killed a man in Portugal," he whispered once, "and fled to England to escape the noose. Father thinks he can trust him, but can he really? Who is to say he will not kill us all in our beds one dark night?"

The boy knows they were just stories made up to trick him into revealing his terror. There was nothing Edward liked more than to drive his brother out of his wits with stories of evil spirits and murder but … you never know.

"Whose house is it then?"

"Your aunt's."

The boy stops eating and looks at Brampton askance. "My aunt's house?" He looks doubtfully around the room, at the plain furniture, the lack of decoration. "My aunt is the Duchess of Burgundy; you can't expect me to believe she lives here."

Brampton tears another strip of flesh from the fowl and chews it, licking grease from his fingers and speaking with his mouth full.

"I didn't say she lives here, you little fool. She owns everything around here; everything and everyone. Her instructions were to bring you here and, if it is indeed the right place, we are to await her here."

The boy puts down his bread.

"She is coming here? Will she take me back to her court?"

Brampton sighs and leans across the table, grips the boy's arm. His face is serious, his eyes dark. For a moment the boy thinks he is sad, regretting that they must part. But then he speaks.

"Listen, boy, you must forget who you are. I keep telling you. It is important. Prince Richard is no more. You will be given another name, another life, and you must just be grateful that you live. Your life in England is gone ..." He snaps his fingers. "Forget it. Your brother is dead; your country has a new king. Your uncle could have ordered you killed; it would have been wiser for him to do so. But he has granted you your life, sent you here to his sister, your aunt, where you will be safe, but in return you must forgo all claim on the English crown. Do you understand?"

The boy nods, just once, but his eyes are full of questions. He swallows, licks his lips.

"What about my mother? Will I see her?"

Brampton ruffles the boy's hair.

"She will write when she can but it is doubtful you will see her. Be grateful that you live."

The boy is silent for a long time. He tears the soft white bread to pieces, crumbles it onto his plate before asking quietly, "What happened to Edward? Is he really dead? Or is that just another trick?"

Brampton's sigh is deep and long. "I wish I could say it were, boy. There was a rebellion. London, the whole of England was in chaos. Your cousin, the traitor Buckingham, tried to take King Richard's place and have you and your brother killed, but Richard got wind of it and ordered me to get you both to safety. I failed with Edward, but you're here. That is the main thing."

The boy cuffs his nose. A tear trickles from one eye; he keeps his head low, sniffs, and hopes that Brampton won't think him a girl. Brampton stands up and tosses the boy a kerchief. It is stained with grime from the road.

"You've done well, boy. We've come all this way and you've not shed a tear till now. I am proud of you."

His hand falls heavy on the boy's shoulder and while he dries his eyes Brampton moves to the door, his ears alert for the sound of approaching horses.

Chapter Six
Elizabeth

<u>December 1485</u>

"You still believe he will marry you, don't you?"

Cecily's voice intrudes into my thoughts and I turn from the window to where she is sewing. She has paused, her needle half in, half out of her work while she looks at me with ill-concealed impatience. "Even though he has had himself crowned and all the nobles in the land have bowed their knee to him, you still think he needs you."

"He does need me."

I do not bother to point out that most nobles did not bow to him at all but were executed or fled overseas to safer harbours. In dating his reign from the day before the fight at Bosworth Field, Henry was able to accuse them all of treason. I try not to think of the noble souls who were punished for supporting their anointed king. There are many things I try not to think of these days.

I pick up an apple from the table but a wasp has been at work on it, the neatly burrowed hole discoloured and brown at the edges. I put it down again and join the women who are working at the hearth. As I take my place among them, a little girl leaps up to fetch me a footstool, and I smile in thanks.

Cecily continues her taunting. "Why does he need you now he is crowned? He can beget an heir on anyone. I've heard he was fond of ... what is her name? Herbert. Maud, perhaps? Or Katherine? Anyway, whichever one it was, the gossips are saying that when they were young he promised to marry her, too."

She examines me for signs of resentment but I keep my face calm, smooth out the irritation caused by her persistent questions.

The other women show no sign of even hearing our conversation let alone joining in. They are well-schooled but I doubt their loyalty. More than half of them are probably spies on Henry's or his mother's behalf. I smile serenely over their bowed heads.

"The king may well favour Katherine, but he will marry me."

"How do you know?" It is a good question. Half a dozen faces turn toward me, trying not to appear eager for my answer. I stand up again.

"Because he promised," I reply lamely as I walk away.

A small boy throws open the door to my inner chamber as I approach and I hear Cecily's footsteps hurrying after.

I am not as confident of Henry as I seem and was taken aback when the arrangements for his coronation began without a word to me. He has punished all those who failed him and honoured all who supported him. His stepfather Stanley is now an earl; his beloved Uncle Jasper now Duke of Bedford and promised the hand of my aunt, Katherine Woodville. Henry has done all he promised; all but appease the remaining Yorkist faction by cementing his claim and marrying me.

As the door closes, Cecily darts in behind me and resumes her attack while I throw myself onto the bed and kick off my shoes.

"You've only met him a few times." She bounces onto the mattress beside me. "How can you possibly know he will keep his promise?"

I don't know, of course, but I cannot allow my insecurity to show. As if Father is before me I can hear him telling me, 'Never let them know what you are thinking, Bess. Smile, laugh and keep your own council.' So, remembering his words, I hide behind serenity.

"I just know."

"Oh, you are so smug sometimes, Bess. You know nothing about him … only gossip. And what about those other things we heard, you know, the bad things about him being cowardly on the battlefield, pissing his hose and all?"

I roll over onto my belly and laugh at her. "You are lucky his spies can't hear you. Oh Cecily, those are just tales, told by our uncle's supporters. You won't hear a good word for a Tudor from the lips of a man of York."

She sighs again, pouts as she pulls off her cap and frees her red-blonde hair. "Who am I going to marry, Bess? Now that Henry has had my betrothal to Ralph Scrope dissolved, who will I end up with?"

When Uncle Richard arranged her marriage to Scrope in the year before Bosworth, Cecily was most unhappy, declaring he was too lowly, too poor, and too mean for a princess of York. Poor Cecily has always found it hard to accept our fluctuating status.

"I thought you didn't like Ralph?"

"No, well I didn't but at least I was betrothed then and given due respect. Now I am in limbo, and nothing is being planned and it won't be until the king has you out of the way."

Out of the way? She makes me sound like a load of dung tipped from its cart into the path of the king.

"Henry will organise it in his own time."

"How can you be so patient?" She sits up and punches the pillow, her face red, her eyes bulging with irritation. She looks like our father.

It must be an hour since noon and Mother is due to arrive. Seeing I am to be allowed little peace, I slide from the bed and smooth my hair, poking pieces back beneath my cap and straightening my sleeves while she watches.

"Don't you have a woman to do that for you?"

"I can't be bothered, and it is no trouble. Come, let me comb your hair, Mother will scold you when she sees those knots."

Cecily meekly crosses the room and sits at my feet. Her bursts of temper mean nothing. I have known her long enough to ignore them, and even her unkindest words no longer have the power to bite that they once did.

Our faces are washed and schooled to obedience by the time Mother and the king's mother arrive. We sink to our knees in a great puff of skirts and wait for their signal to rise.

Mother has lately been restored to her former position of Dowager Queen and although Henry did not pass all her holdings back, she now has over thirty manors at her disposal again. When Mother opens her mouth to speak, Lady Margaret cuts across her as if to assert her position above her. I flinch inwardly, irked at her ill-manners, but I let nothing show. She is mother of the king and as such is not to be crossed. Why, I wonder, is it always the most irritating women who manage to manoeuvre themselves into positions of power?

"Elizabeth, my dear," she says, holding out her hand for me to kiss. "What a pretty gown. We must soon begin looking out some suitable fabric for your wedding."

44

Cecily nudges me and I grab at the chance to reopen talks of my marriage.

"Will the wedding be soon, my lady? The king has been crowned for almost two months, yet still he has not set a date."

She blinks, her expression unchanging, but I sense I have displeased her. "The king will speak to you when he is ready, Elizabeth; you must be patient."

"Oh, we are all patient." Mother reaches out and takes a cup from the tray one of my women is holding. "I imagine Elizabeth is merely eager for some new clothes; she has always been fond of finery – like her father, King Edward. It is what she is used to."

Lady Margaret must be able to hear the latent derision in Mother's words. Cecily and I exchange glances, and I know she is remembering the finery Mother had when she was queen; one room stuffed with velvets, the other piled high with shoes. Whenever we had the chance Cecily and I would rummage through her clothes, trying things on and parading about the chamber as if we were mummers in a courtly play. I remember one occasion when Cecily went to Mass forgetting she had pinned on one of Mother's priceless brooches. The chamber women searched high and low for hours but when it was discovered, pinned to my sister's bodice, we weren't scolded. We were rarely reprimanded; we were kissed and tickled instead and, as a result, we never questioned our position or our place in the world.

But those were carefree days, when the rules laid down for us were far more lax than those we must follow today. Even had Henry Tudor been raised in his mother's house I am sure he'd never have known the carefree romp through childhood that we enjoyed. There was nothing better than gathering my brothers and sisters close for a story of King Arthur and his knights. Often, on hearing us, Father would join in too; throw himself on the cushions among us and listen as avidly as the children. Those former days of royal domesticity, when the royal privy chamber vibrated with laughter, are gone now and I miss them. There is only stiff formality now and only Henry to rule over us. Henry the king and, if he ever bothers to tie the bonds, I will become his stifled consort.

"I hear the king has ordered new coins to be struck, showing the mark of both our houses." At Cecily's words, all faces turn to the king's mother. She closes her eyes, like a nun laying a blessing upon a novice.

"He has indeed, my dear. And therefore we must surmise that his intention to join our houses will be soon."

She goes on to tell us of the new regiment of guard Henry has established. Fifty yeomen to follow him about the palace, dressed in lavish uniforms in a resplendent reflection of his majesty. I see it as a vast intrusion of privacy and we all know it is for Henry's peace of mind, his protection. He cannot hide his fear of an assassin, not in this court.

"How lovely," I hear myself murmur as she describes how many lengths of braid were used on the coats. "I daresay we will see them at the Christmas court. I expect the king is busy with preparations for the festivities, and I hear His Majesty is planning a progress too before long."

Lady Margaret enlightens us further as to Henry's plan to show himself to the people of the north. None of us gathered think this wise. The northern populace loved Uncle Richard dearly, and their love increased once he was their king. They will not give a warm reception to the slayer of the man they prized.

"We will pray for clement weather," I say, plucking at the most innocuous words I can think of.

"The sun shines on the righteous." My mother's face is empty of irony but I can hear it in her tone. I pray God Margaret Beaufort is too full of self-congratulation to perceive it.

Before she takes leave of us, I ask the king's mother to pass on my remembrance to Henry. Perhaps if she speaks of me he will be shamed into action. Before we know it, Christmas will be upon us. I should be wed by then. People are beginning to talk.

She squeezes my hand and says that she will indeed pass on my greeting and we all hold our breath as she leaves. As soon as I can I send my women away, and Cecily and I settle in the parlour alone with Mother.

When they have gone she sinks into a chair and emits a small explosion of ire.

"That woman!" With both hands she thumps the arms of her chair. "You'd think she was the only lady to ever birth a king."

I move to her side, bringing a bowl of nuts.

"I thought you were getting on well."

"Oh, we pretend, but it will never be more than that. Too many injuries have been done; too many and too great to ever be fully forgiven. I'm sure she knows something ... I am always waiting for her to blurt something out ..."

"Have you heard anything, Mother?" I duck my head closer to hers. "Of the boys, I mean?"

For a long moment she looks at me. "Nothing, Elizabeth; nothing at all."

I wait for her to expand but, studiously ignoring me, she picks at a fingernail, nibbling it smooth with her teeth. I know she receives letters. I have seen messengers

47

come and go, unmarked and discreet. She is in touch with people all over Europe and I have always suspected she knows more than she reveals about the fortunes of my brothers.

What is she hiding? What does she know?

Cecily begins to crack nuts, a pile of shells growing in her lap. The flames of the hearth cast shadows on our faces and, as she hands the kernels out in turn, first to Mother, then to me, we eat in companionable silence. It is a peaceful scene, one could even mistake it for contentment, but each of us is aware of the other's restless thoughts. We will never be free from worry; our smooth expressions merely mask a torrent of unanswered questions and unsolved problems.

From the other chamber I hear the muffled voices of my women and know that I should call them to join us where the fire is warmest. But we women of York cherish these moments when we are alone and unwatched. We huddle like a coven about the fire. Each can trust the other; each would stand shoulder to shoulder against a foe; and yet, as we sit in silence, I become aware of something.

Some new change is taking place. It is as if my association with Henry Tudor has undermined me a little, inched me from their sphere and thrown me off centre. I am on the cusp of being apart from them; no longer entirely York but not yet Lancaster either. I am neither white nor red. I am merging; blurred.

*

It is quite late and I am almost ready to go to bed. I sent my ladies away some time ago, even Cecily and Margaret, who has been fidgety with a toothache. I am seldom alone these days and enjoy a rare moment of

48

reflection. The chamber is full of shadows, the fire that burned brightly all day has slumped now and the shutters are closed against the chilly night.

I put aside my needlework and as I do so I notice a tiny tear in the lace of my sleeve. I poke the tip of one finger through so it shows pink beneath the hole and make a mental note to have it repaired tomorrow. I rise from the chair and pick up my book; I am just reaching for the candle when a small sound at the door alerts me. I look up, expecting Cecily or Margaret. My book falls open on the table, and my mouth goes very dry.

"Your Grace." I sink to my knees and wait while he slowly approaches. I feel his hands upon my head but he does not bid me rise. I can see only the royal feet and notice he is wearing slippers, a loose gown. His ankles are bony, hairy and bruised from the stirrup. While I crouch at his knee, his fingers move in my uncovered hair, testing the softness and sending a swathe of goose pimples scurrying across my shoulders.

I shudder and, at his bidding, begin to rise, my eye travelling up his loose night robe, the heavily embroidered yoke, a few stray chest hairs beneath. The ends of his sleek dark hair curl in a frame about his jaw.

His lips are unsmiling, two parallel lines run either side of his mouth; lines that will grow deeper as he ages. My eye is drawn to them. He will tuck his troubles beneath those lines; use them his whole life to conceal his fears with half a smile until the folds of skin become so deep they could be set in stone.

Our eyes meet like strangers, yet I know why he has come. I know I cannot withdraw. I am trapped in a silken cage of his devising. He reaches out and touches me again, locking my prison door.

"You are very beautiful; I think I told you that before."

I nod soundlessly as his fingers continue to move in my hair, down the side of my skull to run lightly along the curve of my jaw, beneath my throat, to my neck. "I hadn't expected beauty." He traces a nail along the surface of my skin and a trail of Judas bumps appear. "They all told me you were beautiful, but people say that of princes, don't they?" He laughs suddenly, the levity out of place in the deathly serious silence of the chamber. "Some people even say it of me."

There is little mirth in his humour. I sense fear and tension, a latent power. He circles me, his eyes absorbing every detail, making me wish I had selected my better bed gown and asked that my hair be brushed to a greater sheen. Suddenly it is imperative that I please him, for if he should find any fault with me, I will not just be letting myself down but the whole of my house, too.

He is standing so close I can see the rise and fall of his chest. He places a hooked finger beneath my chin, lifts my eyes to his. "When I saw you first, I suspected some trick. How can it have been this easy?" His breath flutters in my face. I catch a lingering hint of garlic and wine that reminds me of my father. I lower my eyes. He turns away and I breathe a little more easily, and he begins to pace back and forth, back and forth.

"All my life I've been fighting for this. The crown. England ... you. I'd seen the crown a few times on other men's heads. Even though I'd not set foot here for fifteen years or more I could remember the lush green fields of home, but you, Elizabeth ... you were the surprise. A bonus I'd not expected, and my heart took a leap of gratitude at my very first sight of you."

I follow him with my eye as he continues to pace. He stops at the hearth, lifts his arms and lets them fall again. "There had to be a catch, didn't there?"

I shake my head once, unsure where this is leading, but he does not look at me. He continues to speak, heedless of my response.

"Of course, it didn't take me long to learn what that catch was. Almost right away those who have no love for me took pleasure in telling me of your ..."

I am alert now and curious. "My what?"

He spins on his heel and comes close, pushing his face near; he narrows his eyes and enunciates clearly so as to catch my slightest reaction.

"Your impurity." He spits the words so violently that I pull away from him, a gasp of outrage springing from my lips.

"That is a lie," I shout as the blood surges beneath my skin. My anger swells. I clench my fists, my nails digging into my palm. "Who has said such things of me?"

He laughs, bitterly not merrily. "Everyone. It is common knowledge. Did you think to hide it? Every lowly knave in the palace whispers of how you gave yourself to your uncle; how you flaunted your tawdry nature beneath the nose of Gloucester's dying queen."

Cecily and I had wondered how Henry would be in anger. It affects men in different ways; my father used to bellow and cuff his servants; my uncle Richard became tight-lipped and anxious; Henry, it seems, becomes spiteful.

He grips my upper arm with strong, outraged fingers. "You were to have been my prize," he sneers. "Yet what do I find? A baggage! A rotten, hackneyed gutter-wench! A royal whore!"

"My Lord!"

Summoning what dignity I can, I look down with disdain at his wiry hand digging into the fleshy part of my arm. He relaxes his grip a little. I can smell the wine on him, the sweat of fear and disappointment. His breath comes heavy and hoarse. Trembling with fury, I swallow my revulsion; remember my father's advice to hide my feelings away, play the game for all it's worth and to keep the stakes high.

"Those are lies, my lord."

He maintains his grip on my arm. I speak more calmly, my words clipped and controlled, close into his ear. "Lies and slander to wound you. Those who bear you no love seek to undermine our union. They are trying to break us, my lord, before we are forged. They have their own agenda, sir. Only a fool would listen to them."

As soon as he releases it, I rub my bicep. I will be bruised in the morning. He moves away, stares into the dying embers, his hair falling across his face so I cannot see his eyes. I swallow phlegm; cough lightly to clear my throat and gather all my courage. "Come, my lord," I suggest with great daring. "Will you not take some wine?"

He turns slowly to face me, takes a few steps into the light of the single candle and regards me for a long uncomfortable moment.

"Do you swear it is all lies?"

I fasten my gaze on his and look him directly in the eye. "I do, my lord ..." He makes to turn away again and I speak quickly to detain him. "And I can prove my words are true."

I watch the question form on his lips, knowing that the moment he gives voice to it, I am lost.

"How?"

His eyes are on my mouth as I make my reply. "When I give myself to you, my lord, you will know if I am a maid ... or not, as the case may be."

For a long while he does not speak. We stand in our nightclothes, eye to eye in the rapidly cooling chamber as the last few minutes of my maidenhead tick by.

Then he reaches out and begins to loosen my robe.

Chapter Seven
Boy

<u>Farmstead near Dijon — December 1483</u>

She is tall, very tall, and the skin is pulled tight across the bones on her face. She leaves her retinue outside and enters the room alone. The boy stays in the shadow while Brampton goes forward to greet her with showy grace. "My Lady," he bows low over her hand and offers her a chair but she stands, unsmiling, while her agate eyes dart about the chamber, seeking something ... someone.

At Brampton's summons the boy steps into the light and her breathing, which was audible before, halts. She throws up her hands. He sees long white fingers, pure unspotted palms; she holds them aloft as if she is greeting a small god. The boy gathers his courage and approaches her to make an elegant knee as if he were back in his father's court.

"Edward," she breathes, when he is upright again. Her black-swathed arm reaches out from a voluminous cloak to touch his shoulder. "Edward," she says again.

The boy clears his throat. "I am Richard; Richard of Shrewsbury: Duke of York and Norfolk. Prince of England." He glances at Brampton to see if he did right to confess to his own name but his companion is looking straight ahead, his eyes fastened on the fascination of the Duchess. Her gaze has not left the boy's face. She reaches for him as if she is transfixed.

"York and Norfolk," she murmurs slowly and breathily as her eyes devour him. "Oh, yes, I can see who you are. You are the living image of your father. Brampton, bring me some wine."

The boy, taking no small delight in the ease with which Brampton is reduced in status to a servant, allows himself to be manoeuvred into the light so she can look at him. She takes the proffered cup absently and sips delicately, watching her nephew over the rim while she speaks.

"Do you know why you're here?"

A frown darts across his brow and the bright head lowers. "M-my father ... my Uncle Rich— my brother, Edward ... he – he ..."

Taking pity on his charge Brampton steps forward. "The lad has quitted himself well, Your Grace. He is a brave fellow. He knows of the unrest in England; he knows he is here to be kept from harm's way."

"From harm's way." Lady Margaret has a habit of slowly repeating the last line of any spoken sentence. She swoops forward suddenly, taking the boy by surprise. Her face on a level with his, her dark eyes consume his features. "You are a true son of York. It is a lot to live up to. You must learn. You must do more than learn, you must excel ... at *everything*."

Doubt creeps across the boy's face. He has never enjoyed the schoolroom; Edward was better at learning. The boy prefers to practice with his wooden sword, or ride with the hounds. "I will do my best," he says at last. Brampton looks down at him and ruffles his hair approvingly, winks and flashes his wide smile.

Margaret has turned away. She is counting coins from her purse and piling them on the table. "There will be more, of course, Brampton, in time, but this will be enough for you to reach your destination."

"Yes, Your Grace."

The boy looks from one face to the other; trying to determine the meaning of a grown up conversation in which he has no place although every word, every decision concerns him.

"But, but aren't I coming with you, Your Grace?"

Margaret smiles and squats before him, their faces on a level. Hers is huge and white, lined with worry and grief. The boy's is round and pale, a streak of dirt across his nose, his eyes bright with unshed tears.

"Not today, child. You must be kept out of sight. There are enemies who would have you killed; enemies of York who would destroy us both. You will go with Brampton and live as part of his household, and learn, my son, learn, learn, learn until you can fit not another morsel of knowledge into your skull. I am hoping to send you to join the son of a friend of mine who is studying in Overijsse, you will like it there, it is a good place. But nothing is decided yet. But, whatever happens, by the time you have learned all there is to learn, you will be a man and ready to take your place in the world."

The boy looks doubtful. "Just me ... and Brampton?"

Margaret smiles, her eyes almost disappearing, the crinkles on her cheeks like the rays of the sun. "Brampton is a good man. My brothers, both Edward and Richard, trusted him with their lives, and that is good enough for me. He will look after you and I will send word to you when I can, and visit from time to time. Be a good boy and write to me should there be anything you need. Good fortune, small one."

She lays a hand either side of his head and places her lips on his brow. He feels the warmth of her breath, the pressure of her fingers on his cheek. Suddenly he remembers his mother, the softness of her lap, and wants to cast himself into her arms. But Brampton's hand is heavy on his shoulder and he knows he must behave as a man. "Come, lad," Brampton says. "We can rest here tonight before we travel north."

Chapter Eight
Elizabeth

<u>January 1486</u>

Lady Margaret, the king's mother, swears that Henry tells her everything but I can tell he has not told her our secret. That first night Henry took me with a kind of reverent terror, but in the nights that follow his terror turns to rapture. During the day his hot persistent lovemaking regresses once more to chilly wariness, but I am confident that now he's had a taste of it, he will visit me again.

I am right, his visits become predictable. Each night I ensure I lie alone, and whenever he can he comes scratching at my chamber door as soon as the house is settled.

The first time I wake at dawn in the grip of nausea, my ladies fear I've been stricken with the new contagion that is sweeping in a tide over England. The disease, the sweating sickness, strikes suddenly and usually takes its victim before a day has passed. There is no known cure and the doomsayers swear it is God's vengeance on Henry for the theft of another man's crown.

I hurl the contents of my stomach into a pot, look up in a frenzy of weeping and cry for my mother.

"Hush." Margaret scoops back my hair, trying to salvage it from the ribbons of vomit. "Your mother is coming, Elizabeth. All will be well. Hush."

Cecily, ever useless in a crisis, weeps in the corner, her knees drawn up beneath her chin. "We are all going to die," she wails, plucking at her nightgown in a frenzy of terror. As my body succumbs to a further attack of retching, I wonder if she is right.

"Be quiet, Cecily. Remember who you are." My sister's wails cease instantly as Mother glides toward my bed. "Sit up, Elizabeth, let me look at you."

I struggle, still sobbing, onto my pillow and feebly kick off the covers, suddenly hot whereas a moment earlier I'd been cold. "She's going to hurl again," cries Cecily, pointing from her corner as I lunge once more for the pot.

Mother, unperturbed by my extremities, feels my forehead the moment I am upright again. "When did you last eat?"

"Don't even speak to me of food." I lie back, shudder and roll my head away from her hand.

Mother straightens up and with a jerk of her head clears the chamber of women. When we are alone she sits beside me, and to my surprise reaches out two hands and tests the weight of my breasts.

"Ow!" I pull away, scowling at her breach of conduct. She leans forward, hisses through her teeth.

"You are pregnant." Her face is white, her words clipped and quiet as she thinks out loud. "How could you do this? We must be rid of it. If ever the king were to discover ..."

It is too much to take in all at once. A thousand thoughts flash through my mind. Triumph; joy; quickly followed by fear.

"Pregnant? Already? How is that possible?"

"You tell me." She keeps her voice low, controlling her anger as she glances furtively to and from the door, afraid someone will overhear. "How could you have done this to us, Elizabeth? Who have you lain with?"

60

I look at her, my sickness ebbing a little, my former misery replaced with a sudden euphoria and an irresistible urge to giggle. Mother doesn't know. She hasn't guessed. She thinks I've been sporting with one of the servants like my father used to. I am tempted to prolong her agony, exacerbate her dread, but I am too tender hearted ... too delighted to keep the knowledge to myself. I reach for her hand and give her a smile that is ridiculously wide.

"Oh, Mother, do you really not know me at all? I lay with the king. It is his child."

"The king?" Her lips part. Her face opens further and I watch as relief swamps her and she begins to mentally calculate when we can expect the confinement. "Why did you not tell me? Oh, Bess. I thought for a moment ... the wedding must be soon. Does he know? Have you told him?"

I shake my head.

"He is not a great one for talking, not in the few stolen moments we have enjoyed together."

"Then you must tell him at once. Come, get up, and dress your best."

She claps her hands and my women appear as if from nowhere, the chamber descending into chaos as she orders a bath to be filled and my finest gown to be brushed. Soon I am sponged and oiled and brushed and clad all in dark green velvet and ready to offer up my news to the king.

*

When I am finally given permission to enter, I find the king with his mother. They are seated at a table, papers strewn across the surface. They both look up, the resemblance between them striking. I sink into a deep curtsey.

61

"Elizabeth." Henry rises and comes toward me, takes my hand and leads me toward the table. His brow is furrowed, his face full of questions.

"I must speak with you, my lord," I whisper. His fingers are warmer than his expression but I sense he is not best pleased at the interruption. His mother seems even less so.

"Lady Elizabeth, how gracious of you to join us." Her tone tells me she is anything but delighted, but I smile and incline my head courteously.

"There is an important matter I must discuss with the king."

"Oh Elizabeth, I hope you are not still pestering him to free your cousin Warwick. Really, the child is better off in the Tower, safer ..."

"No. It isn't about my cousin. It is another private matter."

I emphasise the word 'private' and refuse to back down while she looks vaguely in my direction, her gaze not meeting mine. One hand moves across the bundle of papers she has been perusing.

"I hear my son's council; there is nothing you can say to him that he will not relay to me later."

I allow myself a little giggle, feel Henry stiffen beside me.

"I hope there are some things that will remain just between ourselves ... when we are married." I manage to catch his eye and silently impress upon him that he should extricate us from her company. He hesitates, his teeth showing momentarily on his lip. He clears his throat.

"Perhaps we might permit the Lady Elizabeth just a few moments alone, Mother."

Her lips tighten, the lines about them gathering into what my father would have termed a 'pig's arse.'

"Very well." She stands and with a perfunctory curtsey to her son, glides past us, her head high, her servants scurrying in her wake. Before I can speak, Henry drops my hand.

"You'd do well, Elizabeth, not to make an enemy of my mother. She is a good and virtuous woman; one you should emulate."

He has his back to me, fidgeting with the papers on the table. I jerk my head high.

"I have some news I thought you would prefer to hear for yourself first, considering how things have been between us."

He stops fussing with the letters and turns slowly to face me, a dark red flush beneath his skin.

"And your news is?"

I step toward him, brazenly grasp his hands and bring them close to my face, rubbing them against my cheek, allowing my joy to show.

"I am with child."

He becomes very still, the expression in his eye remaining unchanged. He takes a deep breath before he speaks. "That was quick. How very … convenient."

I drop his hands, let him see my hurt. "Henry!"

He moves away, pours a cup of wine and drinks without offering a cup to me. I suddenly realise that in all the weeks I've known him I have yet to see him happy. I have never once heard him laugh aloud for pure joy; a sound I heard my father make every day of his life. This news should make him the most jubilant man alive, yet here he is, still full of doubt, riddled with suspicion.

"I had thought you'd be overjoyed, Henry. I could be carrying your son, your prince, your heir."

He looks at the floor. "Or someone else's."

My breath breaks on a sob.

"Oh, you are cruel. You know I was a maid when you lay with me first. You know this is your child; a prince to link the houses of York and Lancaster and put an end to the wars. You know that! Why must you be so ... so suspicious of everything, everyone?"

He shrugs. I turn away but his next words give me pause.

"I'd say it was my upbringing. Raised first by my enemies, your father's liegemen, the Herberts, at Raglan. Then my teenage years overseas, exiled, on the run, never knowing who was a friend and who a paid assassin. Your people made me the man I am, Elizabeth. Your precious father; I cannot change that. I cannot be joyful."

He speaks the word 'joyful' as if it is a flaw, a defect. I narrow my eyes, spit through my teeth.

"Then you have my pity, sir. I bring you the best news a man can have; tidings of the son your house craves, and still you see demons. For Heaven's sake, why not look upon it as God's blessing on our union? It is what the people want. They are crying out for you to make me your wife and now you should do so before I am shamed before the world."

There is a long drawn silence. He turns and perches on the edge of the table, puts his cup beside him on a sheaf of papers. His eyes are sad.

"Oh, I will make you my wife, Elizabeth. I will not deny you that, but it will be a dark day in hell before I trust you."

With one hand he gives what I have asked for, and takes from me with the other.

"How am I to rule alongside a man who can show me no trust?"

"You will not rule beside me. I will make you my wife; I might even be persuaded to let them crown you if I have to, but you will never rule. York shall have no more influence over the future of England than the colour of our son's first shoes."

Chapter Nine
Boy

<u>Overijsse — 1486</u>

A nightingale sings in the tree outside the window. The boy, familiar now with the smell of ink and parchment, puts down his pen and goes to lay his head on the sill. He closes his eyes, drinks in the sound of the birdsong and waits for Brampton to arrive.

For two years now the boy has been here in monastic quietude learning the delights of philosophical discourse. At first he was homesick, always looking forward to Brampton's next visit or rare invitations to his aunt's court—always incognito, of course.

As good as her word, Margaret has kept the boy supplied with serviceable clothes, good food on his table, and his chambers replete with books.

"It is important," she tells him in her letters, "that you learn to be the prince you were born to be."

He learns fast. There is little else for him to do. Sometimes he even forgets he is an exile, assuming the identity of another until the time comes for him to be Richard of York again. He knows Latin and Greek, philosophy and history and, when Brampton comes, he practices his skill with the sword and in the tiltyard.

It has been many months since Brampton last visited, and the boy is impatient for the sound of his horse in the distance. Brampton brings news from home, word from his mother, sometimes a note written in cypher expressing her love and loyalty. At last, when the afternoon sun is heading west, a swirl of dust appears on the road. He hears a clatter and a cry at the gate and his old friend rides wearily into the courtyard.

Last year when he came, Brampton brought tearful news of his Uncle Richard's inglorious death on the battlefield against the usurping Tudor. The boy wept to hear how the last Plantagenet king was betrayed by his own countrymen. A new regime now ruled in his place.

The boy spat in the dust when he learned of his sister's marriage to that invading king. He remembers his eldest sister with fondness; the rainy afternoons when she read stories of Arthur and his round table. It is hard to reconcile that memory with the woman who is now his enemy, Tudor's queen.

The boy hurries down the steps and they embrace before Brampton ruffles his hair in the same infuriating way he used to. The boy ducks away from him and scowls playfully.

"How are you, boy?" Brampton throws off his gauntlets and summons a passing monk for wine.

"Well enough, what news from home?"

"The Tudor is over the moon now your sister is soon to be lighter of a son. I've heard they plan to name him Arthur." Brampton laughs derisively.

"Arthur, like in the tales?" The boy looks pleased, forgetting momentarily that the newborn will be a rival, son of his deadliest enemy. "Is Elizabeth well?"

Brampton shrugs, surprised to notice a downy shadow on the boy's upper lip. Mentally he counts backwards, working out his age as he makes his answer.

"I don't know, but if she is anything like her mother the child will be brought forth safely, and I doubt Tudor will waste any time before getting another on her. A king can never have too many sons. Look at your father; he

68

had a nursery full of brats, two strapping boys and yet ... his royal line will die out with you. Unless you do something about it."

"Get married again, you mean. My first wife is dead."

Hot from the saddle Brampton eases off his jerkin, untucks his shirt and pours some water into a bowl, rubs a cloth around the back of his head.

"I meant make some preparation to take back your throne – you can't do that with a wife in tow."

"Oh. I am not ready." The boy's eyes are fearful but Brampton pretends not to see it and hopes he will outgrow his cowardice. Brampton, his wet hair standing up on end, plucks a grape and pops it into his mouth.

"Of course, you know what Tudor has done?"

The boy shakes his head, just once, his eyes fastened on the man's face. He watches as Brampton tosses a couple more grapes between his big yellow teeth.

"Think about it. In preserving his own son's claim he reversed that act, the Titulus-something-or-other, that declared you bastard. To marry your sister he had to legitimise her. Yes?"

"Yes." The boy nods, watching Brampton's gyrating jaw as he obliterates the grape. The man reaches forward for the wine again.

"Well, in doing that, he made you legitimate too. As long as you were legally a bastard, the crown was rightfully Tudor's. Now, since you are not misbegotten, you are once more your father's heir. Tudor's only right to the throne is through your sister, Elizabeth, but you, boy, are heir before her." Brampton drains his cup and bangs it on the board. "And legally the rightful king of England."

The boy blinks but doesn't speak. His mind is awash with many things. He is beginning to feel he belongs here,

69

sometimes he thinks he'd prefer to stay put, devote his life to study. There is a girl in the kitchen who smiles whenever she passes; a pretty girl with big grey eyes. He likes it here although memories of home often intrude on his present peace; a distant image of a loving family, a bevy of sisters, all doting and giggling over him.

England; it is like another lifetime, one of privilege until his father died and he and his mother and sisters were plunged into danger, taking refuge in sanctuary. He prefers not to remember the period of uncertainty while he and Edward were housed in the royal apartments at the Tower, awaiting the glorious coronation that never happened; the sudden reversal of fortune.

Uncle Richard came to them in the Tower, his face white and anxious as he tried to explain why Edward could never be king. The boy blinks away tears at the memory of Edward's sharp and sudden anger, his refusal to obey, his denial of food, his rejection of comfort or sleep. The boy flinches physically from the unbidden memory of that last night and his elder brother's rejection of Brampton's attempt to save them. He can never forget the smothering blanket, the fear; the foolhardy escape beneath London Bridge in the custody of the man who brought him halfway across Europe into the protection of his aunt.

Brampton spits on the floor, pulling the boy from his reverie. "Of course, Tudor has no idea you are alive. He is living a fool's paradise and so is your sister, but we will let them continue until the time is right."

"We will not hurt Elizabeth, or her child?"

Sometimes the boy is unsure if he wants that day to come. The thought of raising an army fills him with dread. When he tries to picture himself leading a large troop into enemy territory, his imagination baulks. Why

70

would men follow him? He is just a boy. He likes it here; he wants to pluck up the courage to speak to the girl with the grey eyes, to find out her name.

"Perhaps it is too late, Brampton. Perhaps we should leave well alone. I was not born to be king, Edward was. I am happy enough here with my books. I have thought perhaps I might enter the church."

Brampton roars like a lion and punches the wooden table. "I have spent three years of my life defending you, keeping you safe, giving up my own ambitions for the day we will fight for yours. Don't tell me of your reluctance to leave the cushioned existence you are enjoying here. Whether you like it or not, the day will come and you will welcome it, boy, come hell or high water!"

Chapter Ten
Elizabeth

<u>Placentia Palace, Greenwich — March 1486</u>

Henry is a complex man, warm and cool in turns; one moment an ardent lover, the next little more than a gaoler. In early March, just as the worst of my sickness is passing, he embarks upon a progress north. Constant rumours of unrest, small pockets of demonstration against his rule, force his hand. I do not even suggest I travel with him, although as a young girl I accompanied my parents on many such journeys. There was nothing I liked better than hearing the people in full song as they expressed their love for us. But I sense Henry's uncertainty; he is not yet used to showing himself to his people and is unsure how to get them to love him. He is so fearful of an assassin that when he is in public his shoulders tend to hunch and his eyes dart uncertainly from side to side. It is not an endearing picture of a king.

For days the palace is in upheaval as he prepares for a few months on the road. On the last night he comes to me in my chamber but, fearful of injuring the child, he does not lay with me. As if I am a child that cannot get by for a few weeks without guidance, I am given a list of instruction.

"Be ruled by my mother, she is my mouthpiece in all things."

It is always so, I wonder that he needs to remind me. His mother, who has spent her life fighting for her son's concerns, is not content to be called by the long-winded title of *My Lady, the King's Mother*, but has taken to signing herself Margaret R., as if she is herself the queen.

I do not stoop to fight her; I know I cannot win. She stands upright beside me while the king's horse is brought to him. Henry is fiddling with his gauntlets, shrugging his fur cloak higher about his neck. He glances at me and away again before I can speak or catch his eye.

He is riding north, into Yorkist territory. There may be people there who will speak out against him, or worse. For the first time I feel a thrill of fear as I contemplate the possibility of an assassin. In the crowd-lined street it would be easy for an unknown hand to strike against him ... or a small army of them to rise suddenly. Henry is the last of his line.

My hands travel to my belly. It is flat yet, his child is not yet making himself known, but I am vulnerable ... we all are. Security is not a luxury of kings but for Henry, whose enemies are legion, it is worse. If I lose him now, I will be alone, my unborn child at the mercy of the cruel world.

A sudden craving for his reassurance washes over me. I want to feel his gentle touch on my hair, his kiss on my forehead. I step forward, reach out to detain him and whisper in his ear to keep safe. But before my fingers can grasp his cloak, Lady Margaret steps between us. She kisses him on both cheeks in the French way and issues some last minute instruction, no doubt telling him to be sure to wash behind his ears.

My hands fall to my sides. Through a blur of tears I watch Henry mount; he gives a quick, tight smile and raises his hand in farewell. Then he calls to his outriders and they clatter away, leaving me at the mercy of his mother.

*

I keep to my chambers as much as I can, closet myself with my favourite women. We busy ourselves fashioning tiny garments for the new prince. Anne Parry softly reads a passage from the Bible, and a minstrel strums a lute in the corner. When Anne's voice fails I tell her to put the book away, and to while away another hour, we each take it in turns to sing. When Elizabeth Stafford sings the cuckoo song, I am whisked back to my girlhood when I would delight to sing before my father's court.

Beside me, my cousin Margaret remembers it too and her eyes fill with ready tears. She has been weeping on and off for days, unhappy at the marriage Henry has proposed for her to his cousin, Sir Richard Pole. She has reduced several kerchiefs to shreds as she constantly beseeches me to intervene with Henry, both to delay her marriage and to allow her brother Warwick to leave the Tower.

To alleviate her misery I promise to do all I can, but I don't know how I am to approach the matter. Henry never encourages any intervention from me and, with the constant rumblings of discontent from the Yorkist party, I can quite see why he would want to keep young Warwick close. I wonder if there will ever be peace in England. I had hoped that my joining with Henry would satisfy the warring houses of York and Lancaster, but now I lose hope. In the early days of our marriage I secretly rooted for York, but now I carry the heir in my womb, my allegiance is shifting. I am neither one thing nor the other.

The song comes to an end, Elizabeth resumes her seat, and the minstrel puts down his lute and takes some refreshment. Mother is dozing at the hearth. She spends much of her day with me now, for we are both missing

Cecily. My sister has lately been taken into the Lady Margaret's household, and a fine new wedding has been arranged with John Welles. She is pleased to be getting herself a viscount, but he is an unambitious fellow and, since he is so loyal to Henry, I rather suspect that the king is bundling Cecily out of harm's way. His mother keeps my sister close, as if they fear her Yorkist blood makes her prey for the disaffected faction at court. I know my sister better; her interests do not stray beyond the latest fashion in hoods and sleeves. There is not a political bone in her body. She is not the one they should watch.

I lay a hand on Margaret's sleeve and ask her to pass the bowl of honeyed nuts for which I have a craving. She dabs away a tear and leans forward for the dish, passes it back to me. I offer her one and she absentmindedly takes a handful. We chew contentedly, our attention half on the conversation and half on private matters.

A scuffle at the door and the king's mother is announced. She sweeps into the room and immediately every one straightens up, the atmosphere shifts and thickens. At the sight of her my heart sinks, but then I see Cecily is with her and it lifts again. Mother stirs at the disruption, surreptitiously wiping a trickle of drool from her chin. "Lady Margaret," she says thickly. "Cecily."

They greet me first, as is etiquette, and then Cecily hurries to Mother's side and begins to enthusiastically describe her wedding dress. Lady Margaret lowers herself into a chair, her back straight as she fans herself rapidly, although the chamber is not over warm. She looks distracted, two parallel lines stand sentinel on the bridge of her beaky nose.

"Are you well, Lady Margaret?" I venture, and she turns toward me with a quick movement, like a bird of prey when its hood is suddenly removed.

"Perfectly. I have had word from the king."

I put down my sewing and cock my head enquiringly, determined not to show how annoyed I am that he writes to his mother yet neglects to send word to me.

"And how is he?"

"He is well enough but we fear trouble may be brewing."

It is just as I feared. I lean forward in my chair.

"Trouble?"

"Stafford and his brother have escaped sanctuary at Colchester and are inciting rebellion. Richard of Gloucester's former lap dog, Lovell, is stirring trouble too."

My heart sets up a dull thump that fills my ears, making me nauseous. I swallow a lump from my throat.

"Where is Henry? Is he safe?"

I cannot help but remember another king who believed he had the support of his courtiers. Of all Henry's followers the only one whose loyalty is unshakeable is his Uncle Jasper.

"Henry was at Lincoln when news came. He kept holy week there and now plans to ride on into Yorkshire and put the rebels down."

"Oh, pray God he is successful."

I get up and walk to the window and back to the hearth. My mother's face is pensive, her eyes fixed on the dying flames, but she doesn't speak. It is my mother-in-law who answers.

"Of course he will be. God is on our side. He proved that at Bosworth."

As soon as I am able, I excuse myself and sit down to write my husband a letter.

"I would have word of your well-being, in your own hand, my husband. I fear for your safety. I pray you send me a letter by return. I shall not rest until I hear from you."

Within the week a messenger arrives with his reply. When it is brought to me I am attended by just one maid of honour, a girl of twelve who is soothing my aching head with an infusion of camomile. Her hands fall away as I sit up and reach for the letter; my eyes quickly scan the neatly written script that makes light of my concerns. I can almost hear the derision in his tone.

"There is no need to worry. The good people of York lined the streets in welcome," Henry boasts, *"and cried my name with one accord. You have no need to worry. "*

I glance up at the messenger boy and recognise him from my father's court. I give him the benefit of my best smile.

"All is well with the king … that is good news," I say, but as I am about to return to the letter, I notice he avoids my eye. His expression denies the comfort of Henry's words; my heart misses a beat.

"What?" I demand, leaping too quickly to my feet so that the room tilts a little. "What is it? You must tell me what you know."

As tiny bright lights dance in the periphery of my vision the fellow reluctantly stammers a story of an attempted kidnap at York, and the king escaping by the skin of his teeth when Lovell and the Staffords try to lay siege to the city.

Every drop of blood seems to drain from my head, the room tips. I stagger, grope for the chair behind me and lower myself awkwardly into it.

"The king is safe, Your Grace," the boy assures me. He is on his knees, terrified at his breach of trust, fearful of the king's ire when he discovers it. I blink at him, try to force his swimming features into some semblance of order.

"Don't worry," I assure him. "Thank you for your honesty. The king will never know that I am aware of what has happened."

The boy grovels at my feet, kissing the hem of my skirt, babbling gratitude while my maid of honour frantically dabs my forehead with a damp sponge.

"Go." I push her hand away, wave the messenger from my presence, suddenly irritated. "I want to be alone."

The girl doesn't leave. She fusses around me, loosening my bodice, fanning my face as she frantically seeks to draw me from the brink of oblivion.

"The king will come home now," I murmur, half to myself, but I am mistaken, he does not come home. Stubbornly he continues his progress, making light of the brush with disaster. He writes from time to time with news of pageants and shows of adulation from the people, but never once does he mention the attempt on his life. From Bristol he writes to me of the poverty there and his promise to build ships, to make the English fleet the best in Europe.

I do not let the Lady Margaret know that I have discovered the truth, and she does not confide in me again. I guess that Henry has instructed her not to. It is through other means that I hear of the warrant put out for Lovell's arrest and his flight into hiding. I remember Francis Lovell; he was my uncle's loyal friend. I know his wife, Anna, a gentle home-loving woman. She must be fretting for her husband but there is nothing I can do to save him. Not now he has made an enemy of the king.

My informants also say, although I find it difficult to believe, that Henry has ordered the Stafford brothers dragged from sanctuary at Culham Abbey. Their trial, I am sure, will involve an equal lack of mercy. My dreams are haunted by the screams of dying Yorkists.

The following weeks are fraught with discomfort. The child swells in my womb, my head aches, and I am constantly on my knees praying for the safety of my husband. I seek refuge in my mother's chamber and lie across her bed with my head in her lap. I am finding more and more lately that I want to retreat into childhood, when the sanctuary offered by her lap was secondary only to that afforded by my father. In the face of my fear, Mother remains serene as if she knew no harm would come of the rebellion.

"There is never any peace for those in power," Mother says as she massages my temples. "Your father would have said it was nothing but a fart in the wind, Elizabeth. There is no need to fret."

Her musical voice lulls me into a half sleep, the familiar scent of her bed, the light touch of her fingers making me believe the past few years have been nothing but a dream, and I'll wake any moment, safe in my father's court.

Winchester — September 1486

Nobody told me it would be like this and there is a moment when, with his head stuck fast in my nethers, I think I will never bring the child forth alive. The poppy seed and tansy they feed me offers little relief and my prayers to St Margaret bring no reprieve. My world is a nightmare, a swirling, spinning animal existence of pain and punishment. My body is failing, my knees knock, my back breaks and the blankets are drenched with sweat and blood and tears. I cannot go on.

Someone pours moisture onto my lips; I grab at the cup, take great gulps of water so that it runs down my chin and soaks my nightgown. Then the pain returns with the grip of the devil. I whimper, gripped with a mightier pain than ever before.

Mother comes forward, takes both my hands and forces me to kneel upright as if in prayer. Behind me I hear the soft drone of my ladies asking St Margaret of Antioch to send me the strength to bring forth a healthy child.

"Push, Elizabeth," she demands. "Push, push like a daughter of York. Push as if you are having a shit." There is no time to be surprised at her crudity. Her teeth are clenched as she bears down with me, her gown as damp with sweat as mine, her flaxen hair fallen about her face that shows each exhausted line. I grip her tightly, I clench my teeth as she is doing and, screaming and bawling like a cow in the byre, I push harder than I have before. My child shifts in the birth canal, startling me, making me realise I have the power to do this. I am Queen of England and I will give them a son of York.

The pain relents just for a moment. I squat, still clinging to my mother's hands, and I wriggle my hips as she has instructed. The child shifts again and, when the next pain assaults me, with a great scream I force my son out of my body and into my mother's waiting hands.

I fall forward onto my face, fighting for breath while my women scrabble behind me. There are hands on my buttocks, my thighs, warm wet fluid flowing all around us, the sweet sharp smell of new life flooding the chamber.

While the midwife washes and binds him tight, my son squawks like a piglet. I am still panting and weak when they put him to my breast. I look down at his battered

81

face, his bruised nose and blood-clotted hair, and with a shock, I realise he is the image of his father.

We name him Arthur, after the king of old. The name makes me think of my brothers who loved to listen to stories of Arthur and his knights. I push the painful thought of them away and lower my lips to my son's head. I inhale the heady scent of infant and my senses swim with contentment.

I have all I need.

Arthur is sleeping now, his eyes shut tight, his rosebud lips making sucking motions as if he dreams of my breast. Soon they will take him from me and lay him in his vast gold-encrusted crib of state, but for now I snuggle him close and sink further beneath the covers.

I must make the most of him. The wet nurse is coming tomorrow. Since Arthur is heir to the throne, Henry's mother insists everything must be done by The King's Book. Left to my own devices I could probably persuade my husband to allow me a few more weeks with my son, but I know better than to ask it. It has long been the convention for the royal princes to be raised separately from their mothers. At least he will be nearby for a while but, in time, he will have his own household, away from court. Henry suggests Ludlow on the Welsh border is a suitable residence for the Prince of Wales, and even though my heart weeps at the thought, I do not demur. That day is in the future, for now Arthur is here with us, and I must make the most of it.

I watch Henry with our son, counting his long perfect fingers, feeling his strong kick and although he doesn't say so, I know I have done well.

Chapter Eleven
Boy

Overijsse — May 1487

A bead of sweat trickles from Brampton's brow and into his eyes, giving the boy a chance to undercut his guard. A clash of steel and with a grunt of defeat Brampton stumbles backward to land on his backside in the bracken. "Ha!" The boy waves the tip of his sword before his instructor's face. "I have you."

"So it seems." Brampton shakes his wet hair and with a wary finger guides the sword-point away from his nose. The boys steps back, reaches out a hand to help him to his feet. "You have made progress since my last visit."

"I've been practicing daily. One of the lay brothers was a soldier in another lifetime. He is still agile enough with the sword to keep me on my toes."

The boy flops onto his knees in the grass and fumbles beneath his discarded jerkin for the wineskin. He tilts back his head and, as he drinks, Brampton notices the strong sinews of his neck, the large Adam's apple that speaks of encroaching manhood. The boy hands over the wine and Brampton drinks with him.

Here, where the pine trees form a dense circle about the clearing, the boy is relaxed; there is no sign of his former anxiety. Brampton notices a new confidence. The boy is growing up, maturing into a handsome young man with a striking resemblance to his father. Already, he is better educated than Brampton and his sword skills look set to soon match his.

Throughout his years here at the remote monastery, the Duchess has sent regular tutors both to entertain and to teach the boy courtly manners. He will be an all-rounder; the Duchess has ensured that he can dance, fight, sing and play. It seems that, like his father, he has a natural talent for making people love him. When the day comes for him to go to court and reveal his true identity, the women will fall at his feet.

"How long are you staying this time?" the boy asks. He is lying on his stomach, a blade of grass between his teeth, the sun glinting on his bright hair. Brampton, resting on one elbow, looks at the clear blue sky and has no wish to leave.

"I have no need to be in Lisbon until July. I may stay a few weeks."

"Then we can practice every day." The boy rolls on to his back, his long hair falling away from his face, the strong bones of his jaw prominent. "I dislike being in the classroom when the weather is fine."

"I will be black and blue." Brampton ruefully rubs his buttocks and the boy laughs.

"At least you can't scold me for not being committed." He plucks another blade of grass and examines the emerald green beetle that clings to it. As the creature trundles to the end, the boy turns the blade and forces it to travel back the other way. The insect follows his directive for long moments, running back and forth on the same path until, either bored or frustrated, it flies suddenly away. The boy watches it go before turning his attention back to the conversation. "What news is there from home?"

Brampton begins to speak, hesitates, and clears his throat before opening his mouth again. The boy is immediately alert. He sits up, leans closer. "What is it? What has happened? Is my mother well? My sisters?"

"They are fine, as far as I know. No, there is another matter. A curious thing has happened."

The boy is kneeling now, leaning forward, his loose white shirt stained with grass. The lacings gape at the collar, revealing his chest, which is not yet quite that of a man. A trickle of perspiration hurries down his throat and settles in the hollow of his neck.

"A fellow has turned up in Dublin, claiming to be young Warwick. He has challenged Tudor's throne, declared himself King of England."

"What?" The boy sits up, his eyes crinkled incredulously. "Warwick? You said he is in the Tower."

"So he is, as far as I know. Maybe Henry has some innocent locked up in his place, I don't know."

The boy frowns, his eyes darting about Brampton's face as he digests the information.

"Where did you hear this?"

"I got it from a contact. You don't need to know the details." Brampton brings his knees up and loops his arms around them. "They are now claiming he is Edward of Warwick, but I am told in the beginning they declared him to be you."

"Me? Who the devil is he?"

Brampton shrugs. "Your guess is as good as mine but Lovell and Lincoln are backing him. He has mustered an army."

The boy jumps up, his face red with indignation. "That is tantamount to treason!"

Brampton looks up at him silhouetted against the blue sky. In his rage he looks every inch the fellow his father was in his youth; tall and strong and a match for any man.

Even though he is just a boy, Brampton would think twice before fighting him in earnest.

"Tudor is certainly seeing it as such."

The boy emits a humourless laugh. "I didn't mean it was treason against Tudor. I meant treason against myself. Lovell and Lincoln should follow no one but me!"

"But they think you are dead, boy."

The boy's eyes narrow, his chin juts forward. "But I am not dead, am I? And if I am ever to reclaim what is rightfully mine I need the men of York to fight for me, not waste their blood over some pretender. What is to happen now? Is he marching on London? Will there be a fight?"

Brampton shrugs.

"I await news. I cannot tell the future. We will watch and wait and the outcome will help us decide what our next move should be. A messenger is due from your aunt, who has spies everywhere. You know, she wants you to join her at court very soon."

"Leave here? For her court? Soon?" The boy's eyes are shadowed, suddenly shifty as if he does not relish the thought. Brampton sits up straighter.

"I thought that would please you."

"Oh, yes. It does, it does. I just … no matter."

"Come, we should get back. I will need to take a bath before Mass. I stink like a mule."

The boy looks into the wood, his mind distracted, his brow troubled.

"I will follow after," he says. "I want to check if there are rabbits in my traps."

Brampton picks up his doublet and tosses it over his shoulder. He had no idea the boy had taken to rabbiting.

"I will see you at dinner," he says as his charge meanders into the wood.

The boy raises a casual hand but Brampton doesn't leave at once. He watches as the boy passes into the shadow, sees him shrug into his jerkin and pick up his pace, heading for the track that leads into the wood. And then, as Brampton makes to turn away, his eye is taken by a movement in the trees. He squints into the sun and sees a figure emerge. They meet in a shaft of sunlight and the boy slips an arm around her shoulder before they disappear into the covert.

*

"Must you go, Peterkin?"

The boy extricates himself from her arms and dries his lips that are wet from her kisses.

"I must. I have duties, and so do you." He pushes her playfully and she laughs up at him from the meadow grass. There are seeds and twigs in her hair, the mark of his mouth on her white throat. His heart twists at the thought that soon he will be forced to leave her for good and reside at his aunt's court. Marin will stay behind, become the wife of someone else, grow fat with another man's children, roughened and embittered by her peasant lifestyle. He wishes he could take her with him but his world is not for her.

For weeks now they've met daily, at first just talking and walking until he plucked up the courage to hold her hand. Hand holding soon emboldened him to sink with her into the long grass, the sweetness of her body encouraging him to touch and kiss. But he'd been careful not to harm her. She was young and a virgin still, although for how much longer he could not promise.

Each time they embraced she allowed him further liberties, and sometimes it seemed he would drown in her softness. It was harder and harder to withdraw.

87

He turns reluctantly away from her, pulls on his jerkin while she arranges her petticoats and tugs up her bodice. When she is safely covered he pulls her to her feet, kisses the tip of her nose and sends her on her way.

She runs along the dwindling path and, as soon as he can no longer glimpse the whiteness of her cap through the trees, he turns on his heel and heads for the monastery.

Chapter Twelve
Elizabeth

Cousin Margaret pulls me casually to one side to whisper in my ear. Her tight grip on my forearm is the only sign of her agitation. At first I can make no sense of her words, her breath buzzes in my ear, making me shiver involuntarily.

"Lincoln has fled court."

Our mutual cousin, John of Lincoln, has seemed content to serve Henry since the king pardoned him. As Richard's heir, he could have been punished with the rest of them. I had thought he was grateful for his life. Just last week I danced with him and found no sorrow or discontent in his manner. He seemed to be forgetting and beginning to move forward, but it seems I was mistaken. I squeeze Margaret's hand and draw her with me to my mother's side. Mother looks up from her Bible, surprise wrinkling her high clear brow. "Is anything wrong?"

"Margaret tells me John has fled England."

She closes her eyes slowly and smiles at me condescendingly as if I am still a child.

"And that surprises you? You thought he was content to play second fiddle? He is for York, as always."

She lowers her eyes back to her book and I realise she is not surprised. More to the point, she knew it was going to happen. How can she be so disloyal? I snatch away her book and hiss through my teeth so as not to arouse the suspicion of my women.

"Did you know of this? Are you involved in it?"

Mother's lips tighten and she reaches out to reclaim her book.

"I am not involved, no. Let us say, I guessed something like this would happen. York will never lie quiet under Lancastrian rule."

A fine line of perspiration coats her upper lip and she isn't looking at me. I fear she is lying. I sink to my knees and grip her hands, wrenching her attention from her book.

"Mother, if you are in any way culpable, I will not be able to save you. You must not get involved. Henry does not listen to me."

"No." She cannot hide her disdain. She looks up from the page, closing the book but keeping a finger between the leaves. We regard each other for a long moment.

"Have you betrayed me, Mother, and my son? Does the blood of York not flow strong enough in us?"

A slight movement of her head suggests the negative but I don't know if she is denying the betrayal or the potency of my son's Plantagenet blood.

I open my mouth to probe further but there is a disturbance at the door. The king's mother and Cecily come sailing into the room. They make the necessary greeting and then, throwing courtesy to the winds, Cecily comes forward and grabs for my hand.

"Bessie, did you hear about Cousin John? They are saying he has fled to Burgundy, to Aunt Margaret who is launching a challenge on Henry's throne. She has found a boy to head her army and she says he is Warwick."

"My brother?" Margaret interjects. "But that is absurd, everyone knows the king has him prisoner." She flashes a look at Lady Margaret, half rebellious, half fearful.

The king's mother's smile does not falter. "Not a prisoner, my dear. My son merely keeps your brother safe from the grasp of unscrupulous people like your aunt, who would undermine our rule."

"But how can anyone believe it is Edward, everyone knows he is ... not himself?"

It is the first time I have known Margaret to come so close to mentioning Warwick's difficulties. The poor lad cannot tell a goose from a capon and we all fear he will never be more than the child he seems. He is eleven years old yet cannot even tie a ribbon or count beyond five. He spends his days playing a tuneless melody on his whistle and drawing infantile pictures of kittens. Edward of Warwick will never lead men into battle.

One of my women belatedly brings Lady Margaret a seat. She smiles her thanks and sits down, smoothing her skirts before clasping her hands in her lap, her serenity unmarred.

"What does the king say, My Lady? Does he know?"

"He is with the council. We will know his feelings soon enough."

Like my mother, Lady Margaret is cool. She has learned not to let her feelings show, but I am so stirred up by the news I can barely sit still. All sorts of scenarios and consequences are tumbling in my mind.

"I wonder if the king will cancel his progress into East Anglia and Warwickshire. He may be needed here."

I look wildly from my mother to my mother-in-law and back again. Both women remain infuriatingly calm and collected; only I am flustered. I cannot remain seated. I get up and begin to pace the floor until Mother orders me to sit down again.

"How long will Henry be in council?" I ask, although nobody has any way of knowing the answer. "Oh, I do hope he comes soon. I cannot think straight. Do you think the Duchess will launch an attack? Lincoln is well loved in

England, men may flock to his …" My words fade as I notice the growing fury on the king's mother's face. "But, of course," I finish lamely, "there are many who love Henry, too."

*

A few weeks later we learn my cousin is indeed with Aunt Margaret, but Henry, refusing to show he is at all perturbed by the threat, sets off on his progress as he'd planned. He comes to my chamber the night before. After we have coupled, he rises from the bed straight away as is his habit.

"I am taking Suffolk with me; that should help keep his son in check."

I have my doubts but I do not voice them. Suffolk is John of Lincoln's father, he may prove to be a good hostage to his son's loyalty but I pray that the chains that bind him are made of silk.

"Be careful, Henry," I implore as he shrugs back into his nightgown. "Sometimes I fear we have enemies everywhere."

He looks down at his chest, struggling with the tangled lace fastening at the neck. I move closer, pull his hands away and tie the strings with a neat bow.

"It is ever the way with kings," he says, smiling his thanks. But he is wrong. I was never fearful when my father rode abroad. Everyone loved him. He was a golden prince full of bonhomie, he basked in the love of the people. England will never know his like again.

Henry places a hand on the back of my head, drawing my face close for a brief kiss. "Take care," he says. "Go with my mother to Chertsey and pay heed to what she says."

I nod and watch him slip through the door. I want to call him back. He represents not just my own security but that of our son, too. Our future rests on his narrow shoulders. I climb back onto my curtained bed, hide beneath the covers and lay awake until dawn, wondering if I should tell my husband that my mother may well be involved in this latest plot against us.

Chertsey Abbey — May 1487

Lady Margaret and I are standing on the spot where the body of King Henry VI once rested. It is a peaceful place, fragrant with May blossom, clusters of primroses hiding beneath the hedge. "I used to visit the old king's grave," she says. "But it was never good enough for such a saintly man." Margaret had loved the old king well. "Moving his body to Windsor was the only noble thing Gloucester ever did." She sniffs and dabs a kerchief to her eye.

Richard's name on her lips makes my heart leap a little, a memory of his face, the ease of his presence. I close my eyes and try to conjure the emotion he once roused in me, but although I still feel sorrow at his passing and a lingering sense that, given the chance, he would have made an honest king, I realise my passion for him was nothing but a girlish fancy. Guilt at the sorrow my silly passion heaped upon Aunt Anne swamps me and I send up a prayer for forgiveness.

"Perhaps my late uncle's decision to honour the remains of King Henry is proof of his innocence in the matter of his death."

Lady Margaret sniffs and jerks my hand from her elbow. "It could equally indicate culpability."

She stalks away and I bite my tongue at having spoken out of turn. If only I could forget my origins and begin to think like a Tudor. I am learning that it is more beneficial to keep my mother-in-law sweet than to bear her disapproval.

Since I produced Arthur she has been gentler with me, less inclined to remind me of the debt I owe to her and her son. She is always reminding me I could have been left in ignominy. I lift the hem of my skirt and hurry after her. As we near the outer gate we hear the sound of galloping hooves, and she stops with a hand to her throat, anticipating ill news.

"Your Grace." A dusty messenger falls to his knees, forgetting in his haste that it is me he should greet first. Lady Margaret snatches the letter and tears it open, her eyes flicking back and forth as she quickly scans the page. As she reads the blood drains from her face, her cheeks are paper white.

"We must join Henry at Kenilworth," she says, turning on her heel in the direction of the abbey.

"Today?" I ask as I hurry along behind. "What does the message say? Let me read it."

She throws open the chamber door, tosses the letter on the bed and begins to issue orders to her women. Our apartments are thrown into disarray and as my clothes are dragged from the coffers and thrown upon the bed in a heap of velvet and lace, I snatch up the letter and begin to read.

"Lincoln is in Ireland with Francis Lovell and the pretender has been crowned king of England at Dublin. My informers warn of an imminent invasion. You must join me here at Kenilworth with all haste."

"We must fetch Arthur en route." I look up from the letter. My mother-in-law is already tying up her cloak and pulling on her gauntlets.

"There is no time. Henry orders us to join him at once; he makes no mention of your son."

"Well, I will not leave him to the mercy of our enemies. Lincoln knows very well where the prince is lodged. Do you want him raised with the enemy as Henry was? It will not take us far out of our way. You go straight to the king if you must but I will not budge without my child. Tell the king if you will that you were too rattled by the threat of invasion to save his heir."

She looks at me, cold fury in her eye, her lips pulled so tight they are devoid of colour.

"Very well," she says at last. "Have it your way."

I send a messenger on ahead to ensure the prince and his household are made ready for a journey. I want to tarry at Farnham for as short a time as possible. If we hurry we can reach my son tonight and leave for Kenilworth first thing in the morning.

*

The sun has barely risen when we mount up and ride across country to be with the king at Kenilworth. By midday the sun is so hot that I discard my cloak and wish I'd worn a lighter kirtle. Dust from the road is kicked up by the horses' hooves, coming down again to coat us, cloying at our noses. The nursemaid keeps Arthur's head covered to protect him both from the sun and the dirt. Behind us comes his wet nurse, bundled onto an ancient mare, and I hope the horse's jogging does not curdle her milk; it will not do to have Arthur fractious.

Henry barely greets us when we arrive. He remains closeted with his Uncle Jasper and leaves me to settle in as best I can. Kenilworth is well-fortified and I am satisfied that nothing could breach its thick defences, which are surrounded on three sides by a wide mere. My chambers are luxurious and the great hall is even grander than I remember it from my father's day. I am eager to see the new tennis court that Henry is having constructed, although I am sure there will be little time for leisure while we are here.

But the luxury and security of Kenilworth help my fears recede a little, and my ladies and I make ourselves at home. There are men coming and going at all hours, messengers galloping away in the dead of night. I wonder if Henry sleeps at all.

He certainly has no time for me. I am barely settled into my apartments when it is time for him to ride off again at the head of an army. He has the courtesy to come and say farewell. He kisses me goodbye and bids me care for our prince. When he turns away, I leave his mother to dominate the leave-taking as she always does, and climb a winding stairway to the top tower.

I look down at the mustering men at arms. A few short months ago I believed the wars were over but now, thanks to my cousin's dissatisfaction, there is to be another battle. More men must die. Knights and their followers have ridden from all parts of the realm at Henry's command. I pray they are more loyal than those who followed Richard.

My stomach churns at the thought of what war means but I try to steel myself, push away fruitless tears and pray for my husband's victory. It is better to lose another cousin than to sacrifice my son's throne to the cause of York. I hope, if he is aware of it, my father will understand.

I know my mother won't.

I lean as far as I dare over the parapet and see below me, among the tall glittering knights, Henry seemingly small and vulnerable. From this angle his body appears squat and distorted, like a silver-clad dwarf. He kisses his mother and, as he pulls away I see her reach for him again but he is gone, calling to his uncle who runs, mail clanking, to join his king.

Jasper has supported Henry throughout his life. He is the only man he can wholly trust. They mount up. Henry places a hand on his sword hilt as if to reassure himself it is there. As he does so a sudden breeze snatches at my veil, almost tearing it from my head, and I give a cry of surprise. Henry glances up, white-faced, alert for an assassin. I raise my hand and blow a kiss into the wind and he smiles, suddenly and unexpectedly, and blows one back to me. My heart flips in my chest and a kind of peace descends upon me. I smile despite my fears and lean further over the parapet so as to keep them in my sight for as long as possible. As the king rides out to face his foe he doesn't turn around, but I know instinctively he will come back.

Chapter Thirteen
Boy

<u>Malines, Brussels – July 1487</u>

"Richard!"

The boy, having grown used to the name 'Peterkin,' flinches at the use of his old name. The Duchess rises from her gilded chair and embraces him unexpectedly. He flounders in her embrace for a moment, and over her shoulder sees Brampton smothering a laugh. As soon as he is free to do so, he executes the special bow he has been practicing for this meeting while she smiles indulgently.

His aunt launches into a criticism of the recent events in England, and the boy cranes his neck about the vast hall. It is a long time since he has enjoyed such luxury, if indeed he ever has. Every interior surface, the doorways, the ceiling, tables and chairs are encrusted with gold, or something as much like gold as to make no difference. The hangings are the finest he has ever seen. Beside him, Brampton is unaffected by the splendour. He coughs and nudges the boy, indicating that he should speak.

Peterkin bows again and clears his throat.

"It is good to be here at last, Your Grace."

"Dear Richard," she says again, lifting his chin with her forefinger to examine his face. "So handsome; so very much like your father."

She claps her hands and a serving wench enters with a tray of wine and three cups. She places it on a table by the window. The Duchess ushers them toward it and with a wave of her hand bids them admire the vast formal gardens outside. With a jerk of his head Brampton sends the girl away and begins to pour the wine. He bows as he offers the Duchess the first cup.

"I take it you were behind the fiasco at Stoke, Your Grace?" Although there is no one near, he speaks quietly, takes a gulp of wine and wipes his mouth on the back of his hand.

"It is of no matter. It was an experiment, to test the water. It proved to us that there are many in England who resent Tudor's rule and who will rise in numbers should the right candidate appear."

Brampton puts down his cup. "Not many chose to ride against Tudor on this occasion, Your Grace, but many died. How can that be of no matter?"

She fixes him with a sharp stare.

"They knew what they were doing. Both Lovell and Lincoln knew the boy they used as bait was nothing but a dupe. Had they won, we would have replaced him with Richard here, once it was safe to do so."

She nods toward her nephew. It is strange to be called by his given name again; the boy has grown used to 'Peterkin' or 'boy'. In the early days he saw the rustic name as an insult, but now it has become a term of endearment, a familiarity he has come to enjoy. He has few enough friends and now that he has left Overijsse, he misses Marin as much as he once missed Edward and his sisters. He wonders what she would make of all this. *What is she doing now?* Weeping probably, wishing for his return.

The boy drags his attention away from Marin's charms and back to the conversation; his aunt is speaking, a flush of agitation spreading on her cheek.

"Next time, mark me, things won't go as well for Henry Tudor. Perhaps this time we were a little impatient but we will learn from that. Had Tudor not held Lincoln's father in such close custody, I have no doubt more men would have ridden out beneath our banner. Next time we will know better."

"Tudor is no easy conquest. He is wily and wise; his life in exile has made him so."

"Tudor is not made of the material of kings; he is an upstart and a usurper. He will be no match for us."

The boy wonders how such a weak and feeble king managed to overthrow King Richard, who was one of the finest generals in England. But he says nothing. He can see the Duchess is growing riled. He looks from her to Brampton, listening intently, and for the first time begins to realise that men have actually died for the cause that was lost before it began.

"What of the boy, Simnel, I think they are calling him? What has Tudor done with him?"

Margaret's laughter tinkles like a thousand tiny bells as she seeks to soothe him. "Tudor is a fool. He has set the boy to work in his kitchen; he is too soft to punish him properly, luckily for the child."

Richard is relieved to hear it. It would be hard to hear an innocent lad had died on his behalf; a lad who, so they said, was little brighter than the real Warwick he pretended to be.

"Warwick will never be a contestant for any man's throne. Tudor had him taken from the Tower and paraded through the streets to prove our boy, Simnel, was a pretender. My informers tell me your cousin can barely tell one end of his horse from the other."

She throws back her head again. The boy watches her; the gaping mouth showing broken teeth, a thick coated tongue that wobbles in her throat as she laughs. The Duchess's finery goes only so deep, he thinks, and not for the first time wonders if his quest is worth it.

The boy Warwick, whom she mocks, is her nephew too, and Richard realises he himself only finds her favour because he is strong enough to promise victory. Because of his resemblance to his father, the men of York will flock to his banner, but what are the chances of success? His main supporters are made up of one reprobate Portuguese and a dowager Duchess bent on revenge. The others who promise him backing are as yet faceless, too fearful of the Tudor king to join with him openly. The boy sips his wine, feels the thick red Burgundy soothe his throat.

"We need more support," he says, putting forward his first proposal and moving a step closer to the adult world of intrigue. "France is no friend to England and neither is Scotland. Can we not approach them for backing?"

The Duchess plucks a grape from a piled up bowl and pops it into her mouth. It bulges in her cheek for a moment before she dispatches it to her belly.

"It is all in hand, my dear," she says. "Now, I have had a chamber prepared for you close to mine. Nelken," she summons the maid, "take my nephew to his chamber and make him comfortable. There are matters I would discuss with you, Brampton. I will see you at supper, Richard."

Thus dismissed, the boy obediently puts down his half empty wine cup and follows the girl from the hall. She leads him along great wide corridors and up vast staircases that could take five men abreast going up, and another five coming down. At the turn in the stair she pauses, one hand on the bannister, and looks over her shoulder at him while she waits for him to catch up. He looks about him with his mouth open, overawed at the grandeur of the palace. As they progress side by side to the upper floor, a host of disapproving framed Belgian royalty watch them go, their painted eyes seeming to follow, an arrogant knowing quirk upon their brush-stroked lips.

She throws open the chamber door and the boy enters. The room is vast; the bed in the centre is itself the size of a small ship. There are windows on three sides looking across formal gardens to the wooded hillside beyond. Everything is splendid; dark carved wood, plush rich coverlets, thick bright hangings, and enough candles to illuminate a cathedral. It is far grander than he'd been used to in England and certainly grander than the humble monastery he'd recently left.

He turns from the window and looks on the bed, the promise of downy softness making him yawn. It is a bed made for sharing.

"Are you going to rest now, Your … Sir?"

She is unsure how to address him. After all, who is he? A king? A prince? Or a bastard his aunt has picked up on the streets? At the sound of her voice he turns in surprise. He had not realised the girl still lingered. He gives a half laugh and tosses his cap onto a nearby chair.

"Yes," he says as he sits on the edge of the mattress. "Would you help me with my boots?"

She is pretty, plump and pink and probably fragrant. She kneels at his feet, her skirts swelling around her and begins to untie his laces, glancing up at him from time to time as she works. Her head is covered by her cap but at the nape of her neck a few strands of red hair have escaped. He imagines it flowing, cinnamon red and fragrant, about her shoulders. She looks up again and, from his advantaged position, he can see the swell of her young breasts above her bodice, a pulse in the base of her throat. The shape of her chin, the youthful curve of her cheek reminds him of Marin and loneliness floods him.

"What is your name?" he asks gently and the girl blushes, her face turning as pink as the rapidly setting sun.

Chapter Fourteen
Elizabeth

"Mother? What is happening?" I turn a circle in the centre of the chamber where my mother's belongings are in disarray. Her clothing and books are piled into coffers as if she is preparing for a journey.

She turns to me, her face grey with sorrow.

"The king is sending me from court. It seems I am no longer welcome here."

I move closer, my head whirling as if I am entering a nightmare.

"Not welcome? Why now? I don't understand."

I watch in disbelief as she picks up a shift, examines it for stains and discards it on the floor.

"Then you are a simpleton. Your husband has been slowly ousting my influence upon you. First, in February, he commandeered my holdings and gave me a pitiful pension of four hundred marks a year. Now he is sending me into seclusion at Bermondsey." She sniffs and pulls off her hood, shakes out her hair. I see threads of silver that were never noticeable before.

"Bermondsey?"

The abbey lies across the river, opposite the Tower. There is not another abbey in England more suited to ensure she never forgets for a moment to think about the life she has lost and the suspected murder of her sons. Surely Henry and his mother have not picked it for that very reason? I try and fail to imagine my flamboyant mother cloistered in a nunnery, on her knees in prayer when she could be dancing. Why is Henry doing this? Why now?

"Has he given a reason?"

She shrugs, looks down at the heaped finery upon the bed. She gathers it up.

"I will give this to Cecily. I will have no need of it where I am going."

I step closer, lay my hand on hers and wait until she raises her eyes to mine.

"Why now, Mother?"

"He seems to think I may have had something to do with this latest unrest ... at Stoke."

Unrest is putting it mildly; according to my informers the battle was wild and bloody. Although Henry pardoned any who surrendered to him, the conflict was fierce and the losses high. There is always too much blood in war.

"And did you?"

"Did I what?" Her eyes are indignant now, a hint of colour in her papery cheeks.

"Did you know of it? Did you intrigue against us?"

She pulls her arm away and marches to the outer chamber, ordering her women to hurry up with their allotted tasks. "And find my daughter Bridget and send her to me," she demands. "I would have one daughter about me who has some faith in her mother."

I follow her, halt halfway across the room. "I have to know, Mother. I have to know if I can trust you. I am your first born. How could you betray me, and my son? Are we not Plantagenets too?"

She refuses to answer. Even when I demand it in the name of queen. She gives me a derisive scowl and continues to sort her belongings, angrily throwing some upon the floor and stashing others in boxes. I watch for a while, as unwanted as her discarded linen. After a while I turn away, and hurry to my own apartments.

The fear that she may have plotted against me will not subside. I try to remember who visited her chamber regularly, the people she writes to, but I am not with her constantly enough to recall them all. As I gaze unseeing from the window, I realise I should share my fear with Henry but I know I won't. As long as he is unsure of her involvement she is safe but, my mother or not, the moment he has proof of her duplicity, her life will be forfeit.

I miss her more than I thought. At first I try to persuade Henry of her innocence, but he is immoveable. Without her I am alone; it is not until she is gone that I realise how often I turned to her for support or advice. My sister Cecily has become too close to the king's mother for me to prove a reliable confidante, and my cousin, Margaret, is married now and making ready to accompany her husband, Sir Richard Pole, to Ludlow where they will have the overseeing of Arthur's care. I am wary that she may confide my secrets to her new husband. He is the king's cousin and Margaret is already in despair at his refusal to intervene on her brother's behalf. She says that he has no desire to embroil himself in politics, so poor little Edward of Warwick continues to live apart from all his kin in the grim keep of the Tower of London. I sometimes fear he will remain there for the rest of his life.

*

It is late when Henry pays an unexpected visit to my chamber and I am already half asleep. I have been head-achey and weepy all day and my heart sinks when he takes off his robe and slips naked beneath the sheet. I am not in the mood for his lovemaking but I know better than to demur.

I try to show willing while he grunts and sweats on top of me, but the glimmering attraction I once felt diminishes as my sadness increases. Since he deprived me of my mother I have known little else but sorrow, and even went so far as to ask for little Arthur to come to court. It seems this was wrong of me. Princes should be raised away from courtly intrigue, in a separate household to the king; it says so in the king's mother's precious book. When Henry has done, he rolls from my body to lie at my side. He is breathing heavily as we stare without seeing at the high canopy above us.

"Are you comfortable?"

I jerk my limbs irritably. Why does he always ask that? It is as if he feels his manhood is so vast that I am too weak to bear it. I hide my irritation and answer that I am well.

He pulls himself higher on the pillows and reaches for a cup on the nightstand.

"I thought we could begin preparation for your coronation soon."

At first I think I have misheard. Like so many things, my coronation has long been a bone of contention between us. I had begun to believe he meant to dishonour his promise.

"That will please the people; it is long overdue."

He slurps wine from his cup.

"A king cannot organise his queen's crowning in the midst of a rebellion. The delay is their fault, not mine."

I know that is not the complete truth. Henry has been reluctant to crown me until he himself felt secure. Now he has wiped out most of the lingering Yorkist party, he feels safe to go ahead.

"When is it likely to be?"

"I thought November. That should give us time to arrange everything."

"Mother will be pleased. Do I have your permission to visit her and ask her to attend?"

A long silence, broken only by the crackling of the flames in the hearth and the slight wheeze of his breathing.

"You may visit but do not invite her. She must remain where she is, out of the public eye."

I sit up, shocked from my usual controlled calm.

"Henry, she is my mother. How would you like it if your mother was not there?"

I cannot keep the resentment from my voice, and the words *'your mother'* are replete with bitterness.

Henry remains unmoved. He turns cool hooded eyes upon me. "I would not like it at all, my dear," he says. "But *my* mother's loyalty is unshakeable. She would die for me."

I slide from the bed, my hands shaking as I struggle into my robe.

"And that is what you want, is it, Henry? Complete subjection? Women who will die for you? Well, you won't get it from me."

The corridor, lit only by sconces, is dim; too dim for the guards to see my tears as I dash past them. I burst into the chamber that Margaret shares with my other ladies and locating her with some difficulty, I drag her from her bed.

"What is it, Bess?" She stumbles after me, still stupid with sleep. The other women peer curiously from their pillows and I know that, come morning, my midnight breakdown will be on everyone's lips.

We hurry to a small antechamber and I fall sobbing into a chair. I am shaking from head to toe. I have crossed the king, for the first time I have spoken out against him. He could cast me off; shut me up in a nunnery like he has my mother.

At last Margaret strikes a light, and the candle illuminates her like an angel of mercy. She opens her arms and I fall into them. Her grip is solid and warm as she tries to make sense of my garbled, frightened words.

*

Henry does not come near again. For weeks I hear nothing more of the coronation. I visit my mother and tell her my fears, but there is little she can do to reassure me.

"You should have kept calm. There is nothing inflames a man like indifference. Now he knows your weakness he will use it against you. Warwick, me, the future of your sisters, are all tools he will use to control you. You must learn to turn the other cheek."

I sniff and wipe my eyes on the corner of my veil. Impatiently, she hands me a kerchief. She is right; Henry and his mother use our family as if we are counters in a game. Although my little sister Bridget has made it clear she wishes to become a nun, the king's mother wants to marry her to James, the king of the Scots. In the past she has gone so far as to persuade Henry to offer my mother to the Scottish king, too. Scotland is too close for comfort and, should they ever become a real foe, their court would provide a perfect nest for our enemies. Henry is desperate to get King James on our side.

I look about my mother's humble chamber. It is comfortable enough. There is glass in the windows and hangings on the wall, but compared with the majesty she is accustomed to, it is a bleak outlook; almost as bleak as my future.

I let out a gusty sigh and she takes my hands.

"Listen to me," she says as she strokes my brow. "No matter what sorrows come, there are always methods for making our lives sweeter. Henry has not treated me so badly. I am warm and dry. I am alive. And things could have gone much worse for you. Outwardly, I am nothing more than his prisoner, yet in here," she taps her temple, "I am as free as a bird. No man can tell us what to think."

I blink up at her, the soft tone caressing and sweet, reminding me of the times as a child when I took a tumble in the garden and she picked me up to rub my knees. As the meaning behind her words becomes clear, I begin to feel a little better. She continues to speak and as she does so, something unleashes in my mind and I realise what I must do, how I must behave.

"He married you, didn't he, when he could have kept you under lock and key? And now, you say he plans a coronation. You will be queen, you will have everything. Riches, fine clothes, jewels... Be grateful. It could be a lot worse. Don't be a bull like your father was, be subtle and spin your womanly web like a spider about him, until he is yours."

I find I am nodding, but then I remember the flaw in her plan.

"But he has not been near me in private for months, not since I crossed him."

She laughs merrily at my simple mind.

"He will, my dear. He hungers for another son. No king is safe with just one; look at your father, he wasn't secure with two. You are beautiful, royal blood flows in your veins, and Henry Tudor has always coveted both. He will come to you, once he finds he can no longer stay away."

111

I lay my head on her shoulder, inhale her familiar scent. "I am glad we are friends again, Mother."

I feel her body shake with mirth beneath me. "You are my daughter. I will always be your friend, come what may ..."

I sit up. Our eyes meet, full of love, full of gladness, but as I gaze at her, I realise hers are shadowed. Her smile conceals deeper sorrows than I will ever know.

"Mother, do you know what became of Edward and Richard? Do they live still? I wish you'd tell me." My voice is all but a whisper.

She pulls down a shutter between us and turns sadly away.

"If I knew they still lived, Elizabeth, I'd not tell you for you'd carry it straight to the king. Your son and mine place a barrier between us, but it is only a silken screen. It will not destroy the love I bear you. Be content with that."

Chapter Fifteen
Boy

<u>Malines, Brussels 1487</u>

For the first time, the boy mixes with the elite. When the Duchess introduces him as her "dear boy" the foreign officials bow over his hand and do not enquire as to the details of the relationship. A fellow a few years older wearing a cap encrusted with seed pearls waves a wine cup and declares he is glad to know him. The boy, resplendent in a doublet of the Italian style, smiles and inclines his head this way and that. The evening passes in a blur of heady introductions, half-remembered names. He dances with half a dozen women who laugh and simper, although he has said nothing amusing. He wishes Brampton were here to guide him, put him at ease with his rough humour, but Brampton has little regard for high company. He will be swilling ale in a hostelry with a comely wench on his knee.

Richard, as he can now be called again, leads a young woman with a high plump bosom back to her mother. When he takes his leave she clings to his hand, prolonging his company, but as quickly as he can he disengages himself. The boy likes women, probably more than he should do, but he has only ever desired one at a time. He knows that Nelken will be keeping his vast soft bed warm until he returns, as she has done these last six months.

Nelken is not as innocent as she first seemed. He soon learnt that her blushes and timid ways masked a variety of bolder skills. She dispatched his virginity as deftly as

she removed his clothes. Within minutes of her taking off his boots, he found himself without his shirt and swamped beneath fragrant petticoats. It was a welcome lesson and he was quick to learn it. Poor innocent Marin is forgotten as his head fills only with Nelken.

All the while he is leading the young ladies of the Duchess's court about the floor, he is relishing the moment he can return to the uncultured but lovely charms of the chambermaid.

"Richard, Richard!" The Duchess's voice breaks into his reverie and with a start he realises everyone is waiting for him to answer a question. A question he hasn't heard. He excuses himself.

"I do apologise. I misheard you; the musicians are playing so loud."

The girl with the large breasts laughs, hangs on to his sleeve. "I was saying ..." She lifts herself onto her toes and speaks into his ear so as to be sure he catches every word. Her bosom presses against his arm. "... that you are the most accomplished dancer in the room."

Richard steps back, sweeps a bow and gives her the benefit of his warmest smile. "My dance master will be gratified to hear it, Madam. Now, Aunt Margaret, if I may?"

He holds out his hand and, with a twitch of her lips, the Duchess takes his fingers and allows him to lead her away. The girl watches them go, disappointment marring her expression.

The Duchess's veil floats across his face as they walk side by side to take their position on the floor.

"Really, Richard, what is wrong with you? Her father is the richest man in Brussels; we will need his backing when the time comes."

"I am sorry, I wasn't aware. Who did you say she was again?"

The Duchess's laughter turns the heads of those nearby as they wonder what the boy has said to amuse her. "If I didn't know better I'd think you'd a fancy for the fellows. I swear that girl is notorious; she has sampled every eligible man this side of Bruges."

He smiles, bends his fair head close to his aunt's ear so that none should hear.

"I prefer to be the sampler not the sampled, My Lady; the hunter not the quarry."

There is a pause in the dance in which they are supposed to change partners. They stop for too long, causing a blockage in the promenade. "Sorry." The boy apologises and takes his aunt's arm, moving her to one side to allow the dance to flow again. She regards him for a long half-hostile moment before relaxing and whacking his sleeve with her fan.

"You are a tease like your father, Richard," she laughs uncertainly. "It is almost like having him back."

*

It is late when the last of the guests disperse and the boy is allowed to escape to his chamber. He closes the door quietly; the room is in shadow, the crouching furniture turned into dark assassins by the dim light, the bed in the centre looming like a vast unlit galley. He pulls off his doublet and drops it over a chair, unbuckles his belt and lets it fall. From beneath the bedcovers protrudes a small pink foot. The boy sinks to his knees as if to pray and begins to kiss each toe, one at a time.

She stretches and groans, her toes splaying out as his tongue wraps around them. Slowly, he progresses up the bed beneath the covers. She is naked and warm, slightly clammy with sleepy sweat. As he climbs higher up the bed her legs part to encompass him, her arms reach down, her fingers tangling in his hair.

This is what life is about, the boy thinks. This is why we are put on earth. With each kiss the quest fades further, with each new moist sensation the thought of England and the gilded throne that awaits him there becomes more remote. He doesn't need England, not while he has Nelken. She is more precious than any crown. He should tell his aunt and Brampton that there are more important things.

*

"You look as if you've had no sleep, boy!" Brampton, just back from an early hunt, slaps him on the back, sending a jolt of pain through Richard's skull.

"I've had enough," he mumbles. But the fingers that are separating the orange peel from the fruit are trembling slightly. In truth, he has barely enjoyed a wink of sleep. Nelken saw to that. Once he had loved her and rolled over and tucked his head beneath the pillow to shut out the light of dawn, she had given him no rest. First she prodded, and then she kissed and licked until, against his inclination, he rolled over onto his back, providing her with better access to his body.

He was unwilling at first but sleep was a master easily bested and soon he began to stiffen. She sat up, astride him, and with the early sun on her, she was like a goddess. Her red hair flowed like blood across her breasts as she leaned forward tantalisingly, the tips of her nipples inches from his mouth. Then she laughed, pushed herself upright again, lifting her hair behind her head and arching her back.

"You are a witch, mistress." He spoke through his teeth, fighting for self-control as she raised herself up, coming gently down again to engulf him in her warmth. Tired as he was, he could not pull back.

It was once the loving had finished and they lay on top of the tumbled bedclothes that she really shattered him.

"I am carrying your child," she said. "I am going to be in so much trouble with the Duchess." Her cheeks glistened with tears, her lower lip trembled. "I am ruined," she sobbed, and the boy did not contradict her for he knew that, were he not careful, the path of his life could be altered too.

Chapter Sixteen
Elizabeth

London – 23 November 1487

The river is alive with craft, and boats both small and large jostle to come close to the royal barge. Banners and streamers flutter in the breeze and the surface of the water is sparkling in the winter sun. I order the curtains to be drawn back further, lean forward in my seat and wave to the roaring crowd. All along the banks the people are calling my name, waving their arms. My face aches from smiling.

Close behind comes a splendid thing. A barge carrying a replica of the dragon Cadwaladr—it is huge, painted scarlet and gold, and as it moves slowly along the river it belches forth great spurts of fire. A terrifying thing.

Music fills the air, the finest musicians in the land— trumpets, clarions and drums. As we turn the bend in the river, the Tower comes into view, standing sentinel over London as it has since the Conqueror's time. On the opposite bank I see Bermondsey Abbey, where my mother now resides. My heart falls a little and I wonder if she is watching. Just in case she can see me, I sit taller in my seat, raise my head and wave both hands. She will know my salute is for her, and her alone. It will fill her with joy to see me follow where she led. Her daughter crowned Queen of England after coming so close to ignominy.

Henry is not with me and it is probably just as well. He would not relish this outpouring of love from the public, the calls of "A York! A York!" that pepper the celebration.

He waits for me at Tower Wharf. As we draw close the tall dank walls shut out the sun and I shudder, draw my cloak close about me. When I alight from the barge, he takes my hand and kisses it and the crowd cheer again, their joy following us all the way to the Lanthorn Tower where I am to be lodged. Henry is smiling and for once his good humour reaches his eyes.

That night a great reception is held in the hall and Henry, as is tradition, creates fourteen new Knights of the Bath. There is dancing, music and feasting. Beside me the king is in high good humour, he laughs and seems relaxed and happy, pleased with me. Once he even takes my hand beneath the table and squeezes it.

But later, when it is almost dawn and he comes to lay with me, I cannot respond as I would wish. I am so tired I lay like a wilting lily beneath him, and once he has done with me and rolls over into loud snores, I lie awake in the darkness.

The walls of the Tower seem to be breathing, they press down upon me. I imagine stifled cries, whispering voices, muffled footsteps. As I toss and turn, the remembered images of my brothers, whose crown I have stolen, sit in sulky vigil at the foot of my bed.

24 November 1487

In the morning, I am heavy-eyed and weary. I stifle yawns while my ladies, led by my sisters, dress me in white cloth of gold and a mantle furred with ermine. My hair is left loose, covered only by a coif of the new style, cross laced with a network of golden cord. Cecily, sombre for once, places a circlet of gold on my head to secure the coif. She clasps her hands and stands back to look at me.

"Oh Bessie," she breathes. "I can scarce believe it is you."

"It is me though, Cecy," I whisper fervently, clasping her hand. I reach out for Margaret too, and my sisters, Anne and Catherine, and we all come together in a girlish huddle. "This isn't just my day," I tell them solemnly. "It is a day for all of us; for our mother, and for father, too. Think of them this day for they are here with us. This day is for York—our last day, for afterwards our house will be one with Tudor."

It is a passionate speech that affects us all. Anne wipes away a tear and busies herself arranging my train, while Cecily turns to admire herself in the looking glass, tweaking the ends of her veil and biting her lips to redden them.

"Are you ready, Bessie?" Catherine offers me a kerchief and I tuck it into the pocket that is hidden among my sumptuous skirts.

"I am ready," I say, taking a deep breath to dispel my emotion and calm my raging nerves. I stand upright, take a deep breath and remember how well Mother always bore herself on these occasions. I wish she could see me now. It breaks my heart that she is not here. I must relish every moment so that I may relate it all in detail when I see her next.

In great state we emerge from the Tower and make our way to the open litter that awaits us. It is hung with white cloth of gold to match my clothing, so when I am seated my conveyance appears to be an extension of my skirts. I am glad to find it is well cushioned and comfortable. A knight helps me aboard and I take my place amid the splendour. I am still arranging my skirts when the eight white horses lurch forward. I give a little cry and clutch the sides of the litter while the tassels on the great canopy, borne by four of the newly appointed Knights of the Bath, sway gently above me, as if they are dancing in joy.

My ladies, with Aunt Elizabeth to keep them in order, follow on behind in their own litter. Over the din of the crowd I occasionally hear Cecily's high laughter and, although I dare not look round, I can imagine her waving and delighting in the moment, probably more than I am myself.

Catherine and Anne, who are by nature more sombre, will be more restrained. As we pass into the streets of Cheapside the cries from the populace, already great, grow louder. London is bedecked in ribbons, great tapestries have been hung and velvet and cloth of gold stream from every window.

There is so much to see. I turn my head this way and that, eager to miss nothing, reluctant to disappoint even one of the many who have come here to entertain me. We pass a company of angels; a group of little girls, chosen no doubt for their golden hair and angelic faces. One of them, however, overcome by the tumultuous celebration, has resorted to tears; her mouth is open, her eyes spouting water like a gargoyle on a church roof. Another girl, a little older, distracts her by pointing to me and the weeping child ceases sobbing, cuffs her nose, and waves.

I wave back but my attention is quickly taken by a fresh burst of music. I turn away from the children to a colourful band of musicians; beneath the shelter of a multi-coloured canopy, they let forth a symphony of joy. With my heart surging with love for the people of England, I lean back on my cushions, exhausted but happy. I am unsure how much longer I can wave and smile, and tomorrow will be another day just like this, only better. Tomorrow is my crowning day, the day I will at last feel the weight of England's crown on my brow, as is my birthright.

25 November 1487 — Westminster

"I wish you were coming with me." Margaret is fixing the coif back into my hair. Her hands are gentle and should be calming but my stomach is knotted with nerves.

"I will be there watching with the king and his Lady mother. It is your day, Elizabeth; you are the woman upon whom everyone will be focussed. Besides, Cecily will be right behind you."

At that moment my sister emerges from the closet dressed in a gown similar to my own but of a simpler cut and a different colour. The purple velvet I am wearing is only for princes. She pauses, one hand fiddling with the lacing of her cuff. "You look wonderful, Bessie. Very regal and not like my sister at all."

She comes forward and kisses me. "You look lovely too," I say, putting my hand to my brow while Margaret teases a stubborn knot from my hair.

"I am glad it is bright again," calls Anne from the window. "You need sunshine for a proper pageant. It would have been horrid to be crowned in the rain. Imagine if the poor people had to wait outside in the cold and damp, I am sure they'd never cheer so loudly and the hangings would be dripping wet."

I too am thankful the weather is fine. It is cold, but the sky is clear and the air crisp. The sort of day that makes you glad just to be alive.

When the door opens and the king's mother appears, my aunt Elizabeth, Duchess of Suffolk, claps her hands to gain our attention. The Lady Margaret runs a critical eye over us to make sure we are properly presented, and at her signal my women come forward to tie the purple velvet mantle around my shoulders. It is time to descend to the hall and take my position beneath the purple canopy and wait while the procession forms behind me. My throat is dry. Cecily is fussing with my hem.

"Remember, Bess, I will be right behind you."

I smile my gratitude, lift my chin as high as I can and, just as I have practiced daily for the last few months, try to glide down the stairs as if I am on wheels.

They throw open the huge double doors and immediately the din of the crowd drenches me like a huge wave. The streets are lined with people, the air thick with good wishes. My heart surges and a lump builds in my throat.

I recall my father's love for the people, the easy manner he adopted with them, and I wish I could do the same. I see a fleeting image of my mother-in-law's outrage if I were to abandon decorum and go among the people to shake their hands and let them kiss my fingers. Those relaxed days of my father's reign have gone now. The king demands a stricter etiquette and likes us to remain aloof. I must content myself with a wide happy smile and it seems to serve, for the volume of their cheers increases as I draw nearer.

It is but a short walk to the abbey. Following the regal steps of John de la Pole, I am flanked by the bishops of Ely and Winchester. We pass close by the flag-waving people, their faces a blur of grinning teeth and rosy cheeks. The men toss their caps high into the air, the women and children throw greenery in my path.

We follow the new baize cloth which has been laid to mark my way to the altar and as I move along it, the people surge in behind me to cut it into strips to take home as a keepsake. It is a tradition that's been followed for an age. Behind me I hear their uproarious laughter, screams of hilarity. My smile stretches, my face aching, my eyes moist with happiness.

Then comes a deeper, tortured cry, followed by another of outrage. I half turn but the Bishop of Ely grips my fingers tighter and forces me to keep moving forward.

"Don't look back," he mutters from the side of his mouth. "Just keep walking."

The joy behind me is turning to terror. I hear screams of pain, cries of anger, and the clash of steel. The calls of celebration turn to anguish, "Shame, shame!"

I snatch my hand away from the bishop and manage to turn my head enough to glimpse what is going on over my shoulder. From the corner of my eye I notice Cecily has turned too. We see women fall to the floor, their children crying in fear while their fathers wrestle with the yeoman guard. The crowd surges forward, pushing those before them closer to the procession. I open my mouth to command the guard to show mercy, but the Bishop of Winchester adds his strength to that of Ely and together they all but lift me from my feet and bear me onward to the church.

We pause inside the west door. My heart is banging like a drum, blood surging in my ears. I can hear Cecily whimpering behind me. But the Bishop of Ely's hand is cool. "Be calm, Madam," he says, fixing me with his sagacious eye. "All will be well, you are quite safe."

"It is the people I am worried about. There was no need for violence; that man was bleeding ..."

The doors close behind us, obliterating the sounds of discord. The trumpets sound, blasting out my imminent entrance, and Cecily, still sniffling, rearranges my train. I know I must put aside my distress and continue with the ceremony. There will be time to discover later what became of the injured. In the meantime I can only pray for a peaceful outcome.

We begin to move slowly, step by step, along the nave. My hands are trembling but I rekindle my smile, this time for the sake of the nobility who are seated within. Before me, Henry's uncle Jasper, now Duke of Bedford, bears my crown. I follow him on quaking limbs.

All heads are turned toward me. The voices of the choir soar to the rafters. I raise my chin and glance up at the fluttering pennants, the high gilded ribs of the roof. In the moments before my life is changed forever, I remember all those who have been here before me and, suddenly, I feel very small.

The king remains hidden but I know he is watching, his mother beside him, her sharp eye marking my every move. If I make a wrong step or say a misplaced word she will never let me forget it. I can almost feel sorry for her. It must be hard for her, conceding this much to the house of York; she would prefer all the honour, all the glory went to her son, the Tudor. My presence at his side can only ever serve as a reminder that without me, her son may never have kept his crown.

I am a good wife, a good mother; I have provided an heir and mean to present England with many more. Sons like my father, and daughters like me and my mother. If I have my way we will swamp Tudor's blood with the good stuff of York.

In high ceremony we reach the altar, and the bishop relinquishes my hand. My half-brother, Dorset, recently released from the confines of the Tower, winks at me and raises one eyebrow, forcing me to stifle a laugh. It is so like my irreverent brother to mock at solemnity. I just hope Henry or his mother did not see it. I turn away from him and focus my attention on the solemnity of the moment; my moment.

With Cecily's aid I prostrate myself before the high altar where the Archbishop of Canterbury begins his prayers. When he instructs me, I rise up and Cecily unlaces my bodice. My upper body is bared and, with an intoned prayer, he anoints my forehead and between my breasts. He blesses my coronation ring, and as I am presented with the orb and sceptre, the choir begins to sing again.

Dressed in royal purple velvet, I sit in splendour on the ancient throne. With the elite of England looking on, the crown is lowered onto my head. It is heavy and I am forced to balance it most carefully. As Mass is said I fear I am in danger of losing my crown, so I keep my chin high and look across the nave of bared heads, lowered in prayer.

One day my son will sit here to be crowned king. The blood of York and Tudor run richly through his veins and will flow in his children's too. This is but the first step.

The whole world is watching. I am aware of the king's eyes upon me as well as those of his mother; my enemies as well as my friends are all looking on. I am just a small woman; a few years ago I was a bastard with no future at all. Now, a million eyes are boring into me; the ghosts of my father and uncles, my grandfather of York, together with those who have fought and died for us down the ages. As I achieve their dream to be risen before God to a higher state, all of them are witness to it.

Chapter Seventeen
Boy

<u>Malines – Brussels Christmas 1487</u>

The boy closes his eyes, remembering previous Christmases; his sisters squealing with excitement, his father in blustering good humour. One Yule, he hides behind the drapes of his mother's chamber, watching her woman brush out her beautiful long hair. It crackles beneath the brush and glints in the candlelight. She has forgotten he is there and has put aside her indulgent maternal face and is completely herself. He notices something different about her. She is proud and beautiful as she always is but there is a new expression, something he hasn't yet learnt the word for.

When the door opens the maids bob a curtsey to the queen and scurry out, giggling as they hurry past the king, who takes a playful swipe at the bottom of the last out of the door. Forgetting them immediately, he tosses his doublet on the floor and turns to his wife, his expression altered. The jovial king has gone, replaced by someone new, someone softer and yet more predatory. He holds out his hand and clicks his fingers; the queen rises and moves sinuously like a cat across the floor toward him.

"Elizabeth." His father's voice is husky. With both hands he lifts the mantle of hair from her shoulders, lets it run between his fingers to fall like a sheet of golden rain. He is so tall the top of her head does not even meet his chin. With her back arched and her face tilted to his, she takes a step closer and their bodies touch. The king's hands skim across her, run lightly down her spine and linger at her buttocks. The boy watches entranced as his mother's arms slide about his father's neck. He realises he is seeing a side to his parents he's never known before; a glimpse of a hidden adult world that is forbidden him.

She throws back her head to allow the king to feast upon her long white neck; at the touch of his mouth she gasps, closes her eyes, clutching at his sleeves while his big jewelled fingers dig into her buttocks. Effortlessly the king hoists her into his arms and her legs wrap about his waist. The boy holds his breath as his father carries his mother toward the bed and throws back the curtain.

"What the devil?"

The boy draws back in alarm, thinking he is due for a spanking. His mother squeals as the king tosses her gently onto the mattress before lunging at his son. With a yelp, Richard pulls away and leaps out the other side, crawling beneath the table, waking the dogs and setting them yapping. "You rascal," his father yells. "Wait till I lay hands on you!" But the boy recognises the amusement in his voice and the tinkle of his mother's laughter.

When he reaches the door, he turns and wags a cheeky remonstrating finger at his father before wrestling with the catch and darting into the corridor. As he heads for the nursery, the conjoined laughter of his parents follow him up the tower stairs.

Life is different now. Once everything was multi-coloured, flavoured with saffron; life was soft and comfortable. He was a blessed prince, everyone's little darling. Even the time in sanctuary after his father died was cushioned by the love of his mother and sisters. They shielded him from the worst of the sadness, the danger

130

they were in, and the chilly damp living conditions all seemed part of an extravagant game.

"I will see you again soon," his mother said on the day he was sent to keep his brother Edward company in the Tower while he awaited his coronation. But she was wrong; he never did. The day he left sanctuary was the day his life changed forever.

Since the night Brampton wrapped a rough blanket over his head and carried him kicking and screaming from the Tower, the world had become an unstable, constantly shifting mystery. Now it is difficult to know who he is or what he wants. The only peace he knows is in Nelken's arms and she has spoiled it all by announcing she is carrying his bastard. Now she has no time for him. She spends all her days throwing up into a bucket and he can no longer bury himself in her depths and forget his problems. She is his problem now; the biggest one of all.

*

"Cheer up, boy, it's Christmas!" Brampton claps the boy on the back, making him spill wine down his chin and the front of his jerkin. He wipes the back of his hand across his mouth.

"Damn you, Brampton, you almost drowned me." He puts down his cup and casts a glowering eye around the room. The hall is in full swing, the remains of the feast spread like the aftermath of battle across the white tablecloths. A trio of fools cavort before the dais and the musicians are making ready to play, issuing a sharp discord as they tune their instruments.

Any moment now the dancing will begin, and he will paste on his mercurial, fun-loving face. He has come to detest the endless round of smiling faces, the pointless conversation. Richard's tall bright looks act as a magnet

131

to women both young and old, but he has no taste for what they offer. As he gazes unseeing at the vaulted rafters, a voice breaks into his reverie.

"I hope you manage to find time to partner me this evening, young man. I was quite left out last night."

A middle-aged woman, still bearing the traces of her former glory, drags him back to the moment. He bows politely, kisses the back of her clammy hand and murmurs that she can be sure of it. She opens her mouth to speak again but Brampton grabs his arm, makes a glib excuse to the matron and drags him to one side.

"What is wrong, boy? You've been sulking about something for weeks. Have you fallen out with your hearth wench?"

The boy scowls. "She is no hearth wench and no ... we haven't fallen out."

"Then what is it? I've not seen you this despondent since ..."

"Since when? Since you dragged me from my home, my family?"

His face is hot, his lips tight against his teeth in a sudden ungovernable rage against fate, against Brampton who is his only friend and doesn't deserve it. Brampton draws back, his face stretched with surprise.

"Most men would argue that I'd snatched you from certain death." His face relaxes. "Ah, I see what it is. It's Christmas, the past always seems closer at such times, and old memories have a habit of spoiling the present. Drink up and be merry, boy; there is no need to linger here, go and find your woman and lose yourself in her."

"I can't."

"Why, has she tired of you? Well, there are plenty of others, most of them are falling over themselves to be bedded by the English prince."

A jerk of the boy's head negates Brampton's suggestion. "It isn't that."

"Then what is it, boy? You can tell me." He hooks an arm around Richard's neck, his ear close to the boy's mouth.

"She is with child, as green as a frog and throwing up her guts all over the chamber."

Brampton pulls away, gives a silent whistle.

"Your aunt will be livid, she doesn't tolerate loose living among her servants. How far along is she?"

The boy shrugs miserably. "How should I know?"

"Is she fat yet? Are her tits any bigger?"

"She is just sick and green and won't let me near her. All she does is weep, and no, she isn't fatter, she is thinner if anything. If this goes on it won't be long until she is skin and bone."

"Well, they don't tend to die of it, not at this stage anyway. We will have to find her lodgings somewhere, give her some money to keep her mouth shut. But listen; don't make a habit of it. It won't do to litter the continent with York bastards; they could come back one day and bite you in the heel."

The boy raises his head and blinks at Brampton for a long moment. "I won't abandon her; she isn't a whore."

"She might not be now but she soon will be. How else is she to make a way in the world now? What do you propose then, marry her?" He leans back in his seat, folds his arms and puts his feet on a stool. "She will drag you down. You need take a princess or a rich man's daughter to wife, not a drab. Half the court will have had a go with her before you got there. You have to forget her and look to the future."

When the boy makes no response Brampton continues, speaking quietly and earnestly. "Life is shit,

133

boy, you have to get used to it. Under your Uncle Richard I was a rich man in England, Governor of Guernsey, property in Northampton, but I lost it all when the fates smiled on Tudor. I could have sat down and wept like a woman but I chose to grab what I could and make the best of it. Fate sent me you; our future is bound, boy. You need to grow up. I've a mind to take you with me on my next trading trip—incognito of course; you must leave off your fancy clothes. I will tell the Duchess you need some experience of the world. I will take you to Lisbon where I am having a house built. Your wench will have recovered by the time we return and the brat, if it lives, can be fostered out."

Worn out by the long uncharacteristic speech, Brampton sits back and waits for the boy's reply. In the end Richard rubs a hand over his face.

"I want to stay here; I am needed here."

"No you're not, boy. You are needed in England; the people are restive under Tudor. When the time comes your return will be welcomed, but not if you have a foreign whore on your arm, so forget her and think like a man, like a king."

Brampton's earring glints in the torchlight as he winks, but the boy turns away. His heart is sore; he is afraid of the future, afraid of the man he is becoming.

He gets up and fights his way across the hall, through the celebrating mass of courtiers, almost falls over a tumbling dwarf and crashes into a servant bearing a tray of cups.

"Sorry, sorry!" He holds up his hands and backs out of the room, his pace quickening as he reaches the tower door. As he climbs the stairs, each step he takes grows heavier. He pauses outside Nelken's chamber, hesitates before knocking, pressing his ear close, listening as the seconds slip by. He hears a snivel from within, the sound of retching, a splash of vomit, a groan of misery. After a moment, he turns and hurries quietly away.

Chapter Eighteen
Elizabeth

<u>Hertford Castle – April 1489</u>

I am queasy, my head is light, my belly churning, but I welcome it. Yesterday I realised that I am, at last, in the early stages of pregnancy. I have slept in this morning, detaining my women for a long time over my toilette and lingering to dry my hair before the great fire that is roaring in my chamber. I am staring at the flames, dreaming of my unborn son when Henry comes upon me unexpectedly. He sends my ladies scurrying from our presence.

I rise to my feet, cling to the back of a chair while I fight off an unexpected wave of nausea. "Henry," I smile weakly. "I did not expect you."

"No." He looks uncertainly about the room and I sense that something is bothering him.

"Is anything the matter?"

His answering smile is rigid. He gives a half laugh and looks down, fiddling with a loose thread on his sleeve. With a gusty sigh, he raises his hands in agitation.

"There is always something. No matter what I do, how hard I try to win them over; there is always some new trouble brewing."

He is missing the guidance of his mother who is absent from court, attending to matters of her own. I sense that Henry is in need of someone to talk to, someone he can trust. I take a step toward him, hold out my hand.

"Come, Henry, why don't you sit down and tell me all about it? I might not have the answer but sometimes it helps just to have someone listen. You know you can trust me as you can no other."

Poor Henry craves loyalty. He has not yet learned that, as the mother of his son, I am on his side. The king has recently secured a treaty with Spain with the understanding that their daughter Caterina will be betrothed to our little Arthur when the time is right. It is a fine alliance between our countries and proof of Spanish acceptance of Henry as King of England. This should help to secure his position. If the great heads of Spain accept him, then hopefully others will too.

He follows me uncertainly to the window and waits while I make myself comfortable, but he doesn't join me. Instead he begins to pace up and down, four steps to the right, then four to the left, so that I grow quite dizzy waiting for him to speak.

"The north has risen in rebellion against us," he says at last. I sit up straighter, doing my best to keep my expression bland. It is important that I do not show surprise or fear; he must think I view the odd uprising as nothing more than a necessary hazard of kingship. In truth, fear unfurls in my belly like a sickness. I am no stranger to rebellion and have been close to losing everything many times. The chill memory of my father's exile and my time in sanctuary with my mother and siblings makes me shiver.

"Indeed?" I manage to say calmly. "And what troubles them this time?"

He throws up his hands again. "They sent Northumberland to me in protest against the taxes I imposed. The higher levies are essential. I need to fund the business in France, but they say they are unjust,

138

unrealistic. But it's more than that, isn't it? It isn't just about the money. They resent *me*; they still hanker after your wretched uncle, although he's been four years in his blasted tomb."

Petulantly, he punches a cushion, but I make no answer. I have learned it is best that we do not discuss Richard. After a moment he joins me on the window seat, perching on the edge of the cushion and speaking earnestly into my face, watching my every reaction.

The lines that flank his nose seem deeper today, accentuated by care. His grey eyes are cloudy with trouble. His tongue flicks across dry lips. "I sent Northumberland back to ensure the monies due to me are paid, and the mob turned on him. They dragged him from his horse and ... and they murdered him, like a dog in the dirt!"

"Henry Percy?" I cry, my hands to my mouth, remembering the great earl who was such a friend to my father, and ultimately, an enemy to Richard at Bosworth.

"Yes, Percy. And now the mob runs amok like the misbegotten bastards they are."

"Poor Maud ..." My voice trails off as I think of Northumberland's bereaved wife.

"Aye, poor Maud indeed."

His voice is soft, bringing my head up sharply. Our eyes meet. Henry's are narrowed, as deep in thought he looks away and stares into the corner. Once, so the gossips say, Henry was betrothed to Maud, the daughter of William Herbert, who held him in honourable captivity when he was a boy. The arrangement was stopped by Jasper Tudor's brief return from exile when my father was overthrown. On York's return to power, when Jasper fled once more overseas, he took Henry with him and the betrothal was broken.

139

"Did you care for her, Henry?" The words are out before I have thought them through. He looks up surprised, and laughs; a series of breathy snorts down his long nose, a sardonic smile lingering as he denies her.

"Nay, not really. We were young; it was a tactical match that would have suited her father, but myself? Not so much."

"Not that it matters now," I assure him. "It was all so long ago and feelings change."

I risk a glance at him and see he is watching me. Taking advantage of this new harmony between us, he takes my fingers in his palm.

"They tell me you had a fancy for your uncle once. Do you think of him still?"

My face grows hot. I shake my head, my hair, still damp from washing, falling across my cheek.

"No, of course not; that was nothing but a sly rumour. I am happy with the man I have."

I can see he is pleased. He squeezes my fingers gently, raises them to his lips but says nothing. I have learned not to expect sweet words from Henry, who shows his feelings by way of gifts and actions. If he joins me in my chamber after supper, I can surmise I have pleased him in some way and I have learned to be content with that.

"So, what do you propose to do about the northern rebels, Henry?"

He shrugs. "I have sent Surrey north with an army to restore order. I have instructed him that once they are quelled, he should hang the leaders and then listen to the people's grievances, see if we can reconcile them by answering their needs."

"That sounds a better way of winning them to your side than fighting them, Henry. People respond to reason. When things are quieter you should perhaps take a progress north, let the people see for themselves that you are a reasonable king."

He begins to look happier.

"That is an idea. You must come with me, my dear. The people seem to love you."

My cheeks flush. "I fear I will not be able to, my lord. Not in any comfort."

In answer to his enquiring look, I place two hands on my belly and my smile stretches wider. "I have some hope that I carry another son, my lord."

The summer that follows is long. I am uncomfortably hot and remain at Hertford for as long as possible, enjoying the cooling breezes that blow in off the River Lea. Henry travels from palace to palace, joining me when he can, always with an anxious enquiry as to the health of his child. He heaps gifts upon me: a bolt of black velvet, some lovely russet cloth, and an exquisite squirrel fur that I plan to have made into a hat. He also orders new shoes for my increasingly swollen feet.

I am in lusty health, eating like a horse and fighting a craving for pomegranates. Lady Margaret, when she visits with Cecily, says it is a sign I will prove fruitful and from the way my son kicks and stretches in my womb, I think she may be right. We spend a few days discussing domestic womanly things until a summons from the king sends her scurrying away again. She kisses me warmly, a hand on each shoulder, and I realise she has come to approve of me a little. The birth of Arthur and the imminent arrival of a little Duke of York has helped her to overlook my Plantagenet failings.

I go with them to the door and smile warmly as they mount up, remaining on the steps as they ride away before turning gratefully inside.

There are preparations to be made for my return to Westminster where my lying-in is to take place. By summer's end I must shut myself away from the court and not emerge until the child is born. By my reckoning, I will miss the ceremony that will make Arthur, now almost three years old, a Knight of the Bath. It will be a special day for him and I am sorry to miss it, but it cannot be helped. Both Henry and my cousin Margaret have promised to describe the events in detail.

Within a few days, my coffers are packed and the horse litter made ready for the journey to Westminster. There will be a brief time to spend with the king while I ensure the lying-in chamber has been properly prepared. I look wistfully down at my vast belly and wonder what he will make of a wife who is the size of a galleon.

I need not have worried; his expression when we meet shows no surprise. He takes my arm and leads me into the hall, enquiring after my well-being.

"Is Arthur here?" I ask, scanning the hall hopefully, but Henry shakes his head.

"Not yet; we do not expect him for a day or so."

My face falls. I had hoped to see him before my confinement, but I make no fuss and manage to summon some enthusiasm when my cousin Margaret suggests we visit the birthing chamber.

My apartments that look across the river smell familiar; wood smoke, perfume, a hint of spices, and the fresh tangy aroma of the aloe vera salve I use on my skin. I sink gratefully onto the bed and kick off my slippers. My ankles are a little swollen and the skin feels tight and hot.

Margaret is busying herself about the room, peering into cupboards and examining the array of bottles and potions the midwife has stored there. Alice Massey is to be in attendance to me; she was present at Arthur's birth and proved a stalwart support when I knew so little about what to expect. I don't think I can do without her now.

The bed on which I lie is soft; another gift from the king, the featherbed stuffed with down and covered in the finest Holland sheets. The walls are hung with fine floral tapestries and the ceiling with blue arras cloth starred with golden *fleurs-de-lis*. The pallet bed where I shall give birth is similarly fine, with a high rich canopy of gold with a velvet pall, embroidered all over with red roses. I reach out and feel the fabric between finger and thumb.

"It is very comfortable," I remark, and Margaret turns to me.

"Cousin, it is a chamber fit for a queen." We both break out into silly, girlish giggles.

Westminster Palace – 31 October 1489

Today I must leave the court and retire to my chambers. I may not give birth to the child for a month yet, but convention says I must hide myself away. Although part of me is weary and welcomes the enforced rest, the other half misses court already.

I love the feasting and the entertainments, the fools and players. But I will not be alone, my women will there and Henry has allowed my mother to leave her seclusion to be with me. This morning, to my sorrow, Margaret, my cousin, returned to Ludlow and it is doubtful she will return for some time. Her growing family and the demands of her husband forces her departure. I am sad to lose her but I sense that Henry and his mother are glad that another tie with my past has been loosened.

But my mother is here, and I am grateful to Henry for that. When we embrace she clings on when I would pull away, and I sense a change in our relationship. She has always been the strong one, the woman leading me on, holding my hand, but now the tables have turned and I am the one with the power.

Her time in Bermondsey has aged her. Her hair is less bright, her skin sallow from lack of air, and for the first time I notice the lines of age marring the outer edges of her eyes. "Come," I say. "There will be no formality; come to my chamber and I will send for some wine."

For a while we are mother and daughter again; we speak of confinements. She tells me of the travail of giving birth to Edward in sanctuary at Westminster. "We had no hope then for the future," she says. "Your father was in exile; our lives upside down. I was in despair the day I went into labour, but as soon as he was born and I saw that I had borne a son, I found hope. Edward was sign from God that all would be well again. I had given the king an heir."

I sit quietly, watching her face alter as the memories rush in again. Her face drops, her eyes fill with tears. "But it wasn't all right really, was it?" A tear drops onto her hand, she rubs it away on her skirt. "My son was never destined to rule, was he?"

A memory stirs of my brothers snuggled either side of me while I read to them. Little Richard wielding his wooden sword, his fair hair glinting in the torchlight. "I will be a warrior like Lancelot one day and smite all your enemies, Edward!" It seems like only yesterday.

Mother is openly weeping now. I struggle to my feet and waddle across the room to wrap my arms around her.

"I am sorry, Mother, so sorry." I rock her, as if she is the child and I the woman who bore her. "It wasn't our fault."

She sniffs and pulls away, fumbles for a kerchief.

"Who hurt him, Elizabeth? We know it wasn't Richard. Was it Henry? Are you sleeping with the murderer of your brothers?"

I stand up, step away. "No. No, I am sure of that. He has asked me many times what became of them, where they are. He wouldn't need to ask that if he had ordered them slain."

She stares at the floor; an ageing woman, cloaked in the misery of not knowing.

"Of course, you'd protect your husband. It is your duty."

I shake my head. "No, I wouldn't. You are quite wrong. If I knew the slayer of my brothers I would seek vengeance, no matter who had dealt the killing blow."

That night as I struggle for sleep, memories of my little brothers float through my mind. With so many sisters, they were spoiled and cossetted. Edward was quiet, serious and studious, but Richard was funny, chubby, and the image of our father. He was the noisy whirlwind that flew about the royal apartments with his toy sword, leading the castle dogs into mischief. Full of tales of chivalry and battle, he would have made a perfect supporter for his royal brother. And Edward would have made the perfect king. I have seen him ponder long and carefully before deciding between a honeyed wafer and a sweetened pear just as, had he been king, he would consider each problem from several angles before making a decision. He would have been a wiser ruler than my father and, with Richard at his side to fight his battles, his reign would have been a long one.

I should not mourn them. Their deaths have put me where I am today; had they lived, my son could never be king. In the morning Arthur is to be created a Knight of the Bath, and in a few days will enjoy his investiture as Prince of Wales. But while my child is benefitting from the gap left by my brothers, I am eaten up with guilt for feeling glad about it.

Westminster —All Hallows Eve 1489

In the morning, worn out from little sleep, I make what will be my last appearance at court for many weeks. As my ladies and I make our way to the great hall, Henry's Spanish fool appears in the doorway. With a yell, he takes a sudden leap into the air and, performing a series of backward somersaults along the corridor, lands at my feet. He makes a sweeping bow and offers me something. I reach out warily, knowing his habit of bestowing toads upon unsuspecting ladies for the pleasure of hearing them shriek. His offering is small and furry, and at first I fear it is a mouse and make to drop it, but then I realise it is a rabbit's foot. I open my eyes wide in surprise and give him my best smile.

"For luck, dear Queen." He sweeps another bow and, deeply affected by his humble gesture of devotion, I lean forward and leave a kiss on his brow.

Instantly, he falls over backwards, his hand to the place where my lips touched. "Oh my!" he exclaims. "The lady kissed me!"

Everyone bursts into laughter, the solemnity of the day broken. Our hilarity brings the king, who has been waiting for us within, to discover the cause. His velvet cap appears around the door first and when he sees us all gathered about his stricken fool, he relaxes and begins to smile also.

He offers me his arm and conducts me to St. Stephen's chapel where the Reverend Father in God, the Bishop of Exeter, is waiting to conduct Mass. It is a solemn occasion. I put away levity and prepare to receive the host. Voices begin to sing the *Agnus Dei,* and while the song continues I am led by the earls of Derby and Oxford back to my antechamber. There, beneath the cloth of estate, in the sight of God, the court falls to their knees to pray that I am given a happy hour.

I close my eyes and pray with them; trying to erase from my memory the host of good women I have loved who have died during the travail of childbirth.

And then we partake of a ceremonial meal where further blessings are said. At the end Henry comes forward, puts a hand to my hair and brings my face close for a farewell kiss. Although neither of us acknowledges it, we both know that, should things go badly, this could be our last meeting. I suffered greatly bringing Arthur into this world. I cling to Henry's fingers, hoping he recognises my silent request for his most urgent prayers.

The people depart, leaving me alone with my attendants. The shutters are closed, extinguishing the winter sun, and the fires are stoked. Soon the rooms are stifling, but I know better than to ask for a window to be opened. It will not do for me to be chilled. I must remain here for at least a month, maybe more, until my son has safely arrived and I am churched and made ready to face the world again.

*

"Arthur's ceremony is today," I comment wistfully. I am staring at the tapestry above my bed as I have done every day for almost a month. It is a fine piece of work, come all the way from Flanders. It shows a flowering meadow of daisies and buttercups, a style thought suitable for a woman in childbirth. I am allowed no scenes of action; no figures or faces that might instil fear or bad thoughts. It really is a very pretty tapestry but I am so tired of staring at it. I have been in bed for a week for my feet are so swollen I am forbidden to rise.

Every so often they help me to the close stool or allow me to sit in a chair while my feet are soaked in warm water. As my belly expands, so my need to piss grows more frequent. I sigh and turn over, feeling the sharp dig of the child against my bladder. Heaving myself upright, I call for my mother. "Can you help me, Mother? I need to go again."

The task is far beneath her but she doesn't flinch from it. Gladly, she puts down her sewing and helps me to stand, with my hand in the crook of her elbow she leads me to the screen in the corner where the close stool is situated.

As we cross the room I feel a sudden pop, and my legs are flooded with warm, fragrant liquid. Instinctively, I place my hand on my quaint, like a child who has damped herself. "The water!" I exclaim. "It has broken."

Immediately, the chamber erupts into life. A few moments ago we were all sleepy with ennui but now the air rings with energy. Someone calls for a midwife, another for a messenger to run and tell the king his son is on the way.

"It is Arthur's ceremony," I call after them. "Do not disturb the king."

I don't know if they hear me. As Mother helps me onto the bed, the first fingers of pain begin to squeeze at my nethers. "Oh dear," I whimper, clinging to her hand. "I hope I can do this."

"Of course you can; aren't you my daughter and doesn't the strong blood of Plantagenet run through your veins?"

The midwife orders a brazier lit close to the bed, and when it is blazing she throws on handfuls of herbs. Soon the room fills with a heavy fragrance. "It will ease you," she says and, stifling a cough, I take her word for it.

Someone hands me a drink; a foul-tasting brew which Alice insists will aid me. I empty the cup and hand it back with a wry face.

"It is best you walk around as much as you can, Your Grace," Alice says, pushing my mother aside to place a hand beneath my arm to help me rise again. I do my best; I slide from the mattress and shuffle beside her, up and down, round and round the chamber, stopping only when the pain becomes too intense. I am almost dead with fatigue and feel the pain has been nagging at me for hours. I've lost all track of time.

"It won't be long now," Alice assures me. "Your child will be here before you know it." But she is wrong. For hour after hour, the pain increases along with my fear. The top of my thighs, my loins, throb with a grinding pain that grows stronger with each passing moment. How much can a woman take, I wonder?

I fight for calm, try to breathe, deep and long as I am instructed, but when I find myself suddenly clamped in a markedly strong grip of agony, I groan aloud. My back is breaking.

I lean over the bed, my head resting on clenched fists, and mutter a rapid prayer. "Help me, Lord. Give me the strength I need for this."

As suddenly as it arrived the pain ebbs again, and I am released. Alice ceases rubbing my back and bids me roll over so she can feel my tummy. I can barely move. I am as clumsy as an ox but, with a great cry, I fall obediently onto my back. I do not care when she raises my gown and begins to examine me. I have lost all sense of pride. Her hands are dry and cold on my belly, which is as tight as a drum. I look down to see her busy between my spread knees; my bulging gut and huge breasts make me feel like a cow, but I am unmoved by the indignity of it all.

I just want it to be over.

I greet the next assault with a groan. I can feel it spreading from my loins across my back. My belly is tight, and as it grows even tighter, I fart loudly and a spurt of liquid shoots onto the mattress.

"She will be dry soon," I hear Alice inform my mother. "Dry births are always the worst." With a jerk of her head she urges Mother forward, and I feel her cool familiar fingers slide into mine.

"You are doing well, Bessie," she says, but I can hear the worry in her voice and know that all is not well.

The pain grows stronger, I clench down upon her hand, feel her fingers crunch in my grip as I writhe against the beast that is dragging me down again. My legs thrash, my heels digging into the mattress. With all my might I push and strain, but the child does not budge. I think it will never budge.

I am going to die here.

I am too young to die!

The pain recedes just long enough for someone to hold a soothing flannel to my mouth to wet my lips. I cast an eye about the room, pass a fractious hand across my forehead, and push aside sweat-drenched hair. The king's mother is standing by the hearth, for a moment our eyes

150

meet. Hers are hooded, just like Henry's. I see the scorn in them. I am failing and her white, lined face informs me that I must not fail her beloved son.

They say she suffered badly giving life to Henry; at just thirteen years old she was too small and unfinished to bear a child. Mother told me that Henry's coming ruined her body and left her unable to carry further children, so he became her only son. She steps forward suddenly and I think she means to castigate me. I am not sure I can bear it. My loins begin to tighten again. "No," I whimper, "I can't. Mother, I can't."

Tears drop onto my cheeks. I shake my head from side to side, exhausted and lacking the courage to fight. Lady Margaret takes my other hand.

"Oh yes, you can. You are strong, Elizabeth. You've done it before and can do so again. Now, you push hard when we tell you and let's get this boy out of there. Push with all your strength. Do it for Tudor."

I raise my knees, tuck my chin to my chest and strain for all I am worth. Slowly, the thing lodged in my birth canal begins to move; I grab a few quick breaths and push again, gritting my teeth. At the foot of the bed, Alice Massey peers between my open knees.

"I can see the head," she yells and, putting all my energy into my belly, I strain again.

"Go on!" Mother screams. I lose grip of her hand, flounder for it and grab on again tight. The king's mother's rings are biting deep into my other hand but compared with the trauma that is assaulting my body, the pain is nothing. I rest briefly, pant for breath before trying one more time.

"Wait." Alice leans forward, touches my throbbing, bulging quaint with gentle fingers. "Keep panting, Your Grace. Don't push until I say."

A heartbeat away from real panic, I pant, high and quick in my chest, and feel Mother brush my hair from my eyes. The room is quiet; the other women standing tense around the bed. I notice the strong aroma of ambergris and civet that Alice has been throwing onto the flames. My head begins to swim, my eyes roll backwards.

"Now; not much longer. You can push with the next pain."

The agony builds, slow and strong, rising gradually across my torso until in a great rush my entire body is consumed. Desperate now, I look from Mother to Lady Margaret, lick my dry cracked lips.

"I can feel the pain coming."

Their grip tightens, my knees rise again as if of their own accord. I duck my chin, grit my teeth and with a rictus smile, I bear down with all my might. I am stretching, tearing; my mouth opens in a scream of furious agony such as I have never made before. Then, with a sudden jolt and a spurt of liquid, something shifts.

"The head is born." Alice fiddles between my legs while I gasp and pant like a lunatic. "Push again, Madam, more gently, if you can."

I feel the child turn, a sharp tearing pain as his shoulders are freed and then, with a great slither of limbs and liquid, he slides from my body.

I flop back on the mattress. Mother sits up, wipes a forearm across her brow, leaving a smear of blood. She smiles at me.

"Well done, Bess," she says.

I strain to see, looking down across my ravaged body to where the midwife is waiting for the afterbirth. She frowns and clucks as she prods my belly with calm, capable hands. Lady Margaret is stooped over the bed where a blood-daubed infant is screeching, its limbs punching and kicking the air. The King's mother looks up; her face is puce, her eyes as bright as diamonds.

"It's a girl," she announces and my heart plummets. I feel suddenly sick. I try to sit up, but Mother pushes me down again.

"Oh God," I whimper into the sweat-stained pillow. "I am so sorry. I promised the king a son." I turn my head away so she cannot see my tears, but the bed dips as she comes to sit on the mattress beside me. I look at the red, wrinkled child she is cradling in her arms. My heart lifts, just a little. Lady Margaret looks at me quizzically.

"Why be sorry? There is time for you to give Henry more sons. Besides, every country needs princesses. Look at us. Where would this realm be without women like us?"

Chapter Nineteen
Boy

The deck heaves with the swell of the sea, the sun gilding the tips of the surging waves, spume sputtering like an old man's vomit across the deck. The boy clings to the handrail and looks out across the ocean and cannot help but be invigorated by the freshness of the air, and the freedom of the great canopy of sky.

Until this moment, he had not realised the suffocating confinement of his aunt's court; the clinging embraces of Nelken. He is free now; for a few short months his future set aside. Today he is a sailor, just another member of Brampton's household. He can forget Nelken, forget war, and forget England.

With a gusty sigh, he runs his fingers through his blond hair and feels it thick with salt. His chin is unshaven, for the first time a proper man's beard is blurring his Plantagenet features. He scratches it, relishing the newfound sense of masculinity. For now at least, he is done with foppish court ways.

Turning from the rail, he struts steady-footed across the deck to the cabin where Brampton is studying a map. Brampton looks up when the boy enters, stabs the parchment with a grimy finger. "By my reckoning we should be here."

The boy leans over his shoulder and follows the line of his finger.

"What is it like in Lisbon?" He pulls out a stool and, stealing Brampton's cup, takes a swig of his wine.

"You'll like it. It's a trading port, a gateway to the world where the whores are dark and dangerous."

The boy flushes, not ready yet for thoughts of women. It was not easy leaving Nelken behind. His aunt, having learned of his indiscretion, promised to look after her, but he knows her care will stretch only as far as ensuring she does not starve. Sick or not, she will have to work until the birth is imminent and her child, if it lives, will be farmed out, to be raised by strangers.

He's spared the child little thought, but now, in the gloom of Brampton's cabin, he glimpses a brief bright image of a small boy, wearing the face of his father. He passes a hand across his eyes, erasing the vision, and turns his attention back to the map.

"What do they trade?"

"Everything; spices, wool, slaves. Men gather there from the farthest reaches of the world. They tell some strange tales; things you won't believe."

"Maybe they aren't true? Have you thought of that?"

"Ha!" Brampton takes back his cup. "You, my son, are a cynic. Wait and see. I love Lisbon; it is exotic and wild. You won't want to leave."

*

After the exhilarating voyage, Lisbon harbour is a seething mass of noise and stench. The dock is bristling with masts, the quayside piled high with cargo. Men, their backs bent beneath barrels and sacks, scuttle past like strange exotic crabs. The boy tries to keep pace with Brampton as he weaves his path through the crowd with accustomed ease. Women with painted faces make lewd comments from the sidewalk about the boy's bright hair and athletic build. He snatches his eyes away, reluctant to be drawn by their obvious charms. He thinks of Nelken, tries but fails to remember the shape of her face or the exact shade of her hair. All he can recall are her wandering fingers and the lascivious rasp of her tongue on his skin.

An older woman with threads of grey showing in her black hair calls to Brampton, who stops, pushes back his cap and bows to her as if she were a lady. "The queen of my heart," he says, slavering over her hand, his eyes inches from her exposed bosom. "I shall call upon you later." He jerks his head in the boy's direction. "And find a playmate for my companion, too."

She glides toward Richard, her eyes travelling greedily up and down his body. "Oh, they'll be fighting over you, my lord," she says before opening her mouth in raucous laughter and revealing a set of stained, crooked teeth. He pulls himself away and runs after Brampton who is already starting up the hill toward the cathedral. "Christ," he says. "Who was that?"

"Pilar; she's a fine woman," Brampton replies. "She has been well-used but her lack of youth is compensated by her skill, if you get my meaning. She is still a good-looking woman ... in the dark." He places one finger alongside his nose. Richard knows exactly what he means but finds his stomach turns at the thought of bedding an ageing whore. He is done with women and believes he will stay chaste until he is ready to take a wife. So far, his dealings with them have brought nothing but trouble.

"Where are we going?" The boy fights off the clinging hands of another whore and hitches his pack higher on his shoulder.

"I am taking you to my house."

The boy pauses for a moment in surprise, but Brampton is rapidly disappearing into the crowd so he quickly hurries after.

"Your mother's house?"

Brampton throws back his head, almost losing his cap.

"My mother? My mother died long ago, boy. No, I am giving you the honour of presenting you to my wife!" He makes a mocking bow and ushers Richard down a quieter street and, as they near the end of it, passes through an archway and into a courtyard. There are women, decently dressed, working quietly in the winter sun. One of them gasps and dashes into the house, while the others smile and bob deferentially to Brampton.

"Don't stop! Don't stop." He urges the women to keep on with their work but they continue to cast curious glances at the bright-haired stranger. The boy smiles and lifts a hesitant hand in greeting before following Brampton inside. The hall is dim, an open door revealing a comfortable parlour within. The boy sees a high-backed chair, a lute, and a pile of books, half-finished needlework on a settle.

"Papa!" A young woman comes gliding quickly down the stairs and, regardless of Brampton's sea-stained clothes, she casts herself into his embrace. The boy watches as his friend wraps his arms about her, lifts her from her feet, and spins her in a circle that makes her skirts fly out, revealing fine ankles.

In the meantime the hall fills with other youngsters, all of a similar colouring but of various ages and gender. They clamour about Brampton, pushing and shoving for his attention. He stoops to pick up the smallest girl, settles her on his hip.

"João and Jorge, how you've grown." He tussles the hair of two young boys before beckoning another girl close to leave a kiss on the side of her brow. As he looks on in astonishment Richard counts six children in all, ranging from about seventeen to six. At last Brampton pauses in greeting his family, disentangles himself a little and remembers his manners.

"Ah, let me introduce you to my friend. This is Richard, or Peterkin, call him what you will. He doesn't seem to mind."

The boy flushes and gallantly returns the greetings of his mentor's children.

"Come, Papa, come into the salão. Mama will be so pleased you are home. Maria, send to the kitchen for refreshments."

They all move into the parlour, apart from a girl whom Richard assumes to be Maria. Brampton drops his pack and the smallest boy begins to rummage through it, looking for presents. A cacophony of questions follow, exclamations of delight that fade after a few moments when the door opens and a woman enters.

Brampton breaks away from his children and moves swiftly toward her. For a heartbeat they stand looking at each other before he steps forward and takes her hands, kisses both cheeks.

"It is good to see you," he says, more gently than Richard has ever heard him speak before. "How are you?"

"I am better now but ..." She sees Richard listening. "I will tell you of it later. You must introduce your friend."

She is looking at Richard, her lips slightly parted in query, as if she recognises him from somewhere. Brampton turns on his heel and with a hand to the boy's back draws him into the conversation.

"This is the boy I told you of. He has been with me for a while now, his name is Richard but he answers to Peterkin ... or for much of the time to 'boy'."

She laughs delightedly as Richard bows over her hand and places his lips on her knuckles. "I am glad to meet you, Madam," he says before standing tall again, his head higher than anyone else in the room. She tilts her face, her hand still in his, and curtseys low, keeping her eyes on him all the while.

"I would have known you anywhere. The likeness is remarkable."

"Madam?"

"Your father, King Edward; you are made in his very image. I have never seen the like; it is as if he is in the room with us."

Emotion floods in, making his throat swell, and his eyes smart. "You knew my father? Properly? As a man, not a king?"

"Oh yes. He and Eduardo were very wild together at one time, when they were young."

At first the boy is unsure who Eduardo is, but then remembers it is Brampton's name, or the name he took when he converted to Christianity. The boy smiles and leans forward confidingly.

"You must have stories you can share, Madam. I shall look forward to it."

Her laugh is like a host of tinkling bells, reminding him of home. He examines her more closely as reluctantly he releases her hand. She must be of an age with his mother. Would she too bear the signs of her years about her eyes and mouth? If she took off her cap, would her silvery blonde hair now be tarnished with grey? It makes him sad to think of it and Brampton's wife sees it in the droop of his shoulders.

"I knew your mother, too. She has retired to the abbey at Bermondsey where she can be near the … the queen."

"Ah yes, the queen."

At her instruction, the boy sinks into a chair and smiles his thanks when Maria enters and offers him a tray. He sips rich red wine and selects a wafer from a platter. "How is Elizabeth, do you know?"

"The news is she has borne a daughter, whom they've named Margaret for the king's mother." She accepts a cup but shakes her head when she is offered the plate. He pretends he hasn't noticed her casual use of the title 'king' for the man who stole his brother's throne.

"Have you been back?"

Madam Brampton makes a face.

"No. England is not the same now. I cannot live there under Tudor who has slaughtered, or imprisoned, or placed all my friends in penury."

"How can Bess? If people like you and Brampton cannot tolerate it, how can she? I am her brother, and because of her husband, Edward was killed! How can she live with that?"

The children are looking on wide-eyed at the exchange but she answers as best she can.

"I doubt she has been given much choice. She was there, after Bosworth, in Tudor's hands. If he desired marriage there was no champion to save her from it. I suspect Elizabeth is wise and is making the best of things. Women are more resilient than you might think."

Brampton's children have fallen on the platter of pastries, their happy cries negating the emotion in Richard's heart. As his shoulders sag further, Brampton steps forward and pulls a stool to sit between his wife and the boy.

"It won't be for much longer, boy. Soon you will be ready to take your rightful place. We will treat your sister honourably, but the throne is yours and there are plenty who will back us."

161

"And what about her children? Am I to murder my nephew and my niece to take back what is mine? Or do I condemn them to an existence such as mine has been?"

Brampton sits back, looks at the ceiling where smoke from the hearth is creeping like a thief along the rafters.

"That decision, boy, can be made when we get to it. First we have other fish to fry. We need an army and must seek the support of Tudor's enemies."

After supper, Brampton signals to the boy that they are leaving. "We'll not be long." He kisses his wife and tells his children to go to bed peaceably when they are told.

"Where are we going?" the boy asks as he shrugs into his jerkin.

"You'll see."

Earlier, the boy had enjoyed the luxury of a bath. He'd lain back in the warm soapy water while a servant scraped the beard from his chin. Now his skin feels delicate and soft in the chill night air. Brampton sets up a steady pace, forcing the boy to jog alongside him, and soon he realises they are retracing the path they took that morning.

Close to the dock, Pilar steps quietly from the shadows. "You've come then, you old rogue," she laughs. "I've passed up a pretty penny to be with you this night." Grabbing Brampton by the tunic, she bears him away.

The boy looks on in disbelief. It makes no sense. Brampton's wife is good and clean and loving. How can he neglect her for a bawd like Pilar? He is still standing there, his fists clenched in angry confusion, when he feels a light touch on his arm. He looks down into a pair of large brown eyes.

"No," he says, shrugging her off and fighting to fix Nelken's face on his inner eye. He cannot see her and the prostitute is persistent. She tugs gently at his hand, her eyes gleaming in the darkness until he finds he has followed her to a small dwelling beside the inn. She pushes him down on to a couch, loosens her bodice, and his hands move unbidden to discover small tight breasts. Pleasure floods through him and he closes his eyes, gives himself up to the sin of the moment.

*

"How can you do that?" Much later, he scurries after Brampton back toward the house. "You have a wife who loves you, children that look up to you. Have you no honour?"

He is still tucking in his shirt, shrugging back into his jerkin. When Brampton turns suddenly, the boy draws back in alarm and falls on his arse. The man looms above him, spitting in anger.

"You are full of shit, boy! Didn't you just indulge in the same sin?"

"I don't have a wife and besides, I am not talking about sin, I am talking about love. Why, with a family and a wife like you have, would you sport with whores? You dishonour her; you do not deserve a good woman like her!"

Brampton's lips tighten, his jaw clenches. With furious eyes he drags the boy to his feet and pushes him back against a wall, clenches the front of his shirt so there is but an inch between their faces.

"It is none of your business, boy, but since you persist; without risk to her life my wife can give me no more children. I almost lost her with the last one so, in 'honouring' her with my body, I'd be condemning her to death. Do you understand me now? Do you?"

He wrenches himself away and begins to walk backwards up the hill. As he does so he wags a furious finger. "Don't ever think to judge me, boy. Ever, do you hear?"

Then he turns on his heel and runs uphill toward home.

Chapter Twenty
Elizabeth

<u>Sheen — May 1490</u>

"She is lusty." Henry comes up behind me and places a hand on my shoulder. I cover it with my own. After a long episode of squawking, Margaret is now sleeping. I stand up carefully so as not to wake her and, signalling silently to the nurse, we tiptoe from the room.

It was Henry's wish to name Margaret for his mother, but I content myself that it is after my cousin too, whom I miss more than I'd imagined. Baby Margaret is very demanding and much more difficult than her brother was, but she is delightful. She is fat and rosy, and smells of honey and camomile. When no one is around, I like to hold her close and inhale that sweet baby smell, feel her fat little legs kick strongly against my lap, her clammy hands on my face. She will be a girl to be reckoned with, I am sure of that.

"There is no need for you to spend so much time in the nursery, you know; we have servants for that," Henry says as we pass along the corridor and down the narrow stair.

"I know, but I like to be there. I am glad she can stay with us. I have missed so much of Arthur's infancy. It is hard for me to have him grow up so far from us. Having Margaret close compensates for that."

The guards at the entrance to Henry's privy apartments straighten up at our approach and the doors are thrown open. His hand is on my back as we pass into the antechamber, his fingers creep down my spine, sending a delightful shiver through my body as he ushers me into his private rooms. It is a long time since we've shared the intimacy of his chamber before bedtime. I anticipate a lingering supper, too much wine and hopefully, we will make ourselves a son tonight.

"Henry, there you are. I've been waiting to discuss the plans for the great Church of St Mary's."

My heart sinks. The king's mother is seated by the window, the fading light falling on the building plans she has scattered across the table.

Henry squeezes my fingers in silent apology and moves to greet her.

"Oh, good evening, Elizabeth," she says belatedly. I murmur a greeting but do not join them. Instead I stand before the hearth, hold out my hands to the flames.

Spring is late in coming this year; a chill lingers in the air and around the castle the fields gleam with standing puddles that have been there since February. The sun has forgotten us this season and the rain is incessant; the people murmur of bad omens and God's displeasure. The outbreak of measles that attacked us all just after Margaret's birth is slow to be extinguished and everyone suffers, regardless of status.

I had hoped for a quiet evening. I was slow to recover after giving birth this time, and lately the entertainments and constant envoys from Spain are wearisome. As the strength returns to my body in full measure, I find I am more inclined to welcome my husband's advances— when he makes them. I am eager to give him another son. We have our heir. I have a fat, fractious princess to amuse me, but Henry needs a second son at his side; a little Duke of York. But, if I am never alone with him, the chances of getting one are slim.

Henry and his mother are bent over the plans, a flickering candle revealing the similarity of their long, bony faces, their identical hooded eyes.

They are engrossed in their conversation. I could send for my needlework or my lute to amuse myself while they are busy, or I could return to my apartments and let Henry seek me out there later if he is of a mind. I do not consider joining them. I learned long ago that, although his mother accepts me now as his wife, I will never be accepted as their intimate.

Apart from their hushed voices, the chamber is peaceful. The logs spit and settle in the hearth, the rain patters against the dark windows and, every so often, one of Henry's hounds twitches in his sleep and growls deep in his throat, probably dreaming of chasing deer. I pick at a loose fingernail, sit down, stand up again and circumnavigate the room. Henry looks up and smiles a tight smile that does not quite meet his eyes. "I'll be with you soon, Elizabeth," he says.

"Oh, no, my lord. Do not trouble. I am quite content."

Why do I do that? Why am I not more honest? My mother would have left my father in no doubt that she required his immediate attention. I've seen him dismiss a party of foreign statesmen for the pleasure of my mother's bed. I sigh again, remembering that my husband is a very different man to my lusty father. But at least Henry is faithful.

I sink onto a low stool by the fire and, resting my cheek on my hand, begin to look for pictures in the flames as we used to when we were children.

Cecily and I always saw castles and gardens, fairies and flowers, but my brothers saw dragons and battles. Our visions would give rise to marvellous stories of bravery, my brothers' faces bright with anticipation as I reached the inevitable chivalric climax. If I hadn't been born a princess I should have liked to have been a storyteller, a minstrel or a songster, travelling the countryside to entertain the king.

Sometimes I still miss my younger days with a desperation that is almost a physical pain, but I endeavour to hide it behind a smile. The outside world only sees my serenity, for my inner feelings are not for sharing. But how I crave a confidant; someone I can trust and who will trust me in return. I sigh again, and to my relief realise that Lady Margaret has begun to roll up her parchments.

"I will see that it is done," she says as she stands up and shakes out her skirts. "I am meeting with the chaplain in the morning." She bids us good night. Henry walks with her to the door where her page is waiting to conduct her to her adjoining rooms.

While she is at court she is forever under our feet. I long for the day she will take herself off to her own properties again. She holds a vast amount of land and is the wealthiest woman in England, far more affluent than I. Even though I am queen, I am forced to be very thrifty to make my allowance last; and that is not helped by the necessity of funding my numerous sisters. Catherine is always in need of something, and Bridget is always spending her allowance on the poor.

I look up from my musing as Henry returns, looking sheepish.

"Now, where were we?"

I expect him to join me but instead, he moves to the table and pours two cups of wine. I am not thirsty and when he hands me my cup, I put it down. In the firelight, he is better looking; his eyes that tend to dart about a room seem somehow darker and warmer. As if my body is being operated by some external force, I walk boldly toward him and take away his wine.

"What are you doing?" He is half laughing, half hostile as I place my forefinger across his lips.

"Hush," I say, as if he is not the king and, reaching up on tiptoe, I place my mouth on his. At first he does not respond, but when my arms slide up around his neck and my tongue licks across his lips, I feel him relax a little. His hands slide reassuringly down from my waist to cup my buttocks. I press myself against him, the jewels on his collar digging into my flesh, his codpiece hard against my thigh. With a groan in the back of my throat I kiss him harder, closing my eyes. In the gloom of the chamber he could be anyone ... he could be ... I sever the thought, open my eyes and focus on my husband.

"Come," he says, pulling away but maintaining his hold on my hand. "Come to my chamber."

But I resist him. "Let us do it here, Henry," I say, "before the fire where it is warm." I snuggle up against him again and, putting aside his reservations, we sink together to the floor.

He pulls off my hood and my hair falls around us as I struggle to free him from his coat, pull his jerkin from his back. Suddenly, a picture imprints on my inner eye of how we would appear should anyone enter; the king and queen coupling on the floor like peasants. I begin to giggle and our teeth clash. He makes to pull away but I bring his face back against mine and squirm beneath him. He cannot resist me.

He tugs at my bodice and I relish the pain of the hard bones biting into my flesh. His brow is beaded with sweat. He balances himself, his body forming a bridge above me, allowing me to reach down between his legs. I scrabble at the lacings of his codpiece as he burrows beneath my skirts and wrenches them high.

It has never been like this between us; even our best lovemaking has hitherto been polite and businesslike. The man who now takes me like a hearth wench is a Henry I've never encountered before. When he enters me I cry out and wrap my legs about his waist, cling on as he pounds into me.

At first I am not sure what is happening to my body, but after a while I no longer care. It is as if my mind is possessed by wanton demons, but it is a feeling I relish. I strain upward to meet him, my pleasure building with each thrust. When I open my eyes I see the veins standing out on his forehead, his eyes bulging, his teeth bared, sweat dripping from his brow onto my face. I grab his drenched hair and force his mouth against mine. And then ... an explosion, a roaring fire that rips through my body, consuming me, consuming both of us so that we cry out in unison, his voice hoarse, like a lion's roar, mine high pitched, like a bird's.

We fall together in a heap of sweaty velvet and silk, and as my breath returns and I remember who and where I am, I wonder if our cries of pleasure penetrated the walls to his mother's apartments.

He doesn't speak but stands up, avoiding my eye, and begins to fumble with his lacings. I sit up, my heart still heaving, and begin to gather up my skirts to cover my legs. The peach-coloured silk is smeared with ash, the lace of the sleeve torn, and the petticoats closest to my skin are damp with royal semen.

As soon as he is decent, he hesitates, gives me a half smile before offering me his hand and helping me rise. As our faces come level I notice his eyes are fixed on my breasts which still bounce free of their lacings. There are marks left by his mouth, marks that, when I see them, send a dart of delight deep into the pit of my stomach. He reaches out and wrenches my bodice up to cover them, clears his throat.

"I am sorry," he croaks and makes to turn away, but with a hand on his sleeve I restrain him.

"Sorry, Henry? Don't be sorry, my lord. We should be glad."

Greenwich — Late Summer 1490

My ladies and I, along with a few gentleman courtiers, are enjoying the late summer sunshine when Henry and his mother join us in the garden at Greenwich palace. I pass Margaret, or Meg as we have begun to call her, to her nurse and rise to greet them. I shuffle along the bench and offer the king's mother a seat and she sits down and looks about the garden. Her quick eyes do not miss one of my younger ladies sitting a little too close to Henry Stafford. Stafford shows the ladies much attention, but has never yet come close to matrimony. I've been watching them for a while, reluctant to spoil their fun. Summer was so long in coming and soon it will be over, and the romances that bloom in the warmer weather will fade as the temperature drops. Lady Margaret is watching them with a twitch of displeasure that quite mars the afternoon and reluctantly, remembering my duty, I sit up straighter. The minstrel instantly ceases his tune.

"Emily," I call across the mead. "Can you fetch my shawl, I feel a chill."

The girl, with a reluctant smile at her admirer, rises to her feet, drops me a brief curtsey and hurries toward the hall. Lady Margaret, satisfied that their pleasure is spoiled, settles herself on the turfed seat and begins a conversation with Cecily.

It is some time since I've seen Cecily. She is wed now and the mother of two, as I am. Her children are often ailing and she spends her time torn between her duties at court and those of motherhood. I watch her now, plucking at her kerchief as she responds to the king's mother's questions. The Lady Margaret has taken a great fancy to Cecily; sometimes I think she'd have preferred her as a wife to her beloved Henry, but I know he wouldn't agree.

In a very unkinglike manner, Henry has managed to sidle around the company until he is at my side. He sits beside me, kisses my fingers surreptitiously. "Are you well?"

"I am quite well, my lord." I cannot help but flush, for this question has become code for when he wishes to enquire if he is welcome in my chamber. Invariably my answer is yes.

Our relationship has developed into something closer to that which I've always hoped for. I am slowly unravelling the cocoon of distrust that Henry wraps around himself. I may be born of York but I am Tudor now, and his loyal wife. *Nothing* can alter that.

As we relax and listen to the minstrels, the call of the birds and the chatter of the women, it is good to feel the press of his arm against mine. Meg, as usual, is not far away. She is crawling now, trailing her gown through the dirt and trying to eat the garden soil or sample the flowers. She seems to think that every new thing she encounters belongs in her mouth. Henry and I watch her, and laugh at her antics, confident that the nurse who hovers behind will prevent her from eating anything too unpalatable. We linger in the garden until the sun begins to sink and the air grows chilly, when we move indoors. It is time to freshen our bodies, change our clothes in readiness for the evening entertainments.

As we reach the door, a messenger appears and asks to speak to the king. With a smile of regret, he leaves me to continue to my apartments alone. I do not see him again that evening. I dine in my chamber and the court is forced to enjoy the entertainments in the absence of both king and queen.

It is much later, when I am almost ready to slip into bed, that he comes to my chamber. I can see straight away that something is wrong. Immediately, I think of Mother, a sudden twist of fear that she may be ill.

"What is it? What's wrong?"

His face is pale and I sense he is concealing, or trying to control his anger. My fears increase. He'd not be angry if my mother was ill; it must be something worse, or some political insult he has received. He moistens his lips to speak, glances at me, looks away, and tightens his lips.

"My spies inform me that there is a fellow ... some crazed pretender ... at your aunt's court in Burgundy, who is claiming to be your brother."

"Edward!" My heart turns somersault. "Is it him?"

Henry, his face like thunder, brings his fist down hard on the table.

"No." His voice is harsh, almost a shout. "He claims to be the other one. Richard. But it is not him, is it? How can it be? They are dead, aren't they? You told me they are dead!"

Greenwich Palace – June 1491

In the months that follow I try very hard to regain Henry's confidence but he resists me, pushes me away. When he does come to my chamber it is to perform a duty, the joy has gone from our marriage. Yet, by the autumn, I am pregnant again and once more embracing the depths of my chamber pot. This time the sickness doesn't last as long, and by the time I am mid-term I am thriving and bonny. For the first time I enjoy the 'bloom' of pregnancy that I have previously dismissed as a myth.

Although he is pleased by the news, the edginess between the king and I continues, as does the uneasy truce between me and his mother. My cousin Margaret finds time in her schedule to visit from Ludlow. She has scarcely sat down when she begins urging me to speak to the king on behalf of her brother. Poor Warwick is still incarcerated in the Tower. He is sixteen years old now and I have not seen him since he was a small boy, although Margaret has regular word from his servants.

"How is he?" I ask and pretend I do not see the furious anger that passes swiftly across her face.

"He is well enough but he knows no different. He knows no other home than the Tower. He is content with his picture books and cats but it is no life for him, shut away from his family for no greater sin than being born too close to the throne."

I lower my eyes. I feel so useless, so helpless. I fiddle with my cuff, tracing an intricate line of the embroidery with my fingernail.

"I have tried to get Henry to see reason, Margaret, I really have, but he says it is for the boy's safety. He knows Warwick is not ... not really capable of starting an uprising but that is not the point. There are those who

174

would manipulate him and use him as a figurehead for insurrection. Henry has to be careful, so careful ... especially now ..."

She jerks her head in my direction and slides along the settle toward me so her words cannot be overheard.

"This ... pretender, Elizabeth ... who is he? Do you know?"

I straighten up, my eyes darting around the room to see who might be listening. I shake my head and mutter a reply.

"We don't know but the king is very shaken by it. Henry's spies are busy trying to discover his identity, but so far they have learned nothing."

"Our Aunt Margaret is backing him."

"But she hates Henry; she would back the devil himself if he offered her the chance to displace him."

"But that doesn't mean the boy isn't your brother. I mean, we both know Uncle Richard would not have harmed his own blood. He looked after all of us so carefully. The boys were no threat to him; the king had more reason to ..."

She stops midsentence, suddenly realising she is speaking treason to the Queen of England. Blood rushes into her cheeks, she puts a hand to her face and shakes her head. "Oh, I didn't mean that. Elizabeth, honestly, I wasn't suggesting ..."

"I know." I cover her hand with my own. "It is so hard to speak openly, to anyone. Henry didn't harm them, I am sure of that. He has been frantic to discover the boys' whereabouts since he won the throne. If he had ordered them killed, he wouldn't be so worried now."

"To think it has come to this." She shakes her head sadly. "Our family fragmented, your brothers lost, my brother imprisoned and us, both of us, married to men

175

our fathers would have scorned. Nothing is ever certain, is it? Not in this world."

At that moment the child leaps in my womb, making me gasp. "This little fellow seems very certain of himself," I laugh, in an attempt to break the sorry tension that has descended upon us.

Margaret smiles. "Do you think it is a boy?"

"If it isn't, it will be a princess with very large feet and a kick like a donkey."

Margaret moves even closer, drops her voice to a whisper. "Maybe she favours her paternal grandmother."

We burst into laughter, drawing the attention of my ladies who are sitting a little way off. Cecily detaches herself from the group and approaches us, laughing although she is unaware of the cause of our mirth.

"What? What is it?" She sits beside us, her smiling eyes moving from my face to Margaret's. We both sober.

"Nothing," I reply. "Just a silly thing about … about kittens."

Watching me closely, Cecily's face falls a little and I feel a twinge of regret that I can no longer confide in her as I used to. Her relationship with the king's mother is strong now and she is too quick to carry secrets to her. This is one joke that would entirely fail to amuse the Lady Margaret.

Coolly, Margaret proceeds to admire Cecily's gown. She reaches out to feel the fabric and they fall to speaking of safer, domestic things. As their conversation washes over me, I run my hand across my bulging belly and count the kicks and nudges issuing from within. The child seems to be dancing a saltarello. By my reckoning the babe should be born sometime in June or July, and I have already begun issuing orders for my confinement, which will begin very soon.

The chamber is made up as it was before, with soothing tapestries and yards of sumptuous hangings adorned with red and white roses. I order my needlework, my lute and favourite books to be placed within easy reach, for I know from experience how long and tedious the waiting can be. This is the first time I shall be giving birth in the heat of the summer, and I hate the thought of shutting out the sun and stifling behind sealed windows. When I confide in Cecily how I dread it, she pulls a face.

"I dispensed with all that when I birthed Elizabeth. I realise my own confinements do not demand the degree of ceremony as yours do but, for heaven's sake, Elizabeth, you are the queen. Demand that they open a window if it pleases you."

I hadn't thought of that. My whole life is spent conforming, trying to please the king and his mother, but during labour, when my life and that of the unborn child are at risk, is perhaps the time they will bow to my wishes.

In early June I ceremoniously bid farewell to the world and, with a blessing from the bishops, I retire to my chambers. By the time I emerge again, the summer will be well past its zenith. It will be a shame to miss the last days of summertime. But I am tired and glad for the rest. In the privacy of my chambers I can relax and wear loose-fitting clothing, and be as lazy as I please until the child decides to make his appearance. But I must have made a miscalculation because midsummer's day has only just passed when I feel the first pangs of labour.

I put down my lute and place a hand on my tightening belly.

"What is it, Your Grace?" Anne Crowther puts aside her sewing and sinks to her knees at my feet. I reach out and squeeze her hand.

"I think the baby might be on his way."

She stands up to run and summon the king's mother and tell Henry that the child is imminent, but I grab her wrist, shake my head.

"Don't go yet, Anne. It may be a false alarm. I don't want to worry anyone until we are sure."

But this time it is quick and there is no opportunity to send for anyone other than the midwives. At first I walk about the chamber, but after just half an hour of this my waters break, drenching my petticoats and, almost straight away, the pains begin in earnest. It seems this child is in a hurry to be born. I dig my fingers into Anne's arm and bend over, gasping with pain.

The midwife aids me to the bed and without seeking my permission lifts my sodden clothes to determine the child's position. Her hands are cool and dry. As she examines me I feel the pain returning, my womb tightening and squeezing. With a cry, I clench down on her arm and hold my breath, fighting against it.

"Don't fight it. Breathe, Your Grace. Breathe and try to relax. There is no point in fighting it."

Belatedly I recall my earlier training; it worked before, once I gave in to the inevitable and went with the pain. With difficulty I suck in air, blow it out again, my cheeks puffing like a hearth wench blowing on kindling. Very slowly, inexorably, the pain reaches its peak, begins to ebb. I breathe deep and calm, close my eyes and ride toward the break in the battle.

Anne calls for a drink and between contractions she moistens my lips, dabs my brow with a cooling cloth. "Not long now, Your Grace; I think this little fellow is in a hurry." The midwife stands up, her face pink with sweat. "I can see the top of his head."

"Already?" I try to laugh but another pain is beginning and I break off to breathe and puff like an elderly dragon. The window is open, the sounds of the river floating in on the summer breeze, a strain of music from the garden. I bring my knees up high, hook them over my elbows and, tucking my chin to my chest, I begin to bear down. While the midwife hollers instruction from between my legs, and my women hover in a flutter of concern about the bed, I lose myself in the battle to bring my child into the world.

Deep in my nether regions I can feel his head move like a cannonball along the shaft. I push and he fights with me, inching closer until my quaint bulges and I am fit to burst. I put down a hand, feel his wet pulsing head and, when the next pain comes, I push again. A burst of water and his head is born, filling the chamber with the sweet aroma of birth fluid. Almost screaming with every pant, I cease to strain until the midwife instructs me to continue with gentle pushes. Together, with great care, we ease my child into the world.

"It's a boy!" someone yells. "A great fat boy!"

I scramble up, supporting myself on my hands, and look down at the baby on the bed.

He is very large and very angry, and not at all shy of letting the world know of his displeasure. Puce with screaming, his fists are clenched and his legs, already chubby at the thigh, kick the air in outrage. I lean forward to pick him up, cord still trailing, and hold him, just for a moment.

His toothless mouth is downturned, his chin juddering in grievous protest as I drop my first kiss on his brow and settle him to my breast. Like an expert he latches on straight away, greedy for life, and his tiny fingers clench about my own. Quieter now, his limbs cease to agitate as he feeds upon me. I draw a shawl across him and relax into the pillow.

I have done it. I have given Henry the peace of mind of two sons. We have a Prince of Wales and a Duke of York; what more can he now ask of me?

*

When the news is out the country erupts into celebration. It is hard for me when they take the baby, wrap him in a mantle of gold furred with ermine, and bear him off to church for his christening. He is to be named Henry after his father, but there the similarities end.

It is clear to me, even at this early stage, that little Henry, in build, looks and manner will resemble one man only; my father, Edward IV. I wonder how the king and his mother will like that. So far they are both besotted with him and the plans for his christening are extensive.

My son is escorted by two hundred torch-bearing men, and the church is hung with cloth of gold. The Bishop of Exeter, Richard Fox, is to officiate, and Henry has sent for the silver font from Canterbury Cathedral. Nothing is overlooked; this christening is to be as grand as any there has ever been. I just wish I was there to see it. By the time they return him to me my breasts ache from want of him, and the first thing I do when they place him back in my arms is loosen my bodice and let him feed.

Feed time is the only period that he is truly peaceful. He likes to be held and when I cradle him in my arms to look at his tiny fingers and toes, the pale sandy lashes that curl on his cheek, the red button nose and pursed, sucking lips, he watches me through slitted eyes.

I am determined not to relinquish this child too soon. I would like all my children to grow up close to me. I want to witness their first teeth, their first steps, their first words. I want to teach them their letters and tell them stories of old. It goes without saying that this boy will delight in King Arthur and his knights. He is made in my father's image and every time I look at him, I remember the past and my little brothers of whom we were all so proud. Their memory burns suddenly bright again and with it comes the pain of losing them. This child might go some way toward making up for their loss. I hug little Henry suddenly close, making him squeak, and determine that nothing shall harm this child. No matter what it takes, or what it costs, I shall guard him to my last breath.

Chapter Twenty-One
Boy

<u>Lisbon — Autumn 1491</u>

Brampton's wife is sick and he reluctantly allows the boy to return to Flanders on his own. He finds him a berth on a ship and goes with him to watch him embark. "Stay out of trouble," he says. "Keep your head down."

The boy agrees, suddenly tongue-tied, conscious of a thousand things he should say, a thousand thanks he owes this rough and ready fellow. As Brampton turns and begins to clamber overboard, the boy suddenly grabs his arms and pulls him round to engulf him in an embrace. Brampton thumps him on the shoulder and returns the hug. "Take care, boy," he says throatily. "We will not be parted for long."

It will be a long voyage, the ship calling at other ports and countries to deliver cargo. For the first time, the boy is alone. As the ship slowly moves from the dock Richard finds his throat is tight with regret, his eyes stinging with tears. *Man up*, he tells himself as he forces himself to face the open sea. *Man up and remember you are a king.*

It is a rough few days. For the first time he is seasick, hanging miserably over a bucket, spitting bile. But, as the ship draws closer to land, the swell lessens and he is able to hold up his head again.

He emerges on deck, stumbling a little and hanging on tight to the ship's rail. They pass a remote rock, too small to be called an island, where a colony of gulls set up a ruckus at their passing.

"Where are we?" he asks a passing crew member.

"Just nearing Ireland, my lord, where we will put up for a few nights."

"Ireland!" Richard peers into the distance where a ruffle of cloud cushions the horizon. "Ireland is almost home."

He scrambles back to his cabin and sorts through his clothes, donning his best striped sleeves and topping it all with his favourite cap. He is still strapping on his sword as he arrives back on deck. One of the crew whistles admiringly, but when he turns he cannot determine who it was.

The ship is close to the shore now. He can see green fields, clusters of houses, a church steeple, people swarming at the dock.

The captain stops hollering orders to the crew when he notices Richard's attire. "Are you going ashore, Sir?"

"Yes, yes. I need to stretch my legs."

"Well, you cannot go alone. Brampton would have my head. I will get up a party for your protection."

Twenty minutes later, the boy feels firm ground beneath his feet and inhales the sweet moist air of Ireland. It is almost home, closer than he has been for many years. With a cheerful smile he sets off through the town, walking the muddy streets just for the hell of it. At first he doesn't notice the stir he is making. He doesn't hear the muttered questions. "Who is he? Why is he here?"

He turns a corner into a market square full of livestock, the stench of the farmyard almost making him recoil. A sharp breeze comes from nowhere and takes off his cap, and one of the ship's crew set to guard him runs after it, chasing it like a cat after a mouse. Richard throws back his head and laughs, his bright hair glinting in the sunshine. A peasant steps forward from the crowd and directs a dirty finger in the boy's direction.

"It is the king," he cries. Richard's head jerks up, his blue eyes assessing the mood of the crowd. The crew move in closer, hands to their daggers.

"The king? Don't be daft, man; what would the king be doing here? Hasn't he enough trouble of his own?"

People begin to laugh. A pretty peasant girl runs forward and offers Richard a rose; it is off-white but close enough. He bows politely and tucks it in the lacing of his doublet.

"I don't mean the Tudor King; I mean the real one, King Edward or Richard ... or if it isn't, he looks as damn near like it to suffice."

The crowd falls silent, then a woman steps closer. "I think you might be right, Pádraig. I saw King Edward once and if this boy isn't made in his image then you can call me a donkey."

"You're a donkey," someone shouts from behind, and the town square fills with laughter. The people surge forward, dancing and calling 'A York!' The ship's crew edge closer to their charge, waving their daggers to little avail.

As the Irish surge in, Richard feels grubby hands upon him, smells their unwashed bodies. He flounders, begins to lose his footing and grabs at someone's jerkin to save himself. But before he can fall, he feels strong hands grasp him and the claustrophobic crowd breaks so he can breathe again. His head bursts into the air as he is lifted aloft onto their shoulders, and he looks down on a sea of heads as they begin to march him triumphantly through the town.

Malines –Late summer 1493

Two years pass, years of campaign, years of plummeting fear and soaring hopes. The Duchess works tirelessly. To Richard, now publically declared to be the rightful king of England, her hatred for the Tudor usurper seems sometimes irrational, sometimes he shares it. Barring Spain, they have the support of the heads of Europe and relations between Brussels and England have all but broken down.

Henry Tudor is furious that they are harbouring what he calls a 'pretender' to his throne. The English king may have power, but he is distrusted and scorned the world over. York's star looks set to burn bright again over the skies of England.

Richard is euphoric but when news comes of his mother's death, her life ending in a cheerless nunnery, exiled from the royal court, he is consumed with angry sorrow.

He recalls her gentle hands, her ringing laughter, her soft singing, and his chin wobbles like a child's as he dashes away a tear. He had thought to go back one day, to draw her from her cloistered prison and greet her before the world. Just once more to call her 'Mother' and hear her name him as her son. Now she is gone, her vigour shrivelled, her silver bright hair and high clear brow is shrouded and sealed in a lowly tomb.

He should have been there with his sisters to see her laid to rest. Her life should have been celebrated throughout Christendom, but Henry Tudor, with customary parsimony, keeps her funeral small and mean.

"Why didn't Elizabeth demand a proper funeral as befits a queen?" he asks.

Duchess Margaret turns from the window. "I understand your sister had nothing to do with it. She was in confinement awaiting the birth of her fourth child; a girl, they tell me. She is nothing if not diligent in that department." She sniffs disdainfully, as if she wouldn't welcome a child of her own, whatever the gender.

The boy puts down the letter and flops back in his chair. "I wonder what she thinks of all this, of me ..."

The Duchess leans forward and selects an apple from a bowl on the table, sinks her big teeth into it.

"I doubt she thinks of you at all. Not as her brother at any rate; she will see you as nothing more than a usurper. You can be sure that having whelped four Tudor pups, she will no longer think like a daughter of York."

He tries to reconcile this image with the Bess he once knew and loved. Her bright stories of courage and valour, her firm conviction that York would always be the victor cannot have altered. The knightly king she described in her stories and sang about in ballads was always tall and fair like their father ... just like the man he, Richard, had now become. Surely, when the time comes, she will recognise him as a returning hero and welcome him home? Bess was always the champion of justice, cheering for the underdog, the rightful victor. Surely, a few misbegotten brats with a man she cannot love won't change that?

The Duchess is speaking, gloating over the success of the plot she has hatched with John Kendal, a Yorkshire man in the confidence of Henry Tudor. She has persuaded him to use his position to work for their cause, undermining the English king's position. She chews audibly, apple juice on her lips as she speaks with her mouth full.

"There was a meeting in Rome ..." She pauses to prise a slither of apple skin from between her teeth, "... where they pledged to seek ways and methods to bring about the death of Tudor, his mother, his children and close relations—"

"Not Elizabeth!" The boy is on his feet. "The children I can understand, although I heartily dislike it, but not Bess, not my sister—she and my other sisters are the only family I have left. They are not to be harmed."

"Sit down, Richard. No one has been injured yet. Anyway, I have little hope anything will come of it. My informers tell me that they plan to employ astrology and black magic against them. Personally, if I wanted to kill someone I'd hire an assassin. I've no faith in the mysterious arts."

She examines the flesh of her half-consumed apple, which is beginning to turn brown. Tossing it to her dog, she stands up, smoothes her skirts and turns toward the door. A bevvy of waiting women follow her. At the entrance, she stops and turns. "You need to form a tougher skin Richard, or you'll never get anywhere. Kings, even if they bleed, must never let the pain show. Get yourself some invisible armour or you'll be unhorsed by the first strike."

He sits alone while the busy palace moves on without him. The chamber grows dim, it is almost dark when a servant comes to light the torches. Slowly the room is illuminated, and when she notices him in the shadows, she jumps, bobs a curtsey.

"I am sorry, my lord, I didn't see you there."

"Carry on."

He nods at the hearth and she begins to build the fire while he watches her. She works quickly, every so often glancing up at him as if his presence discomforts her. His thoughts go to Nelken; poor, poor Nelken who did not survive the birth of their child.

Somewhere he has a son, he knows that much, but where the child is now Richard cannot discover. The Duchess refuses to speak of it, will answer no questions. On impulse, he moves forward to crouch beside the girl at the hearth.

"You knew Nelken?" he whispers.

The girl is immediately on the alert, her eyes darting to the corners of the room, checking the door. "I did, my lord, yes. She was a good friend."

"Then you must know what became of her son. Where was he taken?"

She stands up and begins to back away. "I don't know, my lord. Why would they confide in me? I am just a servant."

"Just a servant. Yes, I am sorry, but … he is my son … all I have left. If … if you should learn of his whereabouts, would you tell me? I will reward you well and the Duchess will never hear of it … I promise."

For a long moment she looks at him, taking in his fine figure, his fair hair, his troubled expression. One of his eyes has a slight cast, which gives him the appearance of being troubled, vulnerable. She smiles suddenly, her prettiness breaking through the grime of her workload.

"Very well, my lord. If I should hear anything, I will find you and let you know."

She bobs a curtsey and, gathering up her bucket, hurries away, leaving him alone.

Chapter Twenty-Two
Elizabeth

<u>Westminster Hall – December 1493</u>

Christmas is lavish this year, but I sit beneath the royal canopy and watch the entertainments with fear in my heart. I miss my mother and I badly need her advice. My new born daughter, Elizabeth, is not thriving; she feeds sluggishly and rarely smiles. I bore her in July, just after my mother died. I was not allowed to leave confinement to share Mother's last hours, the king's mother forbade it. She said it went against the guidelines in her blessed book. I wanted to scream at her that they were guidelines only, but I could tell from her frigid looks that my argument was futile. Instead, I fell to my knees and prayed that Mother be taken quickly and painlessly to Heaven.

My mother was a woman of many secrets. Her life was one of political intrigue, and many stories that are told of her are uncomfortable to hear. But I loved her; she was my mother. I just wish that I could have seen her one last time. Perhaps, with God's angels looking over her shoulder, she might have revealed to me the fate of my brothers. I would lay down my life on the fact that she knew of it.

With a heavy heart I watch the tumblers, I applaud the minstrels, and clap my hands with what I hope is convincing glee. William Cornish comes galloping into the hall dressed as St George, followed by a ferocious dragon that spits fire from its mouth. I glance at Henry who is leaning forward in his chair, watching appreciatively as a lavishly garbed 'princess' screams at the monster's approach.

Inwardly I sigh, and long for the night to be over so I can retire to the peace of my chamber. I cannot keep my mind from little Elizabeth. I must find a way for her to thrive. All my children are healthy except for her. Young Henry is growing apace. At eighteen months old he is as loud and demanding as an untrained puppy. He is my consolation. There is nothing I like more than when he climbs onto my lap, puts his thumb in his mouth and nestles up close. Henry and Meg make up for missing Arthur so much, but I am not sure if even they could make up for Elizabeth ... should I lose her.

*

The king is simmering inwardly but does not share his worries with me. I discover by nefarious means that his lack of ease is due to the men flocking from his court. The court gossips whisper that they are heading for Europe, to the standard of the man calling himself Richard of England.

I don't know what to think. Even one of my own household, my chamberlain, has gone, preferring a pretender to me.

But is he a pretender? The fearful question is persistent. It returns in the dead of night, in the midst of the day when I should be at peace; in our marriage bed when my mind should be on other things. *Suppose it is Richard? Suppose my brother and I are ranged against each other? Suppose my husband is forced to kill my brother, or my brother to kill my husband?*

Neither scenario bears thinking of. I hold little Henry tight, lay my face against his fine red baby hair, close my eyes and pray for him. I pray for all of us.

<u>Westminster — November 1494</u>

For almost a year the king is on edge, snapping at innocent questions, suspicious of my every move. He still suspects me of some duplicity, of knowing the truth, or secretly supporting the pretender's claim. His fear eats away at him like a maggot on a piece of rotting meat, tainting everything. It is difficult to get close to him. Time and time again I have tried to explain that my husband and my children come before everything and anyone else. Even if this pretender is my brother, which I hope he is not, I would never choose him above my sons. But I cannot convince Henry.

He sends forth spies to determine the pretender's identity, to disprove his claim to be of the house of York. Between them, Henry and his uncle Jasper decide the Pretender is a Fleming who goes by, or used to go by, the name of Perkin Warbeck. It sounds an unlikely name to me and how would a common foreigner persuade half of Europe that he is a royal prince? I keep quiet and, with admirable cunning, Henry manages to undermine the friendship France has displayed toward the Pretender. Now France's support has been severed, Warbeck will find things harder, but Henry doesn't leave it there.

"There are more ways to win a war than in battle," he says with grim pleasure. I try not to reflect that I never heard such words from my father and applaud when I learn of his plan.

"It was my mother who thought of it," he boasts, and I try not to let my envy bite too deeply. "You will recall that I have already made young Henry Lord Warden of the Cinque Ports and Lord Lieutenant of Ireland, and Warden of the Scottish Marches?"

I nod, keeping my eyes wide and fixed upon him, terrified that whatever he has to tell me might somehow betray me into disloyalty. "Well, now I play the trump card. I plan to make Henry the Duke of York; there can only be one, can't there? It should state quite clearly our disbelief in the Pretender's claims and put him firmly in his place."

My heart flips. This is well and good if the boy in Malines is a pretender, but York is my little brother Richard's title. In bestowing his title on my son, Henry announces, quite plainly, that my brother, Richard of York, is dead. Each time I come close to accepting his death, another question immediately rears out of the unknown: *then how did he die?*

Either scenario is torment for me. Either my brother is alive and threatening all that I hold dear, or he is dead, murdered by someone close to me. Mentally, I strike off the candidates, measuring the likelihood of their guilt.

It cannot have been Uncle Richard, who was so fond of us. I remember a day when he came upon my siblings and I in the royal nursery where I was telling stories. Instead of hurrying off to join the court revel, he sat down on the floor, took my youngest brother on his knee and urged me to go on. When the story reached its climax, he roared with excitement just as loudly as the children.

He was everything to me then, all I aspired to, and all I hoped for. I refuse to believe he would ever harm any of us but, who does that leave? If my brothers were murdered and not by my uncle, then who stood to gain the most?

I push the thought away, unwilling to confront it but, when I least expect it, the question comes creeping back.

*

194

For two weeks, the court celebrates. There is feasting and jousting at Westminster. A special stand is built, draped in blue cloth of velvet, embroidered all over with golden *fleur de lis*.

Baby Elizabeth, too prone to chills, is left at the nursery, but the other children relish the fuss and ceremony. The king sits beneath his canopy of state, garbed in Tudor green and white. To serve as a reminder to those of a mind to stray from our side, I wear mulberry and blue for my own house of York. The colours speak for both houses. Henry is the Tudor king, but I am the rightful heir of York and so are my sons.

Little Margaret, although not yet five, presents the prizes. My ladies, Anne, Elizabeth and Anne Percy, assist her. My daughter, dressed in white damask with red velvet sleeves, steps importantly forward and offers the prize to the three victorious knights.

I am proud to see how carefully she performs the task and how gravely she greets the victor. It is plain to see that, like her brothers, if we can protect her, Margaret will go far. She is made in the mould of my mother, like my grandmothers, Cecily of York and Jacquetta of Luxembourg. They were strong women who overcame the harsh obstacles fate threw in their paths. They survived war, exile, bereavement, widowhood, yet they were undaunted. Nothing overwhelmed them, and they did not fail. As I watch my infant daughter, so confident in the face of the world, I rediscover a little courage and tell myself that weakness is not an option.

Eltham Palace– January 1495

I have been trying to comfort Elizabeth, who is fractious with another cold. She is sleeping now. Although she is approaching three years old, she is still not robust and seems to stagger from one ailment to the next. With a supporting hand beneath her head I lower her into the cot and, signalling to the nurse to watch over her, I tiptoe away.

Henry and Margaret are playing. As I approach the nursery chamber, I can hear the sounds of little Harry trying to stand firm against his sister's bossiness.

"You can't do that, Meg, it is my go. You have to take turns."

"I am taking turns but I want another go."

"Oh, you always want it your way."

I hesitate, a hand on the latch, and recognise the beginnings of a scuffle. When I throw open the door Harry has his hand to his eye, and the ball that has just struck him is bouncing away across the floor. Meg wipes the mischief from her face and puts her hands behind her back with guilt written large.

"She throwed the ball at me!" Henry exclaims. "Look at my eye!"

"She threw the ball," I correct him as I kneel beside him to wipe a tear from his reddened cheek. I cast a reprimanding look in my daughter's direction.

"Margaret. Your poor little brother. I hope you are going to say sorry."

Harry is clasping the neck of my gown, his mouth downturned, but his eye is kindling glee at his sister's disgrace. He gives a theatrical sob, his little chest heaving.

"I am sorry, Harry," Meg mumbles unconvincingly, "but you should play nicely."

"Indeed you should, Harry. If you want to be a gentleman you must learn to be kind to little girls. You wouldn't find King Arthur being unfair to Guinevere, would you?"

He wrinkles his nose. "But Guinevere is a queen. Meg is just my sister."

"And will one day, no doubt, be a queen also."

I hold out my arm and she comes to me. I enfold my children in my arms, inhaling their sweet, puppy dog fragrance.

"What else have you been doing, besides fighting?"

"I did a picture, come and look."

Harry takes my hand and drags me to my feet. Laughing, I follow him to the table near the window where he stabs the parchment with a grubby finger.

"I drew a king on a horse and a castle, and a dog."

I bend appreciatively over the table to admire the representation of a large knight on what appears to be a large rabbit. They both have big smiling mouths and some way above their heads, suspended in midair, is a multi-turreted castle, complete with fluttering pennants.

"Oh, that is very good, and how neatly you have signed your name. You are clever."

He stands up tall and beams at his own brilliance. He has misspelled his name, *Herny*; his hand is round and unformed, the letters unevenly spaced. But it is recognisable.

I have lately been teaching the children their letters. At six years old, Margaret is picking it up well and can now form simple sentences to describe her daily activities. She waves her own paper in front of my nose and I praise her for her neatness.

Henry climbs onto a chair and begins to try to copy his sister's name. He manages the M, A and a passable R but the G defeats him and he throws down his pen. Meg laughs.

"My name is easy, Harry; you can't do it because you are such a little baby."

Harry's face turns puce, his eyes disappearing beneath a furious frown.

"That isn't kind, Meg." I lean over my son's shoulder and take his pen. "Look, Harry, why not write it this way. You can just put 'Meg' so it is easier."

I write the word and hand back his quill, watching as he frowns over the task, the tip of his tongue emerging from the side of his mouth in his efforts to master it.

"There." He sits up with a look of triumph. "I've done it. Now show me how to write Bess."

"That's easy." Meg slides between us and begins to show Harry the letters. I sit back and watch them together. Now their squabble is forgotten, they are the best of friends again.

I am enjoying five minutes contentment when I hear footsteps in the corridor and look up in time to see Henry sidle into the room. He has been king for more than ten years now but still hasn't learned how to enter a room regally. I rise to my feet and greet him with a curtsey and a smile.

"Look, children, your father is here."

They put down their quills and slide from their seats. Margaret performs a wobbly curtsey and Harry the most gallant of bows. Henry smiles at the children and flicks a finger to indicate they should return to what they were doing.

"I was looking for you," he says, as the children move away. His gaze is fixed on something outside the window. "They said you were here."

"I've been with Elizabeth all afternoon. She can't seem to shake this cold; neither of the other children had it half as long."

Henry shrugs. "Some people are like that, one cold after the other, yet they are perfectly strong."

I don't contradict him although I know in my heart he is wrong. This is more than a childhood sniffle; this is something that baffles even the royal physicians.

"She is sleeping now, thank goodness. I have been helping the children with their letters. They are so clever. Why don't you have a look and tell them so."

He hesitates, his sudden smile disappearing as quickly as it was born.

"I don't have the time to dally. I came to find you; I have some news."

"What has happened?" As always when I fear the worst my heart begins to flutter, my palms sweat. He is regarding me, seeing the fear, and I know he is suspecting the worst of me.

"Not here. In my chamber."

My skirts hamper my steps as I bestow hurried kisses on the children's brows and fend off their complaints that I am leaving.

"I will be back soon. If not this evening, then tomorrow. Be good, both of you, and no fighting."

"No, Mother." As I follow Henry from the room, I hear Margaret begin to berate her brother for splashing ink upon the table.

*

Henry sets up a rapid pace to his apartments and, when the doors are thrown open at our approach, he steps aside to allow me to enter before him. The room is sumptuous, masculine, a fire roaring, the table spread with books and parchments, a bowl of exotic fruits. Before the hearth his dog raises his head and drops it to his paws again, too lazy to bother with a greeting. To my relief I note that Henry's mother is not present; this interview is to be between husband and wife alone.

He doesn't speak at first but moves to a side table and pours some wine, hands me a cup, although I am too strung up to drink.

"What is it Henry? What has happened?"

He takes a gulp of wine, looks at his feet and then up at me again.

"I – I … Can I trust you, Elizabeth?"

"Of course." I put down my wine and move toward him, place a hand on his sleeve. "You can trust me absolutely."

He takes another sip of wine, swills it round his mouth before placing his cup on the table. I notice his hand is trembling slightly.

"Where is your mother?" I ask, suddenly worried that some misfortune has befallen her. He shrugs.

"She has gone from court for a few days. I have summoned her back—something has arisen that concerns her deeply." He hesitates, looks at the ceiling and blurts out his worries quickly. "Elizabeth, I fear her loyalty may be compromised …"

"Henry! That is absurd. It is simply not possible. Your mother may be many things but I would lay down my life that her loyalty is unshakeable."

He closes his eyes, seems to sway slightly on his feet. "I know. I know. At least, I thought I did but now … this latest treason comes very close."

"Just tell me what has happened; you are driving me to distraction."

"Do you recall I told you Clifford was working as a spy into the enemy camp? Well, he is back from Burgundy with unsettling news. It seems William Stanley has espoused the Warbeck cause and sworn that if the pretender turns out indeed to be the son of your father, he'll not raise a hand to stop him." Henry pulls a face, halfway between a grimace and a smile, that cannot disguise his disappointment. "So much for loyalty."

"Stanley? Well ..." I half laugh but, realising this is not an occasion for levity, pull myself together in time. "The Stanleys are not renowned for their fidelity."

Long before he was married to the king's mother, it was Stanley who intervened at Bosworth and put an end to Richard's valiant attempt on Henry's life. He has been rewarded well, his coffers are stuffed with blood money, but Henry has never condescended to give him the title he craves. I can see it must be difficult to see his brother rise so high and wed to the king's mother. He is not a likeable man and I push away the little twist of satisfaction that Stanley has been discovered in this new betrayal and will, I have no doubt, suffer the consequences.

I am so engrossed in my dislike of him that it takes me some time to realise the real nature of Henry's fears. I look up and read in his face that he fears his stepfather, Stanley's brother, knew of his planned defection. It is more than probable they were covering themselves for each eventuality, as they have done in the past. With a brother on each side of the breach, the family would flourish and their assets be preserved whatever the outcome.

William's brother, Thomas, now enjoys all the associated rewards of being the king's stepfather but should Henry fall to the Pretender's claim, the Stanley family, with a boot in either camp, would survive and thrive. With sudden empathy I understand Henry's injured pride and, to some extent, his fear.

"What does your mother say?"

"We haven't spoken of it yet but I have little doubt as to her husband's reaction when I execute his brother. There is no other option and I am afraid her loyalties to her husband may outweigh her devotion to me."

"Oh, don't be ridiculous. She has no romantic attachment to Thomas Stanley and even less love for his brother. Had she the slightest inkling of this she would have told you straight away. She has spent her whole adult life fighting for your cause and she isn't going to stop now for the sake of a diplomatic marriage."

I stop abruptly, realising as I speak that Henry and I are the product of just such diplomacy. Thankfully, he decides to overlook my near insult. His hand covers mine, a cool salve to my clammy skin.

"I hope you are right." He sighs and perches on the edge of a stool, looks at the flames crackling in the hearth. "The next few weeks will be harsh, Elizabeth. I want you to come with me, bring the children and your unmarried sisters. We are all going to lodge at the Tower for a time where I can keep an eye on everyone."

*

Henry is right. The next few weeks are bitter. The king keeps me close, his eyes never tarrying for long in one place, or on any one person. He is constantly alert and his anger simmers dangerously.

As soon as she hears of William Stanley's arrest, Henry's mother hurries to London. She stalks into the chamber, barely acknowledging my presence, and launches into a catalogue of reasons why Stanley must be pardoned.

"This man," her voice rasps with disappointment, "plotted and intrigued with me against Gloucester on your behalf and, on the battlefield ... at Bosworth, wasn't it he who plucked up Richard's fallen crown and placed it on your own head? Is this how you would repay him?"

"It is how I repay treason from wherever it comes." Henry's face is passive but I know that underneath he is seething with disappointed fury. I watch them keenly, my eyes flicking from my husband to his mother. This is the first time I have ever seen them at odds. Warbeck's treason is doing its job, sending distrust seeping into the most tightly forged of alliances.

"He is close kin to me. His disgrace will reflect upon my husband and upon myself. Please, Henry, can you not just ... just lock him up, torture him a little and make him suffer that way?"

"No. He has to die and those who aided and abetted alongside him will be punished also."

She sits back tight-lipped and red-eyed and looks dejectedly about the hall. When she sees me in the corner, I lower my head, concentrate on my needlework and hope she doesn't intend to draw me into the debate.

I should have known she wouldn't. I am nothing to her. I am powerless, little more than a broodmare for the next generation of Tudors, and she knows my influence with the king is non-existent. Her gaze floats over me and I glance up just in time to notice tears of frustration and self-pity balanced at the edge of her lashless eyes.

"There is nothing to be done," the king continues. "I put my trust in Stanley and he betrayed me. I can never have faith in him again and, if I show him leniency, others whose allegiance is tested may think me weak. Stanley has to die. He has to be made an example."

Margaret stands up, makes her curtsey with her head held high. "You are the king, Henry, and of course, it must be as you wish. Do I have your permission to leave court or am I to be held here under suspicion too?"

"Don't be absurd, Mother. You are free to go where you will. I know I have your loyalty and your devotion."

He speaks as if his words will make it so and only I hear his doubt. He stands up, and when Lady Margaret makes a knee to him and reaches out to anoint his hand, he draws her close for an embrace and places a kiss on her temple. She turns her head away, croaks something incoherent before scuttling from our presence, the most defeated I have ever seen her.

To my surprise, I feel a pang of pity.

Henry stares into the flames unspeaking, knocks the crook of his forefinger against his teeth. I put down my sewing and move closer to him and he looks up, surprised to find me there.

"That was difficult, Elizabeth," he says. "My mother and I have never been at odds before."

"She will come round. You will be friends again. Once ... once the deed is done and cannot be altered."

I place my hand on his shoulder and he raises his head, stares deeply into nothing, his eyes narrowed.

"Yes, you are right." With a groan he eases from his chair and stretches his back, brings his hands together, interlaces his fingers and makes his knuckles crack. "I am very tired," he says in an uncharacteristic confession of weakness. "Would you take me to bed, Wife?"

Chapter Twenty-Three
Boy

<u>Vlissengen — 2 June 1495</u>

The sun is high in the sky, the port of Vlissengen bustling; a group of horsemen weave a path through flocks of sheep, hawkers, sailors, and whores. They pause at the dockside and the boy cranes his neck to look up at the ship that will carry him to his destiny. Pennants snap and dance in the breeze, the barefooted crew swarm over the decks, stowing weapons and victuals for the impending voyage. The boy is nervous, his belly grinding and churning, but he lets no emotion show. His face is open and bright, projecting hope. *This will be the day*, he thinks; *tomorrow I will be in England to reclaim my birthright.*

He slides from the back of his horse, pausing for one last caress of her long soft nose. His companions follow; George Neville, sweating beneath his cloak, is closely followed by Richard Harliston and James Keating. Other men of lesser status filter through the crowd and follow Richard of England onto the deck.

The boy halts at the ship's rail and looks down on the thronging dock. A sailor loosens a fat tarred rope, the captain cries an order, and a gap appears between the ship and the wharf. Debris, branches, rope and dead birds litter the stretch of dark green water. Soon it will be too broad to leap. The ship lurches and lifts, but he keeps his footing and looks up at the towering mast, remembering other voyages.

This will be the final one. Soon the sails will unfurl, fill with wind, and the salt-laden air will batter his cheeks. *This is it*, he thinks. *I am leaving, I am finally going home.*

It feels strange without Brampton. He has come to depend upon the Portuguean's rough humour, his brusque encouragement, but he has returned to Lisbon where his wife is mortally sick.

Below deck all is chaos. His cabin is small and dark, not fit for a king, but the boy clings to the knowledge that he is not the first dispossessed king, nor the first Plantagenet, to return to England on a humble ship, uncertain of his reception.

Richard was just a small boy when his father told them the story of his own desperate battle to win back his crown. He remembers the glow of the fire, the elated squirm of his siblings as they crowded together to listen to their father.

"I never for one moment believed England was lost to me. Warwick and the Anjou woman had placed mad old Henry back on the throne, but I knew it would be mine again. The day we sailed into Ravenspur I had barely a shirt to my back, but God was on my side.

"We marched first on York, where I was sure of the people's love. Outside the city walls I stood high in my stirrups and cried, "I come, not to regain my crown but to secure my rightful inheritance, THAT OF YORK!"

The people cheered, threw their caps in the air and opened the gates for me and after that, it was easy. We marched swiftly into the midlands, but Warwick refused to fight and beat a hasty retreat into Coventry. So we left him there, my brother George came creeping back into my favour, and we marched on London where they lined the streets to welcome me home. Those were great days, great days."

The memory fades, his father's smile slides away, and his focus blurs. Richard is pulled from the past by the arrival of a servant who has come to light a lanthorn. A few moments later, the cabin door opens to admit James Keating. The boy looks up, his face stretching into a smile.

"James, come in, sit down if you can find a space. I was just thinking about my father. It seems to me my fate is echoing his; we will be landing at Ravenspur just as he did, so pray God that history repeats itself."

Keating picks up a pile of clothing from a chair, tosses it onto the bunk and takes a seat. Richard calls for wine and soon the cabin fills with friends, the table is crowded with victuals. The men gathered here are the remnants of the Yorkist cause, men driven from England by their loathing of the Tudor usurper.

Keating stands up. "Let us drink," he cries. "Let us drink to the rightful king, Richard IV of England ... and an easy victory!"

The small chamber vibrates with cheers and the boy flushes, pushing the small nagging doubts away, and raises his cup.

But the crossing that begins so well deteriorates overnight. A swell builds up and their vessel is borne relentlessly with the tide. Soon the other ships are out of sight, the bulk of the fleet disappearing beyond the heaving sea. When morning comes, the boy learns they are farther south than they had planned to be. His ship is quite alone on the smooth calm sea but soon, on the horizon, one of his lost vessels appears, and the ragged fleet begins to re-muster. The captain, after consulting his maps and compass, declares they are somewhere off the coast of Kent.

"Kent?" Richard scratches his head, tries to quell the superstitious fear of failure. "How far are we from Ravenspur?"

"Half a day maybe, but if we travel north we will have lost the element of surprise, Sir."

"Tudor, even if he is forewarned, won't have time to act."

The boy turns to his advisors and is met by a mixed response. These men have waited years for this day; it cannot be allowed to slip away. Some want to head north, some want to land in Deal; a few even suggest they retreat back to Flanders while they can.

"No! No, we have come this far. I cannot in honour return to my aunt's court like a whipped dog. I must win this day ..." Richard paces the deck. The morning sun is just beginning to burn through the blanketing mist. He looks up at the first patch of blue sky where a lone gull is circling. "Perhaps we could land a small force here, just to test the water, see how we are received. Support in Kent has always been for York, men do not change allegiance so quickly."

A murmur of agreement and preparations are begun. The boy eats no breakfast; his stomach is a churning bowl of fear and hope. He is strapping on his sword when Harliston enters, followed by Keating. "My Lord," Harliston bows. "The men are ready, are you coming to see them off?"

"See them off? I am going with them."

Harliston bristles. "I don't think that is wise, my lord. We don't know how we will be received. You cannot leave the ship until the second landing, or maybe the third."

Keating steps forward, adding his voice to Harliston's.

"Indeed you cannot, sir. It would be foolish."

To his shame, the boy feels relief trickle through his veins, diluting his fear, but he puts up a convincing protest.

"I have waited for this for years, Keating, you know that. How can I send men into the unknown to fight for my cause while I wait here like a scared girl?"

Keating smiles and hooks a thumb over his belt. "It is customary for the leader of an army to remain behind the lines. The men will be expecting it. There is no shame."

Richard doesn't remind them that his father and uncle never remained behind the lines but fought in the thick of battle when they were little more than boys. He relaxes a little, pulls off his cap and tosses Keating a sulky look.

"I suppose I must listen to you; there is little point in me having advisors if I don't heed them. Very well, come along. Let us go and speak to the troops. If I cannot fight, the least I can do is give them a stirring speech to remind them of the justice of our cause."

Three hundred men clamber into small boats and push off toward shore. Richard waits on board, Keating and the others at his side, watching anxiously as the invaders approach land. At first he hears the swish of the oars, the slap of the waves against the hull, but soon all is silent again. He watches the vessels bob on the surface of the sea, riding the waves until lurching onto the shingle. The men leap out, a hand to their swords, crouching low as they move like armoured crabs across the beach.

The hamlet is peaceful, a cluster of wooden shacks sleeping in the morning sun. From his position on board ship Richard sees the standard of York, the white rose, raised high in the sky. It flaps and then hangs limp, a colourful anti-climax to the glory of his moment.

The boy strains his eyes to see, hears the faint echo of a ragged cheer, as men at arms appear from nowhere, crying out in celebration at their coming. A mummery of joy ensues, and the men on board look on bemused until a man, one of Richard's messengers, detaches himself from the throng and makes his way back toward the ship, bringing news.

Richard waits anxiously and, although it is no more than ten minutes, it seems an hour later that the fellow's head appears above the ship's rail. Men grab his arms and haul him on board. He flings himself onto the deck, pulls off his hat and drops on one knee.

"Your Grace." He wipes his brow and looks up at Richard. "They are for York. It is safe to come ashore. They swear to live and die for you and wait to show you great honour. They have cracked open caskets of wine and even now are drinking your good health."

The men on board relax; someone thumps Richard on the back in congratulation. Not a blow has been struck. If they are welcomed like this in every village they pass, London will be theirs in no time.

But amid the celebration Richard pauses, licks his lips and narrows his eyes. He places a hand on the messenger's shoulder and propels him back to the ship's rail.

"Go back, my friend, give them our royal greeting and tell them we will be there anon."

Richard rubs a hand over his unshaven chin and watches the fellow take up his oars and begin to row for the shore. He turns to his companions, his troubled face quelling their optimism.

"I fear a trap, my friends. I don't know why but I will not be disembarking here, not yet. Not until I am certain. We will wait and see ..."

The fellow is little more than a dot on the dunes by the time Richard's attention is drawn back to shore. Undiscernible figures move across the sand in joyous cavalcade but then a sudden shot rings out; a single blast, loud in the still of the morning. At the sniper's signal chaos is born in Deal.

Soldiers appear from nowhere, the Tudor banner unfurls as men stream from the cover of the dunes. Arrows are falling, raining down on Richard's advance army. He cries out fruitlessly as he witnesses them fall, sees their spent blood, and hears their dying screams.

He turns away, seeking his friends; his tears are wet on his cheeks as he screams through gritted teeth.

"Get us out of here! Get us out of here!"

With white knuckles he clings to the rail, watching the destruction of his dreams. Some of the men try to flee. They run leaping through the waves, floundering through the surf in a futile attempt to re-join the ship. But, hard on their heels, Tudor's men follow and the Kentish sea turns red with the blood of York.

Chapter Twenty-Four
Elizabeth

<u>Eltham Palace — May 1495</u>

I cannot believe she has gone. I look down at the letter and the psalter Grandmother Cecily bequeathed to me, and guilt bites deep. I neglected her for too long. She was so upright, so spry, that I failed to realise her years were short. I thought there would be time to visit when my life became peaceful. It is a hard lesson and for the first time I acknowledge that my life will never be one of ease. I may be queen of England but my time is not my own, I will never enjoy the leisure of normality. I dab away a tear and summon my seamstress to make up mourning clothes.

Sometimes there seems to be so much sorrow cast in my path. The loss of Grandmother hangs heavy, mingling with the loss of my mother and the continuing fear for Elizabeth's health.

Henry remains watchful, his temper strung so tightly I can almost hear it. He trusts nobody, not even me, and sometimes his watchfulness is unbearable. When he announces we are to take a progress north, I welcome the news with relief.

Although he does not confide in me I have learned, by nefarious means, that he expects an invasion at any time. His spies run hither and thither, bringing news, gossip and speculation and the threat eats away at him. It will be better away from court, I tell myself. There will be fewer whom he mistrusts, and he may find it easier to relax and breathe freely. I begin to make preparations for the journey, spending more and more time with the children whom I will miss so much while we are away.

It is July before we leave. Harry clings to my knees while Margaret, standing a little apart, sulks at what she sees as my negligence. Little Elizabeth, in her nurse's arms, knuckles her eye and whimpers. She has rallied of late and her growing strength nurtures hope for the future. I have forgotten my desire to get away from court and wish for the power to refuse to leave. In the end I have to tear myself away.

As we journey toward Chipping Norton, my eyes are sore from bidding them farewell. Beside me, Henry looks neither left nor right. He sits straight and proud on his mount, the feather in his cap the only part of him to betray any sign of softness.

We are riding into the north, where the people resent the execution of William Stanley, and their love of King Richard still lingers. As we progress further into the northern territory, I realise why I have been asked to accompany Henry. I am here, not because he desires my company, but because he knows the northerners love me for my father's sake. My presence is a balm to help a little of their love to reflect on him.

I glance at him sideways. His hair is neat and trim, his clothes, although richly made, are sombre; his face is pale, firm and unyielding, the creases on either side of his mouth set in stone. Even I, who know him well, feel his intractability, his steely strength. This is not a lovable king and generosity has little place in the method of his rule, but he is a good king. The royal coffers have never been so well filled.

The roads of England stretch ahead. First we travel to Combermere Abbey in Shropshire, then to Holt and Chester, and then on to Lathom, where the king's mother lives with her husband, Thomas Stanley. I wonder how, as the murderer of Stanley's brother, the king will be received.

The sun is beginning to set when we slide from our mounts to be welcomed into the Stanley stronghold. The king greets his mother warmly, extends a royal hand to Sir Thomas and waits to be shown inside. As we pass beneath the lintel the courtyard becomes a hive of activity. Our attendants and the supply wagons begin to arrive and a dog appears from nowhere. He leaps up at me, barking, his tail wagging and tongue lolling. I grab his ears in pleasure, laughing at his open, drooling mouth that seems to be smiling. It is a warmer greeting than we received from his master.

"Down, Trent!" Sir Thomas yells and the dog reluctantly drops to the floor, sniffs around before cocking his leg up a pile of boxes near the door. "I am so sorry, Your Grace." Sir Thomas bends over my hand, his apology sincere.

This is the man, I remind myself, *who delayed his army long enough at Bosworth to spell failure for York. Action on his part could have saved Richard's life, saved his crown. He was instrumental in securing Henry's claim.* But the thought passes, the man before me now is smiling congenially. I decide to give him the benefit of the doubt.

"It is perfectly fine, Sir Thomas. I like dogs. He isn't very old, is he?"

Our host hesitates, as if surprised at my lack of formality. His smile widens.

"No, Your Grace. He is barely a year old and already a monster."

At his behest we move laughing into the house. It does not escape my notice when the king's mother pointedly takes precedence over me. *This is my house, I am the king's mother*, she is telling me, and I can't be bothered to quibble. I follow her flicking skirts into the hall and look about me, pleased to find a warm fire and plenty of cushions. There are books left open on tables and a goodly supply of fruit and nuts near the settle. It is a warm inviting room and I find I feel quite at home.

We stay for four days and Sir Thomas goes out of his way to make us welcome. He holds a banquet, inviting all and sundry to join us, and after supper a trio of women sing to us, sweet soaring voices that pluck your heart strings and bring unwarranted tears to sting my eyes.

The last song is The Cuckoo; it evokes happier days when I sang to my father for sixpence. My father's court was similar to this, grander and more opulent but just as relaxed and warm. He too revelled in the entertainment of ordinary folk, singers and musicians plucked from the countryside, and not imported from overseas. He enjoyed English songs, sung by English people, for English kings. I wish Henry's court was so relaxed. I lean back in my chair and cradle my wine cup, more at home than I have felt for many years.

The next morning I wake queasily from sleep, my stomach rebelling against the day. At first I think perhaps I ate something bad at supper, but then begin to consider if I might be with child again. I missed my courses last month and the one before that was slight. If I am right it will be welcome news for Henry, who still craves more sons. "Two are not enough," he has told me more than once. "A king cannot have too many sons."

With some satisfaction I look into a glass and notice my eyes are shadowed, my skin pale and transparent. It must be so. If I am right, no one can accuse me of not doing my duty; there are already four children in the nursery and soon, although my belly is yet as flat as a board, it seems there will be five.

After prayer, when I have broken my fast, I begin to feel a little better. Today, the king's mother and her husband are giving us a thorough tour of the house. Sir Thomas is proud of his improvements and the more recent embellishments have been made in honour of our visit.

Lady Margaret is uncharacteristically quiet. She listens without interrupting, showing little interest as her husband enthuses over the lavish windows and the new wide fireplaces. It is as if she feels enthusiasm is beneath her, as if she is slightly disdainful of her husband's pride.

Sir Thomas has my sympathy. Marriage to proud Margaret can be little easier than my life is with her son. I keep close to Sir Thomas's side, demonstrating a keen interest in all he has to show us, and as the day progresses I feel myself warming to him. I have never spent much time with him before, and am pleased to discover not just a soldier but a man of intellect and learning.

"You should see the view from the Eagle Tower, Your Grace," he says, turning to the king. We crane our necks to look up at it, the moving clouds making it seem as if the tower will tumble down upon us.

"Well, lead the way," Henry says. "I shall be pleased to see it."

"So shall I." I am eager not to be left behind with the women and a party of us begins the long climb to the top. Lady Margaret remains below, so there are just the three of us and a few members of the Stanley household to brave the perilous stairs. Sir Thomas's fool maintains a steady flow of ribald jokes as we clamber upward.

I am not even halfway to the top before my breath becomes audible, and behind me I can hear Henry panting like an elderly hound. I keep close behind Sir Thomas, whose sword rattles on the wall at every step. I clutch my skirts in my hand, holding them high to keep from tripping, and my headdress keeps bumping on the low ceiling. I am beginning to wish I'd stayed safely at ground level. Behind me the fool makes jokes about slim ankles and I suppress the desire to send him tumbling to the bottom. When my heart threatens to burst from my chest, I pause with a hand to my side. "How much further?" I gasp.

"We are almost there now, Your Grace," Sir Thomas replies as he throws open a low door, flooding us with daylight. "Just a few more steps." One by one we stoop beneath the lintel and onto the roof, where Sir Thomas holds out a steadying hand and waits while I regain my breath.

"Well," I laugh, looking out across the vista. "The view was certainly worth the climb."

With one hand to my heaving chest and one resting on the low wall, I look out across the landscape. A river slides like a green serpent through trees and meadows where small farmsteads are dotted like toys. My stomach turns rebel at the unaccustomed height so I keep my chin high to avoid looking at the ground. "Henry, isn't it lovely?"

Beside me Henry grunts, a brisk wind blows up and I move a little closer to shelter from it, and his hand rests on my waist.

"That is a new bridge, Your Grace, built to mark your visit and make the passage easier from the road."

I turn my head to reply and notice the fool sidle up to his master's side. Sir Thomas stoops to harken to his whispered words. I have no liking for this little man; his jokes are unfunny and often cruel. With a curled lip he speaks slyly into his master's ear, his hoarse voice not meant for my sharp ears.

"Tom," the fool whispers as he nudges his master and nods toward the king. "Remember Will?"

Sir Thomas's face blanches and, in the long moment of silence that follows, I hold my breath, unable to move or speak.

I am still staring when Sir Thomas straightens up, his face drained of colour, and snaps a few curt words, lunging at the fool. The horrid little man ducks away from his master's swipe and takes himself off, his footsteps skittering down the spiral stairs.

Henry is close to the parapet. It would take but one moment for our host to exact revenge for his brother and send the king plunging to his death. It is plain Henry didn't hear the fool's words. I should warn him but I can't find my voice, or tear my eyes from Sir Thomas. I feel as if I have been turned to stone.

Sir Thomas steps forward. I hold my breath, my heart beating loudly, my stomach churning.

"If you look this way, Your Grace, you can see the house where …"

I release a gusty sigh, my whole body suddenly weak with relief. The balustrade is rough beneath my fingers, my chest tightens and there are tears in my eyes. I mustn't cry. I must not draw attention to my husband's near danger. I attempt to follow the line of Sir Thomas's finger, but my vision is blurred and I can see nothing of the scenery now.

"Are you well, Your Grace?" Sir Thomas notices my lack of ease and is at my side, followed belatedly by my husband. I cling gratefully to the king's arm. Suddenly pleased to feel the solidity of his muscle beneath.

"I think I have a touch of vertigo," I lie. "Please, can we go down now?"

"You should never have come," Henry snaps irritably as he ushers me through the door where Sir Thomas is waiting to take my hand.

The decent is steep and my knees are shaking as if I have an ague. Every so often I am forced to stop. I draw in deep breaths, and try to calm my raging heart. Behind me, Henry places a chilly hand on my shoulder to encourage me not to faint. He believes me to be suffering from vertigo and I do not disillusion him. I give him a watery smile, wishing we were on firmer ground so I could cling to him and share the astonishing truth. Henry may be a troubling, uncomfortable man to live with but I don't want to lose him.

He is all I have.

*

After supper I excuse myself from the dance and sit near the open window, drinking in the fresh evening aromas from the garden. Unusually, the king is on the floor partnered with one of my ladies. His mother is watching with a doting expression, every so often clapping her hands in time with the melody. The hall is filled with laughter, song, and the lingering smells of a well-cooked dinner. Sir Thomas approaches with a glass of wine and I bid him sit beside me.

"You have a lovely home, Sir Thomas. I am glad to have visited you. Thank you."

"It is my honour, Your Grace; a greater privilege than you can guess."

I smile at him and he looks away in confusion.

"What is it?" I ask, my smile beginning to fade. He looks deep into his wine cup.

"I can never decide if you look more like your father or your mother." He drinks deeply, embarrassed by the sudden intimacy.

"My grandmother always said I resembled both, depending on my mood. She had little love for my mother but gave her due credit for filling the royal nursery."

He laughs quietly and then a sudden silence falls between us.

"I loved your father; you know that, don't you?"

"I think everyone loved him. He was that sort of man."

"And you are that sort of woman, Your Grace, if you don't mind me saying so."

"Why should I mind? I get few compliments these days."

"Really?" He looks at me incredulously, his eyes sweeping across my hair, taking in my flushing cheeks. It is my turn to be embarrassed and I dip my face to my own cup. There is something I want to say to him, something I *need* to hear an answer to. I clear my throat and let my upper body lean a little closer.

"Sir Thomas ... today, up on the tower. I heard what the fool said. You were tempted, weren't you, just for a moment?"

He sputters his wine, dabs at his damp doublet with trembling fingers.

"I don't understand, Your Grace. What do you mean?"

"I heard him quite plainly, Sir Thomas, and, just for a second, a look passed across your face, a sort of desperate look. For a moment I thought you were going to act on it."

"Never. Never!" His voice is hushed, urgent, his face thrust toward me. "I am loyal to the king, I swear it, and to you."

"Yet he killed your brother."

He takes a shuddering breath and looks deep into my eyes.

"The king executed a traitor, it was hardly murder."

I lower my head; my fingers are fighting a desperate battle in my lap.

"There are some who believe he murdered my brothers, too."

A silence; brief and pregnant.

"You think them dead?"

I look up, our eyes lock.

"Do you, Sir Thomas?"

His eyes narrow. I can see his thoughts chasing through his mind as he searches for the best answer; the safest answer. Slowly, I reach out for his hand.

"You can speak freely. It will go no further."

There is a long silence before he speaks. He rubs his face with a big calloused hand.

"At one time I thought they were dead, but now? Now, I am not so sure. This ... this boy that your aunt Margaret parades as York, he has persuaded many men to his banner."

"But not you, Sir Thomas."

"No, Your Grace, not me. Never me."

"Suppose things were different and I were not married to the king, on which side would you be then?"

"That is supposition, and an unfair question, Your Grace."

"But, nevertheless, it is one I'd like an answer to."

He shrugs, deeply uncomfortable, and looks away to where Henry is now leading his mother onto the floor. Margaret is beaming on the assembly as if she is indeed the queen.

"I am wed to the king's mother. I am loyal to my stepson."

"Yet your brother was swayed."

"My brother was a fool."

"My brother was a child. I loved him. Should the man now claiming his name prove to be my brother indeed, I will not know what to think, how to act."

He turns back to me, his eyes kind and full of sympathy.

"He must be a pretender, Your Grace. How can a ten-year-old boy have survived?"

"The Duchess claims my father's friends took pity on him and helped him escape. There are many men who serve Henry only because of me. Because I am the child of Edward IV. Perhaps there are those who would prefer to serve his son."

"I cannot know, Your Grace. What do you want me to do, or say? You know I could be taken up just for speaking to you in this manner."

We both glance toward the king who has, for once, let his guard over me drop. I am rarely so unobserved; perhaps the sensation of not being watched goes to my head.

"I am sorry. I had thought you loyal."

"I am loyal!" He rises to his feet, stands towering above me like an oak tree. I hold out a hand and he takes it, helps me rise and, as we walk toward the dance floor, I glance up at him.

"But to whom, Sir Thomas? Which child of York really holds your heart?"

*

I calculate the baby I am carrying will be born sometime next spring. Although I continue to feel sickly in the morning, by lunch time it passes and I am myself again. We are preparing to leave, continue our journey north, and are taking a last walk around the gardens.

Henry is just ahead with his mother, leaving Sir Thomas and I to bring up the rear.

"Your roses are lovely, Sir Thomas," I say, bending down to enjoy their heady fragrance. He waits while I indulge myself, plunging my nose into this bloom and that. When I straighten up, he is smiling, amused at my simple joy.

"They were planted by my first wife, Eleanor. Margaret takes little interest in the gardens."

He plucks a bloom and offers it to me with a bow.

"I believe Eleanor was some sort of relative of mine," I say. "A cousin to my Grandmother, perhaps? I can't quite remember."

"Niece to your grandmother, I believe, but I am no expert, Your Grace."

I see Grandmother's face quite plainly in my mind and open my mouth to express the grief of losing her so suddenly. But my words are stalled by the arrival of a galloping horse. We turn toward it. Henry looks up and, recognising the messenger, leaves his mother and hurries back toward the house.

Exchanging worried looks, Sir Thomas and I follow. As we near the gate Henry signals for us to stay back, and goes forward to meet the messenger alone.

From the garden we see the road-weary man fall to his knee; he is dusty and mired from the ride. I signal to a hovering servant to bring him refreshment. We cannot hear his words but he speaks earnestly, gesticulating with his arms. Henry tears off his hat and throws it to the ground where the thick black velvet is quickly coated in dust, the jewels winking in the sunshine. I lose my patience and, with fear for my children uppermost in my mind, I ignore his order to stay back. I move forward to join him.

"What is it Henry? What has happened?"

He turns slowly and regards me with an expression close to hatred. His face is white, his lips tight, and his eyes bloodshot.

"The boy, the lying brat, has landed a small force in the south. Our army routed them easily and they got no farther than the beach but the boy, God curse him, got away. He is now harrying the coast of Ireland. By Christ, will I never be free of this irritant?"

As Henry stalks indignantly away, Sir Thomas and I exchange glances, his eyes crinkle slightly at the edges and I realise I am relieved. The boy lives. There is still a chance I may look upon my brother again one day.

Sheen Palace – October 1495

I am so happy to be home. The summer has been a long one, travelling from place to place, staying in different beds, different rooms, sampling strange cuisine. I look about my apartments at Sheen, run a finger along the back of my favourite chair that is placed close to the window, enjoying the view across the park. I plan at least a week of doing absolutely nothing but reacquainting myself with the palace that feels most like home.

I am noticeably pregnant now. I run a hand across my rounded belly and feel the child squirm in response. A girl or a boy, I wonder? I hope it is another boy. Henry needs the comfort that only many sons can bring him. For myself, I don't mind either way.

As much as I love my sons, the bond between mother and daughter is different. I share an empathy with them that comes of knowing the difficulties a princess may face. Henry is already negotiating with Spain for a union between Arthur and their daughter, Caterina; and at the same time with France for the marriage of our little Elizabeth and their *dauphin*, Francis.

The *dauphin* is only just a year old, but it seems it is never too soon to make such arrangements. I do not remind Henry that nothing may come of these negotiations. It wouldn't do to upset or offend him, but I know from experience such things are fraught with problems.

When I was a girl my father wished for a union with France and organised my betrothal to Charles when he was *dauphin*. I remember my father's rage when King Louis reneged on his promise. His fury knew no bounds and on the day the news came, I learnt curse words then that I'd never heard before.

Now I am glad it never came to pass. I realise I am fortunate to have remained here in the country of my birth, surrounded mostly by those who know and love me. I should hate to be a foreigner in a strange country. There can be nothing worse, yet it is the normal lot for a princess.

I am watching the sun set slowly in the west when Henry enters. He hesitates near the door and I have to urge him to approach. His habitual manner of lurking like a draper is irritating, but I manage not to let it show. I sit up straight in my chair and stretch my arms above my head.

"I was almost asleep."

He takes a seat opposite, balancing on the edge.

"Why are you alone?"

"I like to be alone sometimes, Henry. Don't you ever grow tired of the constant attendance? It is pleasant to be solitary, so I can slump in my chair if I choose, or scratch an itch if I have one without someone assuming I am developing a pox."

He smiles slowly, and not without warmth.

"I thought we could ride out to Eltham in a day or two."

I sit upright in my chair, instantly alive with joy.

"Oh, I am so glad. I was going to ask if it was possible. It seems so long since we've seen the children. They will be delighted with the gifts we have brought them."

"They will be glad enough just to have their mother back I would think."

"I may stay for a week."

I beam at him, the love we share for our offspring bringing us close. Impulsively, I reach out a hand and he takes it, squeezes my fingers.

We seldom make physical contact outside of the marriage bed, and I feel my body respond, wanting him to move closer. Pregnancy never diminishes but seems to heighten my natural ardour. Affectionately, I return the pressure.

"I wish we could skip supper," I say rashly. "I am so tired of formal dinners, I'd much rather eat here with you … intimately."

It is as close as I can get to ask him to take me to bed. Henry stiffens. He tries to draw away but I cling on. "I am lonely, Henry. Is it so wrong to desire your presence?"

He stands up, tugs the edge of his tunic down and looks away.

"You must be tired … you should rest."

What is wrong with him? I know he has the passions of a healthy man. Why must he keep relations between us so formal? If I were not already pregnant he'd bed me soon enough. Because I am big with his child he sees no need. He is a cold fish but still I try to tempt him into my net, and when he resists I lose my patience.

"I don't feel tired at all. I am well and healthy and if I am tired of anything it is this … this wall you constantly erect between us. I am your wife … why not take pleasure in that, Henry?"

"I have business to attend to. You are excused from the banquet tonight if you wish it but … I have to be there. You get some rest."

I bite my lip and watch him go. I shouldn't have spoken; should never have let him glimpse the lusty side of my nature, so similar to my father's. It discomforts him.

*

We are making ready for our trip to Eltham. I am sorting through small gifts for the children when a messenger arrives. People are coming and going all the time with missives and letters so I pay this one little heed. I am only half aware of the conversation that follows between the king and the dusty courier until a hand falls gently on my arm.

I look up.

The hall is silent, our attendants holding their breath, one or two of my women are snivelling.

"What is it?"

I put down an engraved silver ball and take two steps toward my husband. It is only then that I notice the messenger's livery and realise he has ridden from Eltham. My world begins to crumble.

228

"What is it?" I repeat, rushing forward, my voice harsh with panic.

"Elizabeth; come, come with me." Henry's voice is gentle, his hand is on my right arm. His mother suddenly appears at my left side, her touch firm on my elbow. Between them they urge me to go with them.

"Come with us, Elizabeth." As they lead me away Lady Margaret nods a command to my women, who fly from the hall, toward my apartment.

"Tell me, Henry," I scream. "What did he say? What has happened?"

But I know the truth before they tell me. I can feel it in my heart. Great tearing teeth are slashing at my happiness, ripping my former optimism to shreds.

They push me into a chair. I fight them, scrabbling with my arms, kicking out. I am already sobbing, although the words are not yet spoken. Someone puts a cup into my hand but I thrust it away untasted. I grasp Henry's tunic, wrench him toward me so our faces are level, our breath mingling. He has been eating herring. There are tears on his cheeks, his face is papery white, making him old. "Tell me," I mouth, but no sound emerges.

"Elizabeth," he says and his mother's fingers tighten on my wrist, my head falls onto her narrow breast.

"No." I close my eyes, roll my head against her chest as I try to fight back the agony that tightens like a vice around my heart. "No, please ... not my baby ..."

*

The king's mother says very little but she is with me every day. She offers no criticism; she does not insist that I eat, she does not tell me not to weep. But she is there and, to my surprise, I find some comfort in her presence.

The Lady Margaret was blessed with only one child; Henry. I remember my mother telling me that Margaret was just thirteen when he was born and her body not properly formed. In giving him life she deprived herself of the thing she craved most; more children. Had she been able to have more sons, perhaps her love for Henry might have been less stifling.

As soon as I am able we ride to Eltham. It takes all my courage to enter the hall and make the climb to the nursery floor. Meg and Harry are playing quietly. In fact, the whole palace is unnaturally silent. Henry and I, followed by his mother, slip into the room where the children are at the table, their heads bent over books. Harry looks up first, our eyes meet. His are red and full of tragedy; my heart gives a little leap.

"Mother!" He clambers from his seat and runs toward me, his short fat arms snaking around my neck. I sink my face into his hair and inhale the lingering scent of babyhood, slightly sweaty and sweet. I hold him away a little, push his hair out of his eyes.

He looks peaky.

"Have you been good?"

He nods unconvincingly, so I turn to Meg for confirmation.

"Quite good," she says. "Apart from letting his dog chew a hole in our lady mistress's skirt as she dozed before the fire. And he did eat too many sweetmeats and made himself sick all over his psalter."

Harry looks hangdog.

"I am sorry, Mother."

I manage to laugh, almost choke as, half-formed, the humour turns to tears. Standing up, I try not to look at the door that leads to Elizabeth's apartments.

I smooth my skirts and attempt to rally my courage. It has to be done. As I prepare to move, a small hand slips into mine and my son looks up at me.

"Elizabeth is in Heaven now, Mother."

I struggle for a smile, and squeeze his hand.

"Yes, she is." My voice is husky, my throat closing with grief.

"You still have us, Mother. Don't be so sad." His little face is pink and earnest, his blue eyes glinting with tears. "She wouldn't want us to be sad."

"No." I cannot risk a longer sentence. To my relief, Lady Margaret steps forward.

"No. She would want us to be glad. We must remember that we are fortunate to have enjoyed her for so long. God will send us other compensations."

She draws the children's attention and provides the opportunity for Henry and I to slip unnoticed into the nursery.

In the centre of the room the royal cot stands empty; the canopy already taken down for laundering. I stand beside it, as I have so many times, and my heart breaks afresh. Without my child I cannot properly draw my next breath.

Henry's hand slides gently across my shoulders and I sink my head onto his chest. For once we are united; sorrow has brought us close and his cheeks are as wet as mine.

Perhaps I am unwise to stay so long; perhaps it would be better not to be here where I dwell upon my loss every day. Henry, seeking solace in practical things, is already organising a lavish ceremony and has ordered a tomb of Lydian marble with a black marble cover. Although I know I shall never bear to look upon it, there is to be a copper gilt effigy, and she is to lie at Westminster, as is fitting.

Henry sits at the table scratching his head over the wording for the tomb. For the hundredth time he sighs and scores through the words he has written. I move to stand beside him, reading over his shoulder.

Elizabeth, second daughter of Henry VII, the most illustrious King of England, France ...

If it were up to me I'd want to state that she was our beloved daughter, the joy of my heart, the light of my future; but I know such things must be left to Henry, who remains, first and foremost, even in his grief, the king.

I turn away, listless, unable to settle, and move about the room picking things up and putting them down again. I even go so far as to poke the dog with my toe. He lifts his head, looks at me with miserable bloodshot eyes before dropping it back onto his paws, and soon he is snoring again. I am so bored, so lifeless, so beset with sorrow that I don't know what to do with myself.

I look up expectantly when the door opens and a servant slips in.

"Your Grace." The boy bows low. "Lady Pole is here; shall I send her away?"

"Margaret?" I almost push the boy over in my haste to reach my cousin. I drag her into the room, hugging and kissing her, my tears falling afresh at the sight of her. Henry looks up from his work, gathers his papers, nods his head at Margaret and makes himself scarce.

"I hope he doesn't think I've come to beg my brother's cause at a time like this." She eases off her gloves and lays them on the table. "Elizabeth, I am so sorry. So very, very sorry."

I cannot help it. I am in tears again before she has finished offering condolence. I plump onto a settle,

232

fumble for a kerchief and dab at my eyes while she takes her place beside me.

"My poor Elizabeth, I can't begin to imagine … if it were my little Henry …"

She stops and stares into space, her throat working with emotion. Margaret has borne her husband one son so far and has hopes for further children. "But, soon, my love, you will have another child. Pray God it is a daughter you carry this time to soothe your loss. There is plenty of time to give Henry another son."

I sniff and roll my kerchief into a ball.

"This babe kicks so hard, I am sure it must be a boy."

"Oh." Margaret pats my hand and winks conspiratorially. "There are those of us among the female sex whose kick is as good as any boy's."

For the first time I find myself smiling. Friendship and kinship is healing. From the moment she entered the room I felt better.

"Come to the nursery, Margaret, and see the children. You've not seen your namesake for months."

"I thought you'd named her for the king's mother," she retorts as we leave the room and begin to hurry along the corridor.

I smile for the second time. "Between you and me, so does she."

Harry and Meg are being fitted for new outfits; they are tolerating the tailor who fusses with pins and lengths of wool. A visit from their mother and cousin proves a welcome distraction. Harry wriggles from the nurse's grasp and runs to greet me, remembering just in time to drop his cousin a courtly bow. Meg follows decorously and performs a perfect curtsey.

"My goodness, how you've both grown," Margaret exclaims. "They are not babies anymore."

"No." I realise, a little sadly, that she is right. They are growing up fast.

"Henry is so much like your father, Elizabeth. The look in his eye; the set of his head. It could be him reborn."

I consider my son in a new light, through fresh eyes.

"Do you think so? When he was born I wondered if he was going to be fair, like my mother and I. But the older he gets the redder his hair shines."

"It is the only thing he's inherited from the Tudors, I'd say. And Margaret, what a beauty you are going to be!"

Meg blushes and squirms at the attention, pleased to be so regarded. As she continues to chatter, Margaret draws Harry onto her knee and wraps her arms around him. "You're not too big for a cuddle, are you, Harry?" She gives him a smacking kiss and he wipes it away with his sleeve, making us laugh.

It is a happy family picture, one I crave more of. I seldom see my own family. My sisters have been suitably married and spend most of their time in the country. Cecily comes to court occasionally but she is too close to the king's mother for intimacy, and is kept busy attempting to supply her husband with sons.

"It is good to see you, Margaret." Spontaneously I reach for her hand again. "You must bring your son to visit the next time you come to court. He can lodge here with the children."

"Yes, that would be nice. It would be good for our children to remember they are cousins. My Henry will serve Arthur one day, when he is king. We should always look to the future and plan for it, even if it is an uncertain thing."

I know she is thinking of her brother. Despite my attempts to intervene on his behalf, poor little Warwick is still in the Tower.

"I have tried to get Henry to free Warwick, I really have but ... the king thinks it too risky ..."

"He is little more than a boy, and not himself. He has had no education, has no ambition of any kind. What risk can there be?"

I look down at my hands, my fingers slightly pudgy and over-warm.

"It isn't Warwick himself that poses the danger. Henry knows he hasn't the ... hasn't the, erm, nature to rebel but there are those that would back him. You only have to consider the man Warbeck to realise that."

Her breath is released in a rush and we exchange glances, aware that we've been on the verge of quarrelling. She throws up her hands and lets them drop again.

"Oh, Elizabeth. It is all so ridiculous. We are all walking on eggshells. This pretender, this boy from Tournai— what do you make of it? He has won himself a goodly following and I've heard him referred to often as 'King Edward's son'."

Henry's spies have confirmed that the boy causing all the trouble is the son of a weaver from Tournai, a boy with no learning or nobility but with enough impudence to impersonate a royal duke. Henry seems convinced, but I am not so sure. I cannot imagine how a base-born boy from the low countries could fool a group of disgruntled refugees from my father's court; men who knew my father and his sons very well indeed. Margaret observes me keenly as she waits for my reply.

"I don't know. If I could just see him, or if someone close to me were to see him ... sometimes I am desperate to know. I loved Richard so much but the danger he poses, or this pretender poses, threatens my sons. I am torn between wanting him to be my brother and dreading it being him. I don't know what to think or what to do."

"It must be hard."

"Sometimes it is impossible." I lean forward and drop my voice to a whisper. "The king is suspicious of everyone. It is not healthy. My father saw more than his share of betrayal but he didn't let it eat him up. He didn't suspect everyone. Henry is so watchful that the whole court is on edge all the time. Sometimes I think I will just be glad when it is all over and the pretender is dealt with."

Margaret sighs and allows Harry to slide from her lap. We watch him wander across to Meg and try to steal a handful of nuts from her apron.

"Even if the pretender was caught, I dare say the king would find someone new to be suspicious of."

I fear she is right.

Chapter Twenty-Five
Boy

<u>Scotland — 20 November 1495</u>

A noisy flurry of gulls follows the ship as it glides into dock, the grey green water fleeing from beneath the bow. On deck the boy clings to the rail, standing a little apart from his companions. He looks across the water to a harbour heaving with men, whores, dogs and mules. The stench of the dock replaces the clean, clear air of the sea; reeking fish, stale sweating bodies, clothing that has been soaked by rain and dried by the salty air. A drunken man spews in a gutter, a trio of urchins play tag through the crowd.

Richard looks on, encouraged by the promise of solid ground, of a warm bed, a good dinner taken on a table spread with linen. For the past weeks he has rarely been on deck or breathed fresh air. Most of his days and all of his nights have been spent in the plunging darkness of a ship's cabin, his only light a swinging lantern, his only relief the bottle, and the oblivion of sleep.

After the failure of the Kent landing depression bit deep; half-heartedly he turned his small fleet toward the coast of Ireland, hoping to find enough support there to resurrect his cause. He lingered for a while with the Earl of Desmond, but Tudor's punishment for Ireland's support of Richard in "91 had been harsh. The people were loath to risk Henry's displeasure again and stayed away, turning their backs on Richard. For a while it seemed he'd met with defeat, but Desmond urged him to make one last attempt.

Looking back, Richard realises the siege of Waterford stood little chance of success and the ignominy of the pursuit to Cork, the destruction of his fleet, nags at him day and night. Now, his quest having so far failed, he turns to King James and begs for sanctuary at the Scottish court. His heart is heavy and he has little faith that he will find comfort there.

His fortunes seem to have plummeted since he and Brampton parted; he misses the buoyant support of his long-time friend. Brampton always knew what to do, where to go, whom to trust. Without him and without the support of Margaret, the boy is dithering. Now that the new Duke of Burgundy is seeking a treaty with England, there is little aid his aunt Margaret can offer other than her good will. He feels alone, vulnerable, and inexperienced.

High above his head the sails are furled, and the narrow gap between ship and shore closes. A figure moves to stand beside him and he turns to find Keating pulling a cap over his sleek dark hair.

"It will be a relief to disembark, Your Grace. If I never see the sea again it will be too soon."

Richard smiles slowly, his shoulders relaxing a little.

"I am eager for a bath. I am sure the lice are carrying lice too; and oh, for a properly cooked meal, a finger bowl instead of a bucket."

"And a woman, Your Grace. It's been a long time."

Richard's face falls. "It has," he replies, his mind slipping reluctantly back to Nelken. He regrets not finding his son; the boy will be growing now, crawling or walking perhaps, smiling at strangers.

Richard shakes himself and, pulling his gauntlets from his belt, begins to draw them on, flexing his fingers. They are worn, the embellished trim torn; he could do with a new pair. He grimaces with distaste before taking one more look at the open sky, the stretching grey-green sea. He draws in a deep breath.

"Right, summon the others, Keating. Let us go in search of this Scottish king."

*

High on its crag Stirling Castle waits proudly, dwarfing the ragged party as it rides beneath the ancient gate. Richard, trying to appear confident, cranes his neck at the wet windows and the dark towers where the limp flap of a pennant welcomes him in from the fog.

The courtyard is alive with people; servants, grooms, milling horses, barking dogs. A group of women stand with hands on hips, watching his party dismount. His army is made up of Portuguese, Germans, Burgundians and a few disaffected English, but to the Scots they are all foreigners.

Richard stretches his stiff back and waits for his companions to flank him before they move into the castle itself. His knees are weary from the long ride, his hands frozen inside his threadbare gauntlets. As his horse is led away he pulls off his hat, tries to revive the limp feather that dangles over the brim like a dead fowl.

One day, he thinks, as they progress across slick wet cobbles, *I will make a goodly entrance. One day, when I enter a palace, the people will fall to their knees and count their blessings when I deign to notice them.*

As they reach the outer door a steward steps forward; he bows his head courteously and ushers them inside. They follow him up the twisting stair and, as they go,

Richard notes the sumptuous hangings, the blazing candles, the Scottish royal arms emblazoned on every wall.

"We have put you in here, my lord." The steward throws open a door. "I think you will find everything you need. The king will be pleased to receive you on his return to the castle. If you should find anything lacking, you have only to call."

The man bows and hurries away. Richard looks about the room. It is warm. A huge fire burns in the grate and torches have been lit to fend off the dark that comes so early to Scotland in November.

He sees a table laden with victuals, and comfortable chairs pulled close to the fire. Through an open door he notices a bed with fine thick hangings and a deep mattress. It promises much after the trials of a ship's cabin. A girl is folding back the sheets, another stokes the fire. They are young and comely, no doubt selected for their feminine appeal. He feels the tension drain from his shoulders, throws down his hat, and casts off his damp cloak.

*

Richard tugs at the bottom of the doublet supplied by his host. It is a trifle short and will have to be altered, but it will do for now. The garments may be slightly small but, for the first time in months, he feels clean, respectable and, from what he can tell in the hand-held glass, his royal breeding is now visible.

He follows the steward back along the corridor, down the twisting stair, through the castle to the great hall where the king is waiting. At the end of the room a group of courtiers are lounging in the corners, another group is ranged about the throne.

When the steward inserts himself at the king's elbow, James looks up and spies Richard waiting to be introduced. "Ah, there you are, York."

King James disentangles himself from the conversation and hurries toward Richard. They meet in the centre of the floor. There should, of course, have been ceremony, a fanfare announcing his entrance. Richard should stoop to pay the king homage but James has little patience with formality and, when Richard bends over his hand, he pulls away before the boy is done. The boy hesitates and, when he straightens up, realises he is taller than the Scottish king. They regard each other for a long moment before James speaks.

"It is good to finally meet at last, Richard." He slaps the boy on the back and leads him away from the crowd. "Had fate decreed otherwise, we should have been brothers."

"Your Grace?" Richard's brow wrinkles in confusion and James laughs, gestures to a servant to pour them some wine.

"I was betrothed once to your sister, Cecily, but ... well, it didn't happen. A shame. Perhaps once you have ousted the Tudor, we can negotiate a fresh union between our countries."

"I believe Cecily is already taken, Your Grace, but I have other sisters. I am sure there must be one still unwed who will suit you."

I'll do anything, he thinks. *If you help me reclaim my throne, I will marry you to my grandmother.* As James chatters on it becomes apparent the Scottish king enjoys life and all it holds.

"I was just talking to Campbell here about the possibility of a Scottish printing press. We are way behind England in that respect. You've seen Caxton's machine, I suppose?"

Richard, about to drink, lowers his cup, his thirst unquenched.

"I've not seen the machine but I've seen the books. My father had a vast library. I remember my favourite was *Le Morte d'Arthur*; it coloured my early years ... and my uncle, Anthony Woodville, was involved in the printing trade. I recall his excitement when he showed us the printed version of his book on philosophy."

Richard's voice trails off as he recalls his uncle is dead now, along with the rest of the people there that day, but James doesn't notice. He looks at the boy speculatively, his smile slowly stretching into delight.

"You have a keen memory. I can see we have a lot in common, Richard. I am currently backing research into improving the range and aim of guns. You must come with me when I visit the foundry ... I can lend you a horse. Ah!" He is diverted by a newcomer to the circle. "Do you know my brother, James? Gets confusing, the both of us blessed with the same name, so it's easier to call me 'James' and my brother 'Ross'. He is the Duke of Ross, you see."

A young man with some resemblance to the king holds out his hand, and Richard clasps it but the lad has no time to speak. As James continues to dominate the conversation, Richard wonders if Ross is naturally quieter than the king or if he has given up trying to get a word in. As the three men stroll about the room, the king stops from time to time to make introductions.

"This is the Duke of York," he says. "With our help he will overthrow Tudor and, once he is made king, relations between our countries will blossom."

Richard smiles, his eye skimming nervously over the colourful crowd. It may be dark outside and rain may be lashing the casements, but inside it is bright and warm. More candles and torches than can be counted illuminate the crush of bodies, bouncing from the fabulous gowns and jewels, and reflecting in the mirrors.

A tall slender woman, older than the king, slides her arm through James's and smiles boldly at Richard. He bows slightly, uncertain of her status until the king's hand falls on hers and his smile widens further.

"This is Margaret; Margaret Drummond."

The king does not elaborate but it is clear she is his mistress. Richard bows over her hand as she assesses him.

"We are blessed to have you here, my lord," she smiles. "The young ladies will be fighting for the attention of such a gallant young fellow."

He laughs half-heartedly, uncertain how to reply to such overt flirtation before the king, but is saved by the press of people. They press in, vying for an introduction, and he becomes detached from the royal party. Everyone is reaching out to grasp his hand in greeting and Richard is overwhelmed, warmed by their generosity. *I should have come here sooner*, he thinks. *Why did I wait so long?*

"Ah, Huntly." The king speaks loudly over the din of the crowd, beckoning Richard back to his side. "Richard, you must meet the Earl of Huntly." The boy turns and bows to yet another newcomer. "And his daughter. Where is Catherine? Ah yes, and his daughter, my ... erm ... cousin, isn't it? Catherine Gordon."

The clamouring crowd seems to fall away, their voices are silenced, and the tug of their hands on his doublet is unheeded. A woman is curtseying before him, her head bowed. He looks down upon a velvet hood trimmed with pearls and, as she rises, Richard notices a few strands of bright yellow hair peeking from beneath. She has a high clear brow, a pretty up-tilted nose, flanked by wide blue eyes. His heart lurches, his mouth goes dry and words fail him.

She is the most beautiful woman he has ever seen. Her throat is long and white, her breast translucent. When he bends to kiss her fingers, they flutter in his palm. Slowly he straightens up again, looks into her eyes and fumbles for something to say.

"I—I am … delighted …"

She laughs, a tinkling sound. He remembers the stories Bess told him as a boy and knows he has found his Guinevere.

"They told me you were tall." She tilts her face upward. "But you are almost a giant."

"I think, my lady, that you are very tiny. It makes me appear bigger than I am."

"They say your father was a large man, too."

"Oh, to me he was huge. I was just ten years old when he died. Now, when I recall him, I remember a big man, a laughing man, glinting with jewels with a cup of welcome forever in his hand."

Richard hears his own voice with some surprise. It is as if someone else is working his mouth. He has no idea what he is saying. *Catherine*, he thinks, rolling the word around his mind. The name seems suddenly exotic and wonderful as if he has never heard it spoken before.

There is a flush beneath her cheeks, and her eyes are bright with pleasure. *This is a lady,* he tells himself. Not someone to be taken lightly; not a roll in the hay, or a fumble in a darkened corner. She is the cousin of the king, and expected to marry well. He must tread warily.

"The king says there is to be a tournament tomorrow in your honour. Will you be riding in it?"

His eyes are fastened on her mouth, moist pink lips, straight pearly teeth, and a glimpse of her tongue.

"Me? No; I shouldn't think so."

Richard feels uncomfortable at the thought. Of course, by now he should be a champion at the lists, but he's never had the chance to train properly. He can wield a sword and understands the rudiments of battle, but he has never fought. He will never be a hero, although from the look in Catherine's eyes, you'd never know it. He bows once more.

"Would you dance with me, my lady?" he asks. "I may not be a champion of the lists but I am king of the dance floor."

She laughs gaily and takes his hand. The music begins again as they hurry to take their places on the floor. From his place on the dais King James watches, and raises his glass.

*

In the weeks that follow, Richard attends more jousts and pageants than he has in his life. He rides out with the king and his favourites, hawking and hunting. Wrapped warmly against the encroaching winter weather, they eat *al fresco*, warming their hands at braziers set beneath the rapidly thinning canopy of the wood.

Relaxed, happy and safe, Richard blossoms and for the first time in his life, resists the invitations of the prettier element of the court. It isn't that the women aren't appealing, for King James ensures his attendants are comely and willing. But each time he feels tempted, Catherine's face and Catherine's laughter and the memory of the thrill of her hand, prevents him.

I should stay away from her, he thinks, afraid he will go too far and offend his host. He can't afford to lose his ally in the battle to regain his throne. He determines he will avoid her, pointedly seek the company of other women of the court, but she is always there and, like a fish to a worm, he cannot keep away.

They make a handsome couple, everyone says so. The top of her head is level with his throat, their colouring similar, and something in the way they move suggests they were made to dance together. The court begins to gossip, linking their names, and insinuating an illicit union. Richard is forced to take the matter to the king.

"I swear it is gossip, Your Grace. I have never laid a hand on her or set eyes on Catherine outside your royal hall."

James smiles. "Relax cousin, I never listen to gossip. Although, in this case, I can see there is no smoke without fire. You and Catherine were made for each other, man. Why not take her to your bed and seal our alliance; call it a sort of treaty?"

Richard sputters, begins to speak, but is robbed of his words. He stutters and stumbles until he manages to blurt out, "To my bed? What on earth are you suggesting?"

"Oh, I don't mean you should take her down. I mean, why not marry her? She has good connections; she is my cousin. It would be no shame."

"Of course it would be no shame. It would be an honour, a huge one but ... my position ... my future is uncertain, what can I offer her? Oh ... she would never have me."

"She'd have ye in the blink of an eye, man. She is smitten, it's plain to see. And what could be better for a

246

woman than the promise of the English throne ... unless, of course, it's the Scottish one?"

While James throws back his head and laughs at his own joke, Richard struggles to come to terms with what he is being offered.

"Y-your Grace ..." He stumbles over the words. "You have given me so much; a house, servants, horses, clothes ... I owe everything to you, everything. But this? Are you sure? Suppose I should fail? I can't drag Catherine around the courts of Europe for the rest of her life."

"Acht, we won't fail, Richard. God will see to that. Marry her and be happy, man, while you are still young enough to enjoy it."

Chapter Twenty-Six
Elizabeth

<u>Sheen — 18 March 1496</u>

This time it is easier. Perhaps it has something to do with the alignment of the stars, or it may be because I am not attended by my mother-in-law. Either way I am calmer, and since I know what to expect, I feel less fear than last time. The pain and the bloody fluid does not concern me greatly. I follow the instructions of the midwife carefully, work hard, focusing on the task instead of fighting it. When at last my child slips into the world I am pleased when they tell me it is another girl; a princess to balance the nursery and offer companionship to Margaret.

She lies in my arms, the womb grease still thick upon her. As I examine my daughter's face she grips my finger as if her life depends on it, which I suppose it does. Her face is wrinkled, her nose and forehead showing signs of bruising, and she looks rather cross, disgruntled with the harsh world although we have done all we can to give her a gentle entry.

I loosen my shift and let her suckle, the tenuous tug of her mouth growing stronger and more confident as the minutes pass. After a few moments the sucking stops, and she slips into a doze.

"Let me take her now, Madam. I will make her tidy."

I offer her up reluctantly, sitting up on my pillow, watching as they wash away the megrim of birth from my child. They anoint her with milk and myrrh, dust her naval with aloe and frankincense. All the while she sets up a loud protest, which grows in volume as her limbs are wrapped tight and she is handed back to me, her face redder and crosser than before.

It is not long before the king is announced, and he enters the chamber sheepishly. He kisses my brow and casts a non-committal eye over his daughter.

"How are you, wife?"

"I am quite well, my lord. The birth was straightforward this time, praise God."

He nods, takes a stool at the bedside, clasps his hands between his knees, his eyes darting about the room.

"Have you thought of a name, Henry?"

He looks up, surprised. "No, no. I have no preference. I will let you choose."

I look down at the child again. She has fallen asleep. I expect being born is as exhausting as giving birth. Her bruised nose is decidedly bluer. Her tiny mouth moves as if she is suckling an invisible teat. Quite suddenly a memory is born of my young sister, Mary, who died a year or so before my father. She, alone of all my sisters, never indulged in petty squabbles; she hated disputes of any kind and Father had given her the pet name of Mary the Peacemaker.

"What about Mary?"

"Mary," Henry repeats, as if trying out the name. "After the Virgin. Yes, it seems very fitting."

I realise he has no knowledge of the sister I lost so tragically, but I don't enlighten him. He stands up and kisses my brow again. "I will leave you now. You must need sleep."

I let my head fall back on the pillow and send him a sleepy smile.

"I will soon be up and about again, and things will return to normal. Tomorrow perhaps you can bring the children to meet Mary."

"I will see that they come. Sleep well, my dear."

He leaves me alone. The nurse, Alice, fusses with linen in the corner and my women melt into the shadows leaving Mary and I at peace.

*

My chamber is a haven from politics and intrigue, for a few weeks I am oblivious to affairs of state and if Henry has any concerns about the Pretender, or his dealings with Spain regarding Arthur's marriage, then he conceals them from me. A happy time, safe in our nest, Mary and I become acquainted and day by day she grows in strength and character.

Henry doesn't accompany the children when they come to visit their sister for the first time. Elizabeth Denton, the lady mistress of the royal nursery, brings them. I can tell from their shiny bright faces that they have been thoroughly washed and scrubbed for the occasion.

When the door opens they sidle in and hesitate at the foot of the bed until I beckon them further. Harry needs no further encouragement but comes rushing forward, pushing Meg aside to reach me. His arms clamp around my neck, his lips are wet on my cheek. Meg is more withdrawn, polite and slightly awed. She looks around the room curiously, as if realising this will one day be her lot. It is a woman's lot, especially royal princesses, to bear children, perpetuate the bloodline and give life to future princes. There is no escaping it. My daughter and I exchange secret female smiles before she kisses me, as warmly as Harry although her kiss is not quite so moist.

Mary is placed in my arms and Alice stands back to allow the children closer as I draw the blankets aside to reveal her face. They regard her solemnly. The last time I introduced them to a baby sister they were younger, less aware of the impact a new sibling would have on their lives. Now, of course, still not fully recovered from the loss of Elizabeth, they greet the newcomer tentatively. Meg smiles softly. "She is lovely, Mother."

Harry leans over, examining the baby closely. "She is all squashed," he says. "Why is she squashed? She looks like an old woman."

I laugh and let my free arm slide around his shoulder.

"That is because she is so new; her face has not yet unfolded properly. In a few weeks her skin will be white and smooth. Her eyes will open and she will learn to laugh and speak."

"Speak?"

"Well, not right away but she will make noises. She can yell very loudly already."

"Can she? As loud as this?" He opens his mouth and gives a great shout that makes Mary wake with a start and begin to bawl. Harry is dismayed.

All the servants come running and Margaret puts her fingers in her ears while I fall about laughing. I jig the babe on my shoulder and pat her back, hushing her as the tears subside. Harry knuckles his eye. "I'm sorry," he says, shamefaced. "I didn't mean to frighten her."

"I know, Harry. It is all right. She will grow used to your noise. She will have to if she is to live with you and Meg at Eltham. You will be the best of friends. Would you like to hold her?"

He sits on the bed with his legs straight out, the soles of his shoes threatening the covers, and holds out his arms. Alice looks on disapprovingly as I place the child on his lap. He clutches her, and when she pulls a face and tries to squirm, he jiggles his knees. "Don't cry, Mary," he says. "Don't cry and I will tell you a story. Look, Meg, her hair is the same as yours."

Meg inches forward and settles beside him, her eyes wide with interest.

"Can I hold her now, Mother? You must take turns, Harry. Tell him, Mother. I want a turn."

While they nurse their sister, I probe gently about their progress under John Skelton who was engaged last year to oversee their education. Harry shows much talent in music and dancing, and his handwriting is advanced for his age. Meg is attentive too but seems to lack her brother's natural ability. She is capable and efficient, but displays none of the brilliance of her brother. She hides any sense of inferiority behind a barrier of teasing and bullying but, despite that, the children are very close.

They stay with me all the afternoon until their father arrives and Elizabeth Denton hurries them away. I pass Mary back to Alice and give my husband my full attention. He talks about the coming summer and a proposed progress to the south west of the country. It is too early for me to think with any comfort of leaving Mary, but I do not argue. All queens must learn to put duty before pleasure and Henry is eager to get the people of England to love him.

With a nursery full of little princes and princesses, it should be easy to please them. There is nothing discernible about his person that makes him unloved; as far as the poor are concerned one king is much the same as another. I suspect it is the taxes he levies that makes them resent him. The poor do not understand the expense of maintaining peace and, even if they did, it is doubtful that they'd see it as their duty to fund the king's defences.

As he details his plans for the summer, I listen without argument. His words float in and out of my consciousness while I wonder if the rash Mary has developed beneath her chin is really caused by excess dribble, or if it indicates something more sinister. I make a note to speak to the physician in the morning and turn my face back to the king. Slowly, a few of his words begin to penetrate; names like Warbeck, James, and Scots spark in the darkness of my mind. I sit up straighter.

"I am sorry, Henry. What did you say?"

His face stiffens, his lips clench firmly before he repeats it.

"I was telling you that the boy, the pretender, is growing very thick with King James, and the Scottish people are applauding him as king of the English. How can James support such treason? My spies tell me that Warbeck spends all his days hunting and his nights dancing and all the court have fallen in love with him. And it also seems that the Scottish king is encouraging his amorous advances toward his own cousin."

"Oh."

I don't know what else to say. I don't understand how the common people can fall in love with a penniless boy with a specious claim to the throne. And then I recall my father and my mind betrays me as I begin to toy with the idea that Warbeck may be my sibling after all.

He may not be *Richard*, as he claims, but everyone knows my late father's weakness for women. Perhaps the boy is some bastard-born child who has inherited my father's talent for winning love. Father married my mother secretly, or 'privately' as they preferred to call it, without the consent of his council. Their union sparked another round of fighting in the long war between Lancaster and York. Their passion was so strong, things could not have been otherwise; their need for each other was stronger than duty, stronger than dynastic requirement. And now the Scottish king is supporting a marriage between this man who claims to be my brother, and his own cousin. Surely the boy is a pretender, *surely* a pretender, who has somehow been blessed with my father's face and his way with women.

"What are you thinking?"

Henry speaks sharply, startling me so that I jump and give an unconvincing laugh.

"Nothing really. I was just wondering how much longer this can go on. I am not convinced James really believes Warbeck's claim and surely the boy cannot roam indefinitely about Europe with this treasonous claim. You will stop him in the end."

I add the last few words by way of comfort. Henry sits back in his chair, links his fingers, stretches his arms and makes his knuckles crack. It is a habit I detest, every sinew of my body rebels against it, but I do not say so.

"Oh yes," Henry says quietly. "I will stop him, and when I have him, his ending will not be pretty, whoever he may be ..."

Those words echo long after he has departed. *Whoever he may be.* My former contentment has fled, draining from my body. I can almost sense my optimism scurrying across the floor and plunging from the open window into the dark night beyond. Henry is informing me, quite plainly, that this person who dares to call himself the Duke of York will die, whether his claim is false or not.

*

I re-enter my life as queen, glad to be free of the confines of my chamber but sad to see Mary packed off so young to Eltham, where she will take up residence with Harry and Meg. Her household is vast for one so young, but she is a princess and as such must be well attended. I select women I trust, women of experience, and my directions to them are heartfelt and lengthy. Eltham is not far and I will visit very often, but as the cavalcade draws away, leaving me behind, my heart cries out as eloquently as my body, which yearns to nurse her again.

The king and I leave Sheen in June and begin our journey west. The summer promises much as we pass at a leisurely pace through some of England's finest countryside. As we go, we hand out gifts to the peasants, coins and new bread, a basket of cherries. It warms my heart when they cry out to us in thanks.

We linger at Beaulieu, enjoying the gardens and the soft summer sunshine that is encouraging the roses to put on their best display. When the time comes to move on I am reluctant to leave, but once on board a ship across the Solent to the Isle of Wight, the fragrance of the sea refuels me with vigour. It is as if the flowers of Beaulieu had cast a spell of somnolence upon me for now, in contrast, I feel energised and alive.

Henry and I stand at the ship's rail together. As always he is self-contained, never betraying joy but, although I try, I cannot hide the thrill of the swelling sea as my blood is invigorated by the stiff Solent breeze. The Wight Isle waits, snug and green in the choppy grey sea. As our ship takes us close, on impulse I clutch Henry's sleeve and place my cheek on his shoulder, and he doesn't pull away.

At first the atmosphere is one of a holiday, and Henry seems relaxed and happy, responding to the raucous crowd with grace. But once we are settled in our chambers I sense a change in him. He is tense and scowling again, making it difficult for me to maintain my holiday mood.

A messenger bows his way out of the room and Henry sighs, throws his pen onto the table.

"What is it, Henry? Not bad news from Eltham?"

He lifts his head, his face showing weariness, his eyes are shadowed, the lines about his mouth cut deep.

"No, the children are well. It is news from Scotland."

"What is it now?" I discard my embroidery and rise from my chair to join him.

"That fellow ... Warbeck. I told you James has blessed the marriage to his cousin ... well, I have the report of the ceremony. Apparently it was ostentatious in the extreme, distastefully so. It was clearly intended to persuade the world that it was not a match between some base-born adventurer and a distant relative of the king but of a king to a lesser royal. The wedding bore all the extravagance of a royal celebration and the people of Scotland now hail the pretender with great relish. Look here," he waves a letter beneath my nose. "He was married in purple silk, no expense spared! And all this from the coffers of a king of Scots whose usual generosity makes me seem a spend thrift! The pretender's bride, Catherine or Caroline, or whatever her name is, was dressed up like a queen, and the banquet ... I tell you, James pulled out all the stops. He has gone too far this time. There will be no peace between us now—not until I have that boy in my hands."

I don't know what to say, what to suggest that may both appease and bolster him. I pat his shoulder ineffectually, but he shrugs off my hand. For a while I watch him pace the floor, judging the extent of his fury and how much of it is directed at me. I don't understand why his displeasure is aimed at me for I have done nothing. Perhaps it would be as well to remain silent, but I can't help myself.

"It is just bluster, Henry. Nobody really believes his story. It is all for show ... for—for effect ...to alarm us ..."

Henry turns on me, his face screwed up in ridicule.

"You believe that? You honestly believe that no one gives him credit? What about your damned aunt? What about Maximillian? What about Ireland? The heads of Europe are biding their time, unwilling to pledge themselves to either me or the Pretender until a clear winner emerges. I curse the lot of them. I wish them all to the devil."

"Spain is on your side. Ferdinand and Isabella favour a match between Arthur and their daughter, Caterina."

"Spain," he sneers. "Why do you think Ferdinand is spinning the process out, pretending to negotiate? He is worried, uneasy, and all because of this damned boy. The king of Spain won't send his daughter to us while Warbeck is at large. That boy is a thorn in my flesh, Elizabeth. A thorn I will rip out no matter how much pain it causes."

"Can you not negotiate with James? Perhaps you can make it worth his while to hand the boy over to you?"

I do not speak from the heart and I quail with fear that the Pretender is indeed my little brother. What will I do if it is? I will want him to live, I know I will, even if I dread him being the victor. I know that should Henry lay hands on him he will be shown no mercy, and the thought is killing me. I am torn cleanly in two like a piece of parchment.

That night, after the lights are extinguished, I lay quietly, thinking of the boy and his long years of exile in foreign lands. As always when I think of him, my mind betrays me and it is my little brother, Richard, that I see. His bright shiny face is still round with youth, his eyes still merry. The image is so real I can almost smell the puppy dog fragrance of his skin.

"Oh, Richard," I whisper to the moon. "If you are indeed my brother can you not give it up and travel far away to where you will be safe?" A tear trickles onto the pillow, and more follow. Soon I cannot control them but let them roll like wax down a taper.

In the morning we journey on. When we are alone Henry is distant, his mind on his troubles, but he dons a jovial public face for the benefit of those who come to cheer us. The men who host us along the way are charmed by his courtesy, and the king does his best to be amiable. But I know it costs Henry a great deal to overcome his natural reticence.

I try to add my own easy charm to ensure we are seen as kind and humane monarchs. Without being asked I attempt to silently guide him. I squeeze his arm should his smile slip, or surreptitiously nudge him in the back should he make some small breach of etiquette. The king has not been bred to this life. Before Bosworth his existence was similar to that of Warbeck's, and he too was lost and exiled and alone.

By summer's peak I am growing weary and missing my children. I have regular missives to keep me abreast of their news and often a small note or a picture is folded within. When I am alone I take them out and gloat over the careful spelling and brightly hued drawings. They make me smile.

"Look, Henry." I pass him the latest letters and he casts an eye over them.

"Their writing is improving," he says. "I hope they work as hard at their other lessons."

"Oh yes, the reports are very good. And Mary has grown a tooth."

"That will surely not please her nurse."

I cannot help but smile at the picture his words evoke.

"Ha, yes. I am sure you are right. Once they get teeth they begin to gnaw everything."

"Like little rats."

"Rats, Henry? Is this our daughter you speak of?"

We are still laughing when a boy comes to light the candles and draw the shutters closed.

Henry dismissed my women some time ago and night is almost upon us. We are alone; our bellies replete, our minds mellow with wine as we watch the light dwindle. Henry is close beside me, his hand slides about my neck, his fingers finding my skin. He strokes and instinctively I lay my cheek upon his hand as warmth floods my limbs.

It has been quite a while since he came to my bed, and I relish his unspoken request. I am made differently to my husband, my needs are greater than his, and the long weeks without his company at night can be very trying. But I have learned to hide it and try to match my desire to his.

"Come along," he says, taking me by the hand and leading me to the bed. As he unlaces me, his fingers are as deft as any lady's maid's. My petticoats slide to the floor with a hush of silk, and he holds my hand as I step out of them. There is no embarrassment, no hurry, and little hunger as we prepare each other for bed.

I have long given up hope of a heady passion, an all-consuming desire for each other, but this is comfortable, and I feel secure in his arms now. I want for nothing else, no one else. I know pleasure will come for both of us but it will come later in the full dark when his blood warms and his mouth and fingers grow more urgent. His methods of love are such that I learn only by stealth how much he needs me.

*

Gradually we grow nearer to home, passing through Bristol, Malmesbury, and Woodstock. Our various hosts do all they can for our comfort, some of them must have bankrupted themselves to provide such luxury. They might as well have not bothered for although I try to hide it, I am unimpressed. My desperation to see my children is overriding everything else and is difficult to conceal. I count the days until we can return to London.

Henry remains attentive. We walk in the gardens, and enjoy intimate suppers when we can. When we are forced to bear company he stays close to me, bringing me into the conversation. I am grateful and, for a while, he treats me as his equal. Perhaps it is because his mother has stayed at Eltham to oversee the children and is not here to take him from me. Perhaps our more frequent intimacy at night is spilling over into the daytime. Whatever the reason I find I like it, and welcome this often hidden side to the king.

As my moon-time nears, half in dread, I begin to look for signs of pregnancy. It is too soon after Mary and although more children will be welcome, I am greatly relieved when the bleeding starts and I know I have a little longer before motherhood claims me again. I am enjoying the lack of constraint, the absence of the king's mother's disapproval, and hope the new relationship that has developed between us will long continue.

It is September before we spy the towers of Windsor above the treetops. As the royal cavalcade jogs on through the trees, the late sunshine turns the leaves to gold above my head. "Let us hurry, Husband," I call, and spur my mount forward, outstripping the rest of the party. I am happy to be coming home. I am loved and confident and my husband seems content, too. I can hear his horse's hooves thundering close behind me and I turn my head to smile.

"It is good to be home, Henry," I call gaily and he grins back at me, his face warm with affection, the thrill of the ride casting a pink glow upon his usually sallow cheeks.

Please let this last, I pray silently; *this new warmth between us. Let it last for the rest of our lives.*

Chapter Twenty-Seven
Boy

<u>Stirling Castle — September 1496</u>

Richard rolls over and sits on the edge of the bed, head in hands, trying to dispel his lingering dreams. Morning has come too soon and he is loath to leave the comfort of his blankets. Today of all days he should be ready, his mind should be honed as sharply as a blade but instead he feels lethargic, reluctant to move.

He rubs a hand over his face and squints as daylight pierces the shutters. He has planned and plotted for this day for more than half his life. Today, with the support of King James, he will invade England and, God willing, take back that which is rightfully his. He had imagined that when the time came he would be brave, invincible, but now the moment is here, his overriding emotion is one of fear.

"Richard? Surely it is not yet day. Come and lie with me a little longer."

He turns smiling eyes on his touselled wife as she blinks sleepily, clutching the sheet across her breasts. Her usually smooth blonde hair is snarled and knotted from sleep, and there is a mark on her neck where he kissed her too roughly. He reaches out and grasps the sheet, tugging it sharply from her grasp. She squeaks and giggles until his eyes fasten on the dark hue of her nipples, the bulge of his child in her womb. She quiets, her breath stilled, waiting.

Although the late stage of her pregnancy means he cannot love her as fully as he'd like to, his loins stir again and he falls onto the pillows beside her. He pulls her close, tastes the sweetness of her mouth, feels the tremble of her wanting as his fingers rediscover her willing flesh.

"Be gentle, my love," she reminds him and she is right to do so for when the blood is up it is easy to forget that he cannot take her as he'd like to. Her hands are skilled and willing and in the joy of her touch he forgets the pain of leaving, the fear of defeat, and the uncertainty of the unknown. He rolls onto his back while she delights him, feeling the tension flow away as they drift together on a cloud of pleasure.

Afterwards, when he has untangled himself from her arms and stands half-dressed by the bed, she pulls herself upright on her pillow.

"Don't get up, Catherine. Don't watch me ride away; I am afraid I will lose courage if you should cry. It wouldn't do for me to scuttle like a frightened mouse back to our chamber."

She places a hand on her belly and his eyes follow her fingers as she strokes their growing child. "He may be with us before you return, my lord." Her eyes are huge and filled with tears. "Keep yourself safe for we have need of you." Her voice breaks but he doesn't comfort her. Instead, he turns away to hide his own grief.

"And may God keep you safe too, my Catherine. Look after our son. If he comes in my absence, tell him that I have ridden away to regain his birthright."

His armour clanks and his sword clatters on the wall as he hurries down the stairs and into the sunlight where men at arms and mounted soldiers are gathered, waiting for him.

Richard's eye is immediately taken by a fluttering pennant. The banner of York, the undulating white rose, embroidered by Catherine's hand, declares his identity and his right to contest Henry Tudor's claim. His unease is soothed a little by the sight. He remembers the emblem of York when it blazed over his father's throne, a throne that would have been his had his future not been stolen.

A few days ago James rode forth amid a clarion of trumpets and celebration, clad in a new cloak of crimson velvet and satin. Richard looks down at his newly-forged armour, pulls on his gauntlets and tries to appear as brave, as much in command as James had been. He raises a hand in salute as if his heart wasn't failing.

"Good morrow, friends. It is a fine day for an invasion."

A cheer goes up and Keating brings his prancing horse under control, removes his plumed helmet and bows his head to his monarch.

"The people of England will flock to your standard, Your Grace. Never doubt it. They have no more love for Tudor than we do."

They mount up and begin to ride out amid a chaos of cheers. An impressive array of horse and foot soldiers, padded and armed against the fray. A long line of supply wagons comes next, followed by barking dogs, screeching children who see it all as a lark, a frolic. As he passes beneath the gate, a group of women throw petals from an upper window. He cranes his neck for a last glimpse of Catherine but she is not there; she has obeyed him and stayed away. He wishes she hadn't.

I know nothing of England, he thinks, as the cavalcade passes from town to country, and moves single file along the leaf-strewn road. *I know nothing of the people, their needs and desires. I don't even know how to be a king.*

James and his force are a few days ahead, waiting for them to join him. The cavalcade passes through hamlets and villages where the Scot's people emerge to see them pass. Richard's horse puts down his head and his back end heaves at the din, but Richard reins him in with one hand. With the other he waves to the peasants, blows kisses to the fairest girls in the crowd.

Young as he is, he looks every inch a king, but his appearance hides inner insecurity. Richard bites his lip and hopes he can live up to James's image. It is easy for James; he was born to it, has lived each day of his life as a prince and a king. He has not known uncertainty; even at his lowest ebb he never lost his position, witnessed the death of his brother, or suffered his sister being married off to the usurper of his very throne.

James has never known hunger or cold, or been so saddle weary that death promised the only relief. Compared to Richard, James has led a life of ease. To him war is a game, a relief from the tedium of security.

They pass the bare Lammermuir Hills and follow the course of the river Tweed toward the border. With only a watercourse between him and his birthright, Richard's courage shrinks. He looks at the mercenaries who make up his army; rough men from many countries, with hardly an Englishman among them. Their banter is coarse, often threatening to overspill into civil violence. It does nothing to alleviate his foreboding, his sense that the stars may not be aligned in his favour after all.

The Tweed lies before them, a wide serpent of deathly cold water between him and his goal. The men straggle across in dribs and drabs; groaning at the aching temperature of the churning water. The horses throw up their heads, reluctant to tread an unseen path, but the men curse and kick them forward. One of the baggage carts founders, the draft horses plunging, throwing up great shafts of water, drenching those nearby. The carter raises his whip, brings it down hard.

Richard's face becomes a mask of unconcern, a bland mindless smile as he fights not to let his followers see his lack of courage. As his mount scrambles up the far bank, his legs are mired, his freezing toes screaming with pain. Murky water streams from his horse's flanks, and Richard's boots are brimming over. His once spotless banner hangs limp over his weary army, spattered by mud and marred by rain.

I am in England, he thinks. *Northumberland*. He looks around at the empty landscape where straggly sheep graze unconcerned at the elite company. There is not a homestead or a building in sight; just a vast, rain-lashed landscape that bears no resemblance to the England that Richard remembers. The lush green of Kent does not reach this far north.

"We will make camp here," the boy announces. "Our supporters will reach us in the morning, no doubt. I am assured they are just delayed."

The servants set to erecting the campaign tents; his muddy banner is hoisted above the royal marquee and a brazier lit beside his bed. He settles in a chair with a cushion at his back, glad to be free of the saddle. He feasts upon bread and cheese; the burgundy in his cup dwindling as fast as it bolsters his courage. He thinks of Catherine, safe at Stirling, full of his unborn child, waiting for the news of his victory, of his son's secured future.

He is washed by his manservant, his emerging beard is trimmed, his hair brushed to a sheen, and he slips between his silken sheets like a new man; a man sustained with good food and given hope with rich wine. As he closes his eyes he suffers a brief longing for his wife and the comfort she offers, but he is exhausted from the ride and sleep claims him, closing the door on all his worries.

Morning blows in to dampen his spirits with cold drizzle. His companions shake raindrops from their cloaks as they enter his pavilion to join him for breakfast. He wraps a fur about his shoulders and accepts a cup of wine, passes the jug to Richard Harliston.

"I could wish God had sent us better weather," says Keating as he holds out his hands to warm them at the brazier. "It is colder than a witch's tit out there."

"Where are our English supporters? I thought there'd be word by now, or at least a messenger sent on ahead."

Harliston grunts noncommittally and empties his cup. "They will come, Your Grace."

Richard moves closer to his friends.

"It is these mercenaries. I am uneasy about them and they are growing restive. They have no love of England or its people … or me, come to that. I am afraid that if they see no action soon and no promise of spoils, they will create some activity of their own."

He orders a proclamation to be read promising benevolence, promising peace, but after two days when his supporters have still failed to turn up, Richard's fears are realised. The mercenaries, fed up with inaction, begin to defy orders.

On the brow of a hill a stronghold, or bastle as they are locally known, waits immovably, the people from within working in a nearby field. When the cavalcade rides past, the people pause in their toil to stand silent in the rain.

"This is your king. Good King Richard of York has come to free you from Tudor oppression."

Richard raises his hand, smiles his most winning smile, but the grim expressions remain unchanged. He rides on, his smile fixed, his hands frozen to the reins, relieved to be past so swiftly.

As he moves into open countryside, he hears a scream behind him and the clash of steel on stone. Fearing the worst, he wrenches his horse round and gallops back the way he came.

His men, his so called 'soldiers,' their cloaks blackened by relentless rain, have fired the thatch of an outbuilding. As a grim trail of smoke belches forth the people try to fight the flames, coughing and choking, their eyes streaming. Richard's head turns right and left, taking in the scene, identifying the perpetrators. A group of soldiers have drawn their swords, laid hostage to a group of elders who huddle around a bleeding corpse sprawled in the mud. Men are fighting all around, a woman screams and Richard's head rips round to see a mercenary soldier and hear the sound of ripping cloth. A few ill-clad men rush forward in feeble defence of their daughter; a dagger flies across the clearing, bringing a man to his knees. It is probably her husband. Richard stands up in his stirrups.

"Stop this!" he hollers. "Stop this!"

But they do not heed him. From the corner of his eye he senses movement and instinctively draws his sword. A big bearded fellow has the woman by the hair and is hauling up her skirts, revealing her skinny red knees, her bare-arsed poverty.

"Stop this now!" He is shaking with fury but the fellow pays no heed. Kicking his mount forward, Richard rides fast, his arm raised to strike his first battle blow ...against one of his own.

The soldier falls swiftly but Richard feels no joy. There are tears on his face. It wasn't supposed to be like this. With the back of his hand he dashes the tears away and cries out again as his rabble army runs amok.

"These people are not the enemy; they are weak, defenceless. I come here in peace ..."

He looks down at the blood puddling around the slaughtered man; the grizzling woman has blood on her thigh. She is pulling down her skirts, crawling away toward the blazing shed. As she struggles past she casts a look of contempt at Richard and he notices a great, scarlet gash upon her cheek, her face open to the bone.

Chaos ensues. The Scots, used to border raids, and accustomed to murdering the English, now join the mercenaries to massacre in Richard's name.

Men are fighting; women roll in the mud, wrestling with their abusers while their naked children flee from the belching ruin of their innocence. He sees an infant cut down, an old man, his breast sliced open, slides to the ground beside the well, his eyes staring in horror at the scudding clouds. Richard lets his sword drop; his head sinks to his chest.

It was never supposed to be like this. Where is the glory? Where is the great welcome I was promised?

He does not wait for an end. Like a coward he pulls on the reins and gallops in search of James. Perhaps he can control the men or order his household troop to open fire on them. The carnage has to stop. He does not slacken his pace but rides his horse right up to the Scottish king's tent. He leaps from the saddle and barging past the guard, enters unannounced.

James has taken off his hat and boots and is enjoying a cup of wine, his stockinged feet stretched toward the flames.

"James, you have to help me stop this. It is mindless slaughter and will gain us no advantage."

"Oh, I doubt they can be stopped. We have held them back too long. A few peasants will not be missed; once the men have assuaged their blood lust they will become biddable again."

"They are slaughtering my countrymen, raping the women. This isn't why I've come. I came in peace to free them ... this—this is just ..." His voice cracks, his head drops forward. He is close to tears.

"You'd do well to take my advice and leave them to it. Once darkness falls the violence will stop and we can regain control in the morning."

"In the morning? James! Your Grace, I humbly beg you to stop this savagery of my country and my people. They will never put trust in me now."

"That is none of my concern, Sir."

"I promised you many things, James. I promised you Berwick, I promised to repay every penny of the 50,000 marks I owe you. But never once, never once did I say I would stand for your troops inflicting carnage on my countrymen."

"It is what happens in war. Blood is spilled, lives are lost, virtue is stolen but life goes on. It is the way of things. If you are going to be a king you need to get used to it."

Sickness washes over Richard. Suddenly he sees James with new eyes. *He is a royal wastrel,* he thinks, *an adventure-seeking dissolute who has used me for his own amusement. He cares nothing for my cause, and God curse me if I continue to call him family.*

Richard rubs the palm of his hand over his face; it comes away grimy. He shakes his head, the wet strands of his hair flicking drips around the royal tent. White-faced, he stares at his former ally.

"Well, I won't do it."

He cannot stay here. He will no longer be a part of it. He will ride back to Stirling, alone if he has to, and carry his wife as far away from James as he can get.

As the boy rides closer to Stirling, he begins to forget the colourful horror of the raids. His messenger keeps him informed of James's doings and he knows that the violence continues. The Scottish king, making the most of the chance to strike at England, lays siege to Herton Castle, bombarding it with his big guns until the threat of English troops approaching from Newcastle send him scurrying for the hills.

But Richard will be in Stirling before the king. *I will pack up my things,* he thinks, *take Catherine and the child, if he is born, somewhere far away. I cannot associate myself with the sacking of England. No one will follow a cruel and violent king.*

But when he arrives, reality forces him to rethink. His wife is in confinement, awaiting the birth that is only days away. His friends find excuses to leave the court and he finds himself, more or less, alone. His possessions and what little wealth he has are provided by James, the very man he wishes to disassociate himself from.

During his wild ride Richard thinks only of Catherine, the reassurance of her love the only thing to keep him going. He tries to see her but horrified women turn him away, tell him he must wait. He sends her letters, pouring words onto a page, praising her hair, her face, her skin, her fine bosom. The knowledge of her, and their son, and the jug of wine at his elbow are his only defence against despair.

In the royal corridors they whisper of his cowardice. A king should fight, not run away. Instead of his pity being judged as noble, he is seen as a coward, craven and weak.

Where inside of me does this weakness lodge? he asks himself. His father was strong. Edward IV was a soldier who loved to fight. He never lost a battle and gained only honour by hand to hand fighting, on the field, at the head of his men. Richard is shamed to acknowledge that he is most unlike his father. He tries to remember his uncles who were soldiers, too. Not one of them was ever named a coward. Richard of Gloucester had been called many things but never that, and even unfaithful George of Clarence had seen his share of battle. His mother's brothers, Anthony, John and Edward, had fought bravely, dying for this king or that. *Why then, why can I not tolerate violence*?

By the time James returns, bursting with news of his short campaign, Richard is the father of a fine son. He breaks etiquette and demands to be allowed entrance into Catherine's chamber. Her women look on askance, making outraged Scottish noises at his audacity, but Catherine, looking pale and shadowed beneath the eyes, opens her arms in welcome.

To the continuing scandal of the women, he climbs onto the bed and wraps his arms around her. "Was it very bad?" he asks.

Catherine strokes his hair back from his brow, as his mother used to do.

"Oh, no. Not so bad," she says. "I am sure you had a worse time of it than I."

He sits up, his blue eyes troubled.

"It was bad for me, sweetheart. I learned things about myself. Things a man would rather not know."

"What things?" Her voice is gentle, like a song, and he finds himself confessing to feelings he's sworn never to utter.

273

"I am not a fighting man, Catherine. I find I cannot tolerate bloodshed. I saw men killed and women violated and I did little about it. There was one man, one of the mercenaries I hired, I struck him down. I killed him, Catherine, when I saw him dishonour an innocent girl. After that I had to get away. I couldn't bear to look on him. I still see him, almost every time I sleep, the blood seeping slowly from his skull, his eyes wide and sightless staring at me ... staring right through me, into my soul and seeing me for the coward that I am ..."

"Stop it!"

Catherine's eyes are wide, her face white, tears trickling down her cheeks. He looks down at his hand that clutches tightly on her wrist. He lets go, almost weeps at the red weal his grip has left behind. She rubs it, and cuffs away her tears.

"You have not even asked to see your son," she reproaches, her voice full of sorrow.

"Oh God, my love, I am sorry." He takes her wrist, smothers it in healing kisses as the child is brought to them.

"He is like you," she says, as the infant is laid in his arms. "I'd like to call him Richard."

He smiles. "Some would say it is an ill-fated name. It has certainly not helped me, or my uncle."

"I don't believe in that sort of thing. Your fate and that of your uncle and brother has more to do with your status than your names. How silly men can be sometimes. Do you have a better name for him?"

Richard takes his child's hand, unfurls his tiny fingers to examine his miniscule nails.

"No," he says quietly. "Richard it shall be. By happy chance, he may be the one to alter fate and come peacefully to his throne."

"Amen."

Their eyes meet above the child's head; Catherine's are tearful, Richard's are full of doubt. "Amen," they say together as his hand closes over hers.

Chapter Twenty-Eight
Elizabeth

<u>The Coldharbour – Spring 1497</u>

My mother-in-law sits erect, her hands clasped in her lap, the cup of wine beside her untouched. I am sewing quietly, waiting for her to speak. I know she has called by to impart some news, or perhaps complain of some indiscretion on little Harry's behalf. From time to time I look up from my needle to smile and offer her further refreshment, which she rejects with a brief shake of her head. At length she clears her throat. "Henry is not himself."

I put down my work and give her my full attention, mirroring her position by linking my fingers in my lap.

"Is he not? I know he is concerned about the unrest in the West but he seems well enough."

She sniffs, her lips twitching, her eye not quite meeting mine.

"He is hiding his concern from you. Yesterday, when I questioned him, he suggested you may be with child again."

Blood rushes to my cheeks, irritation that he should see fit to discuss such a thing with his mother before enquiring of me if it is so.

"Well, I am sorry to disappoint but my husband is mistaken."

She sniffs again in dissatisfaction. I try to prevent my fingers from plucking at my skirt but they won't keep still, not until I clamp them together hard. Mary is not yet a year old, surely I am due some respite. To the king's mother, and so it seems the king also, I am nothing but a brood mare; good blood to boost their bastard stock.

"Well," she says, for all the world as if I haven't already supplied England with two heirs, "there is still time for another prince."

"What is wrong with the two we have?"

"Nothing at all," she says, finally picking up her cup and sipping her wine. "But a king can never have too many sons, you should know that."

Whenever I begin to think my mother-in-law may not be so bad, she shatters that belief with small annoyances. Small reminders of the disdain she has for my family; insinuations that little Harry is too naughty, Mary is undernourished, or Margaret too pert. She has been kind to me on occasion and there have been times when I have almost warmed to her. But her sense of superiority and her jealousy of my relationship with her son are always between us. She is eternally present and I try so hard to like her for Henry's sake, but she is cold and unyielding; a yoke that I find increasingly hard to bear.

"What do you make of this unrest in Cornwall? It is not just peasants, is it? Their leaders are prominent men."

After the Pretender invaded with the Scottish king and slaughtered so many Englishmen, Henry declared war on James. To fund it he has levied taxes, harsh levies in which the Cornish, living so far from Scotland, can see no justice. They are protesting loudly and violently against the king, against the crown, and the band of disaffected rebels draws ever closer to London.

The Lady Margaret's eyes are hooded, her hawklike features disdainful. "It will be contained; I have no doubt of that."

"I hope so. I am so tired of conflict. It seems to me that all my life ..."

"All *your* life? It is not just you, Elizabeth. My life too has been fraught with conflict. Imagine being forced to live apart from your son, not knowing if he was properly cared for, if he wanted for anything? Imagine then having to serve the monarch who slaughtered your kin and issued those orders, and then complain to me of your hardships."

"I didn't mean …"

"I am sure you didn't. You speak of things you cannot know."

The conversation is closed. The words she didn't speak ring loud in my ears, far louder than those she uttered. *Your father.* That is what she meant. *Your father did those things and forced me to live apart from my son.* She will never forgive me. I don't know why I try.

I turn my head from her to look from the window to the gardens where the Lenten Lilies nod their gay heads as if war and suffering do not exist. I have a sudden longing to be outside but I do not suggest it. She will say the wind is too chill, or the ground too damp. Later, when she has gone, I may ride to Eltham and spend a day or so with the children. We can ride in the woods and picnic in the grounds. That will cheer me. For now, I must bite my tongue and bear my penance.

As the silence stretches I search for a subject on which we will not clash, but as I open my mouth to speak, we hear a disturbance in the outer ward. She stands up, holds up a finger to silence me while she strains her ears.

"It is the king," she says. "Something is wrong."

The door is thrown open and Henry enters, casts off his cloak and tosses it over the back of a chair.

"Henry." I sink into a brief curtsey, more for his mother's satisfaction than the king's. "What is the matter? What has happened?"

"Mother." He kisses Lady Margaret's hand before addressing me. "Elizabeth."

He picks up his mother's cup and drains it. "The rebels grow close to London. I must ride forth to deal with it. Elizabeth, you are to take the children to safety in the Tower. I have organised a stout escort. You will be safe there. The Tower has never been breached."

I try not to think of the day my brother Richard left sanctuary to join our brother Edward there. I never saw them again, and now Henry wants me to place my own children there *in safety*.

But I do not argue. I never argue.

"When shall we go, Henry? Now? Today?"

"Yes today. The rebel army has assembled at Guildford. Lord Daubeney is there with our forces and I must join them. I must show my face and bolster their courage."

"A rebel *army*, Henry? Surely they are just a rabble?"

He takes my hand, spares a second for a warm look such as I am only accustomed to seeing in our bed.

"They may be a rabble but they are fifteen thousand strong."

"Fifteen thousand? But they won't beat us, will they? You won't let them?"

I think of my father who never lost a battle, my uncle Richard who perished despite his many campaigns, and I think of Henry, my husband. He is a politician not a soldier, but nonetheless he is riding into danger and leaving us behind. I button down my fears and take control.

"I will make ready at once. Lady Margaret, you will accompany us. Your safety is paramount." She nods and for once doesn't contest my authority. "I will send a messenger ahead to ensure our rooms are prepared. If we hurry we can be there before dark."

I whirl around, clapping my hands to summon my women, but Henry grabs my wrist, spins me toward him. His face is dead white, his eyes glowing dark, the lines that flank his mouth deep, grim folds of concern.

His hand slides beneath my hood, his fingers moving in my hair as he absorbs every plane and shadow of my face. For the first time I see love in his eyes. Not lust, or lingering resentment, but love and respect, and concern. My heart leaps like a hind in the forest and I grasp his wrist, close my eyes, waiting for his kiss.

When it comes it is long and full of tenderness. He rests his forehead on mine. "Take care, my wife. Take care of yourself, and our children."

I nod, unable to speak, for there are tears on my face and an immovable lump lodged deep in my throat. He pulls away with a brief sorry smile.

His mother quickly turns away but she witnessed the moment; she knows now that he has a care for me and I fear her resentment will increase.

Henry is at the door, he lifts his hand before passing through it, and I watch him go with a strange mix of euphoria and dread. He may never return. His actions this day may plunge my children and I into a life of exile and fear, but I know one thing. I have been loved. I just never saw it before.

*

The children are bundled into warm clothing to ward off the night air. It is cold for June, the sky lying heavy over London, and the smoke so thick in the air we can taste it, our lungs filling with dank moist filth.

Meg rides behind her grandmother, her white face peering from deep within her voluminous hood, her eyes wide with unspoken fear. Mary is clasped close to her nurse's bosom; she sleeps on, oblivious to the drama, and the terrified prattle of her nurse.

"Be quiet," I snap as I hug Harry tighter and kick my mount to move forward.

We are flanked by armed guards, stern-faced soldiers in full armour. They form a barricade around us as we ride through the empty, rain-washed streets. The slick cobbled road glistens blackly, the sound of our horses' hooves echoing loudly in the dark, setting the town dogs barking.

Harry's hand sneaks up my chest, to grip the neck of my gown. I can feel his little heart pattering; the sound of his breath is quick and fast. With a squeeze of my arm I send him a fleeting smile of encouragement and he returns it, his eyes trusting but afraid.

"It isn't far now, my son," I say. "Look, you can see the river."

The Thames flows thick and black, slapping against the wharf as the grey walls of the Tower loom ahead, silhouetted darkly against the moonless sky. My horse's hooves slither on the wet pavement and I snatch at the reins to steady him.

Beneath my cloak, Harry clutches tighter. I press my heels to my mount's flanks, turning my head quickly to ensure that the king's mother and the maid follow with my daughters.

A sharp cry as we reach the outer wall; a challenge from the Tower guard that is answered by our leader. The first of many gates slides open and we draw a little closer to safety. With each portcullis and drawbridge we cross, I become both more secure and more terrified. One by one they crash closed behind us with a great clanking of steel and grinding of chains. It is as if we are travelling into the bowels of the earth and will never taste freedom again.

How did my brothers feel, coming here alone? What did they think when they finally realised Edward's crown had been taken and they were prisoners rather than honoured guests? They must have known they'd never escape; that their fate was sealed. The Tower is the last place they'd seen.

"It's all right, Mother," Harry whispers. "We are safe now. Nothing can get us in here."

I smile as if I believe him, and pass him into the arms of a waiting guard. A flurry of servants arrive and the children are scooped up and carried into the White Tower while Lady Margaret and I follow on behind. I am halfway up the steps when I remember something and whirl around, run back to the horses.

"Bring me that package," I order the guard, indicating a long box on one of the pack horses. "Bring it now, please."

He bows solemnly and I wait as he unstraps the box and hoists it beneath his arm. I ascend the stairs again, checking every now and then that he is following.

"Put it there and you can go," I say when we reach the inner chamber. I look about the room where the nurse is helping the children remove their wraps. Mary has woken and started to wail, her nurse fussing with her linen.

A fire blazes in the hearth and the furnishings are soft and plush, but I shudder and rub my arms. Everything we need is here, all that can be done for our every comfort has been attended to, but I hate this place. I always have,

283

but now, until Henry manages to quell the rebellion, I must call it home.

Lady Margaret stands in the centre of the room, directing the servants, ordering refreshment for the children. Harry and Meg sit by the hearth, their faces pale from lack of sleep, their eyes shadowed and afraid. Mary continues to bawl in her nurse's arms; I jerk my head, silently ordering her to leave us in peace.

"Here you are, Harry and Meg; have a drink and a slice of pie and then you must go to bed. It is almost morning. We've had quite an adventure but now it is time to sleep."

Meg takes the cup and sips her milk, but Harry just clutches his to his chest and looks about the unfamiliar chamber with large, fearful eyes.

"Have the rebels gone now, Mother? Are we really safe?"

"I am sure we are. Your father would not allow them to come too close to London."

"So why did we have to come here then, if you are so sure of father's victory?"

I turn in surprise at Meg's voice. She is not usually one to question adults. She is obedient and trusting. In speaking out she reveals the depth of her fear. I run my hand over her hair and do not reprimand her for questioning.

"We came here to put the king's mind at rest. We are important to him; he loves us all very much and would not fight so well if he had to worry for our safety. He will be here in the morning and we can all go home to Eltham, you'll see."

Lady Margaret makes a sharp movement. "I am going to the chapel to pray, Elizabeth. I shall see you tomorrow but do not look for me early for I will spend the night in prayer."

"What is left of it," I murmur but she doesn't hear me. The door closes on her whispering black skirts and I breathe a sigh of relief to be left alone with the children.

"Come along," I say. "Let's get you settled."

I tuck them up together in the same bed, finding some comfort in the act. Usually this sort of task is left to servants. I stroke Harry's hair back from his brow and trace the line of his sandy eyebrows with the tip of my finger.

"Good night, my prince," I say and leave a kiss on his brow. "Good night, my princess," I murmur, but Meg is already half asleep and doesn't acknowledge me. I kiss her anyway, and tuck the covers tight about them. "I will leave a candle burning, Harry," I say before I leave, "and the chamber door open just a little so you can hear me. I will be just through there. Sleep well."

I blow him a kiss and he pretends to catch it in his chubby palm and press it to his mouth.

*

I sit alone in the firelight, waiting. Waiting for what, I do not know. It could be defeat, it could be victory. The reports that have managed to reach me are of stalemate but, when I ask, I am relieved to know that there is no sign of Warbeck.

The present threat is not from the Pretender, although he is the cause of it. His misconceived alliance with King James and their attack on the north of England instigated this latest war with Scotland, and now the Cornishmen are protesting at the taxes to pay for it. Rumour has it that Kent, that nest of turmoil and treason as Henry calls it, is rising too. Will the man calling himself my brother take advantage of this and strike while the king is

285

preoccupied? My father would have, and if Warbeck's claims are true, his father would have also.

I sit there for so long that my maid's head nods and she begins to snore quietly, her chin on her chest. The fire slumps, I draw my shawl about my shoulders and try not to notice the shadows that seem to be creeping from the corners. My disquiet soon mushrooms into terror and I cannot rest. I have never been more wide awake.

My eyes travel about the room, scanning the walls that seem to be closing in, breathing loudly, raucously, like a drunken old man. Although the Tower is full of men and servants, I have never felt so alone, so vulnerable.

My heart is beating fast, short and sharp, and my ears begin to ring. I feel something is close, something dark and menacing, threatening my children, threatening me, threatening England.

With a stifled cry I leap from my chair and rummage for the box that the guard left where I'd instructed. I pry open the lid, pull away the straw packing and peel back the wrapping. A sword, my father's sword; the sword that won him England.

It is heavy and there are signs of rust on the blade, but I manage to heave it from the box. As quietly as I can, I open the door and sneak along the corridor to take up a position at the outer entrance to our apartment.

The White Tower is heavily guarded. There are soldiers at every gate, every window. There are armed men on the roof, a ring of barges on the river. And outside the Tower, the whole of London is armed and ready; the outer city wall manned and every gate defended. I am safe, as safe as I can be from earthly foe, but the memory of others who have died here in the Tower will not let me rest.

Old King Henry was murdered a few floors below, murdered by my father and uncles for his crown; George of Clarence died here, killed on my father's order. Warwick, my cousin, little Edward of Warwick, is here somewhere, guilty only of making Henry uneasy; a simple boy, no threat to anyone. I bite my lip, realising I have not visited Edward for months. Suddenly I wonder if he is even still here, or if he has been put to death, his ghost joined with my brothers and other men, both innocent and guilty, who have perished here in the darkness of the Tower.

I imagine their spirits emerging from the walls to flaunt their gory end in my face, holding me to blame, cursing me for loving a Tudor. I suddenly see myself through their dead staring eyes, a traitor to my family, to my blood.

My nostrils fill with the stench of my own fear, my mouth with vomit; my own breath is rasping in my throat. Suddenly weak, the tip of my father's sword falls to the floor. I place a hand to my throat and fight for breath, battling to overcome blind panic. *There is nothing there*, I tell myself, *nothing that can hurt you.*

But there is a figure in the doorway, a small boy, all in white, the light of the dying hearth shining through his shift. His feet and legs are bare, his fair hair is ruffled. My breath ceases. I open my eyes wide, my voice strangles in my throat. I lift the sword and hold it defensively before me, as if I have the power to smite even the dead.

"Richard?" My voice echoes in the dark, alien, full of fear, the terror unmasked and raw. He lifts a hand, knuckles his eye and begins to cry.

"It is me, Mother. What are you doing with that sword?"

A great crash of metal echoes up and down the corridor as I let the sword fall. I drop weeping to my knees and cover my face with my hands. Soon, his arms creep around my neck. He is warm and living; he is my son.

I hold him close, much too close, sobs wracking my frame, tears wetting both of us.

"Oh, Harry," I sob, stroking his hair, touching his dear little face to ascertain he really is flesh and blood. "Harry, I—I thought you were somebody else."

*

Two thousand men lay dead on Blackheath, two thousand *rebels*, I remind myself. They are men who marched against Henry; men who marched against our rule. Henry rides triumphantly back to London where the crowds line the streets to cheer him home.

For once, their outpouring of love is his alone. After giving thanks at St Pauls, he comes to me in the Tower and I am so glad to see him that I hurl convention to the winds and throw my arms about his neck before he has time to remove his gauntlets.

"I was so afraid, Henry."

"Did you doubt me then, Elizabeth?"

I am chastened, I bite my lip.

"No, I don't think I doubted *you* ... but I have lost those I love in battle before and I've learned the hard way that ..."

"I know." He stems my explanation by kissing my forehead. I watch as he pulls off his gloves, unties his cloak and hands it to a waiting boy at his elbow. We move to the hearth where a flagon is waiting and he sits down, holds out his hands to the flames. I notice his boots are mired and beads of moisture still cling to the ends of his hair.

"I will order the servants to bring hot water, Henry. You will appreciate a bath."

There is a long wait while the water is heated and his servants troop from the kitchens with jugs and ewers. I make myself comfortable at his side while he regales me with the trials of the campaign.

We can hear the children playing nearby. Yesterday, they crept about the chamber as if they were trespassing, but now the romp is loud, clearly illustrating that the safe arrival of the king has dispelled their fears. I sit on the floor with my head on Henry's knee, his hand on my hair, and close my eyes, as close to bliss as I have been since girlhood.

"We should give thanks to God," I murmur. "A gift to the church, and a pilgrimage ... to Walsingham, perhaps."

"It isn't over yet, my dear. I still need to get my hands on the Pretender and put an end to his games once and for all. I can make no progress with Spain until he is silenced."

I try to suppress a shudder as a cloud dims my optimism. I know he is right. He thinks as a soldier, a king, and has no room for womanly sentiment. I close my eyes against the picture of my little brother that rises in my mind and replace it with the face of a desperate rogue; a murderer of innocents; a threat to my children.

The door opens and Henry's mother enters unannounced, her face lined with concern. She ignores me and makes straight for her son, both hands outstretched.

"Henry, my prayers are answered and you are back safe. I am so proud ..." They exchange kisses, her eyes closed, her mouth pursed. As Henry offers her his seat, he sends me a fleeting smile and offers his hand to help me to my feet.

"Why are you on the floor, Elizabeth?" his mother says, not bothering to hide her impatience. "Are there not enough chairs?"

She has no concept that she has interrupted an intimate moment between husband and wife. What can she know of that? She has only ever married for advancement, for political gain; she knows nothing of intimacy, or affection. Some people say that after the birth of Henry, she shunned intimacy with any man, even her husbands. I can only think they were glad of it. Bedding Margaret would be like sleeping with a block of stone.

Henry nods to a servant to bring her wine, and I pass her a bowl of fruit and nuts. She chews diligently while Henry describes the campaign and the effective manner in which the rebels were disbanded. Neither of them can see the tragedy of a king turning his weapons on his own subjects. My own father did his share of it in his day, but he was always sorry and wished for a more peaceful way. We should not make war upon our own. Suddenly, I remember Warwick.

"Henry." I turn to him, almost interrupting my mother-in-law's complaint. "I would like to visit my cousin Edward, is that possible, while we are lodged here in the Tower?"

I have spoken impulsively without thinking the matter through, and while Henry considers his answer my heart begins to hammer beneath my ribs. He exchanges glances with his mother, who shifts in her seat, selects an orange and begins to unpeel it.

He isn't here, I think. They have had him killed. I will never see him again. My mind runs amok, imagining a scenario where I have to inform Cousin Margaret that her brother is dead ... at the hands of my husband.

"I don't see why you shouldn't visit him, Elizabeth, but do not stay too long. He is unused to company and may not behave quite as you expect."

Relief floods through me. My hands fall to my lap and I find I am smiling to widely. I drop my gaze and try to school my mouth into obedience.

"Thank you, husband. I will not stay long. I just want to say hello and send him Margaret's blessing."

"They tell me the boy is little more than an idiot, so do not expect too much. He may not even know you."

Edward has always been gentle ... simple, some might say, but I'd not label him 'idiot.' But I do not argue with Henry, I just swallow his words and ensure the smile remains in my eyes.

*

The next day, while the servants are preparing for our journey back to Eltham, I sneak off to spend an hour with my cousin. I have not seen him in an age, and I half expect to find the small boy who was placed here on that uncertain day so long ago, but I find someone very different.

When I enter, the guard waits by the door. Edward is sitting by the window, a tall gangly fellow, his bony wrists exposed by the too short sleeves of his jerkin. I move toward him quietly but he doesn't look up, not even when I speak his name.

"Edward," I repeat. "Do you not know me? I am your cousin, Elizabeth."

He glances up through his fringe, his expression uncertain, and looks quickly away again. I step closer.

"I haven't visited you for so long, Ned, but I did want to. Margaret sends her love. She speaks of you every day and misses you ..."

My voice breaks as I remember the children we were on the eve of Bosworth, squabbling with Cecily while we waited for news.

Edward keeps his chin on his chest but his head turns slightly toward the fire where a cat stretches and shows us his pink tongue. I squat down, so my head is lower than Edward's, and run a finger through soft fur. "Is this your cat? What is his name?"

Edward always loved kittens. He had one poor creature with him on our journey from Yorkshire. I recall his misery when he discovered it was dead on arrival. He moves from the window and picks up the cat, drapes it over his arm and strokes it fondly with the other hand.

"Tibbles," he says. "He catches rats."

"Does he? That is good. I don't like rats."

"No."

Edward shakes his head and leans over his pet, his fair hair hanging down, shielding his face from view. He has no idea how to behave, no courtly manners, no manliness at all. He is childlike. He has stayed as he was on the day he was imprisoned, a passive, uneducated boy.

I make a mental calculation of his age; he must be about twenty-two by now. In ordinary circumstances he would be taking his place in the world, looking for a sweetheart, planning a future. Instead he is here with only a cat for company and a box of crayons as his only source of entertainment. The euphoria of yesterday dissolves in pity for this loveless boy. He is of my own flesh and blood, and kept here in darkness as a salve to Henry's insecurity.

It is not fair.

I look about the room. There are tapestries on the wall, the hangings on the bed are thick and clean, and the fire in the hearth is large enough to heat the room. But the window is high, too high for him to see out properly, and the room is shadowed and gloomy. His only attendant is a drab fellow with a permanent drip at the end of his nose.

Poor, poor Edward. A royal duke, robbed of his wits, robbed of his place in the world, robbed of freedom. I think my heart will break with guilt and regret.

I stand up, fumble in my pocket and hand some coins to his keeper.

"Make sure he wants for nothing. Should he lack any comfort, then send for me. Send for the queen."

I kiss the top of Edward's head but he is busy picking fleas from the cat's coat and does not look up again. "Goodbye, Edward. I will try to come again soon; perhaps I can bring Margaret ..."

The door opens and I turn back once more before I pass through it.

I can never bring Margaret here. She would never forgive me if she knew the truth and I cannot bear to lose another cousin, another friend.

July 1497

The relief after Blackheath does not last long. Henry is soon deep in negotiation again. Spain is still refusing to allow Caterina to come to us until the Pretender is apprehended. They will not marry her to an unstable prince; they want Arthur's future as king assured before they risk their daughter to the voyage. Henry is furious but I do not blame them. If I were Isabella and it was Margaret or Mary about to set off to a new kingdom, a

293

new life, I'd want to be very sure as to her future stability. All Henry can do is be satisfied with a new treaty in which they promise to send her to us in December 1499—providing Perkin Warbeck no longer poses a threat.

Aware that Warbeck is even now sailing with a fleet toward the south coast, Henry gives his promise. In a few weeks a formal betrothal is to take place. Arthur is almost eleven now, tall for his age and well-schooled in leadership and etiquette. When he arrives from Wales for his betrothal at Woodstock, I am shocked by how tall he has grown. He bows formally over my hand and for a moment I am afraid that my boy has gone forever to be replaced by this tall solemn man. But the moment we are alone he puts my mind at rest and engulfs me in his arms.

"You are looking bonny, Mother," he says. "That shade of blue suits you."

It is strange to have a young man with Henry's eyes and Henry's build play the gallant to me. Apart from a few exceptions, my husband keeps his affections for our private times, but I can see Arthur will be different. I watch him with the court ladies; it seems he already has an eye for them but, in the presence of the king and his grandmother, he manages to keep his interest decorously within bounds. Young Caterina is a lucky girl, I tell myself. If Arthur is as gallant and attentive to her as he is to me, she will think herself well-blessed.

In September, with the betrothal festivities at Woodstock now over, we prepare for a formal reception of the ambassadors from Venice and Milan. Henry is eager to make a good impression and show that he is unconcerned by the pretender who is buzzing about his shores like an angry hornet. Arthur has returned to Ludlow, but I order new clothes of cloth of gold and a matching set for Harry, who will be present in a formal capacity in his brother's absence.

Usually I would not be required but since the negotiations concern Caterina, my feminine presence is necessary. I dress with great care, ordering my women to brush my hair to a high sheen before they cover it with my hood. My eyebrows are plucked, my nails scrubbed and my entire body is drenched with aromatic oil. My gown is stiff with golden braid, the petticoat heavy enough to stand alone, and I am lost amid the splendour of my jewels. My ladies follow me along the corridor, giggling and gossiping with excitement, but when we near the great hall they quieten down, and I pass into the room amid a fanfare of trumpets.

Little Harry is waiting beside the king, he is clad head to toe in gold, a brocade hat and a golden feather, golden buckles on his shoes. He is turning his foot this way and that so the buckle catches the sun and sends a shaft of light to dance upon the wall. He stops when he sees me and grins, his chin high and his hands placed grandly on his hips. I hide my smile and greet the king, sinking to my knees in a full curtsey.

I take my place and the court relaxes a little, their chatter rising to a babble from which I can barely discern an odd word or phrase. I can hear the musicians tuning their instruments in the next room, a cacophony of discords and displeasing sharps. Beside me Henry waits, a benign smile pasted to his face, his fingers playing on the arm of his chair. I suppress the urge to cover his fingers with mine and stretch my own smile wider.

Harry is fiddling with his sleeve, tracing the line of seed pearls around his cuff; if they come loose they will spill across the floor like a forbidden secret. I want to instruct him to leave them alone but I cannot catch his eye and his nurse is looking the other way, her eye on a group of courtly gentlemen way above her station.

At last the ambassadors are announced and I breathe a sigh of relief, clear my throat gently to warn Harry to sit up and play the part of a prince as he has been taught.

The Venetian ambassador, Treviso, bows before the king and after his greeting turns his attention to me. He bends over my hand, a glint of admiration in his swarthy eye, and I feel the beginnings of a blush. It is a long time since I have been openly admired. I hope Henry does not notice, but it is not in my husband's nature to lust after a forbidden woman so he is unlikely to notice it in another. I raise my chin haughtily and hope my blushes do not show. I greet Soncino, the ambassador from Milan, and he offers me letters from his mistress, Beatrice d'Este, the wife of the Duke of Milan.

They then move on to greet Harry, who instantly strikes up a conversation in French that I cannot follow. I watch in bemusement as he uses his hands to illustrate his words. What on earth is he telling them? Beside me the king is scowling, his lips a thin tight line at Harry's indiscretion, but then Soncino throws his head back and laughs. I relax a little and Henry smiles, but his eyes remain anxious.

When the ambassador has stopped laughing, I beckon to him and ask what Harry said that was so funny. He frowns a little and tries to reply in stumbling English. In the end I summon Thomas Savage, the Bishop of London, who is nearby and ask him to translate for us.

He bows, one hand to his breast, and closes his eyes. Then he clears his throat and gives an embarrassed cough. "Your Grace, it seems the prince has been discussing your beauty with the ambassador and says he won't consider marrying anyone who cannot match your grace, beauty and wisdom."

I bite my lip. I should be angry. In discussing me so lewdly with foreign visitors to our court, Harry has flown against convention and should know better. He is watching me with an uncertain smile that speaks more of anxiety than glee. My heart softens.

His face is flushed, there is a smudge of something on one cheek and, as I had feared, he has dislodged the pearls on his sleeve and his discarded hat is on the floor at his feet. A glance at the king assures me that Henry has either decided to be oblivious to the incident or hasn't noticed. I make a face at Harry, rolling my eyes and silently begging him to behave.

As the dancing begins and I relax in my seat, there is a disturbance at the other end of the hall. A messenger pushes his way through the crowd. I lift my chin and look over the heads of the gathering. Henry hasn't noticed, he is still deep in consultation with Treviso. It is not until the envoy is at his elbow, bowing so low that he sweeps the floor with his hat, that Henry sees him

"Your Grace," the messenger keeps his head low until bidden to rise. "I bring news from the Duke of Bedford."

"Jasper? My uncle? What is it? Give me the letter." Henry excuses himself from the ambassador and turns away, bending his head over the scrawled message. I wait in agony, my fingers digging into the arms of my chair. Then he looks up, his eyes finding mine. His face is white, his lips colourless and his eyes glinting dark and angry. In two steps he is before me, he leans close to speak into my ear. "The Pretender has landed in Cornwall."

This is not news. We have known for days this was going to happen. I frown and shake my head as if to help clarify his concern.

"But we knew he was coming, Henry."

"Yes," he replies through clenched teeth. "What we didn't anticipate was that he would have himself crowned king in Bodmin."

Chapter Twenty-Nine
Boy

<u>Bodmin – July – September 1497</u>

A merchant vessel, a small unarmed craft, sails south toward the Cornish coast flanked by two Irish ships. The day is bright, the ship buoyant in the clear blue sea, the sails full as the prow cuts cleanly through the water. On deck, Richard squints into the sunshine. On a day like this it is hard to bear a heavy heart. but he is as despondent as the day Brampton first carried him from the Tower.

For months he has lived at King James's expense; housed, clothed and fed while the heads of Europe conspired to possess him. His liberty means uncertainty for England, insecurity for the king who is desperate to form an alliance with Spain. The joining of Arthur, the Prince of Wales, and Caterina of Aragon is delayed and his very existence a thorn in the side of the English king. The resulting war between Scotland and England has made him an uncomfortable guest. Since Henry is demanding that James hand his friend over, Richard is grateful and agrees to leave when James requests it. Ashamed now for having doubted him, the boy's friendship with James strengthens. In refusing to give him up and allowing him to leave, the Scottish king preserves the honour of York.

Richard departs with far more than he arrived. His wardrobe is that of a prince, the trappings of his horses are those of a noble, and his wife, the cousin of a king, is the fairest in Christendom. For weeks they have been in Ireland, marking time until it was ripe to leave for England.

299

Catherine stands beside him, clinging to his elbow, her beauty untarnished by the rigours of childbirth. Their son, Richard, is sleeping below deck, watched constantly by his nurse. Richard is proud of his son who is a mixture of his parents; his fair hair and bright blue eyes equally Plantagenet and Gordon. When he sleeps he takes on the charms of an angel; peaceful, cherubic and good. But on waking, he casts off those virtues and leads his elders a merry dance. Before he was mobile, the swaddling bands restricted his natural curiosity, but now he can crawl and nothing and no one is safe.

A sailor calls out that the coast of England is in sight, a green haze on the horizon beneath a bank of cloud. Richard peers across the sea, the sense of longing increasing as his confidence descends. James has assured him that once he lands in Cornwall where the feeling runs high against the king, supporters will flock to his side to swell his band of mercenaries. He can rely on the few noblemen left in his train but he is uncertain if the Cornish will join him. He suspects the English people have forgotten him. Why would they follow an exile who has no way of proving his identity?

"It is a shame that royal princes are not stamped in some way, marked at birth as a legitimate son." He speaks without intending to and Catherine laughs.

"Like a potter inscribes his pot, you mean, or a carpenter leaves his mark? An extraordinary idea, my love, but I think you should not worry, you are marked very well. Made in your father's image, so they say."

Richard allows himself the pleasure of looking at her. She is waiting for his reply, her face tilted to his and the sunshine, bouncing from the surface of the sea, would reveal every imperfection, if she had any. Her skin is smooth like cream, and her lips as finely shaped and as delicately hued as a petal. She is his single token of good luck. He lifts a hand and traces the line of her cheek.

"Unfortunately, Catherine, my father was … indiscriminate when it came to women. He left many sons in his own image and all but two of us illegitimate."

"What was Edward like?"

Richard's face clouds, he looks away and shrugs.

"I hardly know. He was raised at Ludlow, as befits the Prince of Wales, while I remained at court, in the care of my mother and sisters."

"But you were together in the Tower … at the end?"

"Yes. We were becoming acquainted. Edward had ambitions to be a good king. He hoped to embrace the new learnings, the new style of art emerging in Europe. He was disdainful of the raucous nature the court had adopted under our father and meant to change things. He was educated by our uncle Anthony who was a poet and a scholar as well as a soldier."

With a rustle of skirts she moves to perch on a pile of hogsheads beneath the mast.

"What happened that night? Why was Edward not rescued with you?"

Richard snatches off his cap, engrosses himself in examining the fine white feather. It takes him some time to find his voice.

"He thought we were under attack. London was in uproar, we'd seen the furore from our window, so later that night when cloaked and masked men stole into our chamber, we took them for murderers and fought hard against them. Edward screamed and kicked and while they were trying to overcome him, he tripped and fell, knocked his head. He didn't get up again."

Catherine touches his knee, her face swathed in pity.

"You were such a little thing, you must have been terrified."

"I didn't know what was going on. I thought they were assassins too ... at first. Since that day, since the time we realised that Edward's throne was lost, I have hardly known a moment's security. All my life I've been looking over my shoulder, wary of spies, afraid of a cloaked dagger."

"I know ..." Her voice is soft, full of tears. Richard takes a deep breath, tries to dispel his remembered grief. He clasps both her hands in his.

"Catherine, if this next attempt fails, and if I escape with my life, we will sail away and forget England, forget the crown. I swear it. We will find a dwelling somewhere and live an ordinary life; a family of cottars. Can you love me if I am not a king? Can you love an ordinary man?"

Her face widens into a smile, her eyes brimming with tears.

"You are a fool, my husband. You can never be ordinary, not in my eyes."

*

Richard is friendless now, or at least the heads of Europe who do back him do so quietly, promising support should he prove successful. It is now he needs their aid, but even those who secretly detest Henry and want to see Tudor overthrown, bide their time and wait for the outcome. When darkness falls and they are alone in their cabin the boy unties his wife's lacing, lets down her hair and makes love to her as if it is the first and last time. She undulates beneath his touch, weeps at their climax and clings to him when it is time to rise.

With a sense of fate, Richard allows the weeping Catherine to help him buckle up his armour. He puts on his sword, tucks his helmet beneath his arm and looks at her for possibly the last time. He takes a deep, shuddering breath.

"When I am gone the ship will take you along the coast to safety. I will send for you when it is safe to do so. Have good care of our son."

She nods, her words stolen by the tears that drench her face. He steps away, their fingers still clasped, and with a heavy heart wrenches away his hand. He knows she is watching from the deck, he wants to turn, to see her one more time, to wave, but fears it will unman him. He sets his sight on the shore and closes the door on his emotions.

A white stretch of sand draws closer. Already there are small boats on the beach, and men, some eighty Irishmen that accompanied him over the sea, are swarming toward the dunes. The sun is hot on his back, cooking him in his armour as the launch grates onto land, jolting him. He steadies himself, stands tall to scan the horizon for possible foes, and places one foot over the edge of the boat and onto the beach. His boot sinks in Cornish sand. Water, English water, floods between his toes.

England. This is England.

Richard has come home.

It is not a place the boy recognises. He has never been to Cornwall before but he knows it, or a place very much like it, from the Tales of Arthur. He always imagined it to be a land of magic and myth. He expects kings and dragons, green men and knights, but the men who emerge from their humble homes are rough, their tongue strange to his ears. Instead of mythical castles and jousting, he finds tin mines and fishing. The life here is harsh and the people as dark and resilient as the wiry heather that clings to the cliff face.

Richard is bright-haired and tall, and stands out among them like King Arthur come again; a man worth following even if his words are foreign to their ears. But he looks at his followers with a twinge of regret. They are simple men, strong men and honest, but they lack the power he needs. They lack war skills and they lack money. It is the great landowners he needs behind him, the churchmen and the gentry, but they are sworn to Henry and too fearful of Tudor retribution should they show support for a Pretender.

Richard marches his rabble across the rocky moor. At Penzance, when they raise his standard and when he sees it leap and snap in the brisk blue sky, his heart swells. Three thousand more men flock to his cause and with little trouble they capture St Michael's Mount. He sends word to Catherine, tells her to go to the monastery there for safety, and in return she sends him a kerchief. He holds it to his nose, inhales her scent and tucks it beneath his tunic.

It is too easy, he thinks as he marches across country to Bodmin, where the people proclaim him King Richard IV; King of England, Wales and Lord of Ireland. For a while he basks in glory; women throw flowers at his feet, men cheer and children race beside the cavalcade as he marches through town.

It is too easy, he tells himself again as they cross the Tamar and enter Devon. He sends out stern orders that there is to be no looting, no pillage or rape. These are his beloved subjects and everything his army uses is to be paid for. His numbers are steadily swelling and when the sheriff of Devon orders his men to stand against him, they refuse to fight. They throw down their weapons and cheer the conquering King Richard.

The boy smiles. He uses his charm and makes magnanimous speeches full of wild promises of prosperity for all. If they will only help him overthrow the Tudor, he will give them anything. He swears the first English town to admit him will be made into another London, promises unimagined prosperity. He boasts of his son, his heir, and another soon to follow. Sons who bear the good blood of York, untainted by bastardy, untainted by Tudor.

News slowly filters to him. The Tudor king is at Woodstock and offers Perkin Warbeck a pardon if he will surrender.

"I know nobody by that name," Richard declares and marches on, the king of York.

Henry then puts out a reward, promising one thousand marks if the Pretender is taken alive. The Tudor is desperate to have Richard in his power, but the boy sees through Henry's trickery and knows that once in enemy hands his days of liberty will be short.

Richard and his army surge like a tide across the West Country, but at Exeter his path is blocked. The city holds firm and King Richard halts at the gates, almost perplexed at this delay. He takes a few moments to collect himself and then, undeterred, he surrounds the city. While the good men of Exeter turn their guns upon his army, he fires back with rocks, tries to batter down the defences and orders his men to set fire to the north gate. The fight is long and desperate, his eyes sting with smoke, his stomach groans from lack of food. Each time one of his men is stricken down he bites his lips, sends up a prayer. *Let it be quick, Lord. Send me victory but let it be swift.*

Richard urges his men on, spurs them on to breach the walls but slowly, inexorably, they are beaten back. Although they put up a desperate fight, no impact is made on the stout defences. It seems they have lost until, on the eighteenth of September, they finally break through the barricades and flood into the high street.

Later, he snatches some time to write to Catherine.

Dear heart,

A fierce battle at Exeter, where Courtney held fast against us and there was much loss of blood. My men were exhausted by the time the walls were breached, as were the enemy. But Courtney and I have reached a truce, a chance to recoup.

It goes hard with me to shed the blood of my own countrymen, my own subjects, but the Tudor forces my hand. I learned in Northumberland that softness wins nothing; I must show myself to be a hard leader if I am to lead at all. But if they would only join me and turn against Tudor, I would pardon them all. Life would be sweet for all of us.

I hope you keep well, sweet wife. You can go to your rest knowing that I will send for you soon.

A strange state of calm washes over him, a sense of fate. Richard shrugs off Henry Tudor's promise of pardon. He knows the usurping king will never show him leniency. He surveys his army, now eight thousand strong. These are men who are prepared to fight for his cause, prepared to die for it.

It is now or never, he thinks. *By the end of this day I will either be king or I will be dead.*

The thought does not alarm him. He is detached from himself; it is as if he watches his massing army from above, as if his real 'self' is suspended some way above the earth, watching from the sky. He can see his own men, a rabble of mercenaries and disaffected Cornish with no heavy guns, patchy armour, and some without boots. *Can we really overcome the royal army?* He pushes the thought away and squints into the distance.

The royal cannon have been ringing out across the valley all morning in demonstration of Tudor's greater strength. Richard looks toward the opposition where Henry's standard snakes threateningly in the darkening sky, and shakes off fear.

He manoeuvres his horse forward, stands high in his stirrups and calls for silence, waits for the cheering to die down to a rumble.

"I am your rightful King," he cries. He holds up a roll of parchment, tied with ribbon. "I have here a papal bull declaring before God that I am the son of Edward IV and the rightful king of England. Henry Tudor is a usurper and a brute and we will tolerate him no longer."

His cheering supporters drown out his wavering voice; the sound of their adulation floods across the valley to where Henry waits ... and grows uncomfortable.

Richard's men are ready, their energies wound tight, ready to burst forth as soon as the order to charge is given. His commanders watch him, waiting for their leader's word or the raising of his hand.

But it does not come.

Richard dismounts without warning from his side-stepping stallion and disappears into his tent. He pulls off his helmet, throws his gauntlets on the bed and snarls at his attendants to get out. Inside his armour his body is bathed in sweat, his hands are shaking and vomit churns and bubbles in his throat. He spews his breakfast, draws the back of his hand across his mouth and slumps to his knees.

I cannot do it. He is weeping now, consumed by the fear he has been denying, and knows that his father, looking down from his place in Heaven, will be ashamed. Richard has failed. He is a coward. He may have inherited his father's looks and pretty manners, his courtly charm, but he possesses not a drop of his military genius, his prowess in battle. His fair head falls forward, tears— stupid, womanish tears—drip onto his breastplate. He does not bother to hide them when the tent opens to admit Skelton.

"What is it, my lord? The men are waiting."

For a long moment Richard makes no answer, then slowly he lifts his head, and does not attempt to hide his utter defeat. Skelton takes a step back, gesticulates feebly toward the entrance. "Tudor is just there, waiting. Now is our time, Richard. We can destroy him today; you can be on your throne by morning."

Richard shakes his head. "The omens are wrong," he lies, taking refuge in superstition. "It is not the time to do battle."

"What ...?" Skelton is robbed of speech. He has followed the boy all round Europe; for years they have dreamed of this day, lived on it. He placed what little he owned on the chance of Richard one day supplanting Tudor. He takes a step back, pauses. "Give yourself an hour, pray, search for strength; but I warn you, Richard, if you do not fight today, your cause will be lost."

Richard does not move. He stays on his knees, sometimes praying, sometimes giving in to despair. As the day stretches toward dusk, his men begin to sneak away. In the morning just a stalwart few remain.

*

Across the valley the Tudor king sends out spies to ascertain the cause of the delay. He waits uncertainly, frowning and snapping at everyone until, leaving Jasper in charge, he returns to his lodging. *Tomorrow then,* he thinks. *Tomorrow I will have him.*

But, when the damp, chill morning dawns, the opposite hill is empty and the eight thousand-strong army, finding itself without a leader, has dwindled away. Warbeck is nowhere to be found.

Henry throws down his plate. "Find him!" he yells with unaccustomed fury. "Find him and bring him to me alive!"

Chapter Thirty
Elizabeth

I am praying for my husband's safe return, but before I rise I add a short plea for the fate of Warbeck, if he be my brother. The past weeks have been hard. Waiting is always difficult but this time my inconstant heart cannot wish unreservedly for the battle to go in Henry's favour. There is always that question; that *'but suppose it is Richard,'* that I cannot ignore.

I cannot concentrate, and even the joys of the nursery cannot distract me from constant worry. When Cecily and our cousin Margaret come to see me, I greet them thankfully. Although we cannot mention him, I know that deep down we are on the same side, but I do not speak of the Pretender.

Cecily is deeply attached to Henry's mother and if I were to unburden myself to her, I do not trust her not to run straight to Lady Margaret with the tale. I greet them warmly, kiss their cheeks, and admire their gowns before we settle ourselves at the hearth. Cecily is a little pale and I remember her daughter Elizabeth has been ailing.

"How is little Eliza, Cecily? Did she like the books I sent her? I hope they help to relieve the boredom of the sick bed."

My sister flashes a smile that dies as soon as it is born. She looks down at her hands and shrugs her shoulders.

"She rallies and then fails again. Sometimes I despair, sometimes I have hope. The physicians can determine no cause for her malady."

I reach out to place a hand on Cecily's shoulder, as if physical contact can ease her pain.

"She is in my prayers, constantly."

"And mine," Margaret adds. "And the king's mother prays for her, too. I am told God holds her in very high regard."

It is no time for levity but Margaret's poor joke makes me smile. As yet, neither my sister nor my cousin know the pain of losing a child and, remembering my own experience, my heart twists with pity. Elizabeth has been ailing for months with no sign of real improvement. I fear she will die and, not for the first time, I wish that being queen provided real power; the power of life over death. All we can do is pray.

"I saw your brother, Edward, a few weeks ago. He is tall now and seems content." A shadow crosses my face as I recognise the crassness of my words. How can anyone be content incarcerated in a living tomb, even if it is well furnished with cushions and picture books?

Margaret's face opens, a half smile plays on her lips. "He is well? Did you give him my love? Oh, how I wish the king would let me see him. What harm could it possibly do?"

Her words send a squirm of guilt through me, guilt that my husband, the man I have come to love, can inflict such suffering on my family. A devil sits on my shoulder, pouring poison into my ear. *If he truly loved you, wouldn't he honour your family instead of punishing them?* I bite my lip, jerk the imp from my shoulder and turn the talk to other things.

"I will speak to the king again, Margaret, but I will wait until he is in a happier frame of mind. He is much distraught over the Pretender and when he is with me I need to soothe his spirits not agitate them."

"I understand," Margaret answers, her eye on the window, but I know she doesn't. She can never have any idea what it is like to be me, and what marriage to Henry entails.

"I will be glad when this fray is over. The Cornish are so troublesome. I fear Henry's punishment will be severe this time and who can blame him? There has been one uprising after another and he does his best to be a just king ..."

Two pairs of eyes are upon me. They are wondering when I changed and what changed me. Cecily shuffles in her seat.

"The king's mother says there will be no clemency this time. Once he lays hands on Warbeck and his followers, he will hang them all."

Our eyes meet, our gaze holds for a long moment, and we are both wondering if indeed Warbeck might be who he claims to be. If he is, how will we ever sit by and watch as Henry murders him? My reticence dissolves.

I lean forward and they meet me halfway, two blonde and one dark head together, like a trio of conspiring witches. "I will know when I see him. If it is Richard, I will beg Henry for leniency. I will not let him kill our brother."

We sit up in unison and regard each other with wide, frightened eyes and I can see that neither of them has the least faith in my influence with the king.

An hour of desultory talk and then the door opens and the guard announces my mother-in-law. Cecily and Margaret rise to their feet, make the required obeisance, although they both ignore etiquette when in private consultation with me.

"Cecily; how lovely to see you." The king's mother kisses my sister on either cheek and greets Margaret rather more coolly. "Elizabeth," she bows her head to me so discreetly she may as well have not bothered. "I have a letter from the king."

I am on my feet. "What does he say? Is he safe? Has he caught up with the Pretender yet?"

She waves the sheet of parchment beneath my nose. Henry's familiar scrawl is covering the sheet and I long to snatch it from her. Instead, I bite my tongue, quell my impatience and wait for her to relate the contents.

"The king caught up with the Pretender but there was no fight. It seems the churl took fright in the night and fled with his closest companions, leaving his army to face the wrath of the true king. Henry and Jasper have followed their trail and expect the pretender to be in their hands very soon."

She beams about the room and we try to look happy that the boy is soon to be within Henry's grasp. I feel sick and long for her to leave us, but she summons a chair and settles herself for a long stay. The rest of the afternoon is spent listening to her embroidering Henry's many virtues. He is described in such glowing terms that I quite fail to recognise my husband who, although beloved, is often short tempered and very seldom glorious.

By the time she leaves us, Cecily and Margaret also have to leave. I walk with them to the door where Margaret clings to my hand. "Try and speak to the king on Edward's behalf. Once the Pretender is captured and his own position more secure, he may think differently. I would take Edward away from court; the king need never lay eyes on him. He is my brother, Elizabeth."

She clings desperately to my hand while I nod whitely and promise to do what I can. As she and Cecily take their leave, my thoughts turn to my own brother and reflect that his fate may very well now be as perilous as Warwick's.

314

For the next few days I am jittering with nerves. I can't settle, neither to sleep nor to prayer, and my meals go back to the kitchen untouched. In the end I take a few of my favourite women and ride to Eltham to spend some time with the children. When they hear me arrive they tumble from the palace to greet me; Harry reaches me first and throws chubby arms about my waist and buries his head in my skirts. Mary's arms are round my knees hampering my progress, but Meg waits, hands clasped decorously before her, and I remember the King's mother has been overseeing her deportment.

When the children give me the freedom to move, I ignore her outstretched hand and kiss her cheek, drawing her into an embrace. She relaxes against me gratefully, glad that I forego the formality insisted upon by her grandmother.

With Mary balanced on my hip and Harry's hand clasped tightly within my own, Margaret and I follow Elizabeth Denton up the stairs to the hall.

I spend a happy hour or so playing and drawing, teaching them new words, telling them stories. Elizabeth Denton is always quite scandalised when I put off my queenly dignity and sit with my children on the floor before the fire. Perhaps I should heed her disapproval but part of me delights in shocking her.

Mary is in my lap, Harry and Meg close by as I tell one of the stories from Arthur. When I get to the part where Arthur casts Excalibur into the lake, Harry leaps to his feet, his face pink with heroic joy.

"When I am a man I shall find the lake and dive down to the bottom and find Excalibur and carry it into battle!"

"No, you won't Harry, don't be so silly. This all happened ages ago, the sword will be all rusty by now."

Harry's face falls, his bottom lip juts out.

"Then I will have one made. When our brother Arthur is king I will be his right hand man, like Lancelot, and guard him against his foes."

"Just make sure you don't steal his wife."

I open my mouth to reprimand Meg for such a pert suggestion but Harry precludes me.

"Why would I do that? What do I want with a wife? Girls are silly."

"Kings need sons, Harry. A king isn't a proper king without lots of sons."

I watch them, fascinated in the turn the squabble has taken. I should put a stop to it at once but it is revealing, their hot words telling me far more about them than a polite conversation ever would.

Harry's face turns puce as he searches for a clever riposte. Margaret, two years older, is far wiser and more aware of the way the world works than her brother. I note the glee in her eye as she folds her arms across her chest as he grows crosser.

"Well, all right then. I will have a silly wife but I won't visit her. I will let her live in a palace on her own and she can fill it with princes."

Meg laughs, a tinkling sound like my own used to be. She raises her eyebrows to me in mockery of her brother's lack of worldliness.

News of the conflict with the Pretender has not reached the royal nursery, and for a few hours I am able to forget it. Although, every now and then, Harry's face, or Harry's expression, or Harry's comical conversation reminds me of Richard, the brother I once loved.

Walsingham – October 1497

I decide not to cancel the long standing arrangements for my pilgrimage to Walsingham, but I leave court with a heavy heart. As I ride the roads of autumn, showered in leaves of gold and red, my mind wanders back down the years. I have come far. I have overcome many obstacles, thwarted many foes to arrive where I am today; queen of England, mother of the next king. It is time to give thanks rather than dither between resentment and joy.

It is late when we arrive at the abbey. I am tired out and more than a little grubby from the rigours of the road. I ask for a bath to be prepared. Anne Say helps me out of my gown, rolls down my stockings.

"I feel so tired." I smile at her as she lays my clothes on the bed. Then I sit on a cushion while she loosens my hair and begins to brush it. The rhythmic strokes of the brush are soothing. I close my eyes and listen to Catherine Hussey strumming the lute.

What will be, will be, I tell myself. There is no point worrying about it. Perhaps when Henry brings the Pretender back he will be a stranger, a vile usurper who ill-wishes my husband and my children. Then I shall be glad of his death. I clench my fingers on the arms of the chair as my whole body begins to stiffen.

"Are you all right, Your Grace?" Ann has stopped brushing and has placed a hand on my shoulder. "You are suddenly very tense."

I smile at her. "I am fine. I am just worried about the king. I will be glad when we can be reunited. I hate fighting and sometimes I feel there has been nothing else for my entire lifetime."

"It will cease now the king has the pretender in his hands. We can all relax."

She begins to brush again and Catherine starts to sing, her soft voice lulling me into a sense of easement. By the time the water has been brought from the kitchens and the tub is filled, I am reluctant to stir. I force myself from the chair.

Fresh clothes are laid out in readiness. I cross the chamber, let Ann help me from my shift and step naked into the warm water. It engulfs my tired limbs, laps against my aching breasts, soothes my chaffed thighs. The water is scented with lavender and chamomile to help me relax and, as I lay there, some of the worries and the fears seep away to be discarded with the dirty water. By the time the water has cooled I will emerge clean and strong again.

As I am made ready for bed, a letter arrives from the king; the messenger has ridden hard from Devon. I order him to be given refreshment and a bed for the night. My eyes scan quickly over the customary greeting to the real news.

As you will have been informed, we have the Pretender in our possession and are riding to London, where he will be placed in the Tower and hopefully forgotten. We need worry no more, Elizabeth; our son's inheritance is safe. I have one more prisoner, however, who is more difficult to throw into a dungeon. I have Warbeck's wife, Catherine Gordon, a close relative of the Scottish king. I have no desire to undermine our recent treaty with James and so will house her gently, as befits her station. I request that you take her into your household and treat her with the respect she deserves.

It is no little relief to have dealt with this matter at last. The marriage negotiations with Spain can now move on and, God willing, the Infanta can be welcomed to England soon.

I will send this letter ahead and arrive soon after it, where I will be glad to be in your company again. I hope, wife, that this letter finds you well.

Henry Rex

So, I am no sooner arrived at the shrine than I must ride back again. I spend a day giving thanks for my children, asking that God send little Elizabeth good rest. I thank Him for the happy outcome of the conflict and also just before I leave, I ask for the joy of another child. A son; another son, just like my Harry.

*

For once, when Henry greets me, he makes no concealment of his regard. As soon as it is fit to do so he gives his excuses to his mother, sends my women away and we retreat, almost directly, into the dark sanctity of our marriage bed.

Even at his most passionate I have found him a reserved lover, the peak of our loving passing quickly to polite companionship. But there is something different about him now; a new urgency, a sweet, hot, welcome thirst that is new to me. I open myself to him, glad that our souls can now touch, relieved that the removed threat of the Pretender has allowed this new side of Henry to emerge.

After he has taken me, he lingers in my bed, curling my hair about his fingers; tracing the line of my breast and laughing when my nipples rise to greet their king. He is almost gay, and in return I am relaxed and happy to discover this new husband, this new lover. I cannot help but let him see how much I welcome and revel in our loving.

When we finally rise from our bed, we are both rosy from our romp. He helps me into a loose gown, and even goes so far as to brush the worst of the snarls from my hair so that my ladies do not remark on it. As I meet his eyes in the glass, he looks different, his reflection somehow altered. I blush beneath the heat of his gaze. *What has happened to Henry?* Surely quelling the uprising and ridding himself of Warbeck's threat cannot have unleashed such an uprising of lust? *Has his insecurity been obscuring his true nature for all these years?*

Sheen Palace – November 1497

I am dressed in my finest; a gown of white cloth of gold with a regal train. From my ears hang two of the world's most enormous pearls. Ann hands me my fan and my prayer book, and we make our way down to the hall for supper.

Customary trumpets mark my arrival and the court falls to its knees while I take my place on the dais. I cast my eye about the hall, looking for Henry. It is unusual for him to arrive after me; he is usually in his place, discussing matters of state with his uncle Jasper.

I locate the king's mother first. She is speaking to the archbishop, probably complaining about some breach of his service. I link my fingers and wait with back erect for Henry to arrive. And then I hear him laugh. I jerk my head in the direction of the sound. It is a laugh quite unlike anything I have heard from him before; usually his amusement is sparing or at the expense of others.

He is hidden from my sight, screened by a curtain that is suddenly pulled back to give him admittance. He steps into the torchlight, a half smile on his face, his eyes soft and relaxed, as if he has just risen from my bed. This evening he looks every inch a king.

He is splendidly apparelled in purple velvet, his hair falling in a smooth curtain to his shoulder. And on his arm is the most exquisite woman I have ever seen. She is chatting, embellishing her words with long white fingers, and he is leaning toward her, entranced by what she is saying, something I cannot hear. He laughs again, and the court titters in accompaniment, happily surprised to see their king so relaxed.

He notices me watching him and his smile widens.

"Elizabeth, my dear." He moves forward quickly, bringing the woman with him. When they are before me he keeps a hold of her hand and stands tall while she curtseys, extravagantly low.

"Your Grace," she greets me in a voice like honey. "I am very grateful to you for welcoming me into your household."

She is so beautiful, so young, and Henry is obviously besotted. She is all in black, festooned with pearls, the whiteness of her cap lending luminosity to her wide blue eyes. Alarm bells ring in my head. The whole court is looking on, eagerly awaiting my response.

Catherine Gordon is as I was ten years ago and instantly I feel old and fat. My heart begins to splinter, but I realise everyone present is waiting for my next words.

"It is good to have you here," I answer woodenly. My eyes are captivated by the sheen of her skin, the rise of her forehead, the plump invitation of her lips. I drink her in and she curdles like poison through my veins.

Henry is still staring at her. I notice he has maintained hold of her hand far longer than is required, and he is delicately stroking her long white fingers with his ink-stained thumb. Jealousy strikes like a dagger, so sharply I almost cry out against it.

The change I have detected in Henry isn't due to me, or Warbeck, or our victory over the Cornish. He didn't make love to me with a new vigour because of anything like that, or from a newfound appreciation for me, his wife, and all that I have sacrificed for his happiness. No. His passion is not for me at all, and all the time he made love to me, he was wishing it was her.

*

It is not easy to pretend all is well, but I do my best. Years of training to conceal my real feelings come to the fore. I continue the charade and push all my jealous rage deep down inside me and paint a serene smile on my face.

I open my arms to Catherine and welcome her into my household as if she is dear to me, but my heart is closed to her. Each time I look on her face I am reminded of Henry's defection. I have no idea if they are lovers or not. She professes to be in love with her husband, Warbeck, but that does not prevent her from hanging on my husband's arm, or sharing long, intimate hours with him over a chess board. He used to play with me; I always made sure his ego remained high by ensuring he won. But Catherine beats him. She takes loud satisfaction in felling his queen and, to my astonishment, Henry doesn't seem to mind.

The Pretender is now safely in the Tower; the king and our sons are safe from him. Several times it is on the tip of my tongue to ask Catherine about him, but so far I have resisted the temptation. I know Henry would not wish it. Any curiosity on my part would suggest I give credence to Warbeck's claim. So I sit quietly, watching her from the corner of my eye and wondering if she is the wife of a pretender, or if indeed she is my sister-in-law.

During the day, Henry comes to my chambers much more frequently but it is not to see me. For the first time in all our married life he sits among my ladies, takes an interest in their needlework and, on one occasion, holds a skein of wool while Catherine Gordon rolls it into balls.

I bite my tongue, plead a headache, and send her for some salve to rub into my temples. Henry sits back, displeased, and sends me a sharp look, but he does not reprimand me. Instead he turns the conversation to the forthcoming marriage of Arthur and the Spanish Infanta.

"I had imagined that once I had the Pretender under lock and key, Ferdinand and Isabella would agree to let the Infanta travel here, but still they prevaricate. Still they do not trust me."

I pluck a few crooked stitches from my work and begin again. "You don't think they give his claim any credence do you, Henry? I mean, if it were Margaret or Mary I should hate for them to go to a foreign country unless their future was assured."

Henry shifts his limbs irritably. "It is clear he is a pretender, he has made a full confession to the fact. He is a commoner from Tournai, not a drop of royal blood in him."

He crosses his ankles, folds his arms defensively. I smile soothingly.

"I know that, Henry. Of course I do, but perhaps the Spanish need a little more persuading."

I bow my head over my sewing again and silence falls between us. From the antechamber come the sounds of a lute, muffled giggles, the light thumping that sounds to me like one of the fools tumbling across the floor. While I sit here talking politics with the king, my ladies are enjoying themselves.

"It will all come right, Henry," I say. "Do not worry."

He stands up, stretches his arms, arching his back before shrugging on his cloak and smoothing the fur collar. He bends to kiss my cheek and I resist the impulse to cling on and prolong the moment.

"I must see my mother before she retires; there was a matter she wished to discuss with me."

He is going to her, I think. I look down at the neat stitches that represent my empty hours and the work blurs, a tear blots the fabric. With a deep breath, I raise my head, wipe the tears away.

"Are you all right, Madam?" Catherine moves forward from the darkness. "What is the matter?"

Relief floods through me. I had truly believed he was making excuses to leave me so he could go to her. I smile blindly and shake my head.

"Nothing, I am just being silly."

She sits on a low stool beside me, her dark skirts ballooning around her.

"It is never silly to cry, Your Grace. I cry often. I miss my husband more than I'd miss my right hand."

Our eyes meet. Another tear drops on my cheek. I try to blink them away and her hand reaches out to cover mine.

"Tell me about him," I hear myself saying. "Tell me about Perkin."

After a long silence she begins to speak, her voice husky with emotion.

"I call him Richard, of course. Despite his confession I can think of him only as the Duke of York ..." She stops, her face white, her eyes luminous in the firelight. "Do I have your permission to speak freely, Your Grace?" She looks toward the door, shuffles closer on her stool. "Can I speak from the heart?"

I nod once and cold fear creeps through me and takes hold of my heart.

"I believe his story. He told me so many things, small things about his life before ... before your father died. He spoke of you, your mother and sisters, the death of your father, your time in sanctuary. His descriptions were so real, so vital; they cannot have been the invention of a boy from Antwerp. I am sure of it."

I am frowning, pain is in my heart and tears spout from my eyes. I cannot help it. I have no control. If Henry were to come back now and see us together, he would know at once that we were discussing the forbidden.

Catherine is leaning forward, clasping my hand, her eyes earnest, and I see now that her flirtation with the king, her light-hearted gaiety, is all an act; an act to fool the gullible king. I fumble for the desire to defend him.

"Some men are very good liars."

She sits up straighter, her indignation plain.

"You do not know him, Your Grace. Honour and chivalry are the closest things to his heart. He wanted to be the second Arthur; he intended to rule like the kings of old, like King Arthur. He is not a violent man. His one desire was to stop suffering, to bring peace, but all he has brought is death and insecurity. That is the thing which is killing him ..."

She breaks off, her voice cracking into sobs. I watch her shoulders shake for a while but then, unwillingly, my hand creeps out to comfort her. As she weeps into my lap, my own tears spill over again but at length she sits up, dabs her face with a kerchief.

"I have tried to persuade the king to allow Richard to come to court. He is wavering. I tried to convince him that if the courtiers saw them together that Henry's nobility would outshine my husband's and he would be clearly seen as a pretender."

Her eyes are penetrating deep into mine, manipulating my thoughts, urging me to speak against the king, against my husband. When I do not reply she lowers her voice, tempting me like a devil to betray my husband's trust. "The king is considering it but, Your Grace, if he was allowed to come, you'd see him for yourself. If anyone can identify him, it is you."

*

"You are not to make any attempt to see him. If I discover you have disobeyed me in this I will send you from court, do you understand?"

I keep calm and try to present a placid face to Henry's back as he paces up and down the chamber.

"I will obey you, as I always do. I have no wish to meet a pretender who has caused us so much grief."

"And cost us so much money. My coffers are low because of him. I shall let the court and any who care to look see him for the pretender he is. A low-born foreigner sent by the Duchess Margaret to be a thorn in our flesh. Well, that thorn is well and truly drawn now."

"Indeed, my love." It is better that I do not say too much. He must think me content to be ordered to stay in my rooms on the nights Warbeck is in the king's company. Henry must think I have no ambition or curiosity to look upon the man at all. But, in truth, my blood is boiling. After all these years I am desperate to know the truth. "When Warbeck is to join you at supper I shall keep to my rooms; it is good sometimes to dine quietly and take my leisure in my own apartments, but I trust you will visit me as usual, whenever it pleases you."

I flush as hotly as if I am propositioning a stranger, and Henry laughs quietly and bends over my hand.

"Of course, wife; that goes without saying."

I am still uncertain if he has taken Catherine as his mistress. Never in all our years has he shown a flicker of interest in another woman and it is strange now, to see him so besotted. She is constantly in his company, when she is not in mine, and her merry laugh can often be heard issuing from his apartments. I cannot ask her. I cannot reveal the extent of my jealousy, my despair that having taken so long to fall in love with my husband, he now develops a passion for someone else.

The royal court vibrates with excitement about Warbeck's presence. We are all curious, all surprised that instead of condemning him to a lifetime in prison, the king has instead decided to make a mock of him. But I recall Henry doing this before, with another rival to his throne, a less dangerous one but a threat nevertheless.

Lambert Simnel was, for a few years, made a mockery of at court and then when the king tired of baiting him, was sent to work as a turn-spit in the royal kitchen. He now works in the mews where he shows a talent with the falcons. Simnel was a puppet, pressured by others to act against the king, and Henry could afford to be lenient. Warbeck is different. He has dogged Henry for years, caused him sleepless nights, stolen some of his closest subjects and cost him an enormous sum of money.

On the day he is brought from the Tower, I keep to my chamber. My women bring me news of him and tell me that he has been installed in the King's apartments where his every movement is shadowed by two burly guards. He sleeps in the royal wardrobe, the chamber where Henry's gowns and royal robes are stored. I imagine he is searched regularly for weapons for, at such close quarters, I am surprised my husband manages a wink of sleep.

The gossips say Warbeck is very handsome but his spirits are low, his hopes so dashed he scarcely raises his head. Catherine is allowed to speak to him in company, but marital relations between them are forbidden. That must suit Henry very well. My informants describe how the king continues to commandeer her attention, leads her out to dance in my absence. The only comfort I have is that he continues to visit my chamber, sometimes lingering until morning, and we both nurture hopes for another child.

The strange situation continues, all of us in limbo, each knowing that things cannot continue like this, something has to happen.

Christmas is approaching. Harry, Meg and Mary are expected from Eltham very soon and I begin planning New Year gifts for them. I am embroidering a fine new doublet for Harry and elaborate sleeves for Meg. After a few weeks, particularly once the children have arrived, I find I treasure the intimate evenings I spend in my apartments with those closest to my heart. Only Henry is missing; Henry who has come to mean so much. I try not to imagine where he might be.

It is dark outside, the sound of the revels in the hall echo through the palace, reaching me in my chambers. The children are in bed and I have supped well and am enjoying a little peace, going over the events of the day in my mind.

Harry has been naughty again, letting the king's monkey into his grandmother's chamber where the beast tore the drapes about her bed and set her servants screaming. I hide my amusement and look reproachfully at Harry but my mother-in-law, who sees the boy as the devil incarnate, scolds him harshly and sends him early to bed. I am made of less stern stuff and as soon as she departs I go to him and read him stories until he grows sleepy. I hold his hand until his eyelids droop, then I quietly extract myself and creep from the room. At the door I turn and he opens one sleepy eye and mumbles, 'Goodnight, Mother."

Apart from that one incident, it has been a long pleasant day, a companionable evening, and I am happily tired. I stretch my arms and legs and yawn, opening my mouth wide in a way I would never do in public.

"I think I will go to bed," I say, putting my sewing down and rising from my chair. "It has been a long day."

My ladies follow me to my sleeping chamber and the long preparation for bed begins. I am disrobed, sponged, my hair brushed, fresh nightclothes put on. Ann tucks me beneath the sheets and draws the curtains about the bed. I am cocooned, womb-like in the dark, the small sounds of my women tidying the chamber slowly fade and my eyes droop, my breathing slows.

"FIRE! FIRE!" People are screaming, my chamber a riot of half dressed women, dishevelled servants. The bed curtains are torn open. "Your Grace, wake up! There is a fire; the king's chamber is alight."

"The children!" I am out of bed in a moment, pulling on my robe, running barefoot toward the door. "Is the king safe?" I shout over my shoulder. Catherine Gordon is there, gorgeous even in her distress.

"I don't know but the children are; Mistress Denton has taken them out. We must evacuate at once, Madam."

I run from their voices, my plaited hair bouncing heavily on my back, my feet bare in the rushes, treading in God knows what as I hurtle along the corridor. Catherine follows. I can hear her breathing, fast and quick, just behind me.

The king's outer chambers are alive with activity. No guards at the door. I rush in, spin around on my heel, absorbing the chaos, the destruction. Thick smoke belches from the inner chamber; from the room that houses Henry's bed. Men are shouting, heavy footsteps, servants fruitlessly dousing the flames with ewers of water. The palace will be ashes in no time.

"Your Grace, we must leave. The king has already gone." Catherine is behind me, beseeching me to move, but I ignore her. I peer through belching smoke, my eyes streaming with tears.

"Where is the king?" I scream. "Where is the king?"

A hand grabs my wrist, spins me round, and I crash into a broad bare torso; the torso of a man. Slowly, my eyes travel up his body, past the thick column of his neck, past his strong chin and generous mouth, until I meet a pair of well-remembered eyes.

He is dishevelled and grimy, a streak of soot mars his forehead, but I'd know him anywhere. Just as he did when he was ten years old, he pushes back a lock of fair hair that has flopped over his forehead

"Elizabeth," he shouts. "You have to leave. You have to leave this moment. The king has already been taken to safety."

"Richard?" I whisper. I forget about the danger, about the belching smoke, the roaring flames. I forget about the legion of spiteful eyes that may be watching. I am transfixed by his beloved face. "Oh my God, Richard; it *is* you."

"Hush." Catherine steps forward, ordering me to be silent. "It is not safe. Be quiet, or all our lives are forfeit. Come," she says, jerking her head in farewell to her husband. "We must all get out. I will take the queen this way; Richard, you go by the back stairs. The king must not know you have met."

I am led away in a daze, her hand clamped hard about my wrist. Waves of shock and stifling smoke make my head so thick and heavy I can barely think, but as my mind begins to clear, I wonder how Catherine knew about the back stairs that lead to and from my husband's chamber.

*

Henry and I stand in the courtyard, a group of dishevelled courtiers ringed about us. A cluster of smudged sooty faces raise their eyes to the leaping flames that are consuming the palace. My hand slides beneath Henry's elbow and he knows, without looking, that it is me.

"Thank God we are all safe," he says but, still stunned by the fire and by my recent encounter with my brother, I remain silent, my head reeling.

My face and the front of my body are warmed by the raging fire but December frost bites at my bare feet, creeps up my nightgown to gnaw at my buttocks. I shiver, more from shock than cold, and huddle deeper to Henry's side.

Close by, the king's mother is bullying Elizabeth Denton to take the children into the old royal manor complex that lies just beyond the moat. "We must all assemble at the old manor. It will be safe there," she is saying. "The fire cannot cross the water."

As Mistress Denton hurries the children away followed by a fleet of sobbing nursery maids, I can hear Harry excitedly relating all he has witnessed.

"Did you see the flames, Meg? They were like dragons, great orange dragons. I liked it when all the windows smashed and the glass fell tinkling to the ground like ..." His high pitched voice dies away and I am confident they will soon be warm and safe again. I shudder and move closer to Henry, rubbing my face against the warm fur of his cloak.

The king's profile is outlined against the light of the flames; his face is set firm, his lips a tight angry line, his eyes narrowed. I squeeze his arm.

"It will be all right, Henry."

He turns and looks at me, a quizzical frown on his brow. "Just think of what we have lost this night, Elizabeth; not just the building but the rich hangings, our royal apparel, even some of our crown jewels. Those things are irreplaceable. I can rebuild the palace, and I intend to do so, but the treasures lost this night cannot be remade."

"But Henry," I try to explain, groping for words that fail me. In the end I plump for the plain truth. "At least no one was hurt, no lives were lost. We must thank God for that."

Chapter Thirty-One
Boy

<u>Westminster – Spring 1498</u>

The boy has never been so cast down; even at his lowest ebb when he was far from home, there were people who named him 'Prince.' Now, as Henry Tudor's captive, he has no friends, no status, and very little hope.

Ostensibly, the king is lenient. He could have left him in the Tower, shut him away from the eyes of the world, but instead he has allowed him the freedom of the court, the company of men. But Richard quickly realises he is Henry's dupe, no better than his fools, the tumblers and leapers, the malformed idiots that noblemen love to mock. His companions are a bearded woman, a Scottish midget and a giant girl from Flanders. The former golden prince of York is reduced to mingling with the dregs of the court.

He sleeps in a closet within the king's royal apartment, the door locked at night, his guards ever-vigilant at the door. He has no real freedom, he cannot stroll in the gardens, or visit his wife, or take his ease with the courtiers. No, he has to stay close to the king, ready to do his bidding, answer his questions, reiterate his false confession. "I am a pretender, born in Antwerp, not a son of York at all."

Each time he speaks the words he hates himself a little more, almost wishing Tudor had left him in the confines of the Tower where at least he would be away from the eyes of men. Now, on top of the contempt and the mockery, he is suspect.

The gossips whisper that he set the fire in the royal apartments and tried to burn the king alive. Richard sneers at such a suggestion. Had he set out to murder Tudor he would have succeeded, he would have lit the fire directly beneath the royal bed.

The king, for all his leniency, does not trust him and constantly tests him. Ever watchful for a chance to punish him further, Henry leaves doors unlocked, windows unlatched. He watches, waits for his captive prince to run.

Richard is allowed to see Catherine but they are never alone; she is chaperoned. Two of the queen's women wait at the door and his guards hover nearby watching them, eavesdropping on their conversation. Sometimes they smirk and make loud kissing noises should he so much as hold his wife's hand.

"I hate this," she whispers. "The strain is killing me. I miss you so much."

He squeezes her hand. "You are sure the boy is safe and nobody knows? No one suspects?"

She shakes her head. "I am sure of it. He is safe in Wales. I sent him there with my trusted servant before we were taken from the Mount. I could not let Henry lay hands on him."

"He is the one thing we have left. York's last hope."

Her head is bowed. "I am sorry I lost the other, Richard. Two princes would have served you so much better than one."

"Hush," he says. "The blame does not lie with you. I should have left you in Scotland. James would have kept you both safe."

A tear drips from the tip of her nose and splashes on their joined fingers. She raises her head, mops her face.

"I swore I'd put on a brave face. You do not deserve my tears."

"Does he treat you well?"

She knows he means King Henry, although he will not speak the name if he can help it. She nods her head.

"He is very good to me. I have fine apartments, clothes, and am accorded every courtesy due to my station. He desires that I play him at chess every evening and loses often ..."

"In his apartments?" Richard speaks through tight lips, his face pale, and his eyes glistening with envy.

"Sometimes," she confesses. "But we are always chaperoned."

"He wants you, doesn't he? He desires you as his mistress?"

"I don't know, Richard. He hasn't suggested it, or behaved improperly. He is attentive and kind, and that is all I know."

She draws her hand away, injured by his lack of trust. She looks at the door, as if making ready to leave him.

"Don't go." He reaches out to restrain her. "It is hard for me, cooped up in here until he sees fit to show me off to the court. Come, let's talk of something else. Tell me of Elizabeth; has she said anything? I thought she would try to see me ..."

"She is not allowed," Catherine hisses. "She is watched as carefully as you and I."

"Does she speak of me? Has she questioned you?"

She shakes her head. "Sometimes I think she is about to but there is always an interruption. Her apartments are busy. She is the queen, you know."

"She knew me at once. I know she did. She has scarcely altered at all; a little older, a little stouter but still Elizabeth, just as I am still Richard. Why won't she support me?"

One of the guards at the door coughs and spits onto the floor, Catherine grimaces with distaste before turning back to her husband.

"You surely cannot expect her to. She is the queen; if she backed you she'd lose her position, her crown, and her son would be deposed. You have to try to see things from her perspective too, Richard. Just hope that she doesn't reveal your identity to the king because I believe you are safe only for as long as he believes you to be Perkin."

Richard snatches his hand away.

"He knows who I am," he snarls. "That is why he mocks me, just as the Lancastrians mocked my grandfather when they decorated his severed head with a paper crown. He knows I have more right to his throne than he does himself and that is why he is terrified to have me killed. He labels me as Warbeck and pins the blame for the death of the princes on my Uncle Richard to make himself a better king. He is wily and sly, not to be trusted ..."

"Time's up." The guard approaches to usher Catherine from the apartment. They both stand up, she falls into her husband's arms; his lips are on her forehead, his hands about her waist.

"So soon, Richard?" she moans. "We spent too much time speaking of foolish things."

"Next time, sweetheart. Next time will be better, I swear it."

He smothers her face in kisses, tasting her tears until the guards grow impatient and take hold of her arm.

"I will come as soon as I can, my love. I will keep you in my dreams."

Her voice fades, she slips through the door and he is left alone. He looks about the small empty chamber, the abandoned lute, the dying fire, and the untouched fruit on the table. He slumps onto a stool and buries his head in his hands, alone with his fears. He has time, too much time with the bitter knowledge that while he is imprisoned with the royal robes, the king seeks to make love with his wife.

<u>April 1498</u>

It is good to be out of the palace and on horseback again. In the company of the king's fools, Richard joins the royal cavalcade as it progresses around Kent. He has always loved the spring; the roadside is burgeoning with primroses and Lenten lilies, the trees coming into bud, the willows yellow with blossom.

As the royal party moves through the countryside, the people come out to cheer. Henry makes sure they know Richard for the pretender Warbeck, and he is forced to rise above the cruel comments, the crude suggestions of where he should bury his head. He tries to focus on the fine blue skies, the undulating meadows, the full and gushing streams. *This should all belong to me*, he thinks. *I should be king over all of it, as my father was.*

"Ooh, look at the pretender," a gap-toothed woman screams from the crowd as they enter Canterbury. "Let me give tribute to the counterfeit king!" She stoops down, scoops up a handful of mud and hurls it toward him. Richard ducks out of the way, his tunic is spattered as the clod of earth sails past him and strikes one of the fools in the middle of his chest. The crowd screams with delight but the fool scowls and Richard knows he will feel the brunt of his resentment once they are settled for the night.

You'd think that the lower echelons of Henry's court would show some sympathy for the boy, who has committed no crime against them. But, afraid of offending their king, no one dare befriend him and he is denied access to the ring of friendship.

Up ahead he catches sight of the king's cap, the feather blowing gracefully in the breeze. Beside him rides Catherine, her gloved hands lightly on the reins, her gay laughter light in the spring air. Richard's gut twists with jealousy. She is forgetting him, enjoying the notice of the Tudor king, regretting her hasty marriage to an ill-fated Pretender.

Why do I stay? Richard wonders. *If I try to escape and they capture me, kill me, will it really matter? And if I do get away? Perhaps I can board a ship, sail away from it all and forget who I am, become a peasant, or a pirate. Catherine will not care.*

Westminster Palace — June 1498

It has been raining and the king's privy garden is glistening in the morning sun. Drops of moisture hang like jewels from the roses, puddles litter the gravel. Small birds emerge from hiding to hop and twitter as they peck about on the mead. Richard strolls along honey-coloured paths, deep in thought, his hands clasped behind his back. The king's privy garden is the part of his prison he favours most. He remembers walking here with his mother, in happier days. He can almost hear the laughter of his sisters, the whisper of his mother's skirts on the grass. Richard reaches the end of the path, notes the pears that are beginning to swell on the tree and turns to walk back the way he has come.

338

The guards waiting near the hall are talking to a trio of women, a noblewoman and two maids. His heart leaps as he recognises his wife and he hastens toward them. Catherine glides forward, one of the maids in her wake; she is smiling but he detects a new strain about her eyes and mouth. "Richard."

He takes her hands, kisses her proffered cheek.

"I had not looked to see you today. This is a fine surprise." He is kissing her hands, reaching out to cup her face, but she pulls away.

"Richard, please. You must listen. I—I have brought someone to see you, but you must be brief." The servant at her side raises her head, stares at him unsmiling, her large eyes swimming with fearful emotion.

"Elizabeth!"

He drops his wife's hands and goes to take his sister's, but Catherine pulls him back.

"No, you mustn't. Keep your attention on me. The queen will hear and speak to you but do not look at her. I do not know how long Ann can keep the guard's attention."

A glance toward the house reveals the other maid servant laughing and chatting with the burly guard. She has thrown back her cloak and is loudly remarking on the glorious sunshine. Richard turns back to his wife.

"It is dangerous, but I am so glad to see you, Bess. Are you well? Does he treat you well?"

"Very well. He is a *good* husband. A good *man*." Her voice has not changed, it retains the lilt, and even in her misery he can discern a hint of laughter beneath the surface. Catherine places a hand on his arm and they begin to walk sedately along the path, away from the house, toward the bower. The queen places herself at her brother's left elbow. He looks at the ground, watches the toe of her boots appearing and disappearing beneath her skirts. He can scarcely believe she is here; there is so much to say, so much to ask, but she forestalls him.

"What happened to you? Where have you been?"

"All over the place; the courts of Europe know me well. They believed me; they would have backed me had fate not turned against me."

"And what then, Richard? What would you have done with me and my children? Locked us in the Tower and let fate take its course? Condemn them to a life like yours has been?"

They stop in the centre of the path and, careless to the danger, face each other. Her face is white and hostile, his is red with confusion but they are so similar, the truth of their relationship is plain.

"I would never harm you, Bess, or your children."

"But you'd murder my husband. Did you start that fire? Did you burn down Sheen?"

"No! Don't be ridiculous. I am watched every second of the day."

"As you are now?"

He turns his head. The maid is leaning against the wall, laughing up at the guard who, abandoning his post, is doing his best to peer down her bodice.

Richard shrugs and all three move toward the relative secrecy of the rose bower. They sit on a damp chamomile seat among fragrant blooms, scattered petals, and at last he reaches for his sister's hand.

"Believe me, Bess. I mean you no harm. I just wanted my birthright but now, now I would settle for my freedom; the freedom to live in peace with my wife and ..." he almost says 'son' but manages to stop just in time.

"You should have settled for that before. Now Henry will never let you go. You will be another Warwick, held captive for the sake of the Tudor dynasty. Henry has dreams of the Tudor line stretching far into the future."

"You could speak to him on my behalf. Tell him you saw me; if you like you can claim I am a pretender, it is what everyone believes anyway. All I want is to leave here with Catherine to live in obscurity."

She looks down at their joined hands. His nails are bitten to the quick, the knuckles large and bony; she remembers the plump white fingers of her infant brother.

"What happened in the Tower? What happened to Edward?"

Richard takes a deep breath, his eyes glazing as he recalls the horror of that time.

"You will recall the uprising when Buckingham made his bid for the throne?"

Elizabeth nods, lowers her head. She has heard of it, of course, but cannot quite recall it. At the time of the uprising she'd still been in sanctuary with her mother, her life in turmoil. Richard continues to speak.

"Well, it was at that time. We knew of the unrest but not the cause of it, and when armed men came stealing into our chamber we took them for our enemies. We fought hard against them and Edward fell, struck his head against the settle. He never got up ..." He runs his fingers through his hair, his fringe flops forward.

"Brampton. It was Brampton who saved me. He threw a blanket over my head and carried me away, took me to Aunt Margaret. She educated me, clothed me, fed me and made me swear on my life to avenge the crimes committed against the house of York. I was lost, Bess. I wanted to come home, to Mother, to you, to England but it was all gone ... destroyed ..."

He stops, a little breathless. "I haven't had a day since when I haven't been schooled, cajoled, and bullied into

341

deposing Henry and taking back my throne. I am not even sure I want it now."

The queen is very still, the only movement that betrays she still lives is the gentle rise and fall of her breast. She turns suddenly, her eyes boring into his.

"Nothing is the same now, Richard. I can never claim you as my brother; you can never take your rightful place in the world. If I speak to my husband on your behalf, he will instantly suspect who you really are and find a way to have you put to death. It is better if you escape. Somehow get away from here to a secret place and Catherine can follow after but, if I help you, you must swear never to attempt to claim my Arthur's throne. The day of York is over. I am of the house of Tudor now. Do you swear it?"

The boy is beaten. He bows his head, almost vomiting the words, "I swear it, Bess."

"I cannot see you again." Elizabeth stands up but he keeps hold of her trembling hand. "Catherine will act as my messenger, until we can get you away."

The boy kisses her hand, reluctant to let go. As she walks away his last sight of her is blurred by his tears.

<u>Westminster Palace —9 June 1498</u>

Richard is alone in the king's closet staring at the open casement, uncertain if he should go or stay. Catherine brought word from the queen, instructions that a door would be left unlocked, but this is a window. It could be another of Henry's lures; the promise of freedom to tempt him from his prison. He throws back the covers and steals forward, looks out into the night.

There is no moon, the garden is wreathed in shadow, the only sound is of the water playing in the fountain; a joyful, buoyant sound. He pushes the casement wider and leans out. It is not a long drop to the ground: ten, maybe twelve feet. The boy bites his lip. He might snap his ankle, break his knee. He pulls it closed again and turns back toward his narrow bed. But the fragrant stench of his comfortable prison sickens him; the sweet herbs and pomanders meant to keep the king's clothes smelling fresh fill him with nausea. With great stealth he begins to pull on his jerkin, searches for his boots. He has no sword and feels naked without one; venturing into danger without a familiar blade at his hip is madness indeed.

One leg over the sill and panic seizes him again. He pauses, takes a deep, shuddering breath. It is now or never, and the thought of living out his days as Henry's lackey, Henry's dupe, gives him the courage he needs. He slowly lowers himself from the window.

The rough ledge scrapes his belly, he clings to the wooden frame, legs dangling and, as he releases his grip, prays for a safe landing. As he hits the ground, his ankles give way and he rolls onto his back, jarring his elbow on the gravel. His landing was loud enough to rouse the guard. He crouches, listening, ready to flee, but there is no sound of approaching feet, no alarm bells ring out. The garden gate will be locked, he tells himself. Like all his other plans he expects this attempt to fail.

It is open. He sidles through it, pauses to scan the palace grounds, straining his eyes for signs of life. It is empty; no movement. He takes no time to consider how unusual this is, he just keeps moving. Driven on, he keeps to the shadows as he runs, his body doubled, crouched low. He heads for the river and begins to follow the course upstream. He has no idea of his direction, no notion of the terrain through which he flees. The need to escape, to finally free himself of Henry's grasp, is all consuming.

He blunders in the darkness, plunges unseeing into puddles and mud. His cap is lost, left hanging on the low slung branches of a tree but he does not wait to retrieve it. His breath comes fast, a pain in his side like a knife, a trickle of blood runs from the knee he grazed in his climb from the window.

With a hand pressed to his aching side he comes suddenly upon the river, splashes through marshy ground and falls to his knees to take his first rest. He looks about him, peering through the semi-dark. A faint stripe of pink bleeds into the horizon, betokening the dawning day. Somewhere a cockerel calls. *I must move on*, he thinks, *but which way? Where do I go?*

Catherine said there'd be a horse waiting, a servant to ride with him to safety. He must have missed him, taken a wrong turn … unless, unless he was not following the carefully laid plans of the queen after all, but a malicious, deceitful trap laid by the king.

Chapter Thirty-Two
Elizabeth

<u>The Palace of Westminster – June 1498</u>

"Summon Catherine Gordon, I would speak with her." The maid curtseys and hurries to do my bidding while I wait in agitation for Catherine to arrive. There is no one else I can confide in, no one I can ask for confirmation.

When she finally enters, remembering the proper genuflection, I can immediately see from the whiteness of her cheeks that the rumours are true. I beckon her close and flick a hand to dismiss my other women. "Sit down," I say, "before you fall down, and tell me if the tales are true."

"They seem to be," she sobs, pulling a kerchief from her sleeve and dabbing her eyes. "Although I don't understand why; why didn't he wait for our instruction?"

"I don't know." My mind races through a dozen scenarios but none of them make any sense. Plans were in hand for a faultless escape; a horse to take him to a ship. He should have sailed far away from England to begin his new life. Why would he leave before I sent the final word?

Since one of my women told me of his departure this morning, my heart has been leaping and starting in my breast as if I am ailing. I am in terror that Henry has known of our plot all along and has forestalled me. Every footstep in the corridor has me starting up from my chair, expecting the king's guard to come and take me to my fate.

"They are saying that the king has sent out a party to seek him. He has set guards at every port and demanded each ship be searched."

"Where will he go?" I whisper, more to myself than Catherine, who has subsided once more into tears.

"If they catch him," she sobs, doubled up in an agony of grief, "they will throw him in the Tower; he will never be free again. All we want is an ordinary life. All he asks for is liberty."

"He should never have come here, he should have stayed in Flanders." I speak through clenched teeth. My head is aching, my stomach rebelling from the early stages of pregnancy.

Catherine sits up. "I would never have known him had he done that; he would never have known what it is to love."

My heart softens. "Even if his freedom is lost, at least he has known that and had it returned full measure. Take comfort from that."

*

When I next see Henry the effect of Richard's escape is very apparent. "You look peaky, Husband," I murmur when he joins me for a private supper.

"Are you surprised? That blasted boy has interrupted both my sleep and my digestion. I swear my belly is full of poison."

I look up, alarmed, but he is speaking figuratively. I pretend a confidence I do not feel.

"They will catch him soon. No man on earth would turn down such a high reward for a felon."

"Hmmm." The king picks over the food on his plate, selecting a choice cut, spearing it with his knife. He chews slowly, watching me, and I feel my cheeks reddening.

"How are you feeling now? Has the megrim passed? When can we expect the child?"

I feign a delighted smile. "Early next year, I suspect. This time it is sure to be a son."

"A royal Duke; an Edward, perhaps ..."

"Or perhaps an Edmund, by way of a change."

A slow flush spreads across his face. He puts down his knife with a pleased smile.

"After my father? That is a good thought, wife. My mother will be pleased; I shall pray for a son."

I breathe a sigh of relief, glad to have regained his confidence. Perhaps he wasn't suspicious after all. Perhaps he has no idea of my attempts to free Richard. I watch him from beneath my lashes as he continues to pick at his dinner. I notice he drinks more wine than usual. A knock on the door and he puts down his cup and calls to whoever is outside to enter.

The servant bows with a flourish. "The Prior of the Charterhouse wishes to speak to you, Your Grace."

Henry shows no surprise, he lifts his cup again and takes a long draught.

"Show him in," he says with a wave of his hand. The prior, Ralph Tracy, edges into the room, genuflects low before his king.

"Well?" says Henry. "What is it, Ralph?"

"Your Grace, I have to inform you that the fugitive, the man calling himself the Duke of York, has taken refuge at the Charterhouse. He begged for shelter, which I promised him but having him safe, I then thought it best to inform you of it."

"Ha! You did well, Ralph." He gets up and embraces the prior, the splendour of his robes outshining those of the Carthusian. "I shall see you are well rewarded." He shouts for the guard, calls for his Uncle Jasper to send a party to apprehend my brother.

"Will you break sanctuary, Henry? Is that wise?"

He turns toward me as the prior disappears through the door, his eyebrows are raised but I can see he is pleased, silently congratulating himself. My pleas for caution will be ignored.

"Break sanctuary? If I have to; after all, it was good enough for your father after Tewkesbury, wasn't it?"

What can I say? There is no defence against that and I can hardly beg for him; I can hardly step from my usual placid role to plead for the life of a pretender. After all, the captive is not my brother.

*

Henry orders the Pretender to be put in the stocks at Cheapside where the common people vent their scorn upon him. At Westminster, still smeared in the detritus that was thrown at him, he is made to repeat his false confession. He is now in the Tower, in a deep dark cell where Henry swears he will see neither the sun nor the moon again. As soon as it is done and my brother is held fast under lock and key, Henry turns his attention to Spain. He panders to their demands, promising Ferdinand and Isabella that it is now perfectly safe for Caterina to come to us.

But, as confident as my husband feels, his health has taken a turn for the worse. He is not ill but he is ailing. His teeth have become troublesome, his hair is thinning and his digestion continues to bother him.

"I am getting old," he growls when I show my concern, but he is not much past forty. I am seized by sudden panic that he will die and I will be left at the mercy of his mother.

"You must let us coddle you a little, Henry. Stay in bed longer of a morning and take more exercise. I shall order the cooks to prepare you a nourishing broth ..."

"You will do no such thing. I am not a child to be swaddled. I shall do well enough; this year has been fraught with worry, that is all. Next year will be better."

His eye drops to my belly, a smile plays on his lips. "We are young yet, plenty of time left. I will give you enough sons for an army of Tudors."

I move behind his chair, drop a kiss on the top of his hair and try not to notice how grey and thin it has become.

"And I will do my best to bring them all forth in safety."

Windsor Castle — January 1499

Before I am confined to my birthing chamber, my cousin Margaret calls to see me. She sinks to the ground, her skirts pooling around her. "Get up, Margaret, get up. What are you thinking?"

She straightens up with a hint of her old smile but I notice she is pale. Is everyone around me ailing? I glance at her belly to determine if perhaps she is with child again. Her son Henry is no longer a baby, it is about time she produced another.

"How are you, Margaret? Keeping well, I hope?"

"Yes, I am well. I—I wondered if you'd seen Edward again? I write to him but he never replies ... well, I don't suppose he can but sometimes I wonder if he has forgotten me."

"He remembered you the last time I spoke to him, I am sure of that. But no, I haven't been. I am reluctant to go to the Tower now."

"Because he is there; the Pretender? Why should that bother you?"

"It doesn't. I didn't mean that. I've never liked the Tower, it gives me the shudders and now I am with child it is important to stay away from such places. I try to think only happy thoughts."

"That isn't easy, is it?"

I look up sharply, try to read her expression, but her face is bland, her eyes shuttered. As I trace my hand across the bulge of my belly I wonder if she ever encountered my brother while he was at court. I wonder if she knows he really was Richard and I have allowed an innocent man to be imprisoned. She seems to deflate suddenly, looks toward the fireplace.

"Everything seems to be going wrong. Did you know that John Welles is ailing, likely to die?"

"No." This is a shock. Cecily's husband is not yet fifty; a strong athletic man who appears to be in his prime. "What is wrong with him?"

"He took a fever, apparently, and now one of the girls is sick too. Anne, I think."

"Oh, my God. Poor Cecily must be frantic." I wrack my brains for a solution but can think of nothing. I feel helpless, wanting to help at least one of my siblings overcome their trials.

"I will send the royal physician. He must have the best care. He is the king's uncle, after all, or half uncle." I summon a clerk who hurries to my presence to quickly dictate a letter for the doctor. "Send it straight away, there is no time to be lost, and when you have dispatched it, come back and I will send a letter to my sister."

When the door closes on him Margaret brings a bowl of fruit from the table and we sit in companionable silence while she peels an orange. She hands me a segment.

"That Pretender; Warbeck. You know there was another one?"

"Another?" The child kicks ferociously. I put down the fruit. "What do you mean?" My mind is racing, my thoughts tumbling in confusion.

"Some fellow has been declaring himself to be the real Duke of Warwick." She shakes her head sadly. "Sometimes I think it is as well Edward will never know the troubled times we live in. Apparently this new fellow claims his real identity was revealed to him in a dream. I am told he was quickly taken up by the guard and they say Henry interrogated him personally."

"Henry has said *nothing* of this to me. What else do you know?"

She shrugs as if she doesn't care, but her eyes are dark, glittering with fear.

"I know he was hung with great haste. Oh, Elizabeth, I fear for my brother. If the king should take it into his head that keeping him alive is too dangerous, what could we do? How could we prevent it?"

She is right to be afraid. My own blood is running cold through my veins. For too many years Henry has kept my family down for no other crime than their Plantagenet blood. Warwick, a child, an idiot boy, is kept in prison; my sisters are married off to the king's most trusted; my brother put to the stocks and then locked away from the eyes of the world. Margaret must also fear for her son, her unborn children who will be too close to the throne for comfort. Sometimes, as much as I love him, it seems my husband is running scared and will destroy us all if we let him. I stroke the dome of my stomach, the nurturing womb that cradles the royal child. It must not be so, I murmur. I will do all I can to stop him.

<u>Greenwich— April 1499</u>

It comes as a great relief when I can quit the confines of the birthing chamber and enter the world again. I have done my duty and the royal nursery is now home to another boy. After a difficult pregnancy, the birth was straightforward and my son born plump and healthy. We named him Edmund and Lady Margaret stands as his godmother—she is proud and honoured to have him named for her first husband. When she greets me she is almost warm as she gives me a prickly kiss and squeezes my arm.

"I hope you are well, Elizabeth. The boy looks healthy. Oh damn, look, he has spewed on my bodice." I smother a laugh as she dabs at a white stain on her pristine gown. "I understand Cecily is returning to your household. It will do her good, she is peaked and wan after her double loss."

"Yes, poor Cecily. It is hard enough to lose a husband but a daughter also …"

I have to stop mid-sentence as grief robs me of words. I have wondered if it is the right thing for Cecily or not. If it were me and I were widowed and lost a child I'd want to stay at home and hug my sole remaining daughter and never let her go. I asked Cecily to join my household more from formality, I hadn't expected her to agree, but Cecily has always enjoyed the hum of court life. Hopefully it will do her good.

Usually Cecily arrives in a flurry of excitement and giggles, but this time she is in my presence almost before

I am aware of her. She seems somehow smaller, lost beneath her clothes, and her dead-white face is pinched beneath an unbecoming hood.

"Cecily …" I rise from my chair and hurry to greet her, holding her for much longer than the etiquette of a simple greeting demands. When she pulls away I link my arm through hers, lead her to the fire and fuss about, offering her food and drink. She waves it all away.

"No. No, thank you. I am quite comfortable."

She doesn't look it.

"Cecily, I am so sorry …"

"Please." She turns her tragic face toward me, her eyes blind with tears. "Don't speak of it. Don't be nice to me, Elizabeth. I couldn't bear it."

"Very well." I fiddle with my rosary, searching my mind for something to say. I am reluctant to speak of Edmund or ask after Cecily's other daughter for fear of reminding her of her loss and making her weep again. Usually when my sisters or my cousin Margaret visit I drag them off to the nursery to admire the children, but that will not do today.

I remember my grief when Elizabeth died; how it would suddenly swamp me like a flooding tide and leave me wretched. She must be feeling the same. I don't know how to help her.

"The king's mother should be joining us soon. She is happy to have you back at court; she is very fond of you."

"And I her." Cecily answers in monosyllables and I can't think of a thing to say. I take up my sewing and then put it down again, remembering it is a tiny bonnet for Edmund.

"Shall we walk in the garden?" I ask, suddenly inspired. "The spring flowers are so pretty …"

"Elizabeth, please. Treat me normally. Don't fuss and bother with me. I need normality. It would be more comfort were you to scold me for not sitting straight or for having allowed too much hair to show beneath my cap."

We stare at one another for a long moment. Her eyes are wide and glistening, ringed with dark shadows. I moisten my lips with my tongue and let my hands fall into my lap.

"Am I usually such a scold?"

"Yes!" She smiles for the first time. "A dreadful scold—worse than Mother."

My chin wobbles. At first I am unsure if it is with suppressed grief or laughter but then the amusement bubbles in my belly, my lips clamp over my teeth as I try to keep it in. Cecily snorts. I look at her, still holding my breath, but then she smiles and, for the first time, I glimpse the old Cecily.

My returning smile is watery as she reaches out to grip my hand tight. "I am still Cecily. I will recover. Just treat me as you always have. Normality is what I need more than anything."

*

The marriage between Arthur and Caterina is to take place by proxy in May at the palace of Bewdley in Worcestershire. For months now the betrothed pair have been corresponding, and I've seen Caterina's competent round handwriting and her hesitant hopes for the match. At least they are of an age; I am not sure how I could have countenanced it if they were mismatched in any way.

I dread the day when I have to send one of my own daughters away to be wed to a stranger, but that is usually the way with princesses. I was lucky. I resolve to be a second mother to poor exiled Caterina and try to coach her on the requirements of being an English princess. That is if she is ever allowed to come.

Ferdinand and Isabella continue to baulk at actually sending her to us. I can understand it is a difficult decision. If it were me I'd not send Meg or Mary until I was certain their future was secure. The latest pretender was dealt with at once; my brother is under lock and key, unlikely to ever see the light of day again. Our throne could not be more secure and Henry is furious with the Spanish for the delay.

"What more can I do?" he rails at me. "I cannot please everyone. I try to be lenient, try to prove myself a merciful king. You know what they require, don't you?"

I shake my head but I do know, I just can't put it into words. They want the realm cleared of all possible claimants to the crown. He looks at me, his eyes clouded, his mouth tense.

"I think you do," he says before leaving me without another word.

Chapter Thirty-Three
Boy

<u>The Tower of London — 1499</u>

The boy sits hunched against the wall and stares at the square of sky high above his head. He craves to walk in the sunshine, feel the breeze on his skin, and inhale the fragrant air. Although it is just a matter of weeks, he feels he has been incarcerated here forever. Careful of his bruises, he lays his face on his raised knees and sighs, tries to picture Catherine's face, remember the soft timbre of her voice. "Dear Catherine," he whispers but his voice, so hollow in the darkness, increases his sense of isolation, his loneliness.

Somewhere in the world he has a son; he imagines him plump and blond, playing in the fresh air with a puppy at his heels. *Does he know of me?* Will he grow up not knowing he is born of a royal prince? Perhaps that will be just as well. No man deserves to be the son of a felon.

The idleness is killing him. He has no books, no instrument, nothing to do but ponder on his sorry life, his useless, futile existence. The only brightness has been Catherine and now she is denied him.

He will never be released from here and can only look forward to a long and slow death. *How will I endure it? What will Catherine do?* She will be shunned as the wife of a pretender, a liar and a braggart. A tear escapes his eye, trickles onto his knee.

The Tower is a noisy place. Booming guns; clanking chains, grinding locks, tramping feet, the occasional cry of a prisoner and, every so often, a lion roars in the menagerie.

Henry has his armoury here. There are constant comings and goings, deliveries of produce, ammunition, fresh prisoners arriving. The Tower is heavily manned, impenetrably guarded. Richard remembers it well from his time here as a small boy. He recalls the excitement of his first few days, his infantile joy in the flea-bitten lions, the roaring leopards, the sounding guns. Later, as he and his brother realised they were prisoners, he remembers fear, a longing for his mother, but then, at least he had Edward.

Together, the princes had hope. Today he is alone, and has none. There will be no stealthy midnight rescue; no big brave Brampton to pluck him from certain death. Not this time. This time he is friendless.

He raises his head and cocks his ear to listen to the approaching footstep. The key rattles in the lock, gruff voices and the door opens, the dark cell lightens to gloom. "I brought your dinner." The gaoler is rough but not unkind, and Richard suspects someone has ordered he be treated gently.

The tray bears bread that is edible, baked yesterday or this morning, a hunk of cheese, and a flagon of wine, which if not the best, is at least palatable. In the weeks he has been here the diet has not varied, but Richard is grateful to be given wholesome food. He has eaten worse.

He begins to tear the bread apart and poke it into his mouth. The gaoler lingers, ostentatiously turning the keys on their ring. "You must be lonely." He sniffs and wipes his sleeve across his nose. "The other fella, Warwick, he is in a cell just below, you might have heard him singing. He gets lonely, too. He is not all there." The gaoler taps his temple and winks one eye. Richard lowers the flagon and wipes his lips.

"Warwick, my cousin."

"Ahh," the gaoler wags a finger. "Not your cousin, is he, my lord? We knows you ain't who you said you was, don't we?"

Richard makes no answer. He could argue that if he isn't the Duke of York, why does the man address him as 'my lord?' He takes a bite of cheese, chews slowly, savouring the strong flavour, wishing there was more. The gaoler sniffs again. "Sometimes, in the clement weather, we lets young Warwick out for a breath of air. Maybe you'd enjoy a turn about the green too, ay?"

Refusing to let himself hope, Richard makes a non-committal comment and turns his full attention to the rest of his meal. When the gaoler shuffles away, the silence falls heavy on him once again and the food loses its flavour.

The patch of sky is dimmer now, the clouds building as night falls. Richard pokes his teeth with the tip of his tongue, trying to dislodge pieces of cheese. Soon, while the royal court prepares for a night of revelry, the boy will settle for the night, stretch on his comfortless pallet and dream of better days.

Having no idea how long he has been imprisoned, one day is much like the next. The same patch of sky, sometimes blue, sometimes grey, and sometimes white. The same boredom. The same fear runs like a thief through his head, robbing him of sleep, robbing him of hope. But this afternoon is different.

When the gaoler comes to remove the tray, a companion is with him. He picks up the empty plate while the other man jerks his head. "Fancy some fresh air?" Richard jerks to his feet, at once wary, suspecting a trap. "We lets all our prisoners out once in a while."

The gaoler ushers Richard along the corridor, down the twisting stair to an outer door. The boy has never heard of prisoners being given any privileges. It must be a trap. He fears an unscheduled execution; an illicit, hole-in-the-wall hanging. Henry would pretend outrage but he'd secretly be pleased.

What will Elizabeth say? The boy does not let that thought take hold; he has long forbidden himself to hope for help from that quarter. She is helpless. She has her own security to look to. He expects no action from her and feels no resentment for her lack of influence on the king. She has her own battles to fight.

The outer door swings open. The boy lifts his arm, shielding his eyes from the sun as he steps outside. He recalls playing on this green; shooting the butts with his brother, Edward, and sulking when he could not best him. They ran races too, before the course of their life was altered. He can still smell the aroma of the grass, see the daisies that starred the lawn, see the beads of sweat on his brother's brow. Those times are past. Edward is long dead, and his own life has been consumed by the need to redress his death.

He has no family now.

"Hello. Have you seen my cat?"

A man, tall and thin, is on his hands and knees at the perimeter of the garden. He is clad only in hose and tunic, his shirt untucked, a grass stain on his rump. "Puss," he calls gently. "Puss." He makes kissing noises with his lips.

Richard recognises him at once. It is his cousin, Warwick, taller, thinner but no more mature than their last meeting. Richard narrows his eyes and tries to calculate what year that was.

"It is a tabby cat, about so-big." Edward kneels up, his head cocked to one side. To all intents and purposes he is perfectly normal. He shows no sign of being an idiot. His eyes are bright and intelligent, his face bearing the traces of his father who was a good-looking fellow. It is as if Edward's mind ceased to function on the day he was taken from his nursery and his life tipped out of control. *We are two of a kind,* Richard thinks. *Only I kept my wits and fought for my rights, while Edward forgot he ever had any.*

Richard perches on the edge of a low wall and after a while his cousin joins him. "He will come back, I expect, when he gets hungry."

Edward smiles brightly and nods his head vigorously. "What is your name? I've not seen you before."

"Richard."

The boy doesn't try to enlighten him as to their relationship. He will not understand. Instead they talk of other things. Cats and kittens; and Edward shows him a drawing, dragging it from inside his tunic, crumpled and grubby from much examination.

For a full half hour the cousins enjoy the sunshine, pick flowers, and stare up past the towering buildings to the wide indigo sky above. Only Richard knows the real width of the sky, the joy of the horizon, the edge to edge blueness of an ocean voyage. Edward, enclosed in his tiny world, knows nothing.

"Goodbye Richard." Edward waves vigorously when they are parted. He returns happily to his cell, chatting to the gaoler of his new friend. Richard watches him go, bites his lip, unrest churning in his bosom. *Why have they been allowed to meet? To what purpose? What is Henry Tudor plotting now?*

*

Two days later, the gaoler lingers while Richard eats his meal. He seems to watch him intently, noting his manners, his bearing, his features. At length the gaoler clears his throat, jerks his head. "My mate and I think you shouldn't be in here, my lord. We don't fink it's fair."

Richard looks up, instantly wary, runs his tongue along his teeth to clear away a few clumps of pappy bread.

"Is that so?"

The gaoler moves closer, squats at Richard's knee. "Indeed, my lord. We was rooting for you before you was taken. I fondly remember your good father, sir."

"Indeed." Richard is reluctant to commit himself and fearful of a trap. The gaoler shuffles closer, lowers his voice.

"We was talking the other night, trying to think of a way to get you out of here and back to Flanders where you can take another shot at the king."

A long pause, pregnant with danger, while Richard considers his answer.

"I doubt the support would still be there. My aunt is all but powerless now and most of Europe now believes I am a fraud. Even the Scottish king has signed a treaty with Henry. No, it is over. Might as well face it."

"Never say die, sir." The gaoler stands up. "I will speak to Tom; see what we can come up with. Maybe you can get your cousin out of here too. Poor fellow, mad as they come but harmless. I'll see what I can do, sir."

The gaoler backs away, relocks the door, and Richard hears him whistling as he tramps along the corridor.

He tries not to think of it; tries not to put his hopes into thoughts of escape. It is dangerous. Stupid. Probably a trap set by the wily king. He closes his eyes, tries to sleep, but images of freedom peck at his mind like a thousand sparrows on a tray of crumbs.

Three sleepless nights, followed by mind-numbing days, and then it happens. The gaoler sidles into his room, hands him a large iron key. It lays in Richard's palm, as tempting as cake to a starving man. Against his better judgement his fingers close around it.

"The way is clear. That key will unlock anything. Tom is releasing Warwick but he may have trouble getting him to leave if his cat has run off again."

Richard watches unseeing as the gaoler disappears through the door, leaving it swinging open. For a full five minutes he stands in a pool of moonlight, thinking; considering the options. If he can only get across the sea, he can send for Catherine; they can send for their son and live an ordinary life. Together. He can stay and rot, or he can run and maybe die; but maybe he would live!

He snatches up his coat, struggles into it as he slides into the night. Following in his gaoler's footsteps he heads through the door, along the corridor, down the stairs. The outer gate is open. He slips silently through it and keeping to the perimeter makes his way to freedom.

The tower precinct is quiet; unusually so but the boy doesn't think it strange. There is only one thing on his mind now—freedom. Bent low, he feels his way along the outer wall.

In the Lanthorn Tower Tom the gaoler tries to persuade Warwick to leave. "Your friend Richard is waiting for you. He will take you to his house. I am told he has lots of cats."

Warwick sits down and folds his arms.

"I am not going anywhere," he pouts like a child. "Not until Puss comes back. She is my favourite. I cannot go anywhere without her."

Richard sweats. It runs into his eyes, down his back, dampening his shirt. He begins to scale the wall that seems suddenly much higher than before. He skins his knee, his fingernails break as he claws a way to freedom. A shout behind him and an alarm bell rings. Footsteps; running footsteps, yelling voices, and burning torches fill the formerly silent precinct with surging life and noise.

"Oi, you! Halt in the name of the king!"

Richard clings to the wall for a moment, wanting to go on but knowing he is lost. He was wrong to have trusted them. He should have known Henry would never allow unreliable men to guard the Tower prisoners.

With grief and self-disgust in his belly, he releases his grip, drops to the floor and rolls to a halt at the feet of the Yeoman guard.

The Tower of London — 23 November 1499

The boy prays. His knees are sore, his limbs aching from the hard cold stone, but he does not cease. He does not pray for mercy, or for a sudden redemption. He prays for Catherine; that once he is gone the king will treat her well and, if it is her wish, allow her to return to Scotland. He prays for his son; that he will enjoy a full and carefree life, never knowing his parentage. He wants his boy to thrive and be free. Royal blood is a curse and a shackle. When they come to call him, he quickly asks God for one other favour.

"Let it be quick, Lord," he prays. "Please make my ending quick."

He steps from the Tower, his hands shackled like a felon's, and squints against the late November sun. *It should be raining,* he thinks. *My ending should be a damp squib, a rat drowned in mud, for the sun never shone on me in life.*

There is no point in resisting. He fights to keep calm as, unworthy to tread upon the face of the earth, he is lashed face down to a hurdle. His eyes are clamped shut as the horse lurches forward; the crowd howls as he begins the interminable journey toward the Tyburn tree.

He tries to focus his mind on higher things. Often, in his exile, he dreamt of riding through London to the adulation of the public. He imagined soaking up their joy as they welcomed their new king home. *Well, I have their attention now,* he thinks.

Instead of rose petals, they shower him in cabbage leaves, rotten apples, rancid carrots and other, unspeakable things. The stench of the gutter fills his nose, the unbearable weight of the people's disgust.

"Pretender!" they scream. "Traitor!" "Son of a cur!"

Oh, my father would not like that.

He is glad his mother has not lived to see this. He hopes Catherine is safe, with Elizabeth in her palace, screened from this terrible day. They will need each other when the news of his death reaches them.

The horse begins to strain uphill. His wrists ache, the ropes about his ankles are tied so tight he can hardly feel his feet. Agony as the cart rumbles over cobbles before lurching to a stop; he hears the sound of footsteps, someone fumbling at the ropes that bind him. The people laugh. "Come on; time to get up."

He tries to stand, a stinking cabbage hits him beneath the ear and his knees buckle, a hand clenches his elbow, holding him up. "Come on, lad."

The gaoler is not known to him. He wonders where Tom and Robert, his counterfeit friends, are. He hopes they are proud of their dirty work. The only comfort he can take is that Warwick stayed behind. He can live on in the Tower, unaware of the wrongs done in his name, oblivious to the life that should have been his.

A path opens through the crowd and he passes through unseeing, his knees quaking as he climbs the makeshift steps. The raucous crowd grow quieter while the rope is tied about his neck.

It will be no noble death. As a commoner he will die by the rope, no honourable death is due to him; the son of John Osbeck of Tournai. What they will do with his body afterwards he cannot bear to think.

A priest steps close and begins to babble in Richard's ear. He jerks his head to dislodge him, as one would a persistent bee. He is done with praying. He made his peace with God in his cell and would rather not express regret to this baying crowd. He has forgotten Henry and the vengeance he will wreak on Catherine if he does not make the required false confession. He takes a breath, the crowd simmer, eager for his words, his perjury.

Richard is to be seen as Perkin Warbeck: a traitor, a coward who has tried to usurp the king's rightful place. The words stick in his throat; the knowledge that he will be remembered only as a failure, a bogus prince.

If he had the strength Richard would argue that, as a citizen of Tournai, a man from Flanders, he cannot, in law, be a traitor to the English king to whom he owes no allegiance. But he says nothing. His fight has gone; he is tired and ready to die.

"I am not an Englishman, but a Picard from Tournai. My name is Peter, I am the son of the late Peter de Osbeth."

He looks out across the massing heads of the crowd. The people he was born to rule have gathered to watch him die; men, women, children, waiting for his blood. He closes his eyes as if to hide from God and tells his lie again.

"I named myself the second son of King Edward; this is not true." He stops, his throat awash with vomit. He swallows, takes another breath. "I ask forgiveness of the king, and any other man I have offended. I am ready now to face my God."

He cannot breathe, cannot fill his lungs with air. He takes one last look at the world before closing his eyes again and waiting for the inevitable. There is nothing more to do.

A sudden shout and a jerk, as a void opens up beneath him. He scrabbles with his feet. He chokes, his head seeming to explode as the rope cuts into his neck, cutting off his air. A warm sensation on his thigh as his hose is soaked in sudden piss, an excruciating pain that fades quite rapidly into nothing.

The rope strains.

Quietly in the November breeze, the boy kicks and turns.

Chapter Thirty-Four
Elizabeth

Margaret screams. She falls to her knees, clasping her hands, begging me to save the life of her brother. *What can I do?* I was unable to save my own, what possible hope is there of securing a reprieve for Warwick? He was captured, halfway across the Tower green, seeking to escape. Or so we are informed.

Richard, or Warbeck as I must remember to call him, was hung two days ago. In the end I begged my husband, I bribed, threatened and pleaded but he would not be moved.

"He is a traitor; he has to die," he said, and then he walked away, leaving me grieving. In all the years since my parents died never, *never* have they haunted my dreams the way they did that night. I have allowed their son to die. I did not do enough to save him. I have failed. And now Margaret is condemning me, too.

Her face is ravaged, her hood fallen from her head, her hair snarled, and her nose running. I offer her a handkerchief, a thoughtless, pointless gesture and she throws it to the floor.

"Please, Margaret, hush. If the king's mother should hear ..."

She looks up at me, rage and disappointment written clearly on her face. She opens her mouth to condemn me again but Catherine intervenes.

"Margaret, it isn't safe. There is nothing we can do, nothing. If there was don't you think we would have saved my Richard? The king and his council will not be happy until all claimants to his throne are destroyed. The Spanish marriage is paramount in the king's mind."

Margaret droops into Catherine's arms and, over her head, my eyes meet those of Richard's wife. She smiles, somehow. I feel I can never smile again. She has been so strong. It is unlikely she would ever have sat back and let her husband commit the crimes that Henry has. She would have made a better queen than I.

I am married to a harsh man, yet I love him still. There is nothing I long for more than to live in peace with him. If I can ever forgive him. Each time I try to move on, to act normally, the face of my little brother rises before me, a face so like Harry's that my heart breaks anew.

I knew nothing of Richard's arrest, nothing of his impending execution until it was over. Henry kept it from me. He claims it was to protect me, to prevent me from being part of it. I consider how I would have felt had I known; what wouldn't I have done to stop it, if I could?

I stand up, smooth my skirts.

"Margaret if you will cease crying I will speak to the king. I can't promise it will do any good but I will try. It is the least I can do."

I leave her in Catherine's arms, still weeping. Catherine lays her face on Margaret's hair. "There, there," she whispers. "Do not cry ..."

*

To my great relief I find Henry alone. He looks up when I enter, puts down his pen and closes the lid of his coffer. "Elizabeth? Is everything all right?"

"You know it is not."

I decide not to beat about the bush. He looks down at his linked fingers with a sigh that speaks volumes. He has no wish for this conversation. I will be lucky to get past the first sentence. I move toward him and perch on the window seat, smoothing an imagined crease in my skirt.

370

"You say you could not spare my ... Warbeck. You say he had to die for the security of our sons and I accept that. The alliance with Spain, Arthur's future, depended on his death."

I keep my eyes fixed upon his. He looks away first, his lips clamped tightly over his teeth.

"Yes," he says and waits for me to continue. I take a deep breath and send up a silent prayer for God's help.

"My cousin is no such risk. He has never made any attempt to defy you before. Margaret and I believe he was searching for his cat, not attempting to escape. You don't need to be rid of him, Henry. Please, spare his life; if you have any love for me at all, spare my cousin's life."

"I cannot."

"You are the king! Of course you can!"

"He is a threat to our throne, our sons. Do you have more care for your cousin than for them?"

I toss my head, speak through clenched teeth.

"He is all but an idiot, Henry. He can never do you any harm. Show him off to Ferdinand and Isabella, let them see he is simple, an infant. For the love of God!"

I am shouting now, standing up, my hands balled into fists, leaning forward and berating him as I never have before.

"That's enough." He stands up, grips my upper arm and turns me around, compelling me to walk toward the door. Before he can push me from the chamber, the door opens and his mother appears.

"I thought I heard voices," she says smoothly. "I am sure the whole palace heard them, too."

Henry's hand drops from my arm, his face flushes.

"We were just having a discussion."

"About Warwick, no doubt."

She turns to me, ushers me back toward the hearth and places a sympathetic hand on my arm.

"Elizabeth, I know it is hard for you. I know you feel betrayed by us, but it is for the best. It is the only thing to do."

"It is a mistake," I hiss. "He is a royal Duke and has committed no crime. The people will not stand for it."

"It is never a mistake to be rid of a rival." She pours a cup of wine, the liquid flowing thickly like blood, and hands it to me. I look at it as if it is poison.

"Henry was your father's rival, and your uncle's. Imagine if they had done the sensible thing and rid themselves of him, your uncle Richard would still be king today. You'd not want a similar situation for your son, would you, Elizabeth?"

Henry, now equipped with his own wine, lifts his cup and quirks his brow waiting for my reply. He seems like a stranger.

"Of course not." My voice rasps, my heart breaks. I put down the cup without drinking and move toward my husband, place my face very close to his. I speak quietly, my words for him alone.

"I have come to love you very much, Henry. You are my dear, dear husband but you have destroyed my family and continue to do so. I have turned the other cheek; I have tried to understand but … not this. Destroying Warwick is like smothering a babe in arms and God will punish you for it. I too, will punish you for it. If you do not spare him, you will never be welcome in my bed again. Any future sons I bear you will be born of rape."

I turn my back, raise my head and walk from his presence without the respect due to a king.

But, of course, Henry's pride does not allow him to seek my company if I do not wish it. With cold dispassion, he executes my little cousin and turns for comfort to another.

*

Catherine Gordon is my sister-in-law and my friend, but now she is my rival too. Before the whole court Henry follows her like a puppy. He laughs at her jokes, showers her in gifts and somehow, although I know her heart is broken, she seems to welcome him. I have never felt so lonely in my life.

Margaret asks permission to leave the court. I miss her visits, miss her company and fear she will never forgive me. I can scarcely forgive myself.

Since finally ridding himself of his rivals I had expected Henry to be in celebratory mood, but instead he seems to shrink. Since I forbade him he does not come to my chamber now, and we only see each other on formal occasions. I try not to mind, try not to miss him, or to care how he is. But, after a separation lasting several days, I am concerned to see him looking peaked and wan.

His mother is at his side, constantly advising, giving her opinion, trying to rule him. Usually Henry is responsive; he enjoys a political debate and has often claimed she has the most astute mind in the court. Today he merely nods and looks glumly about the hall. No doubt he will cheer up when Catherine comes, but when she appears some time later, I notice no improvement in his spirits. He does not dance after supper, he does not engage Catherine in a game of chess and he does not closet himself away with his courtiers. He slumps in his chair, apparently watching the tumbling fools, but he forgets to applaud when they have done.

My concern grows. I catch the eye of Catherine Gordon and she comes to my summons. "Sit with me, Catherine,"

I wave her into a nearby chair. "How is the king? He seems listless and pale."

"Oh." She looks toward the king. "He hasn't said anything."

"Can't you tell? You spend enough time in his company. Is he happy? Is he eating? Is he sleeping well?"

Her face floods, her eyes grow hostile.

"I would describe his appetite as sparse but I think that is natural for him, and as to his mood, he seems to desire comfort, reassurance. As to the last, I would not know. He does not make me privy to his sleeping habits."

She is upset, offended that I have heeded the rumour that she is the king's mistress. I reach out for her hand and she doesn't pull away.

"I am sorry, Catherine, but please, be frank with me. Does the king really sleep alone?"

"As far as I know, Your Grace. I can only confirm that he does not share a bed with me."

Relief floods through me. For weeks now I have lain awake at night imagining him taking his pleasure of her. "That is good to hear." My voice is husky with gladness, my eyes mist over, the room dissolving into moving patches of crimson and gold.

She relaxes a little, looks away toward the dancing. "Are you well, Catherine, is there anything you need?"

"No." She looks down at her lap. "No. The thing I desire cannot be returned to me."

"We have all lost something," I say. "Every one of us. You lost a husband, I lost a brother, Margaret lost a cousin and Henry, well, Henry lost his self-respect."

"And his wife?" she whispers, her words not just a question but an accusation.

A new century, a time for looking forward, but my heart is heavy and I can only look back. I feel old. I am growing stout; my face is showing signs of age, signs of sorrow. Henry, nine years my senior, is ageing too, his health deteriorating. He has trouble with his teeth, and his digestion. Toward the end of last year he spent a few months confined to his chambers. His physician says he came close to death, but Henry dismisses it and claims the doctor is seeking glory for having saved a monarch's life.

Henry has never been more secure on his throne. He should be happy yet he complains constantly of the cold and hunches deep into his furs, huddles close to the fire. In comparison I am well; it is just my spirits that are lacking. I am filled with a sadness I cannot dispel. I try to cheer myself with the knowledge that Caterina will soon be on her way to us from Spain; there will be a royal wedding, celebrations throughout the kingdom. There are preparations to be made; new clothes to be ordered.

But the plague that has raged unchecked all through the winter suddenly comes too close and Henry, always nervous of sickness, orders the children to Hatfield where they will be safe from contagion.

"I think I'll go with them," I say, dreading to think of them so far from me.

"No, Elizabeth. A meeting is arranged with Duke Phillip in Calais, I need you there with me. We will be discussing the betrothal of Mary and Charles."

My heart leaps. Mary is not yet four years old. Although I know that the day will come, it is too soon to even think of her leaving. Planning makes it somehow too real and too close for comfort, but I know better than to argue. I stand up.

"I will oversee the children's packing." I hurry from the chamber, toward the nursery where preparations for the journey are underway. I peek into the room first where Edmund is sleeping. He is sprawled on top of the blankets; his tunic rucked up displaying his round milk-filled belly. His mouth is slightly open, a trickle of drool on his chin. My heart fills with maternal pride but I do not wake him. Gently, I draw the blanket higher. He snuffles and shifts but does not wake. Kissing a tip of one finger I press it to his forehead and tiptoe away toward the main bedchamber.

The first thing I see is Harry, his sturdy legs sticking out from beneath the bed. He is unearthing various playthings and throwing them to Meg who is gathering them in her apron. She sees me first and tips the collection of toys onto the floor and hurries toward me, remembering, almost too late, to stop and curtsey.

She is eleven now and blossoming beautifully. She is quieter than Harry and Mary, and very aware of her status as elder sister. She does her best to mother them although, quite often, she is rudely rebuffed.

"Good afternoon, My Lady Mother," she says breathlessly before coming forward for an informal kiss. Hearing her, Harry gives a shout, bangs his head on the bed, before wiggling from beneath, his hose covered in dust.

"Hello, Mother," he says, grimacing as he rubs the back of his head. "We are going to Hatfield, did you know?"

"I did. I have come to wish you goodbye. I thought we could finish that story before you go."

"Oh yes." He runs to fetch the book as Mary skips in from the other room.

"Mam," she says, using the name she allotted me in her infancy. She makes a clumsy curtsey as she has been taught, before I scoop her from her feet and into my arms.

In a few weeks I am to meet her future husband, arrange the details of the alliance. It is absurd to think of her married to anyone. She is yet so fat, still such a delicious baby. I balance my chin on her head and inhale her fragrance, close my eyes and wish life could always be this simple.

But my reverie does not last long. When Harry returns with the book, Mary wriggles from my lap. Much to Meg and Harry's disgust she refuses to sit still and listen; she runs about the room, ignoring my pleas for her to join us. Mistress Denton has complained in the past that she is headstrong and difficult to handle. I am beginning to see what she means. I watch Mary for a few moments. She throws a soft ball in the air, fails to catch it, and chases it beneath the settle, hampered by her long skirts.

"Oh look, Harry; look, Meg," I say, cupping my hands around an imagined treasure and beckoning them close. "I bet Mary would like to see this, wouldn't she?"

The children, quickly understanding my ploy, join in wholeheartedly.

"Oh, it is lovely, Mother, where did you get it?" Meg gushes.

From the corner of my eye I see Mary sit up, forget her ball, and look in our direction, her curiosity piqued.

"Would you like to stroke it, Harry? Be very, very gentle."

Harry winks at me and bends over my empty hands, making cooing noises, as if he is stroking the most endearing creature ever seen.

Mary takes a few steps toward us.

"What is it?" she demands.

"Come and see," I say. "Before it flies away."

She runs across the room, launches herself at me and I raise my arms, open my hands, fluttering my fingers.

"Oh, it has flown away! What a shame."

I grab her and she yells, realising too late that she has been duped. She wriggles and squirms, Harry and Meg rolling with laughter while, holding her arms so she cannot move, I cover her furious face with kisses.

"I wanted you to sit with me," I laugh. "You are going away tomorrow and I will miss you. Sit with us, Mary, and listen to the stories. You can play with your ball any time."

She submits, becomes limp in my arms, pokes her thumb into her mouth and nestles against my bosom. Harry holds out the book and Meg settles once again close to my knee, and I begin to read.

"In May, when every lusty heart flourishes and burgeons, for the season is lusty to behold and comfortable. So man and woman rejoice and gladden of summer coming with fresh flowers, for winter with his rough winds and blasts causes a lusty man and woman to cower and sit fast by the fire...."

Meg's eyes are bright, she absorbs every moment as if the pictures my words are forming are teeming through her mind. Henry sits bolt upright, his eyes alight with joy but, after a short while, too small for such worldly things, Mary's head nods on my bosom, her thumb slips from her mouth and she begins to snore gently. I lower my voice, Harry and Meg shuffle closer.

These are the moments that make it all worthwhile. My children are the only people that really matter; even cousins, even kings are nothing compared to them.

They tell me the crossing to Calais is smooth but I have never been across the sea before and to me the swelling ocean seems like a tempest. I keep to my cabin, unable to eat or drink, and pray we will reach Calais in safety. I have fifty ladies with me, all adorned in their best, and half the court comes with us; lords, ladies, knights and yeoman all set to make a good impression on Archduke Phillip.

He is married to Caterina's sister, Juana of Castile. Although undoubtedly very handsome, he is rather too grand, too aware of his own importance. They tell me he leads a dissolute life, and from the easy manner he adopts with my ladies it is easy to believe. If my cousin Margaret were with us we would probably mock him in private and laugh at his rather long nose. But since she isn't here I keep my observations to myself and tolerate his conceit with a smile, and the fervent hope that his son is not made in his father's mould. I would never wish that on poor Mary.

Much to Henry's chagrin, the Archduke is more than a little taken with Catherine Gordon. She seems to be in fine fettle; you'd not know she was the wife of a convicted traitor. In public she glows; her gowns, her jewels, her manners are as glittering as a queen's.

When Phillip leads her onto the dance floor, Henry scowls and mumbles something derogatory. I do not ask him to repeat it. Whenever Catherine is in my company Henry never seems to be far away, and people mutter about their friendship. I hide my jealousy beneath a proud smile. This is how my mother must have felt when Father paraded his whores before her. Yet Catherine is no whore and swears she does not share the king's bed, but his desire for her is obvious and hurtful.

Once the dancing is over and we retire to my private apartments, Catherine allows her shield to drop. She seems to wilt and re-immerse herself in a coverlet of sorrow. It is apparent she is not recovering as well as she'd like the world to think. My heart softens. It is not her fault if she has taken the king's fancy; she did not set out to catch him. It is my fault for growing older, for telling him he is no longer welcome in my bed.

The next weeks pass in a whirl of entertainments until I am quite weary of pageants and feasts. By the end of forty days I am tired, and longing for home. I have had news of the children, of course. Arthur has been unwell but his letters say he is rallying now and looking forward to meeting his bride in a few months. The other children write to me too and send me their drawings, and Meg has sewn me a lovely purse that I tuck their letters into as a precious keepsake.

Reports from England say that the plague is under control now, the number of victims dwindling. Henry, when he deems it safe, says we can return to London. He plans a summer progress, but I am not eager for that. I want to be near the children, who are growing so fast I am reluctant to miss a second.

I don't mind the crossing home so much. Perhaps my mind is on the welcome we will receive, the joy of being reunited with our family. Henry and I may have our differences but we share a deep love and joy in our children. We travel straight to Greenwich and plan to move on to Hatfield in the morning.

"Are you not too tired?" Henry asks, and I laugh aloud.

"No, my lord. Never too tired to see our children. I have missed them so much I can barely recall their faces."

"Every time we see them they seem to have altered; Harry is growing like a weed and Meg is less like a little girl and more like a woman every time."

"I know. I wish they would slow down. I wish I could fold them away and keep them as babies forever."

Henry looks up from the letter he is reading.

"Forever? That might be too long. There is much satisfaction in seeing them grow. It makes me feel as if I have at least done one job right. No one can argue that we have not kept the royal nursery full."

I go to bed happy and rise early, eager to make preparation to journey to Hatfield. I have just eaten breakfast and am in the process of getting out of bed when the door opens and Henry enters.

I drag on my robe. "What is it? Henry, what is the matter?"

He is so grey I think him ill. He clutches at the yoke of his nightgown, bunches it in his fist, his face distorted. *It is his heart.*

"Catherine, call the king's physician quickly!"

She runs from the room, the door banging in her wake. Henry slumps onto the side of my bed. "Henry, Henry. What is wrong? Where does it hurt?"

He bangs his chest with a feeble fist and looks at me with despairing eyes.

Don't die, I think. *Don't die, I love you.*

"I am not sick, Elizabeth." His voice is coarse, grating. "It is Edmund."

"Edmund!" I stand up, begin to back away, not wanting to hear it. No, no, not Edmund. Not again, I can't bear it. I fall backwards onto the settle. My women flap about me, fanning me, trying to take my hand.

381

"Get off!" I cry in rage. "Leave me alone. Fetch my clothes and help me dress. I must go to him. I must ride to Hatfield right away. Hurry."

It is not the joyous journey I had imagined. I am not glad to be in England. The countryside that I ride through is glorious and green, the birds singing joyfully. I want to scream at them to shut up. I want to shout at the sky, summon the clouds, beg for a day of dreary rain to match my mood.

Cold, constant, unrelenting rain.

*

His coffin is so small. His funeral so vast. Henry salves his pain by organising a lavish state affair. Our son's coffin, complete with marble effigy, is brought from Hatfield on a black-draped chariot, drawn by a team of six horses. The common people come to watch him pass, they weep at the roadside, and in London the people, led by the Lord Mayor and the guildsmen of the town, line the sorry streets.

My Edmund never had a chance to grow into a proper boy. He was still a baby, had not yet mastered many words or learned to ride his pony. I will never see him grow. I can't bear the pain. Henry and I wait at Westminster Abbey, I try to school my face into acceptance, present a composed face to the world. The funeral dirge rings in my ears, a dirge that will haunt me until the day I die.

They carry him to the altar and some prayers are said, then they take my child, my baby, the second I have lost in five years, and lay him in Edward the Confessor's chapel.

They seal my Edmund in a dark, cold tomb; shut him forever away from the world when he should be playing in a sunlit garden.

Afterwards, when he is closed away, they lead me back to the palace and sit me in my favourite chair beside a cheerless fire. The flames struggle in the grate, as I struggle to breathe.

I will never smile again.

<u>Sheen Palace — Autumn 1501</u>

But I do, of course, smile again. It is my duty and I have other children to think of. Human nature is curious and, almost against my will, I find myself healing, acting and speaking normally. Sometimes I go for long intervals in which I forget to grieve, forget I have lost my youngest son. As October approaches and Caterina's arrival is at last around the corner, preparations gather speed.

Arthur arrives from Ludlow and he and his father ride to meet the Infanta in Hampshire. Henry is almost as eager as Arthur to see her for himself. He will not accept an ugly or malformed bride for his heir; she is the future mother of Tudor kings and as such must be flawless. It seems she is so for Henry and Arthur arrive at Sheen in glowing spirits.

"What is she like?" I ask as soon as we are settled together in the king's apartments.

"She is very fair!" Arthur speaks before Henry has a chance and the king quirks his brow in amusement. "Her face is very sweet and she seems to be of a willing disposition."

"I am glad she found favour with you. When does she arrive?"

"She is travelling slowly to London so the people can get a good look at her and she doesn't arrive in London too tired. Her voyage from Spain must have been exhausting. I understand Harry is to formally greet her and escort her from Kingston to the city."

"Yes, he is very pleased to be doing so and has practiced his welcoming speech so well that he recites it in his sleep."

"I was wondering, Father," Arthur turns to the king. "If perhaps on the day of the ceremony, Harry could escort Caterina into church, if he manages his first task well, of course."

Henry grunts, swills wine around his mouth and goes to speak but, worried that he will dismiss the idea and spoil the afternoon, I intervene:

"Have you seen the improvements your grandmother has made to Coldharbour House? It will be the perfect home to take your bride to after the wedding. Oh Arthur, I am so pleased for you. So excited for the future. After all the woes your father and I have recently suffered, the wedding brings some welcome cheer for us all."

Arthur rises from his chair and moves to the window. "I am excited too," he says. "It is a shame we have to go back to Ludlow so soon. You will scarcely have time to get to know her."

"Oh, we can visit. In the summer I could bring the children. Harry would love that."

Arthur turns from the window. His smile is like Henry's but much cooler. He has never known the insecurities his father suffered and is a mixture of the best of both of us, bearing his father's looks and my optimism.

*

No expense is spared for the wedding of Henry's heir; the future king and queen of England emerge from St Paul's with the bells ringing in their ears. The whole of London celebrates while Henry and I watch the ceremony from behind a screen.

Harry, dressed in silver tissue embroidered all over with gold roses, leads the Infanta to the altar with so much pride he could be mistaken for the groom himself. Impulsively, I reach for Henry's hand and draw him forward for a better view. My heart is filled with renewed affection for him. We have made mistakes, but God is smiling on us again this day. I don't mind taking a back seat for this is Arthur's triumph, and that of his bride. It fills my heart with joy to see them so well-received, and Henry is not afraid to show his pleasure either.

"They will do well together," Henry murmurs in my ear. "Arthur will rule well."

"Yes." I watch our son take his bride's hand and swear to love and honour her, and Caterina, blushing and buxom beside him, smiles up at him with adoration.

From her build and apparent health, she should prove very fertile. I have a sudden image of grandchildren; the royal nursery replete with babies once again. My days of childbearing may be ending but Caterina is still a girl; she has years of motherhood ahead of her.

Harry leads the procession back to the Bishop's Palace for a grand feast, where we eat from gold plates and drink from jewelled cups. As the wine flows the company becomes wilder, and I watch with astonishment when Harry takes to the dance floor. I am amazed at his grace as he leaps and tumbles like an expert. His face is flushed and his hair is sticking to his head like a red cap.

Henry leans forward, frowning, as if to summon him from the floor, but I put out a hand to stop him.

"Leave him, Henry. The people are loving it, look."

And I am right. To Harry's delight, the court moves back to clear the floor, giving the boy centre stage. They clap their hands to the rhythm of the music and cheer each time he makes a giant leap into the air. My son is a natural, if he were not the Duke of York he would make a fine entertainer.

When the night draws to an end, the time comes for the traditional ceremony of putting the newly-weds to bed. Caterina cannot conceal her worry; she has obviously heard some hair-raising stories about our English rituals but, thanks to my intervention, Henry has warned the men not to go too far.

The Infanta is led away by her women to be made ready and Arthur is dragged to his own chamber, red-faced and sweating, by the men of his household.

Poor Caterina, we must seem so strange to her. When Henry rises to hurry off to witness the bedding of his son, I bid him good night. The hall is quieter now. The decorations hang limp, dogs are sniffing beneath the tables for scraps, and servants are collecting cups, and mopping up spilled wine. I yawn and suppress the need to stretch my limbs. "Come along, Anne," I say. "Take me to my bed."

After a week of celebrations, the royal couple leave for Ludlow just before Christmas. After the rigours of the wedding, I am not sure how I will cope with the jollity of Christmas. I see the newlyweds off, hard pressed to conceal my sorrow at their leaving.

"Goodbye, Arthur; goodbye, Caterina, my dear. If there is anything you need, just write to me and I will see to it."

Henry kisses her on both cheeks and we stand together as they mount their horses and prepare to ride away. I raise a hand in farewell and Caterina waves back.

Arthur takes her reins and kicks his horse forward, the Infanta jerks in the saddle but laughingly, quickly regains control. I watch until they disappear from view. She is laughing and chattering to him, her face alight with pleasure and Arthur is smiling back, the feeling in his heart echoed on his face.

Richmond Palace — January 1502

It seems I must prepare to say farewell to all my children. No sooner have we married Arthur to Caterina than it is time to put the seal on the treaty with Scotland.

Margaret is now thirteen and almost ripe to be a bride. Henry has coveted an alliance with Scotland almost as much as he wished for one with Spain. Now it seems all his wishes will be realised.

James is not yet thirty, but I am troubled by reports of his dissolute life and many mistresses. I do not think he will prove a good husband to our daughter, but Henry will not listen to my concerns. But, much to my surprise, the king's mother seems to be on my side.

"The marriage must go ahead," she insists. "But it should not be consummated until Margaret is older. You must insist upon this, Henry."

She fixes him with her authoritative stare. She doesn't need to remind him of her own experience as a child bride in the hands of an insensitive husband.

"Very well, Mother. I shall see a clause is added." That at least comes as some relief, although Catherine assures me her cousin, the Scottish king, is a kind man.

"He is fond of women, Your Grace. He will cherish and spoil Margaret, I am sure, and will want what is best for her."

Somewhat mollified, I begin to school my daughter into the ways of men; it is a difficult lesson and one I do not relish teaching. I see unspoken questions in her eyes and pray she does not demand answers that I cannot give.

Margaret is wise, self-assured and obedient. When the time comes for the formal betrothal, we assemble beneath the canopy of state. Henry and I are seated, Harry and Mary on stools at our feet. Margaret, my little Meg, stands tall and straight before us and when the Archbishop asks if there is any impediment to the union, she replies clearly that there is none.

I am so proud. She is so grown up, so elegant and composed.

"Are you then content and without compulsion and of your own free will?"

"If it please my lord and father the king, and My Lady Mother, the queen."

Meg will not leave for Scotland until September next year, but already that seems too soon. I resolve to spend as much time with her as my other duties allow. My children are slipping away; some go to God, others to husbands and new lives. I worry that she is too little to travel so far abroad, for although our countries are physically attached, the journey there is perilous and long.

Meg takes a great deal of pleasure from the new address that everyone must make to her. From now on she is known as "Queen of Scots," and she is my equal in status. Whenever she is in public her head must be covered and her behaviour impeccable; no more squabbling with her little brother.

There are feasts and dancing and gifts exchanged and, when the ceremonies are all over, I am left feeling empty and sad; but Margaret seems content. She is endowed with more than a little Tudor ambition and seems to relish her new role. She enters into the preparations with alacrity, deciding on her trousseau and overseeing the ordering of it. She makes a list; a crimson velvet gown with cuffs of fur, white and orange sarcenet sleeves, and she asks for a portrait to be made of herself, with the king and I, to present to her husband on her arrival in Scotland.

My little girl is suddenly adult and serious, and I am a little overawed to realise that I have done a good job in raising her.

My father would be proud.

February 1502

Troubles seldom come singly. I am consumed with worry for Arthur's health, for news has come to us that he is ailing again. He has been sickly for some time; nothing specific, just a general weakness of the limbs and his pallor is wan. Coming so soon after his wedding, gossip begins to circulate that he is indulging too much in the marriage bed. This is, of course, ridiculous, but I have learned that royal families are never free of speculation and rumour. If Arthur was to neglect his marital duty to Caterina they would say he wasn't fully a man; now he is obviously taking pleasure in his new role of husband, they criticise him for doing so.

I pray for his quick recovery and send two priests on pilgrimage to make offerings on my behalf. When I lost Edmund, I saw it as God's judgement on us for our treatment of Richard; I am not prepared to let anything happen to Arthur. He is our prince, our heir, and represents his father's hope for the future. His megrim fills me with terror that it may be something more.

I want to discuss it with Henry, express just how culpable I feel, how afraid I am that we are to be punished. But the king is busy with state matters, his henchmen busy making arrests and imprisoning suspected traitors in the Tower. At first I take little notice, I am too concerned for Arthur who is so far away. But then Cecily brings the matter to my attention.

I notice she is restless and cross about something. It is not like Cecily not to make loud complaint should something be troubling her, but all I have heard from her for the last half hour are gusty sighs and a lot of fidgeting.

"For goodness' sake, Cecily. What is the matter?"

She opens her eyes wide. "You mean you don't know? Doesn't the king tell you anything?"

It is my turn to sigh. I tighten the rein on my conscience.

"I haven't spoken to Henry for a few days, so why don't you tell me? It is clearly troubling you."

"He has excommunicated our cousin."

"Suffolk?"

"Yes."

I am so tired of this fighting. The wars should be over. Why can they not see it? My cousin is close to the throne, his elder brother John was made my Uncle Richard's heir, killed at Stoke battle soon after Henry came to the throne. Although he has kept an eye on him, Henry has allowed Suffolk to be an active participant at our court.

He was with us in Calais last year and more recently at Arthur's wedding. He is a popular, good-natured fellow and I had thought him Henry's friend, but it seems he has been harbouring resentment all along. He fled in high dudgeon to the court of Maximillian in Austria, who has let it be known he'd aid anyone with a drop of York blood should they wish to contest Henry's crown.

I sigh deeply and put a hand to my forehead. I have been suffering from headaches lately and whenever I hear bad news or something upsets me, it begins to bang in earnest.

"Henry should have made him Duke, as was his birthright. If he had really trusted him, Suffolk would have been loyal, if only for my sake. I am sure of it. Nobody desires war."

"Well, that isn't all, Bess. Other men have been taken to the Tower, our sister's husband among them."

I raise my head, stare blankly at Cecily.

"Who? You mean Will? Oh for heaven's sake, what had he to do with it?"

Cecily shrugs. "I think they have taken up his friends, whether they are involved or not."

"And our sister, Catherine, have you seen her? How is she?"

"I don't know. I was hoping you'd know better than I."

"I will summon a carriage we must go and see how she is."

"Shouldn't she come here? Henry might not like you venturing into enemy territory."

"I hope Henry will not hear of it, and besides, he isn't that unreasonable. Once I explain, I am sure he will relent and free Will. He can hardly execute my brother-in-law."

"He killed your brother ..."

I pretend not to hear as I busy myself preparing for a short journey to Warwick Lane, where my sister lives with her family.

I find her in a state of disarray. She is in the hall, pulling on her gloves. She almost falls when she sees me.

"Elizabeth, I was just coming to see you. You must help us."

I take her proffered hand and we move into the front chamber. Her servants are tidying up, a child is screaming on the upper floor. The house resonates with fear. "Please, Sister, speak to the king. Will has done nothing against him."

"I will, I promise. I will do what I can but, you must know my influence is not great. Perhaps if I speak to his mother first …"

"How can he lock a man away for having the wrong friends? We did not know what Suffolk was planning. You must make him understand, Elizabeth."

"I will try. Is there anything else you need? Do you have money?"

"No. Not enough, not now."

I hold out a hand to Cecily and she places a purse in my palm. I pass it to Catherine. "It is all I have just now. I will try to arrange an allowance for you until Will is released, but I do not have a vast amount."

"And Bess already gives so much to charity." Cecily takes a seat beside Catherine on the settle, but I remain on my feet. A feeble shaft of sunlight finds its way through the window, showing up the dust that lays like despair in the corners. My sister needs looking after; better servants, a decent nursemaid. The child is still crying upstairs, the former distress turning to anger.

"What is wrong with your child?" I demand. "Why doesn't his nurse see to him?"

Catherine shrugs. "She left, as soon as she found out about Will. She was unwilling to stay in a house of traitors...."

She dissolves into tears. Cecily pats her hand and I turn on my heel, hurry up the stairs in search of the nursery.

A child is on the floor, unattended, her face wet with tears, her nose streaming with snot. She stops bawling when she sees me and sinks her chin to her chest, tries to hide her face. Her cheeks are red with what looks like a teething rash.

"Hello," I say, misremembering her name. "What's the matter with you?"

I hoist her into my arms, my back protesting at her weight, and balance her on my hip while I wipe her nose with my best kerchief. She snivels, her chest juddering, and looks at me from large wet eyes. She reeks of piss and her skirts are damp. "Where is your brother?" I ask, although she can make no reply. After opening various doors in search of her sibling, I carry her downstairs. Catherine barely looks up.

"We must arrange care for the children, Catherine. You can't go on like this. Come back to court with me; you can have lodging close to mine and I will find someone to care for them. Where is your son?"

"In the kitchen probably." She wipes her eyes and stares up at me tragically. "He goes there a lot."

"Fetch him, Cecily." I send a servant to find outdoor clothes for the children and bear them all home with me.

On our arrival back at court, I am beset with a further worry. Cecily tugs at my sleeve and begs a private audience which I grant readily, surprised at the formality of her request. She is barely seated when she leans forward and begins to speak rapidly.

"Elizabeth. Did you know that some of Will's friends have been taken up as well?"

"Yes, of course I do, why?"

She sits up, checks that there are no servants close enough to overhear.

"One of them, Tyrell, Sir James Tyrell, has confessed to the murder of our brothers in the Tower, in 1483."

At first I do not comprehend the meaning of her words. She must be mistaken. I know my brothers' fate. I know that Edward died an accidental death at the Tower during Buckingham's uprising, and that Richard escaped. He died a felon's death, just last year. What can this mean?

"I don't understand ..."

"Oh, Elizabeth, stop pretending! You know as well as I do that Richard survived. Warbeck's identity was as plain as the nose on my face. He was no pretender. I saw him myself."

"You did? You never said."

"No, I never said. I have learned that in this court, it is best to keep one's own council."

She sits back and waits for me to speak, the only sign of agitation her fidgeting fingers in her lap.

"I don't know what this means. Have you spoken to the king's mother?"

"No."

"Then please don't. Keep this knowledge between ourselves."

"I don't understand why a man would confess to a crime he did not commit. He must know the penalty will be death."

"Unless he has been tortured, or promised otherwise ..."

I cannot bear to think that Henry would go this far to prove that the man he hung last year was a pretender. It is a clever ploy. He wants to be rid of Tyrell, just as he wanted to be rid of Richard, and by concocting this story he can justify the judicial murder of both. But I am sure that such actions will not be condoned, not by God and certainly not by me.

Greenwich Palace — March 1502

It is all becoming too much. I cannot turn around without stumbling across some fresh disaster, some new mischance. I want to ride to Ludlow to be with Arthur, to discover for myself the extent of his illness. I write to Caterina asking for news of him and she sends straight back to me, reassuring me that he is on the mend and was well enough to wash the feet of fifteen poor men on Maundy Thursday, as is tradition.

The physicians recommend plenty of rest, and as much food and fresh air as he can get. Caterina promises she is doing all she can to ensure he follows the advice. Her words mollify me a little, but I send back a note full of motherly advice for his treatment. I am halfway through composing it when the door opens and Henry comes in, holding a letter. I put down my pen.

"What is it?"

"A letter from Rome, regarding the canonisation of Henry VI. You will recall I spoke to you of it."

Henry has been pursuing this idea for months now; you'd think he could find more important things in this time of crisis. I sit up, ready to listen with feigned interest. He drones on about the late king's goodness, his charity, his piety, and all the time his unspoken accusation screams in my ears.

My *father* had the old King Henry put to death. He was a rival, a claimant to the throne with many followers, just like my brother was, just like Suffolk is. It is Henry's way of illustrating that he has no option, no choice. But I ask myself how many more must die for the sake of a gilded chair and a circlet of gold?

*

While the king is occupied with worldly things I am beset with worry about my son, about God's opinion of our rule. I am tormented with fear that He may seek vengeance upon us.

I send up prayers, I make offerings, I send money I cannot afford to the church, to charity, to the aged woman who was once a nurse to my little brother. And when I am alone, I wring my hands, as close to despair as I have ever been.

I need a break, some respite from court, from Henry, from the constant fear that haunts me. I break into his conversation and he stops, his words suspended to hear me speak. "I am going to spend a few days with the Daubeneys at The Hospitaller's House. It is quiet there, a retreat from all this madness, but I will be close enough should I be needed. I am sure they will welcome me."

"Oh."

He looks away. He is surprised and stutters a few words, approving my request as if I had asked his permission.

I have escaped to The Hospitaller's House before in time of need. It is at Hampton, on the edge of the river; a moated house with lovely gardens. Since they were given the lease, the Daubeneys have spent much time and money improving the place, but it retains a sense of monastic peace. It is that peace that I need, in a place where I can feel close to God and perhaps appease His anger a little.

Greenwich Palace – 4 April 1502

I have not been gone for more than a fortnight but it seems I have been missed, for Henry greets me warmly on my return. My husband excuses himself from council to share dinner with me in his chambers. The firelight, the soft music, and the undulating curtains at the open window recall our earlier days when I still had hopes of romance between us.

He smiles at me above his raised glass. "It is good to have you back with us, Elizabeth. We have missed you."

At moments like this it is easy to forget his previous sins. He is a charismatic man when he sets out to be. I look around the chamber. It is masculine and comfortable, open books on a side table, a lute left on a chair, his dog sleeping before the fire. I realise I have missed him too; as much as he sometimes enrages me, it seems I would not be without him.

"I am sure there were plenty to keep you company."

He chooses to ignore my hinted accusation. I can see no sign that a woman has been with him but, in my absence, Catherine Gordon will have seen to most of his needs. I am always afraid that the day will come when she eventually capitulates. He is, after all, a king.

"Can we go to see Arthur?" I blurt the words out when I had planned to lull him into a good mood first and then make my request meekly. He puts down his wine and sighs.

"I am busy this week but perhaps we can travel to Ludlow on Tuesday next."

For the first time in what seems like an age, my smile is genuine. It reaches my eyes. I can feel my jaw ache, my lips almost splitting with the unaccustomed expression.

"Thank you, Henry. I was so afraid I would have to go alone."

When we have eaten our fill, the trenchers are removed and our wine glasses refilled. We move from the table to sit at the hearth and, as is my habit, I sit on the floor, close to the fire and watch the images in the flames.

The black and red heart of the fire is like a living story book, inhabited with goblins and dragons. Henry sighs, stretches out his legs. It is growing late and I should really go to bed, but I am reluctant to leave. I want Henry to ask me to stay. I want him to put his arms around me, offer me his comfort and his body.

I straighten my back and swivel around so that most of my weight is on my right arm, for the left has lost all sense of feeling. Really I should face the fact that I am getting too old to sit on the floor.

Henry sighs again and shuffles his feet and I am tempted to shift my position so I can lay my head upon his knee. But I cannot be so forward. If he desires me, he will have to ask.

I open my mouth to ask how his communication with the pope is going when we notice a disturbance outside the chamber. The king puts down his cup and I sit up, wondering who would disturb the king so late.

We expect to see his attendants, perhaps the gentleman of his bedchamber come to put him to bed, but the figure that emerges from the gloom wears the sombre hues of a friar. I recognise him as the king's confessor.

He takes two steps into the room, stops just outside the ring of firelight. He seems to tremble. His hands are tightly clasped, his fingers digging deep into his flesh.

"What is it?"

Henry stands up, takes a step toward him and then stops, half turns and reaches for my hand. Slowly, I struggle to my feet. Henry's hand is cold; his fingers dig into my flesh. We both know, without being told, what news the confessor brings.

"Your Grace. I am afraid ..." He stops; I see the fear in his eyes, the utter regret of the words he must speak. "We have had news from Ludlow." He pauses, clears his throat. "It seems that after a lengthy battle, your son, the Prince of Wales ..."

"No." Henry slumps into a chair, his head to his hand, defeated before the words are out.

"... has departed to God."

The friar looks at me helplessly, bows his head and begins to pray, mumbling about God sending us good things so that we may endure the bad.

My mind is screaming: *when in all my life has God ever sent me one good thing, and allowed me to keep it?*

I cannot speak. I cannot move. I am rooted to the spot; my knees tremble, my head is reeling, my stomach curdling. Madness beckons.

And then, the king's mother is there. She is in her nightgown, her hair in a long thin braid. She appears suddenly old, her eyes are red, her face as wrinkled as a dried up grape.

"Send for the queen's women," she commands as she takes me by the arm and gently leads me to a chair. She pushes me into the seat. Slowly, I look at her and wonder who it is that is crying such heartbroken tears. I turn my head and see it is the king.

Henry's head is buried in his folded arms, his back is heaving. He is crying as loudly and as angrily as a thwarted child, harsh, anguished sobs that are breaking my heart. Lady Margaret abandons me and moves to his side, runs her old woman's fingers across his back.

"Hush, my love," she whispers. "Hush, my son. Tears will not help."

"Nothing will help," I say, and we exchange hollow glances, my eyes locked in hers. Tears are tracking down the grooves of her furrowed face. I never thought to see the king's mother cry.

They are all weeping. The father confessor, the king, the king's mother, my women, who come racing through the door to bear me off to bed. Everyone is shedding tears.

But my own eyes are dry. My head is clear, my mind as sharply honed as a bloodied knife. I can see the bleakness of my future, the futility of my past. My heart is quite broken but I am too wounded for tears.

I want to sleep. I want to bury myself away, close myself off from the world and curl myself into a ball and give in to the cloying misery. But I can't. I am queen of England. Henry though, forgets he is king. For the first time in seventeen years, he ignores his status and collapses into an orgy of grief. I am alone in my apartments when the king's mother comes to me. She still bears visible signs of sorrow, she is swathed in black, the only relief to the darkness of her figure is her parchment white face.

"Elizabeth." Her voice is cracked. She sinks into my chair without permission and, resting her elbow on the arm, rests her head in her hand. "You must go to him. He will not respond, even to me. He needs to see that your hurt equals his and that Arthur is not his loss alone."

She has healed enough to speak his name. I cannot bear to even think it. I place a hand on her shoulder and walk from the room. In a sort of trance I glide along the passages, servants and courtiers falling to their knees at my approach. The whole palace wears an eerie air of sorrow; it is as if we are all enchanted. There is no noise, no music, no laughter, just an awful strained, painful silence.

But, as I approach the king's chamber, I hear one sound; the rasping, heart-wrenching sound of a defeated man.

I open the door.

Henry, still in his night clothes, is alone. He sits at the table, his plush velvet gown open, revealing sumptuous night-rail. He has pulled off his cap and thrown it to the floor and his thinning hair is standing up like a crown. He does not look up when I enter.

"Henry," I say, but still he continues to weep. "We should comfort one another, Henry. He was my son, too."

When he finally looks up his eyes are red, his face as white as his linen.

"He was more than a son," he says, with almost a snarl. "He was my prince. The royal flag; King Arthur come again; the proof of God's favour upon us and now ... now, there is nothing."

"There is Harry. He will be king now. Think of it, Henry the Eighth—it has a good sound to it."

My voice does not sound as convincing as my words.

"He was always your favourite."

"Henry! That is an awful thing to say, to suggest that I ..."

He waves his hand to silence me but I am done with his self-pity. "I loved Arthur just as well as the others. He was my first born, my salvation! If I have not been as close to him as the others it was because *you* sent him away. It was more important to you and your mother that he was raised a prince ... but he was my baby, my little boy, and you sent him away. If he hadn't been in Ludlow maybe ..."

I stop there. I will not follow the path of recrimination, of blame. The breath leaves my body; quite suddenly I can fight no more. "Henry, *share* this with me. We have lost our son; we should not fight, not now. We need to hold each other up. Henry ... I am *broken* ..."

I am on my knees, folded up, my arms crossed around my middle, where the pain seems to be seated. It is not my heart that is aching, it is my gut; the womb that nurtured him is mourning, screaming for him. I groan aloud. I cannot breathe. I cannot fill my lungs. In the periphery of my vision, bright lights and colours begin to conglomerate. I rock back and forth, a dirge of longing that begins somewhere in the back of my throat.

And then I feel a hand on my hair. I raise my head, turn into my husband's arms.

"Why does God punish me so?" Henry whispers. "What have I done?"

Pushing away a sudden vision of my brother, and my cousin Warwick, I grip the back of his gown and the plush red velvet is soft beneath my fingers. The bones of his shoulder dig into my cheek and my legs are cramped, but I do not move. As we rock back and forth on the floor before the king's hearth, I recall that this is the very spot were Arthur was conceived.

"I can give you another son, Henry. You still have an heir and I will bring forth another ... if you will let me."

*

I am ailing. The court is swathed in black damask; each lady has a handkerchief to her eye and every gentleman a sorrowful demeanour. Grief is like a tightening band around my chest. I go through the motions of being queen. I speak, I walk, I eat, yet all is undertaken with a terrible weariness, a reluctance to go on.

Even little Harry is sad. When I see him, after the formalities of greeting and offering condolence, he snuggles up for a cuddle. I rest my chin on his head and stare into the flickering fire.

"So I will be king then, Mother," he says after a long period of uncharacteristic silence.

"Yes. Perhaps, if Caterina is not yet with child, one day, you will. You must work harder now at your lessons just in case."

He frowns. "I would rather continue to be Duke of York. It is hard to be a king, I think. It makes you frown."

"Frown?" For the first time since the news came I find a small bubble of amusement fermenting in my belly. I should have come to see Harry sooner.

"Well, Father frowns and always has some worry or another. I think I would prefer to be a prince, or perhaps just a knight. I want to learn to joust and be a champion of the field."

His round red face is earnest, his enthusiasm for his sport belying the mark of dried tears on his cheeks. I ruffle his hair.

"You can be a champion jousting king then, my love."

"Can I? Is that allowed? Father doesn't joust."

"Father doesn't care for it. My father jousted in his younger day, when he wasn't waging war."

"Did he? Tell me about it."

He settles back and I begin to speak of my father, of long past days before I was even born. Stories he told me of his glorious youth. Harry listens with shining eyes, his arms clasped around his knees, his red hair glistening in the firelight.

The one good thing to come from Arthur's death is that Harry will not now be sent away. Last year Henry set plans in motion for Harry to take up his own household at Codnore Castle in Derbyshire; a long way from court. It was an idea I hated from the start and, sneakingly, I am glad that he will now be staying.

<u>May – June 1502</u>

The annual calendar of the court does not allow for royal grief, and our duties continue. I present a brave face to the public but, in private, I throw off the deception and my sorrow becomes almost a comfort. Henry spends more time with me. We seem to absorb each other's grief, salve one another's pain, and he makes love to me with a desperation born of fear and regret.

Soon I am able to ease his sorrow further with the news that another child will be born to us in February. Although nothing can bring Arthur back, the knowledge of a new baby lifts our despair—just a little.

For the first time in months I begin to see the good in the world and, although I am not filled with joy, I can at least find a little pleasure in the gardens, and the sunshine. But then I hear the news that Tyrell has been convicted of treason and executed. I know without doubt that Henry has condemned and executed an innocent man. My emerging happiness is crushed and my newfound faith and love for my husband plummets again.

How can I trust him? How can I ever have faith in him when his duplicity is so transparent? I have the overwhelming urge to run away, but queens do not run away and, besides, there is nowhere for me to run.

*

From the start, my pregnancy is fraught with trouble. I suffer sickness as severely as when I carried Arthur. The king's mother assures me this is because I am carrying another boy, and I pin my hopes on that. A boy is crucial for Henry's stability, Henry's dreams for the future.

The king tries to forget his trials by burying himself in state business. He persists in his attempt to secure sainthood for the old king Henry VI, and have his remains moved to Westminster. I indulge myself by continuing with the plans for a remodelling of Greenwich Palace.

I intend to have a private riverside residence for myself with a garden and orchard. I crave somewhere to escape to when I wish it; a place where I can be quiet, away from court, away from the public eye, somewhere to be myself. A place where I can think.

My privy purse is quite empty so I order my old gowns to be turned and made larger to accommodate the growing child. For a while I contemplate cancelling a planned progress into Wales, but my need to be away from court is too great. I *want* to go. I rebuff the king's mother's advice that I am overtired and not as well as I should be. The strange impulse to quit the court will not be denied.

Spain is trying to persuade Henry to send the Infanta home. At first he says she is still too unwell, too grieved to travel, but he summons her from Ludlow and insists she stay at court.

Poor Caterina; her status is altered. She is no longer the Princess of Wales, the future queen. She is an impoverished widow, a dowager princess, and the court no longer falls over themselves to oblige her. Where once she was showered in gifts and affection, now she is largely forgotten.

I wish Henry would agree to send her back to Spain; she has her whole life before her, but he refuses. He is reluctant to part with her dowry or to lose the bargaining tool she represents. My concerns are raised further when the Spanish ambassador proposes a match between Caterina and little Harry.

Enough time has passed now to be sure that she does not carry Arthur's child. Although I am shocked to hear it, Spain is declaring that she is still a virgin and her wedding to Arthur unconsummated. Only Caterina can know that for sure but I remember the post marital joy of my eldest son, and the reports that came to me the next day of him having enjoyed his night 'in Spain.'

Poor Harry, to be saddled with his brother's widow. I hope it comes to nothing. I have more care for Caterina and Harry's future happiness than I have for state politics. As fair as she may be, she is almost six years Harry's senior and I rather suspect that, like my own father, my son would prefer to have the choosing of his own bride.

My head is whirling with too many problems. Every day I receive news, worse than the day before, and on a sunny morning in May my husband comes storming to my chambers, rousing me from sleep.

"Did you know of this?" he bellows as I drag myself upright in my bed.

"Know of what?" I squint at him, holding up a hand to block the sun that is streaming in through the open shutters. "What has happened now?"

He thrusts a piece of parchment at me and I frown at it. The hasty scrawl seems to be by the hand of one of Henry's informants, one of his spies. I have to read the content twice before I can make sense of it.

"Oh no ..." My heart sets up a heavy thud. I put my hand to my chest and stare up blankly at Henry.

"You didn't know."

It is not a question. He can see from my reaction that Cecily has not taken me into her confidence. If only she had done. I would have tried to help her. Now, I know without being told that she will need all the help she can get.

"Who is this man?"

"This man is nobody. Just a self-seeking social climber looking to bed a princess."

"You make it sound worse than it is. They are at least legally wed. At least that is better than her becoming his mistress."

"How can it be worse? She is your sister. She is a royal princess and a Viscountess, and she is acting like a trull, sullying herself with a man of the lowest degree."

I begin to suspect he is secretly enjoying the disgrace of yet another member of my family.

"Not the lowest degree surely, Henry. You are overwrought, and not thinking it through properly. It is true it is an unwise marriage, but he is a respectable knight. I can't imagine Cecily forming an attachment for a common man."

He scowls at me, his lips tight.

"She must be punished. She cannot just marry whom she pleases. I will not have my subjects disobeying me.

She has deliberately gone behind my back to consort with this ... this ..."

Words fail him. I throw back the covers and begin to slide from bed.

"I will discover the truth of the matter, Henry. Then we can decide what is to be done."

"I have made my decision. I am done with people overriding my authority. I am the king. She will be banished from court and her late husband's lands and wealth confiscated. I will not have it, I tell you."

I watch him quietly. There is no point interfering. He will not listen. He will go his own way and, if that entails the destruction of my entire family, it will not deter him.

There are so many problems, so many worries that my head sometimes reels with the weight of them all. I need time to come to terms with everything that has happened. I long to get away; I want to escape court, escape politics and most of all, at this moment, I want to escape Henry.

<u>July 1502</u>

People are grumbling that it is a mad idea for a woman in my condition to travel so far, but I am queen. Only the king can forbid me, but he seems content that I should go. Perhaps he is as glad to be rid of me as I am to leave.

I give orders for my lying-in chamber to be made ready at Richmond. By the time I return from Wales, my confinement will almost be upon me. Perhaps things will be better after my son is born; perhaps we can rebuild our marriage then.

At the last moment I decide to take my sister Catherine with me. She is still smarting after the arrest of her husband but, since Henry has not yet ordered his execution, we both harbour hopes that William Courtney's life will be spared. To ensure that he is offered as much comfort as is possible in the chilly damp confines of the Tower, I order winter clothing and warm bedcovers to be sent for him.

Catherine is grateful and as we set off toward Buckinghamshire we are both in reasonably good spirits. I feel sickly and bloated but it is pleasant to be away from court, to feel the fresh air on my face again. The countryside has a healing quality and even Catherine looks a little less peaked by the time we reach Notley Abbey.

The Abbot's lodging is comfortable and, as always, the victuals are tasty indeed. I eat more than I've been accustomed to of late, and then Catherine and a few of my ladies settle down for a comfortable evening in the chamber.

Anne takes out her lute and begins to play, and after a while Dorothy begins to sing in accompaniment. I am as close to contentment as I've been since we received the news of Arthur's death. I lay my head back and close my eyes.

When a servant enters with a letter, nobody pays him much attention. He hands it to Catherine with a bow and hastily quits the chamber. My sister moves toward the fire where the light is greater and tears it open.

There is no one close enough to catch her when she falls. I leap from my chair, my head spinning at the sudden movement. Catherine is lying like a broken flower on the hearth. My ladies gather around her, their frightened cries like a flock of startled birds.

He has done it, I think. *Henry has waited until our backs were turned and taken the first opportunity to have Will Courtney killed. Poor, poor Catherine.* I pick up the letter that has fallen from her hand and begin to read it. My hand is on my chest, it creeps up to my neck, and my throat fills with grief. The words stand out harshly against the page; the news is even worse than I had imagined.

Little Edward Courtney was just five years old and too young to die. Lately, everyone's attention has been on his father; no one noticed that the child was ailing. The news of her son's death compounds Catherine's existing grief and brings her down heavily. She begs leave to return to Havering for the arrangements for his burial and, of course, I grant her request. I give her my warmest cloak to wear and promise to pay for the funeral, no expense spared.

As she rides away I stand at the window and watch her grow smaller; a tiny black figure on a large white horse. *When will it stop?* I wonder. *When will my family cease to suffer?*

*

We have not travelled very much farther when I fall sick. I am just too weak to carry on. My ladies create a great fuss, declaring I should have listened to the king's mother and stayed in London. Ladies in a gravid condition have no business gallivanting around the countryside, having fun. I am too sickly to argue or order them to be quiet, so I just lie back.

I am breathless and tired, the least exertion too much to even think about. A physician arrives from court and plies me with a foul concoction. I do not dare ask him to enlighten me as to the ingredients but swallow the physic obediently and stay in bed as he advises.

The next week or so is spent resting and praying. There are so many souls, both living and dead, to pray for. I send offerings by proxy to many shrines and churches, and pay five priests to say five masses for Arthur's soul and for the safety of my unborn child. I need all the heavenly help I can muster.

It is August before I am well enough to continue, and we make leisurely progress toward Monmouth, resting at the Forest of Dean. At Monmouth I present the prior with a red chasuble, embroidered with the finest work, and a cope embroidered with the Assumption of the Virgin. I cannot shake the belief that if I can only appease God, perhaps bad fortune will stop afflicting both my life and that of my kin.

Apart from the infirmities of pregnancy, the longer I am away from court the more pleasant life becomes. I begin to forget the conflict of loyalty, my overbearing mother-in-law, my difficult and demanding husband. I play cards with my companions, winning far more than usual and revelling in the unexpected boost to my coffers. I am always short of money; there are so many demands on my income. I have a large family to support and, if I can, I never turn down a request for financial help.

But my primary role is that of queen and my duties cannot be entirely forgotten. I hear regularly from court. Henry is still delaying the return of Caterina to Spain, and I am pleased to learn she is now recovering from a recent megrim. Once my child is born I plan to befriend her, perhaps take her into my own household. She must be so lonely, so disappointed that all her plans have come to nothing.

As I pass through various counties, I am sent gifts of oranges and pomegranates for which I have developed a passion. In Henry's absence I am at liberty to encourage the devotion of the people. It is good to hear the odd cry of 'A York!' as I pass through the busy streets.

By the time I return to London my condition is visible, even in the looser gowns I am now forced to wear. To my physicians' concern my ankles and hands are swollen and my face is puffy, but I feel better in myself. It is as if the fresher air has gone some way toward repairing my injured spirits.

One of the first things I do when I return to Richmond is to visit the lying-in chamber to check that all is in readiness. If I have to be confined in a dark room for weeks on end I am determined it shall be as pleasant a room as possible.

A new richly-hung bed is in place, the hangings embroidered with red and white roses, edged with satin. I begin to look out for suitable nursery staff, cross-examining the applicants myself and asking for their previous experience.

But it is the children I am dying to see. Since I am too tired from the trip to ride straight away to Eltham, I ask for them to be brought to me.

They arrive in a flurry of suppressed excitement. Mary, at six years old, is as pretty and as confident as a pussycat. Her nurse tells me that of all the royal children, she is the most difficult to handle, the most determined to have her way. She forgets that a princess should keep her eyes downcast and her expression meek, and she confronts me with a bold happy smile. I can't help but love her for it.

In readiness for her departure to Scotland, Margaret now has her own household. She approaches me in a regal fashion to demonstrate that she has been attentive to her lessons. She is tall and already showing the promise of future beauty. She curtseys demurely and takes a seat close by while Harry bows, already displaying poise and elegance. He is eleven now and I am confident that he will make a good king, if God will only allow it.

"How are you, Lady Mother? My sisters and I have missed you."

I reach out and draw him close, denying him the opportunity to display his formal training. I knock off his cap and pull his face down for a kiss. He stands up again, puzzled and a little flustered.

"My teachers tell me I must be polite and formal at all times, Mother."

"Not with me, Harry. I am different. Why, when I was a child my father would romp about the floor with me on his back. He made a most noble steed."

Harry half laughs, almost disbelievingly. It is probably outside the bounds of his imagination to think of his own father behaving in such a way.

"Everyone addresses me as Henry now; or My Lord Prince—even Meg is supposed to."

I move my head conspiringly close to his. "Not in private, surely they didn't mean that."

"I think they did." He looks troubled; he is less buoyant, less hearty, and my heart twists suddenly with anxiety. I place my hand across his forehead.

"Do you feel quite well? You are pale. Have you been eating properly and enjoying the sunshine?"

"As much as I am allowed. Father wants me to attend more to my lessons than hunting, now I am to be king."

"Hmm, we will see."

413

I am cross with Henry. Angry that he should try to stem our son's exuberance, and try to fashion him to his own mould. Harry is one of the brightest, most intelligent children I know, or am ever likely to meet. I determine that when I next see Henry, I will let my feelings be known. Our son deserves a better balance of work and play. It is imperative that we lose no more children and I have never seen my Harry look so wan.

<u>January 1503</u>

Christmas is gay this year. The court makes a determined effort to put sorrow aside and give thanks for what we have. The long shadows that trouble us are pushed purposefully aside to let the light pour in. There is the usual dancing, feasting, merrymaking and entertainments, and when the New Year arrives and gifts are exchanged, I begin to think that perhaps we can all be made anew. Perhaps this year will be a new beginning and the dawn of an age of hope.

In January, with Christmas behind us and a new year still unspoiled, I am rowed back to Richmond Palace. Soon it will be time for my confinement.

I have given birth many times now but never before has the thought of my lying-in period been so welcome. I have never felt so tired and I eagerly look forward to an end to the pregnancy and a long peaceful rest. It will be good to be lighter of this child, perhaps then my feet will return to normal size and, with a new heir in the royal cradle, I will feel light-hearted again. Until then, I continue to tire quickly and I know I will need all my energy for the coming birth. Once Candlemas is over and the time comes for me to retire, I will be more than ready to go.

Henry waits at Westminster for Catherine Gordon and I to arrive, and then we set off for the Tower. As always when the grey walls loom above us I cannot help but shudder. I look up at the windows, where countless unseen faces may be looking down, and wish I were somewhere far away. This place has always filled me with a sense of unease, a sense of foreboding. So much has happened here and I fear there are too many more dark events to come.

My husband must be aware of the bad feelings connected with the Tower but, with his usual lack of sensitivity, he is keen to show off the improvements he has made. He has extended the lodging in the Lanthorn Tower, adding a new bedchamber and privy closet and a new tower, a square one, that Henry has dubbed the 'King's Tower'. It has a private chamber, a library and large windows that look out across the river. While he makes himself comfortable there, I take up residence in the Queen's lodging that lie adjacent to Henry's.

We plan a lengthy domestic time in which, hopefully, leisure will be a high priority. The king's mother is at her house at Coldharbour, so although we will see her often, she won't be popping in and out of our privy quarters at all times of the day and night.

I spend most of my time in my chamber, trying not to think of my sister's husband who is closeted away somewhere within the confines of this place. I try to ignore the echo of my brother's memory, and the unseen presence of my little cousin Warwick. I push them away and order the shutters to be opened wide, to allow as much light as possible into the corners.

415

I write letters and then settle down to put the finishing touches to a cap I am embroidering for the baby. It is almost bedtime when Henry comes to bid me goodnight. I watch him in the torchlight, the shadows leap and dance on his face, belying the lines of strain and worry. I stand up and he takes my hand, holds it while I raise myself on tiptoe to kiss his cheek. Just as soon as my lips touch his skin, I feel a pop, and my legs are suddenly doused in warm, sweet smelling fluid. We both look down and the king sputters in astonishment while my head reels with embarrassment. I am horribly humiliated that he should be witness to such a thing.

"Henry!" I exclaim. "It is the child."

"It is too early, surely ..." He shouts loudly for the guard to send for Alice Massey, the midwife, who is thankfully installed somewhere in the Tower. Soon, summoned by the scurrying guard, my ladies come rushing in. Henry stands helplessly by as they hurry me to bed. As they bear me off, I raise a hand.

"Goodbye, Henry," I say, as if I am going for a walk in the park.

*

The birth is quick; too quick according to Alice, who prefers a woman to suffer a little. I barely have time to prepare myself for the task before it is over. While the child is whisked away to be made presentable, Alice dithers over the afterbirth. She carries it away, for some reason unhappy that it has come away in pieces. Soon I am washed and dressed in a fresh gown, and they hand the child to me.

She is tiny. I look down at her delicate features, her bruised forehead and tiny wrinkled fingers. According to Alice she has come a little early, but she appears to be healthy, if rather small. She feeds but slowly, often falling asleep before she is properly full.

"Shall we name her Catherine?" I suggest when Henry comes to look at her. He is so relieved that the child and I have both come through our ordeal safely that he quickly agrees. I have now managed to name each of my daughters after one of my sisters, and I lay back with satisfaction.

Henry is leaning over the cot, examining his offspring for flaws. I am satisfied he will find none. He straightens up and grunts in satisfaction as he returns to my bedside.

"I was worried for you, my dear," he says. "I think we should risk no more children, not for a while anyway."

I am almost thirty-seven. The anniversary of my birth is just a short week or so away; I doubt I have many more years of childbearing left to me. I say nothing. I let him continue his dream of another Tudor prince and the great dynasty he longs for.

"You look tired," he says, standing up and shrugging into his coat. "I will leave you to rest."

He creeps away as if afraid of disturbing the child, and I roll onto my side and close my eyes.

Sometime later I am woken by the king's mother. She comes creeping into the chamber and leans over the cradle to admire her newest grandchild. I drag myself back to consciousness to greet her.

"Sorry," she says loudly. "I didn't intend to wake you. I just wanted a peek at her. She is very small. Is she feeding properly?"

"She is not the little piggy her siblings were but is doing well, I think. She is slow; the wet nurse will have to be very patient. A woman is coming tomorrow."

My breasts are full of milk. Already the conversation has made it begin to flow; I can feel it seeping through the bindings, a growing stain appears on the front of my nightgown. I hope the king's mother doesn't notice.

She stands up. "You have done well, Elizabeth. A son would have pleased the king more but he seems very content for now. Well done."

I am still basking in her praise when Catherine wakes, her tiny mews making my milk begin to flow afresh. I cradle her to my breast, enjoying the pull of her mouth, the touch of her tiny hand on my skin.

<u>9 February 1503</u>

I open my eyes to darkness. I am cold, shivering, yet my pillow is damp. My head aches and my throat is parched. I call out for a drink but I can make no sound; my voice is hoarse. Nobody comes.

I drag myself onto my pillows and peer through the darkness into the antechamber where I can just detect the outline of my woman, her body humped in sleep.

There is a jug of wine on the table, just out of reach. I stretch out an arm but it is too far. Throwing off the covers, I swing my legs from the bed and put my foot on the mat. The room tips, the floor coming up to meet me as a gush of something wet and warm floods from beneath my petticoats. Instinctively, I reach down; my fingers come away sticky, stinking of blood.

It is then that I begin to scream.

My woman leaps from her truckle bed, rushes into the room, takes one look at me and pushes me back down on the mattress. "I will fetch help, Your Grace," she cries before she leaves me. I hear her running along the corridor, shrieking for help.

I close my eyes and groan. "Not now, Lord; not now, not like this."

Henry is in my chamber, his nightgown showing white in the gloom. He shouts for a light, for a physician, for the midwife. Everyone is shouting. Alice comes, the king's mother behind her, her hair a thick grey plait like a horse's tail. She takes control of her son, propels the king from the room. I can hear her telling him loudly that everything will be all right, the queen is in good hands. I draw comfort from her words; the king's mother is a wise woman. She is always right.

Alice is wrenching up my shift, examining my tummy, while my women thrust cloths between my legs to staunch the flow. They illuminate the chamber with torches and candles, and the fire is poked back into life. As I look upon the scene I feel detached from it, as if it is all happening to someone else.

Poor Henry. As his physicians battle their way across country to get here, I am leaving him, little by little; as the blood flows faster, my strength grows less. I feel strangely detached from them all, cannot understand their tears. The pain has passed now but my head feels light, as if it is stuffed with muslin. When they tell Henry they can do no more, he hangs onto my hand, kissing it, telling me over and over that all will be well. He is the king, he has commanded it.

"The children, Henry. Look after the children. Let them marry well and Harry, he is young, let him fly, Henry. Do not hold him too tightly or you will damage him. He is our heir, let him grow strong."

"Yes, yes." Henry has tears on his cheeks; the parallel lines that flank his mouth become conduits for his sorrow.

"I tried to be a good wife, Henry. I did my best, all I could. I never meant to cross you."

"No ..." His voice cracks, he tilts his face to the ceiling and I am sure he is praying. There is a movement at his side and I notice his mother. She is weeping too; I never expected that. I thought she resented me but I suppose I must have been wrong. I hold out my hand and she takes it, her fingers are dry and cold.

"Look after them," I beg her. "They are so small. Do not be too harsh with them."

She dashes a tear from her cheek and turns her face away. My hand drops to the counterpane.

"Where is Catherine?" I ask. "I want to speak to Catherine."

There is a rustle of silk and a woman appears. Henry steps away. It is not my sister, Catherine, whom I had asked for; it is Catherine Gordon, my brother's widow.

"Your Grace?" Her face is so fair; so ethereal, so delicate. "You wanted to speak to me?"

I hadn't called for her but since she is here I grip her hand and urge her closer. I try not to notice how she flinches from my tainted breath. I must stink of death.

"He will be lost without me," I whisper. "Look after him, give him your comfort."

For a moment she is stunned, she blinks rapidly, her mouth working, her tears dropping onto our joined hands.

"I will," she says.

A priest is mumbling a prayer. There are cold fingers on my face, on my lips. Someone is sobbing in the corner. A baby is crying, a feeble cry like the sound of a gull tossed in the wind.

I slip into a sort of dream. I see Harry's face; he is teasing Meg, laughing because she is in a rage with him. Close by is little Mary; she is tormenting a kitten, trying to make it fit into a jewelled box. My children; I have filled the royal Tudor nursery with children of York. This is the one thing I have done well.

I try to wake, to open my eyes. There is something I need to tell Henry. I open my mouth to call him. I see him turn, his face illuminated by the light of the fire. *He is old.*

I start up in the bed but darkness encroaches from the periphery of the room. It pushes me back, heavy on my chest, constricting me, pressing me down, down into nothingness. There is only darkness.

Light the torches, please.

12 February 1503

The divide between life and death is narrow. Sometimes it creaks slowly back and forth, like an old door; one moment promising darkness, the next plunging us back into the blinding reality of this world. Other times, when we least expect it, the portal opens quickly, drags a victim through and slams shut, forming an impassable rift between loved ones.

A boy in black velvet, edged with lambskin, creeps along the corridor, his new black shoes soundless on the stone floor of the Tower corridor. He looks over his shoulder. He must not be seen. He reaches out, grasps the latch and pushes open the door.

His mother's chamber is empty now; the cot that held his baby sister for the few short days she lived is still in its place, close to the bed. But his sister's cries are silenced now and his mother breathes no more.

The room is bleak, the fire cold, and the table at the bedside is littered with an array of medical instruments; a small glass phial, a knife, and a stone bowl. He wrinkles his nose at the acrid, bitter smell pervading the air and knows it for the aroma of death.

Empty of feeling, Harry steps further into the room and stares at the empty bed. Someone has tidied it; the lace-trimmed pillows are plumped, the rich velvet coverlet has been smoothed. At the foot, his mother's prayer book is open, the bright illuminated page a gay mockery of his bewildered sorrow. Her robe is folded across a chair, her slippers partnered neatly beneath. A white scrap of embroidery has fallen to the floor.

Only his mother is not here. She has abandoned him.

He reaches out, tentatively rubbing the soft fabric between his fingers, and her fragrance wafts from the disturbed folds. Lifting it to his face, he buries his nose in the fur collar, and, as if some giant has taken hold of his heart and is squeezing it dry, his tears erupt.

The heir to the English throne drops to his knees and casts himself onto the bed. He pushes his face into the counterpane, smearing it with tears. To escape the terrible ache in his heart, he squirms, consumed by sharp twisting agony. He bunches the coverlet in his hands, screwing it between his fingers, and sends a gasping prayer to God.

"Bring her back, God. Please, just bring her back. I need her. I want my mother."

But God doesn't answer; He is deaf to the pleas of children. Boys, even princes, even kings, cannot counter-command death, or dictate the will of God.

Author's Note

I have always been fascinated by the idea of Perkin Warbeck being one of the Princes in the Tower but I never thought I'd have the pleasure of imagining it in detail. The true identity of the man hanged at Tyburn in 1499 will now remain a mystery. It seems incredulous that a foreign commoner would be able to pull off a credible impersonation of a royal English prince. He gained the support of half of Europe which, to me, suggests either his claims were true, or people really didn't like Henry.

To create this story I have ignored Warbeck's confession, which seems to have been largely a construction of Henry VII's. Most of The Boy's story is the work of my imagination, aided only by a few recorded facts. Please bear in mind that it is a work of fiction. There are some easily accessible non-fiction books detailing every perspective of the story, which I list below.

Elizabeth was a much easier character to access. She is well documented and the few portraits that do survive show a pretty, confident and quietly determined woman. On the surface she may seem to have deferred to all that life threw at her, but it was part of a princess's training to conceal her feelings and I prefer to think that is precisely what she did.

She was family orientated. David Starkey is quite convinced that Henry VIII's handwriting proves that his mother had a direct hand in his education. Throughout her life she supported her sisters and remained close to her cousin, Margaret Pole. Margaret is, of course, the Countess of Salisbury whom her little cousin Henry VIII executed for treason in 1541 when she was in her late sixties. A fact that makes the scene in the nursery when she dandles little Harry on her knee that much more poignant. As to Elizabeth, as is often the way with women, I think history has undervalued her place in world events.

425

Unlike her son, Henry VIII, and the granddaughter named in her honour, Elizabeth of York isn't a household name. When viewed against the backdrop of other Tudors she is far less splendid than her children; she is conventional, and appears obedient, even cowed perhaps. Her portraits show a pretty, plump and resigned-looking woman who doesn't adhere to our imagined picture of the mother of a king, the grandmother of a king and two queens. Her husband is usually given the credit for founding the Tudor dynasty, but he could not have done it alone. He needed her Plantagenet blood.

Elizabeth was born on February 11th 1466, into the bloody era now known as the Wars of the Roses. She was the first child of Edward IV and Elizabeth Woodville. To everyone but the couple involved, it was an unconventional and unpopular match, but unlike other queens, Elizabeth Woodville was to prove satisfactorily fertile.

It was a time of upheaval and when Edward was forced to flee the country to Burgundy, the child Elizabeth joined her mother and sisters when they fled into Sanctuary at Westminster Abbey. There, safe from conflict but estranged from the exiled king, the first of Elizabeth's brothers was born. (Edward would later earn his place in history by 'disappearing', along with his brother Richard, from the Tower of London, igniting a mystery that continues to burn today.)

Meanwhile, the exiled king gathered his forces and with the aid of his brother-in-law, Charles the Bold of Burgundy, returned to England to resume the battle for his throne, finally defeating Warwick and Margaret of Anjou, and having the old king Henry VI murdered. This initiated a time of relative peace.

For Elizabeth, now five or six years old, it was time for her education to begin. As well as the skills of running a huge household, she was also taught to read and write, and given some instruction in accounting. Contemporary reports describe her as pious, obedient and loving, and dedicated to helping the poor.

In 1475, when Edward made his peace with France, it was arranged as part of the treaty that on her twelfth birthday she would go to France to prepare for marriage to Dauphin Charles. But before this could take place, France reneged on the deal and married Charles instead to Margaret of Austria.

Things ran smoothly for a while, or as smoothly as they ever do in royal circles until, on the unexpected death of the king in 1483, the queen, taking her children with her, fled once more into Sanctuary at Westminster. Richard of Gloucester took his place as Lord Protector, and her brother, the Prince of Wales, was brought to London to await his coronation, as was tradition, in the royal apartments at the Tower.

Shortly afterward it emerged (whether true or not is another question) that Edward IV's marriage to Elizabeth Woodville was bigamous due to a prior contract of marriage. All children of the union between Edward IV and Elizabeth Woodville were pronounced illegitimate. As we all know, Gloucester was declared King Richard III and at some point between 1483 and 1485, Elizabeth's brothers disappeared from the record. (That is not proof however that they disappeared from the earth – there are any number of possible explanations).

How must it have felt to one moment be the princess of the realm, Dauphine of France, and the next an illegitimate jilted nobody living in exile from court in the squalor of Sanctuary?

And what of her brother's fate? Elizabeth would have been ignorant of that, and the resulting uncertainty, mixed with grief for her father, would have been terrible. It is possible that her mother knew, or at least believed, the boys were safe. Why else, after scurrying into the safety of

Westminster in fear of her life, would she suddenly hand her daughters into the care of the very man suspected of injuring her sons? We cannot know the answer to that, and that lack of historical clarity provided the catalyst for this novel. The numerous 'what ifs' in this period are invaluable for an author of historical fiction.

Elizabeth and her sisters returned to court to serve Richard's queen, Anne Neville, where they were treated with every courtesy. Queen Anne was ailing and clearly dying. It was at this time that rumours emerged of a relationship between Richard and his niece, Elizabeth. It is now impossible to be certain of the truth behind the allegation, but at the time gossip was strong enough for Richard to publically deny the accusation. Whether the claim was true or not, Elizabeth would have suffered some degree of shame, but she seems to have continued to be prominent at court, serving the queen until her death in March 1485.

In August, when invasion was looming, Elizabeth and other children from the royal nursery were sent north for safety while the king dealt with the threat from Henry Tudor.

Henry Tudor, the Lancastrian heir, was aided by his mother, Margaret Beaufort, in England. Margaret had devoted her life to her son's cause. She served at court but untiringly devised methods to secure the throne she saw as rightfully her son's. In order to muster support from the Yorkist faction, Henry promised that, if he became king, he would marry Elizabeth of York and unite the warring houses of York and Lancaster, putting an end to the Wars of the Roses forever.

After Richard III's defeat at Bosworth in 1485, Elizabeth was taken to Margaret Beaufort's house at Coldharbour but Henry was slow to marry her, and slower to crown her. This can be seen as reluctance, but we should consider the logistics of arranging a royal wedding, although his son never seemed to find it an obstacle. To some it is almost as if the king wished to deny that she had any influence on his claim at all.

They were married in January 1486. Elizabeth gave birth to their first child, a son whom they named Arthur, in September of the same year, scarcely nine months later. She had no further children until two years after her coronation, which took place in November 1487.

Henry Tudor's reign was fraught with rebellion. Pretenders emerged throughout; some were swiftly dealt with but one in particular, Perkin Warbeck, claiming to be Elizabeth's younger brother, Richard, harried the king for years. We will never know his real identity, although the king went to great lengths to provide him with a lowly one.

Elizabeth is always described as a dutiful wife and devoted mother. She took no part in ruling the country and there are no reports of her ever having spoken out of turn or 'disappointing' the king. Henry appears to have been a faithful husband; his later relationship with Catherine Gordon, wife of Warbeck, was possibly no more than friendship, but she did very well at his court.

Although Prince Arthur was raised, as convention dictated, in his own vast household at Ludlow, Elizabeth took an active role in the upbringing of her younger children, teaching them their letters and overseeing their education.

When Arthur died suddenly in 1502, both Henry and Elizabeth were distraught, the king thrown into insecurity at having been left with just one male heir. Reports state that the king and queen comforted each other and, although there are some hints of a possible estrangement between the royal couple, Elizabeth promised to give Henry another son. She fell pregnant quickly and gave birth to a girl, Katherine, ten months later, but succumbed to puerperal fever and died on her birthday, 11th February 1503.

I believe Elizabeth deserves more credit. There is as much strength in resilience as in resistance, and I believe she was both strong and resolved, bound by duty to serve her country as best she could.

Her union with Henry negated the battle between York and Lancaster, and the many children she bore provided political unions with France, Scotland, and Spain. If a king dies dutifully on the battlefield, serving his country, he is usually credited with heroism. Ultimately, Elizabeth died in exactly the same manner, doing her duty to England.

Further reading

Alison Weir: Elizabeth of York: The First Tudor Queen
Amy Licence: Elizabeth of York
Lisa Hilton: Queen's Consort
Christine Weightman: Margaret of York
Elizabeth Norton: Margaret Beaufort
David Baldwin: Elizabeth Woodville
D.M. Kleyn: Richard of England
Ann Wroe: Perkin
Ian Arthurson: The Perkin Warbeck Conspiracy
David Baldwin: The Lost Prince
Elizabeth Jenkins: The Princes in the Tower
Michael Hicks: Edward V: The Prince in the Tower
Peter Hancock: Richard III and the murder in the Tower
Williamson: The Mystery of the Princes
Thomas Penn: Winter King
James Gardiner: Henry VII
Robert Hutchinson: Young Henry
David Starkey: Henry, Virtuous Prince
Also see http://www.richardiii.net/ for countless articles on the era and the people.

For more information and articles visit my website
http://www.juditharnopp.com